ZARA DUSK

A Court of Caprice and Decay

First edition

ISBN: 978-0-6458008-6-9

This book was professionally typeset on Reedsy. Find out more at reedsy.com

This book is for those among us who are attracted to the dark

This book has some dark elements. If you're concerned, check the content warnings at https://zaradusk.com/content-warnings/

Contents

Delph

If Joey the Bull didn't give me this job, I would punch him in the eye.

I may never have worked on the docks before, but I'd worked the streets plenty. Stealing cars, selling honest-to-God-legit-I-swear cell phones, you name it. I was tall and strong, and I could hold my own. Who cared if I didn't have any experience?

Obvious answer? Joey the Bull. He would definitely care about my absolute fuck-all experience. He was the overlord of the docks, at least in the circles I ran in. He had no official title, but that didn't mean shit around here. The truth was, if you needed something or someone, you'd only get it through Joey the Bull.

The pungent smell of salty seawater surrounded me as I swallowed a shiver and continued along the damp cobblestone path climbing to the stone house on the headland.

My breath fogged the early morning air, and I tugged my black leather jacket closer around me while the rippling waves sparkled like emeralds below. The view from here was amazing. I could see all the way out across the glittering green water to the distant haze shimmering in the air, the barrier between our lands and the fae realm.

I looked away fast, avoiding its supernatural pull. I might

be a superstitious idiot, but I hated looking at that barrier. It gave me the creeps. So I kept my gaze on the winding pathway up the headland, letting the pounding of waves wash over me.

Before I was halfway to Joe's villa, the man hiding badly behind a shrub leaped out. "What are you doin' here. Get away, girl, before my blade finds your belly."

He displayed yellowing teeth in a snarl he probably thought was intimidating while his vile body odor assaulted me. He practically danced around, trying to get the weak morning sunlight to glint off the dagger at his belt.

His idiocy pissed me off. Man, I should be mellowed out by now. I always thought I'd have my life sorted out by the time I hit my mid-twenties, but every day I seemed to get angrier. "None of your business," I snarled. I kept walking, keeping an eye on the sentry, waiting for his inevitable lunge.

He telegraphed it like he was trying to play fair, but I knew he was just incompetent. His arm was high above his head, and his rotund belly was exposed, so kicking him in the chest was a piece of cake. I listened for the satisfying whomph of air evacuating his lungs as he doubled over in pain.

I smiled sweetly. "Like I said, it's none of your business."

He waved me through with a hand as though gallantly allowing me to pass.

I didn't bother to hold in my snort as I walked past, nearing Joey the Bull's magnificent stone villa, its sheer size enough to make me feel small and insignificant.

I was good with my fists—and feet—but words were another thing.

Lead settled in my belly. I should have planned what I would say to Joey the Bull and thought this out better. But typical fucking me, I just plowed in without a plan and hoped to God

2

it worked out.

The path led me around the far side of the villa, the dew-covered grass crunching beneath my feet. The front door overlooked the glittering ocean, but looking at the shimmering barrier to the fae realms across the sea gave me the damn creeps, so I locked my gaze on the foreshore to the piers and docks lining the harbor. It was pretty damn quiet down there, even for this hour of the morning, with only faint seagull cries in the distance. Not a ship in sight.

The ships didn't cross to the fae lands, of course—nothing could get through that barrier. They hugged the coastline, transporting goods to other harbor ports. It was a big business, and I wanted a piece of it.

I didn't know what I'd do if I didn't get this job. My savings had run out, and Grandma couldn't afford to dip into her own. She'd told me that plenty of times. The salty breeze brushed my cheeks like a whisper from another world, warning me that failure wasn't an option.

I was surprised when the oak door swung open before I could even knock. Framed in the small doorway was the huge figure of Joey the Bull. Gray beard, bushy gray eyebrows atop glittering green eyes the shade of the sea, and a face lined with age.

His gravelly voice matched his sea-dog appearance. "I saw you take out my man."

Crap. He'd been watching when I kicked his sentry in the guts. Had he also seen me pocket the man's dagger? It was hard to know if witnessing my violence would anger or impress him, but there wasn't much to be done about it now. I was at his mercy.

Silence scraped between us until a gull screeched overhead.

Joey the Bull nodded curtly. "I could use someone like you."

I bit the inside of my cheek to keep from grinning. That was a job offer, no question about it. Now we just needed to negotiate my salary. I figured my strongest strategy was to shut the fuck up and let him do the talking, so I let that jagged silence crust around us some more.

Joey the Bull's eyes narrowed, and he looked more like a sea beast than a sea captain. "I'll give you room and board in exchange for your services."

My heart leaped. Room and board. I could finally move out of grandma's house, which I'd been itching to leave since I landed there twelve years ago.

Before that, I lived with my uncle Jackson. He kept me on when he had his first daughter, Lexi, when I was five. But when he became father to twin baby girls, he kicked me up the line to his mom's place, and I'd been scheming to get the hell out of there ever since.

So the prospects of having a roof over my head—somebody's other than my grandma's—sounded good. Fucking enticing, to be honest.

This could be my chance. Grandma wasn't exactly oatmeal cookies and hot chocolate. She once slapped me so hard I broke a tooth when I came home after curfew. Apparently, I was headed down the same road as my mom, which was about the worst thing I could do. Mom was the poster girl for failure in our house. A drug-taking teen pregnancy ingrate who went missing long ago, presumed dead. Not exactly a role model.

My dad wasn't on the scene at all. I didn't have a clue who he was or anything about him, except he knocked up my mom and fled.

But the truth was, Grandma was getting on, and she needed

me more than I needed her. I wasn't sure if I could leave her rattling alone in her big old box of a house without company. She wouldn't last a week without me to cook and clean for her.

Grandma had drummed into me often enough that family belonged together, so I supposed I belonged with her, even if it didn't feel like it.

Whatever. I just knew I had to do better for my family than my mom did, even if it broke my fucking heart. As though forcing my head through molasses, I shook it.

"I can't do board. I already got somewhere to live," I said. "I need cash instead."

The lead in my chest weighed more heavily. Had I really just given up the chance to leave grandma's home and strike out on my own?

Like a coward, I couldn't hold the Bull's gaze while he considered my fate. I roved my focus down toward the sea and along the Docklands to the piers jutting into the bay like broken teeth. The sun was stronger now, casting full beams along the shore like a broad spotlight. It reflected off a pair of golden-haired girls that made my heart stutter.

For a moment, they looked exactly like my twin cousins, Kayla and Razelle. But they would never set foot in this part of town. Only the hardiest twelve-year-olds would survive down here, and my cousins definitely weren't that. They were sweet and naïve...and just about foolish enough to think exploring the Docklands would be an adventure.

I couldn't focus on Joey the Bull's words when those twin golden heads disappeared into a tunnel. I kept my gaze glued on the other end, waiting for them to emerge, needing to confirm it wasn't my cousins.

The Bull's tone broke through my reverie, a barked command laced with anger and delivered with spit. I needed this job. Man, I needed this job.

But first, I needed to make sure those damn cousins of mine weren't at the Docklands.

Finally, they emerged from the tunnel, traipsing, bubbling, and bobbing up and down like two tiny lost boats. I could almost hear their giggles from here. It might still be early, but those innocent girls would be like magnets to the dockland's worst scoundrels.

And it was definitely them. There was no mistaking Kayla's light skip or the raspberry beret that Razelle wore everywhere.

"Fuck it," I spit.

I spared a glance for Joey the Bull, whose brow clouded in fury, then I sprinted away toward the glowing golden beacons of my foolish damn cousins, leaving the overlord spitting in rage behind me.

I had to keep my cousins alive. They were the most important things in the world to me, more so than Jackson, who'd brought me up, more so than myself. And now the damned fools were in trouble.

As if their lives being in danger wasn't bad enough, to add icing to the shit cake, I'd just pissed off the Bull and made an enemy of the most powerful underworld figure in Hebes.

I flew down the hill as fast as I could, my boot pounding, leaping over branches and avoiding holes as I took the shortcut over the grass. The rush of wind against my face blew my long black hair behind me like a sail.

When I was level with the ocean, plunging into the heart of the Docklands, I could no longer see the girls.

They'd better be okay. If anything happened to them, I... No, I couldn't let myself think that way. I forced more energy into my legs, ignored my squeezing heart and screaming lungs, and sprinted through the alleyways toward where I'd last seen them. My boots pounded on the cobblestones, and I tore through those streets like a hurricane.

I would fucking kill those girls when I found them.

I rounded a corner and slammed straight into a huge muscled chest. It was covered in leather and about as hard as a tavern wall.

"Ow!" I didn't have time to check for bruises, so I darted around the leather mountain of a man and raced past, but his fingers closed around my upper arm like a vise.

I spun fiercely. "Let go of me." My cousins needed me, and I didn't have time for this man's crap.

His face was unsmiling but somehow graceful, the porcelain beauty of a vase. He had to be fae. His unnatural stillness told me that as surely as his pointed ears.

I tried to tug my arm free, but his grip was iron. "Let me go, fae."

The male just scanned me from my toes and back up. "You are of childbearing age," he commented like some kind of freaky android, without inflection or expression.

"And you're old enough to know better than to accost a woman in the streets," I spit, still struggling in his grip.

If I didn't get to my cousins soon, somebody else would, and the streets of the Docklands were not a nice place for naïve twelve-year-olds. Even I'd been wary about these parts at that age.

I twirled close to the man, resting my back against his chest as though preparing to be spooned, then stamped the heel of my boot hard on his toes.

He didn't wince. He didn't even fucking wince.

His voice, a chilling monotone, sent shivers down my spine. "Come with me."

Spitting and dragging and kicking, biting any flesh I could reach, I was pulled away from the pier, away from my defenseless cousins, and there wasn't a damn thing I could do about it.

"Where are you taking me?" I screamed.

I had to force down my writhing and howling to hear his monotone answer.

"You are of childbearing age," he said. "And the fae prince needs a new plaything."

Delph

The oversized fae dragged me the half mile to the center of town, with me spitting and fighting every inch of the way.

He'd make a mistake soon, loosen his grip or readjust, and when he did, I'd be free.

He pulled me all the way to the town square, a cobblestone plaza that used to be quaint but was now lined with cell phone stores and fast food joints. But right now, it was lined with women.

Of childbearing age, I thought, frowning.

I scanned the line of women, searching frantically for Kayla and Razelle. I sagged in relief when I saw them, looking excited as though this was all part of their grand adventure. Razelle adjusted her deep-pink raspberry beret and whispered something to Kayla, who nodded energetically, her hair reflecting golden in the sun.

I sagged against my guard, who was shocked at my sudden relaxation.

When he released me, I moved toward the twins but was jostled into line before I could reach them, shoulder to shoulder with the other women of the town. I took the time to scan for my other cousin, Lexi. She thought she was a major badass, so I was surprised she wasn't here. And relieved. If she was here, she'd definitely get herself into trouble somehow.

A huddle of fae soldiers stood on the other side of the town square, with more standing at the exits. What the hell was going on? In an echoing voice that boomed magically across the plaza, although I couldn't see a microphone, one guard explained that we were there to be honored by the fae prince and that one of us would be chosen to accompany him to the fae realm.

Obviously, I'd missed the memo because most women clearly knew this was happening. They were dolled up more than usual, and the floral perfume was almost suffocating.

A guard started at one end of the line of women and made his way slowly along like he was inspecting cattle. He stopped to chat with everyone, so whatever twisted competition this was, it clearly wasn't entirely based on looks. That was something, I supposed.

The seed of annoyance in my belly bubbled into anger as the women beside me preened. Not all of them, of course, they weren't all ninnies. But plenty were.

Why would they imagine a stranger could assess their worth within one thirty-second conversation? Why would they primp and preen and push forward their chests, trying to be selected to be a prince's plaything?

Why would they think there was any honor in that?

The fae didn't technically have any power over the mortal realm of Hebes, but we sure acted as though they did. They were right up there with movie stars and pop stars, revered for no reason other than their lucky birth.

Beside me, a woman giggled to her friend as the guard approached. "Isn't he handsome? Imagine what he could do with those fingers."

Her friend held a hand to her mouth. "I hear they're so strong. And have a lot of... stamina." Both girls giggled behind their hands, and my anger rose.

I cleared my throat. "The fae also have excellent hearing."

That shut them up.

As the guard drew closer, I scrutinized him. He had gray hair though he didn't look a day over thirty. He moved like a warrior, much more competent than any of the Bull's men. Smooth and sleek, as though in perfect control of every one of his hundreds of muscles.

He didn't speak long with each woman. I overheard him ask their name and age, nothing more.

When he got to me, I curved my back, hollowing out my chest, and stooped, letting my black leather jacket fall flat down my front. The last thing I wanted was to be chosen as the prince's plaything. I wasn't the prettiest or the smartest girl around, so I just needed to slouch and slobber and let this guard go past, and I should be okay.

Then I could head back to Joey the Bull and beg forgiveness. I needed that damn job.

The fae guard wore a red leather jerkin artfully engraved with a rearing horse. That must be his prince's emblem. My hand twitched at my side, every instinct roaring at me to pull the dagger from my hip and wield it, but I knew it would be useless against fae.

The soldier smiled, a perfectly orchestrated movement of muscle and skin. "What's your name?"

Instinctively, I wanted to lie. To pretty much any question asked by anyone, and definitely to authorities. The cops had almost caught me dozens of times, and I wasn't stupid enough to hand out my deets like lollipops.

"Jade Johnson," I said dismissively. He didn't need to know my name was Delphinium Smith; he didn't need to know anything about me.

"Age?"

"Twenty-seven." I made myself a few years older, just for shits and giggles. Like I said, he didn't need to know anything about me.

As I expected, the guard moved swiftly past me, heading along the line toward the far end. The far end, where my young cousins stood.

As the fae approached them, my fury grew. Kayla and Razelle were technically of childbearing age—barely—but they certainly weren't mature enough to be royal concubines. My relief at seeing them saved from the docks, safe and sound from that criminal underworld, slipped away as I considered what might become of them. Not the swift death of a blade to the guts but the drawn-out degradation of being an older man's whore.

I clenched my fists as the guard neared the twins. I hissed at the nearest women to be quiet, so I could overhear the girls' responses. I hoped to hell they were smart enough to lie, but I knew deep down they weren't. They were naive and unworldly and didn't have a self-preservation bone in their young bodies.

Kayla tossed her golden hair, and her words floated through the warming air. "Kayla Smith," she said with a giggle, and my heart dropped through my boots and into the cobblestones at my feet.

Even the carefully crafted fae couldn't hide their responses. Their porcelain faces turned ever so slightly upward at hearing my cousin's name. Or maybe I was imagining it, burdening the silence with too much meaning, my fear coming to life around me.

I released a sigh. I must have imagined the change in the atmosphere because the guard didn't snatch Kayla from the line. He kept moving along and asking the women—and girls—for their names and ages.

Razelle gave her real name, too, like a damn fool. I added it to the list of reasons for fucking killing those girls when this was over.

As the guard moved away, I released my breath and sagged, scraping a boot over the cobblestones. A waft of cinnamon floated to me from a donut shop, and my belly growled. I would buy a cake and then eat it slowly in front of the twins without sharing, and that would only be the start of their punishment.

First, the idiot twins wandered into the Docklands without me, then they were stupid enough to give their real names to a bunch of armored fae. I wouldn't buy them a damn donut for a year.

After the head guard finished his sweep of the women, he glided to the front. He briefly conversed with a second man, and I waited for this charade to end. Most women were desperate to be chosen, and if they wanted a life as a fae prince's sexual slave, then more power to them. I wouldn't waste pity on them.

A hush fell over the crowd. That sugary cinnamon scent was so distracting I wanted this to finish so I could chow down a donut, but when the guard pointed toward the line's far end, the sweet smell turned sour.

Surely they wouldn't choose a twelve-year-old to be the prince's plaything. Anything but that.

The guard's voice penetrated my soul. "Kayla and Razelle Smith, you may step forward."

13

A murmur swelled through the crowd.

My body hollowed out, leaving an empty skin suit with a ringing in my ears. *No.* I turned my head through molasses, looking for the twins, the plaza and luminescent stores spinning around me.

The girls' faces were ashen, paler than usual, clammy, and bloodless. They realized their adventure was deteriorating into a nightmare, and they couldn't escape.

Nobody crossed the barrier and came home. Ever. The only creatures that could pass between the mortal and magical realms were the asshole fae themselves, and they did so rarely enough.

If my cousins crossed over, I would never see them again. They might be damn fools, but they didn't deserve this.

Before they even moved, I stepped forward. My heel caught a crack between cobblestones, and I almost fell, a ludicrous contrast to the perfectly orchestrated movements of the fae, but I righted myself and kept walking.

The fae turned toward me first, watching my progress across the town square, then the humans noticed me. My boots scraped across the stones like I'd forgotten how to walk, and all I could think of was my cousins' young bodies trapped beneath a sweating old fart.

My voice was croaky. "Take me instead."

Some women laughed, imagining I wanted to be made a fae queen just like they did, believing I was soulless enough to think a future in Arathay would be sweet when I knew we were witnessing a slave trade.

I spoke again, my voice steadier. "Take me and let the girls go."

But the head fae guard watched me closely, and a small smile

14

kissed his lips. He let me cross every inch of the space between us before he spoke. "And what is your real name, mortal?"

I forced a half-truth between my cracked lips, "Jade Smith." They didn't need my first name, but I figured having the same last name as the twins proved why I was offering myself up.

I rammed steel into my spine and stood tall, though I was no match for the guard's height. His engraved red jerkin was at my eye level and didn't move as he spoke. "An older woman would be more fitting for the prince's needs. Fine. You will come to Arathay to meet your future king."

A buzzing swarmed around me, and darkness clouded my vision as I fought to stay upright. The last thing I saw in Hebes was my cousins' faces, pale and scared, staring at me in horror. Perhaps they had finally learned their lesson, and my absence from their lives would be their ongoing punishment.

Delph

I barely had time to spit on his boots before the massive fae male rose into the air, climbing steadily like a Goddamn hot air balloon. No flapping, no sign of wings, just rising straight up like smoke.

I didn't know fae could levitate. What the fuck?

I was so stunned I forgot to struggle, my legs hanging limp below me and my heart thudding. It was pounding so hard I bet the guard holding me could feel it. After all, my back was pressed against his chest, and my rib cage was probably vibrating like crazy.

When I remembered, I cast a final glance down and saw Kayla and Razelle being ushered out of the town square. I only hoped they were being taken home and not back to the dangerous Docklands.

The other fae guards rose around us, and, like a flock of birds, we all changed direction in the same instant and shot forward.

Cold wind whipped my face, and my long black hair slew out behind me. I hoped like hell it was annoying my captor and smiled when he spit out a mouthful. That probably made me a bitch, but hey, I was the one being kidnapped.

Although, technically, I volunteered to go. I couldn't have

the evil fae prince getting his talons on my baby cousins, that was for sure.

Within moments, we left land behind and soared above the glittering green ocean. My stomach spun like we were tumbling in circles, maybe taking a trip in a washing machine, but I supposed the flight was smooth enough.

I got up the nerve to look directly at the shimmering haze hovering over the ocean in the distance, marking the border between Hebes and Arathay. I'd always hated looking at that border, never treated it with the fascination that a lot of other folks did. Something about it felt off, unnatural, like a sixth finger or a brain tumor, and I wanted no part of it.

As we flew closer, dread bloomed in the pit of my belly.

The horror thickened and spread, weighing me so heavily I worried the fae would drop me and I'd plunge into the green waves, leaving behind nothing but a rising trail of white bubbles.

Man, I had to get my head together. I was a freaking mess.

But the sense of despair only thickened as we flew closer to the barrier. If I had any control, I'd turn and flee from that magical wall. There was something very wrong about it, and I sensed I would die if I passed through it.

Rumors abounded of humans crossing to the fae realm and never returning. Those same rumors said that time passed differently over there, and that's why humans never returned. Because they lived full lives and died over there while we were just sleeping or something.

The truth was, nobody knew. Knowledge was scarce, and facts were rare.

As we neared the barrier, certainty settled within me. Nobody returned because nobody survived. That knowledge settled into my bones as the shimmering haze widened to take up my entire field of vision.

If I passed through that wall, I would die.

"Stop wriggling, or I'll drop you." The harsh tones of the fae guard bellowed through me, his lips mere inches from my ear.

I realized I was writhing again, squirming, trying to escape his grasp.

I could barely breathe. I just nodded, meaning good, drop me. I didn't want to get an inch closer to that barrier—I'd rather take my chances with the sharks in Requin Strait even though I could barely swim.

The male tightened his grip and grunted, and the sense of my imminent destruction grew stronger, until we were inside the barrier.

My heart stopped beating, and coldness seeped through me, soaking into my flesh and bones, freezing my lungs so I couldn't breathe.

In another moment, I would die. No heartbeat, no breath. No chance of escape.

At least I'd saved my cousins from this fate. That might be the only accomplishment in my entire life, but it was an important one.

Then we were through. I inhaled deeply, filling my lungs with sweet fresh air, wiggling my fingers and toes, sagging in relief.

My fae captor grunted, and I was pretty sure it was directed my way and wasn't a compliment, but who cared? I was out of that damn barrier, and I was alive.

We continued soaring over the ocean, time seeming to stretch as my eyes sought familiar landmarks below. I strained to pinpoint differences in the expanse beneath us from the coastline I knew so well. The ocean was a slightly different color, a brighter green. And was that a massive shadow beneath the water's surface? I could only imagine what horrific beasts lay in the depths of the fae ocean, and I shivered despite the warm sun on my face.

Land appeared in the distance, at first a smudge on the horizon, then an oil painting of smudged forest, then actual trees, rocks, and earth.

Our troop of levitating fae came to land on the shore, choosing a rocky beach with pebbles instead of sand.

My guard released me, and I spun away, looking around, but there was nowhere to run. I needed a boat to return to Hebes, but the thought of crossing that barrier again filled me with despair, and I figured the return voyage could wait a moment or two.

Taking a deep breath of salty air, I turned to my guard. "Why are we stopped? Is this where the prince lives?"

"No, girl. This is the Realm of Fen. We are headed to the Realm of Caprice, where my prince awaits you."

That was more syllables than I'd gotten out of this dude all morning, so I kept pressing my luck. "There's more than one fae realm?"

He nodded. "Yes." The other fae eyed us sideways and sidled away, like they were scared of getting into a conversation with me. I didn't miss the amused glances they threw at my captor.

Since he was in a talkative mood, I kept pressing him. "What's your name?"

His jaw seemed to be ticking with the effort to keep quiet, but he answered me anyway. "Captain Peterson. I'd rather you didn't ask any more questions."

I'm sure he would. But something about passing through that barrier had made him chattier, and I wasn't about to let go of that advantage. The smell of brine lingered in the air as birds cawed overhead while out in the distance, a wave lapped against the shore. I ran my eye along the line of vegetation growing by the beach, seeing the strange shapes of the trees that grew there, and the unusual coloring of their leaves. Light green, dark green, gray, and even some purple-blue. I wanted to lose myself in the forest and become one with nature.

I snapped my gaze back to Peterson. "Can I go into the forest? I'd really like to run away from you guys, and I think I could lose you in there. Then maybe I'd explore a bit, then make my way home to Hebes once I feel brave enough to cross that barrier." I bit my lip hard to stop myself from talking, then mumbled aloud, "Fucking shut up, woman."

Peterson laughed at me. But, surprisingly, he answered my question. "Yes, you can go in the forest, and we wouldn't follow you, so you'd definitely escape us, but you'd never come out again. The wildlife around here isn't friendly."

That didn't sound great. I opened my mouth to speak again, focusing hard on asking for information instead of blabbing every thought that passed through my thick damn skull, but he cut me off with his own question. "What's your real name?"

For some reason, I blurted out the full truth. "Delphinium, but my friends call me Delph. Well, I don't have a bunch of friends, but my family calls me Delph. I like it. It's shorter, easy to manage, easy to say. Delph. Delph." I rolled the name over my tongue like it was strawberry cream.

I was rambling like a lunatic. What the fuck had gotten into me? Since when did I share truths with strangers, let alone foreign fae who'd kidnapped me? Sure, I'd told that one guard

20

my real last name, but I hadn't planned on telling them my full name and my entire cunning escape plan.

A murmur of laughter spread through the guards, and I wondered what the hell was going on. Obviously, passing through that barrier had made my lips as loose as Peterson's.

He nodded. "And are you really twenty-seven?"

No way would I tell him the truth. At least I could cling to that one lie. I opened my mouth to say yes, absolutely, I was born twenty-seven years ago, that makes me twenty-seven. But instead... "No. I'm twenty-four. I only told you I was twenty-seven because I don't like telling the truth to strangers. I'll keep lying to you too."

Fucking hell, I sounded like a damn idiot. I was babbling like a fool, and honestly, my truth made me sound like a petulant toddler who'd been taught not to speak to strangers. It did not make me sound cool. I couldn't hold my tongue still or my lips closed and had lost all control over my words. They just overflowed my mouth like a bottle of shaken coke.

Peterson opened his mouth to ask another question, but I cut him off with a raised hand. "No way. No more questions." I clapped a hand over my mouth just to make sure I didn't fizz any more truths at them.

He raised his brows, and another guard called out, "She's a fast learner."

I felt like I'd passed some kind of test, but that didn't make me feel any better about handing over my details to these guys.

Peterson pulled out a small vial from a pocket in his pants and knocked back the contents. The other fae did the same. I figured it was an athlete's gel or some kind of energy boost.

Moments later, Peterson pulled me against his chest, wafting his soap smell around me, and rose into the air. I looked around. Taken less by shock this time, I craned my neck to watch the other fae ascend, searching for a sign of beating wings or helicopter blades. Zippo, zero, zilch. These dudes were just levitating like a magician's assistant, only without the smoke and mirrors.

As we flew over the forest, I peered down, trying to take in my surroundings. After all, it wasn't every day you got to check out Arathay, and I wanted to soak up as much information as possible to tell Lexi and the twins. Especially Lexi, who was far too adventurous for her own good and would lap up my stories like a cat on cream.

But from up here, I couldn't see a lot. Just the oddly colored forests and some strange formations in the distance that could be rocks, lava, or giant creatures made of horsehair, for all I could tell.

After hours of flying, my chest ached where Peterson's arm crossed it, holding up my entire body weight with just one forearm. My ribs were ready to lodge a formal complaint.

But finally, we started losing altitude, and a magnificent city resolved in the distance. At its center was a huge spike that initially seemed purely ornamental, but as we got closer, I saw it was a building, clearly designed to intimidate and impress. Check and check.

Was that where my evil fae prince lived?

It didn't look like it. Peterson flew us—levitated us?—to a huge and beautiful building in a different district from the spike.

It was a palace straight out of a children's faerie tale book. Towering white turrets with slate gray peaks and an intricately crafted façade seemed to reach into the sky while a moat of emerald green grass and vibrant flowers surrounded the castle.

Honestly, this place was so freaking beautiful that even my most naive cousin, Kayla, wouldn't believe it was real.

We landed on a gravel pathway with a loud crunch, just outside a grand set of doors inlaid with mother-of-pearl handles. As they opened wide, the smell of ancient wood mixed with fresh lavender wafted out. A cloaked figure swept out, tall and broad-shouldered, and wearing a long ivory cloak. With a flick of his wrist, he flung back the hood, and intense lavender eyes locked onto mine.

My breath hitched as my body responded instinctively, coiling and loosening, and I couldn't drag my gaze from his piercing pale purple eyes. His hair was a perfect match, a gentle lavender against porcelain white skin. I had a stupid instinct to run up to him and put a forefinger to his cheek to see if that flawless skin was real.

But mostly, the expression on his stern face made me want to run away.

The fae around me swept into deep bows, but I remained rooted upright, unsure how to proceed. I sure as fuck wasn't about to bow to the male who'd kidnapped me, but every instinct in my body wanted me to prostrate myself on the ground and beg him to adore me.

Instead, I quirked my lip. "Hey."

The prince's lavender eyes widened. "And what have we here?" he asked in a rumbling voice that reverberated through my bones.

Delph

The fae prince swept down the stairs as smoothly as if he was gliding. I mean, every fae moved with style and grace, but this guy was especially impressive. How could he pack such a huge package into such a smooth ride?

His long ivory cloak and alabaster skin made me feel underdressed in my black leather jacket and jeans, but I refused to be cowed. This dude was bound to be an asshole. So, I waited for more assholery to spill from his mouth. After all, what kind of an opening was *what do we have here*? A pretty shit one, if you asked me.

Irritation lanced through me at considering what might happen next. Would this prince throw me in a dungeon? Would he slap me about? Or would he require my...services immediately?

Despite myself, my lips twitched at that last thought. No way would he take me unwillingly, not if I had anything to say about it. But the closer he got, the more I suspected I would go willingly. If only to chalk it up to a victory, one more notch for the bedpost. A prince and a fae, that's two off the bucket list. I mean, who wouldn't?

Unless he turned out to be an asshole. Which he probably would, what with the kidnapping and all.

He swept up my hand and pressed it against his full lips. "Thank you so much for coming," he purred. His voice was as smooth as his movement, and those lavender eyes locked unnervingly on mine. He even smelled of lavender, or did I imagine that?

His lips were warm, and his hands too, surprisingly so, given how white they were. I half-expected them to be carved from ice.

I lost myself in those lavender pools for a moment before remembering myself and withdrawing my hand. I folded my arms across my chest. "I didn't exactly have a choice," I spit. "This is the last place I want to be. Your men forced me."

Anger flitted across the prince's face at those words, and he glanced over my shoulder at the guards behind me. "I explicitly told you only to bring her if she came willingly," he said, his voice controlled but edged in steel.

The tension within me unraveled at that admission. "Oh, thank fuck," I said. I pulled myself together and rose to my full height—still a good foot less than the prince's. "You see, I didn't come willingly," I explained. "These dickwads forced me to come. So take me home now."

Even as I made the demand, I wondered if I should stay a day or two before leaving. I mean, I was in a fae realm, for fuck's sake. Nobody else I knew had ever been here. And it turned out I was a competitive, boastful bitch because I wanted to go home and tell everybody about all the delights I'd seen. But first, I had to see some.

The prince seemed to read my mind. His smile warmed me, melting away the last of the chill in my bones. "Of course you can. I'll have my males take you home immediately if that's what you want." I noticed he slightly emphasized the word 'males,' as though correcting me, and I realized I'd used the term 'men.' I wasn't used to the correct language for this realm. I supposed saying men and women was human-centric. "But," he continued smoothly, "you are most welcome to vacation here for a few days first."

Well, perhaps I'd have the opportunity to discover more about their ways. I breathed deeply, inhaling a floral scent I couldn't identify, probably coming off those amazing vibrant orange flowers that edged the grand stairway to the front doors. "Maybe I could stay a little while," I conceded. "But on my own terms."

The prince smiled warmly and held out his hand, not sweeping it up like he had before but waiting for me to make the first move.

It already felt like a language was forming between us. He'd gently corrected my use of the word men, and earlier, I'd gently corrected his presumption by retracting my hand from his.

Now he was asking if I would take his hand. And yes, yes I would. Hell yes.

I put my hand in his, and we climbed the stairs. "This is a nice house," I told him. Understatement of the year, but I wasn't about to tell my kidnapper how beautiful his home was.

His laughter rumbled around us as he led me into the entrance hall. "Most people call it a palace," he quipped, gently correcting me again.

And I could see why. Every surface shimmered like gold dust, and everywhere I looked, there was something more exquisite than the last—sculptures with lifelike features carved out of marble, magnificent paintings with jewel tones dripping from the canvas, and even one tasteful marble design that seemed to defy gravity, hovering in the middle of the room above us. With the aroma of candles wafting through the air, the space felt warm and welcoming despite the opulence, and I sneaked another look at the prince's face.

He was watching me, monitoring my reaction, looking to see how I would take it in. Damn him. He was attentive and thoughtful and kind... I could be in a hell of a lot of trouble.

I was already in danger of falling for the not-so-evil prince.

"Do you like it?" he asked.

"It's gorgeous," I admitted, practically gushing, unable to hide my admiration. I breezed away from him, regretting the loss of his warmth on my hand but unable to resist moving beneath the floating marble artwork. "How does it stay up?" I asked. "Is it magic?"

I sounded so unlike myself I barely recognized it. Lighter, somehow, like someone had removed a weight from me. I knew myself as a bitter woman struggling just to survive and battling her way through life. That was the person I'd always been in Hebes, especially since I'd gone to live with Grandma. She didn't provide food or comfort, just a place to rest my head and a vague sense of family. I'd always relied on myself and nobody else and needed to construct a hard shell.

But here, in the Realm of Caprice, I could be anyone. I already felt the promise of becoming a new person, that the wonder and joy of the world might soften me. If I stayed here for a few nights, I might rub away some of my jagged edges.

Here I was, with childlike wonder, asking if magic existed.

The prince's laughter rumbled again, not mocking but kind. "I'm afraid it's just held up with fine fae thread. It's as thin as a spider web, spun like gossamer, but as strong as steel," he said.

I whistled through my teeth. "Impressive," I breathed. "Advanced technology is almost as good as magic, right?"

The prince walked around me in a wide circle, his hands clasped behind his back, smiling, assessing me, and I felt from the warmth in his face that he was enjoying my company as much as I was enjoying his. "I'm glad you approve," he said.

I looked at a painting on the wall next. It was like the Mona Lisa but on steroids. The texture and swell of the figure were such that she watched me as I walked across the room, her pupils dilating and focusing as I came nearer. It was beautiful but terrible, all at once.

I peered, trying to detect if it was fae technology or magic and wondering if there was any difference between them. "And the flying guards," I began. "Were they suspended by a gossamer thread as well?"

I looked around, just checking the prince and I were alone and that none of the guards would overhear my ridiculous question.

It was just the two of us, and the prince laughed, a full-throated and decidedly un-kingly laugh. "No, those fae ascended into Hover, which gives them the ability to–"

"Let me guess. Hover?"

The lavender in the prince's eyes glittered with amusement. "Exactly."

"And can you hover too?" I asked.

"No. I chose to receive Healing magic rather than flight."

I dropped my hands to my sides, honestly astonished. So much information was packed into that statement.

Firstly, not all fae could fly, only the ones who chose that power. Secondly, fae could choose what magic they received.

That was about the coolest thing I'd ever heard. "How do you choose your magic?" I asked, practically panting with excitement. "Does it come in a box or something?"

The corners of the prince's eyes crinkled. "During your Ascension rite at age twenty-five, you give yourself up to Gaia's power and let the earth's magic flow into you, enhancing your inner power."

That sounded cool, but it wasn't exactly heavy on facts. I brushed a lock of hair from my face. "Um, and how exactly do you do that?" I asked.

His lavender irises locked onto mine. "You kill yourself," he said.

"You fucking what?" I spluttered, and a fleck of spittle flew from my mouth onto the marble floor. I hoped the prince couldn't hear it land.

"Those who wish to ascend to Hover must fall from a great height. Those who wish to become Wolf Shifters must suffer a wolf's fatal bite. Those who wish to become Magirus must deliberately starve. Only through death can we come into our full power."

I didn't have a clue what a Magirus was, probably something to do with food, but the whole thing sounded awful. "No way. Fuck that," I said. I adjusted my footing uncomfortably, looking at a marble bust of an old dude on a gold pillar. "Count me out."

"Humans can't ascend," he commented mildly.

Well, obviously. I figured. But my mind was reeling about this terrible ritual the poor fae had to endure—I'd never been happier to be human. Although I supposed it wouldn't be so bad if they killed themselves and automatically came back to life. "Does everybody make it?" I asked, a chill tingling my skin. "Do they all come back to life?"

The prince took his time before answering. His voice chilled me further. "Mostly."

I exhaled slowly. That was a no. As I took the information in, I circled the entrance hall slowly, my feet leaden and boots clunking on the parquetry-and-marble floor. My arms hung limp at my sides, but I managed to keep my jaw off the ground.

Fae could ascend into any power they chose, but they had to fucking kill themselves to do it. And not all of them survived.

The prince had chosen to Heal. Completely fucking selfless. I would definitely choose something cool like flying or fighting skills, never something that would solely be useful to others. But the prince had chosen the ability to heal others, which made him about a thousand times more noble than me. More noble than I could ever be.

Holy hell, I came here expecting to meet an asshole who wouldn't be good enough to kiss my boots, but I found the opposite.

He was a prince among men, literally. And the asshole was me.

Concern creased his forehead as he stepped closer to me, his lavender scent lingering. "Are you all right, Delphinium?" he asked.

His use of my name freaked me out further, and I stepped back a pace, trying to get away from him as though the taint of my selfish personality would rub off on him. "Why am I here?" I demanded, trying to mask the guilt consuming me. "And what's your name, or am I supposed to call you Prince?"

Honestly, even if I was supposed to call him Prince, didn't I need a surname to go with that? Like Charming, perhaps?

The prince nodded gravely, taking my change of mood

seriously. I was glad he wasn't flippant or frivolous, trying to dismiss my concerns with laughter or a quip. I sensed he would answer my questions in good time, so I didn't press when he just bowed his head slightly and said, "Please, follow me."

Delph

The prince motioned for me to pass through an ornate door-way into a reception room with elegant furniture woven from the finest threads I'd ever seen. Honestly, they were like living gold.

I couldn't resist. I scampered across the room and sat my ass onto one of his beautiful chairs. It reconfigured beneath me, growing, morphing, changing until it fit my body perfectly, its contours transformed to match my own. I moaned in ecstasy. Seriously, there could be nothing more comfortable in the entire world than this chair—and it looked like a work of art. I'd sit on it if it looked like a turd.

"Where can I get one of these?" I groaned, closing my eyes, my fingers tracing the golden threads of the chair's upholstery.

The prince laughed again. "You can take this one home when you go," he said.

My eyes flew open. "Seriously?" Polite words formed on the tip of my tongue... Oh no, I couldn't possibly, oh it's too much, oh I have to refuse... But those sweet words wouldn't come out of my mouth. Instead, I grinned wildly. "Thank you! Prince...?"

A gentle reminder that he still hadn't told me his name.

This dick had just kidnapped me and hadn't even introduced himself. I mean, where were his manners?

He reached out a hand for me, a pure gentleman right down to his fingertips. It wasn't like I needed help rising from my seat, so I ignored his hand and stood under my own steam.

His lavender eyes locked on mine, then flitted down my body and back up very deliberately, leaving a trail of heat over my curves and hollows. "You may call me Jayke," he said, gently touching my shoulder.

"Jayke," I murmured, focusing on the heat of his touch.

Leaving the elegant furniture behind, he guided me to the next room. He showed me through dozens of rooms in his palace, each more wonderful than the last. Wooden chandeliers that grew directly from wooden ceilings and glowed with living light. And an Aroma Room that apparently provided the scent your body needed at that moment in time.

"And what scent does my body need?" I asked, smiling over my shoulder. That probably counted as flirting, but the guy was hot and my needs were many, so why the hell not?

Jayke leaned in and inhaled deeply, his own musky scent rolling over me he was so close. "You need nothing," he murmured. "You already smell divine."

Despite my street bitch self, I smiled at his comment and walked into the room anyway, expecting at least a couch so I could sit and sniff appreciatively, or whatever the hell I was supposed to do in here, but it was standing only.

"You need to try it," Jayke said and popped out, leaving me alone. The room was about twice as large as my bedroom back home and utterly empty. He switched off the lights and left me in darkness, kind of like a sensory deprivation tank, I supposed.

A charred smell, like woodsmoke, filled the room the moment Jayke closed the door behind him. I inhaled deeply, wondering why the palace thought I needed to smell burning wood. Although a cozy fire would be nice, so perhaps it was just trying to make me feel at home.

Moments later, Jayke returned with a grin and a tall glass of something peachy pink that smelled sweet. He handed me the glass and asked, "What did you smell?"

I sipped from the glass, and another moan escaped my lips. The nectar was so sweet I never wanted to stop drinking. So far, Caprice was a sensory paradise, and the visual perfection of the male before me was no exception.

On impulse, I ran a finger along his jaw. It was so perfect and so close that I couldn't resist, like Temptation herself had forced my hand.

I ran my hand down his perfect white cheek all the way to his lips. "I smelled smoke," I said with a laugh. "I guess I need a firepit."

Jayke's lips tightened, a movement so slight that I wouldn't have noticed if I hadn't been touching them. My comment definitely pissed him off. Apparently, firepits were off-limits. Or maybe he didn't like me feeling his face like an inappropriate weirdo. I snatched my hand away.

His jaw ticked again, but his voice was as smooth as ever. "There is one last thing I'd like to show you," he said smoothly.

He turned and walked from the room, and despite his fluid grace, something about his posture seemed tense. Was it how he carried his head, tilted slightly to one side as though he was considering a difficult issue? Or a stiffness in his gait, hips, and tight round butt. He'd removed his ivory cloak back in the entrance hall and wore a finely woven shirt and pants in a deep port-wine color that played off the shade of his hair and eyes. With every step, the material pulled off his glutes and his pronounced butt cheek for one glorious moment before he took the next step, and my attention shifted to his other cheek.

I was in full perv mode and didn't pay attention to where we were going. The heat in my body from his touches and lingering glances had my cheeks warming and my toes curling.

"This is my mother," Jayke said solemnly, kicking me from my fantasy. We were stopped in a cozy room. A large daybed with white silk pillows occupied a good portion of the space, with a stately marble fireplace at one end. Jayke was looking up at a huge painting of a female above the fireplace.

She was beautiful, with black eyes, black hair, and a regal tilt to her chin. This work's artistry made it feel like she were in the room with us. Art appreciation was not my forte—hell, I'd never seen the inside of a gallery. But something about the painting moved me. "She's wonderful," I whispered.

I didn't just mean beautiful, and I didn't just mean the artist was skilled. But the painting felt as though it had captured the soul of this female, and I could tell by looking at it that she was remarkable in every way.

Jayke sighed heavily, and I could see he'd been blowing himself up for me, putting me first, making sure I felt relaxed and comfortable despite the pain he was clearly feeling. "She would have made a wonderful queen," he said, his voice showing a tiny hint of a crack.

I searched his face for clues about what he meant. "Would have?" I asked gently. The softness of my tone didn't match the street bitch in my heart, but this man deserved a little kindness, even if his guards had kidnapped me. I would save my temper tantrum for later.

"All I want to do is to make Caprice a fair and just realm," he said. "My mother would have done exactly that. She had such grand plans to make everybody's lives better. Not just the High Fae, but the lesser faeries too. She had so much good in her but never got to share it with the realm."

I chewed my lip, desperate to know more but unsure if I should ask. But he was the one who'd brought me to see the painting, so I figured he wanted to talk about it. "What happened to her?" I asked.

Jayke stepped backward and sat heavily on the day bed, leaning back against the cushions and staring hollowly at the intricate ceiling. A single tear traced a path down his alabaster face. "Her enemies in House Athar defeated her and stole the kingship," he said. "She was the rightful ruler, but she never got the chance to reign."

Sadness welled up within me, rising in my chest and forming a lump in my throat. Looking at the painting of his mother, I could see the truth in his words. And my anger at House Athar, whoever they were, sizzled through me like a lightning storm.

The prince looked so forlorn on the daybed, so lonely, and I could see that the pain of his mother's loss, and the kingdom's loss at never having had her as queen, lived on within him. I wanted to tell him I was sorry for his loss and pain. That I understood his grief. But I wasn't good with feelings, and if it wasn't anger or disappointment, I didn't know how to express it.

So instead, I just crossed and perched myself beside him awkwardly. No words came to me, and I didn't dare reach out and touch him, not after the way he'd flinched last time, so I just sat there like a fool, feeling like a tit on a pumpkin.

He smiled faintly as he looked at me, trying to restore his mask of hospitality and charm, but I didn't need that from him anymore. I wanted to comfort him but didn't know how. So I kicked off my boots and hoiked myself beside him, wriggling my butt backward, then lay down.

Our heads were level and mere inches apart. Our bodies weren't touching anywhere, but I was aware of every atom of space between us, of the heat of his skin.

He stared straight up at the whorls and contours of the intricate ceiling, painted with leaves and flowers that seemed to grow and move out of the corner of my eye, though I could never catch them moving.

"That's why I asked you here," Jayke said eventually. "King Athar is dead."

My leg muscle twitched involuntarily. That was the last thing I expected him to say—this conversation was giving me whiplash. First, he told me I wasn't a prisoner, then he said his mom had been killed by House Athar, and now King Athar was dead? And that had something to do with me being brought here?

The flying guards had said they were bringing somebody to be the prince's plaything. That was the exact phrase they'd used. The prince's plaything. So what the fuck did that have to do with a dead king and a dead mom?

I'd volunteered to come because I hadn't wanted Kayla and Razelle forced into sexual slavery beneath a sweating old fart. Then, when he'd turned out to be a gorgeous gentleman with morphing furniture, I thought I'd hit the jackpot. Figured I'd been selected to have neverending orgasms with this man, not for some political ploy.

Disappointment and relief warred within me. No neverending sex with a fae prince, then. But what the hell was I supposed to do about a political situation? I knew nothing about Arathay and less than nothing about fae kings and queens.

Plus, the prince's mood made no sense. If the evil king who killed his mom was dead, Jayke should be rejoicing. He should be dancing around the room and singing to the heavens because this was his chance to regain the rule of Caprice.

But as I mulled over the situation, a new feeling bubbled up inside me—a sense of purpose. I turned to look at him, staring into his alabaster cheekbone. "Then you should be the next king," I said, hoping to turn his mood around. A tinge of annoyance still simmered in my chest at the idea of me comforting my kidnapper, but that was all just a weird misunderstanding.

His marble-white face remained still, absorbing my words. Eventually, he spoke, his voice steady and determined. "Yes, that's the conclusion I've come to as well. I owe it to Caprice to fight for her, to bring justice to the kingship lacking these past thousand years."

"Thousand fucking years?" I blurted out.

Jayke's jaw twitched at my interruption—or perhaps my crudeness—but he continued smoothly. "Yes, Athar has ruled for too long, and I need to be the next king. But my enemies think otherwise."

My body tensed as electricity sizzled through me. This was becoming intriguing—although I still had no clue why the hell I was here. "Your enemies...you mean House Athar?" I guessed.

Jayke nodded ever so slightly. "Yes, and House Davin. Balance is maintained in Caprice by sharing power among three Houses. House Athar, House Sansett, and House Davin. Only one House has the official rule, but the opinions of all three should hold weight in important matters."

I was starting to get the picture. Three Houses, a tiny circle of democracy, but one House had gotten too much power for too long and had gotten fat and lazy. Just like the rich assholes on Capitol Hill.

"And let me guess," I drawled. "King Athar hogged all the power and never consulted the other Houses."

Jayke nodded, his mouth curving minutely. "You're a fast learner, Delphinium."

I settled onto my back and stared at the ornate ceiling, trying to catch the leaves and flowers growing while I pieced it all together. The cushions were as soft as clouds beneath me. I chewed my lip. "And which House are you?"

His lips curved slightly, and my black heart clenched to see that trace of a smile. "I am the royal candidate for House Sansett. There is no candidate from Athar, but the Davin candidate is a cruel male who would plunge the world into chaos if he ever got onto the throne."

Heat sizzled along the narrow gap between our bodies, and determination vibrated through me like a gong. "Fuck that," I hissed. "You have to win."

His smile blossomed, transforming his face, and I couldn't keep peeking at him from the corner of my eye, so I turned my head and watched his beaming face. "I was hoping you'd say that," he said. "That's where you come in."

Really? What the hell did I have to do with a campaign to be king in a fae realm I'd never even heard of until today? I wanted to tell him he had it all wrong, that I was the wrong person and couldn't help him with anything...but I also wanted to do whatever I could to help. "I don't see what I can do," I murmured. My voice was quiet, but his hearing was good.

The prince rolled toward me, rested his head on his hand, and propped up on an elbow. His knees now touched the side of my calf muscle, and the heat that poured through that tiny point of touch was unbearable. His lavender eyes locked onto mine, and I got lost in their swirling depths.

His voice was deep and low. "I asked my guards to find a mortal who would be willing to fight for freedom and equality here in Caprice," he said. "With the support of Hebes, my position here would be stronger, and I'd be more likely to win back my family's throne. I just needed someone who could put justice first. I never imagined they would bring me somebody as...right...as you."

My chest fluttered, my insides squirmed, but only because I wasn't the person he thought I could be. His guards had fooled him. They hadn't vetted women for their passion, eloquence, or ability to get shit done. They'd only looked them up and down and asked their names. I wasn't a diplomat. I was a damn street rat.

Grease coated my tongue. Jayke was heading into battle against his enemies, and even the soldiers on his side were doing him a disservice. Despite being brought here against my will, I was prepared to help him but didn't know how.

He was a pure prince by name and nature, and I was just some asshole girl who slashed tires and stole shit to survive.

I couldn't be the person he needed me to be.

But I was too much of a dick to admit it. His lavender eyes held such promise and hope that I couldn't dash his dreams by admitting my failings. All I could do was lie still and stare at his perfect alabaster face, feel the heat of his breath as it warmed my cheek, and wish I were a better person.

He said it again, making my gut squirm with guilt. "You are perfect for this, Delphinium."

I liked him using my full name. Back in Hebes, I insisted that everybody call me Delph, always detesting the fussiness of my full name. But on this fae's lips, it sounded divine.

Jayke's knee burned into my calf, and he leaned forward, tipping so smoothly that he might've been a clockwork piece, and his lips met mine, soft and warm.

The heat between my legs instantly drenched the guilt in my gut.

Delph

Jayke's kiss was like nothing I'd ever experienced. His lips were firm and insistent, confident like I'd expected, and strangely unyielding.

Was that how all fae felt, or was this particular to Jayke? Perhaps his long life as heir to the throne had forged everything about his personality, including his kissing style.

What was my kissing style? I'd slept with a few men and gotten heavy-handed with a couple of women, but none had reported back on my style. I mean, I assumed I was fucking awesome, but who knew for sure?

I'd also assumed a prince fae would be awesome, but Jayke and I were still figuring each other out.

I put a hand to his cheek, feeling his jaw working as he kissed me, a little uncomfortable in our intimacy.

"Are you okay?" He asked, his lavender-scented breath warming my face. Seriously, did this guy eat flowers?

The barrier between us thinned at his kind question, and I realized I'd built it myself. Some of that guilt from feeling like I shouldn't be here prevented me from enjoying this kiss the way I should.

"Yes, I'm fine," I replied and leaned forward, placing a hand into his soft lavender hair and pulling him closer, focusing on the fullness of his lips and the perfection of his porcelain skin.

He hesitated ever so slowly and pulled back. I'd blown it. Here I was with a sexy-as-fuck fae prince, and I was being all weird about kissing him.

The male barely moved a muscle. He was so perfect and pre-ordained in every movement that I knew his small furrowed brow must be deliberate. "You're hurt," he said, his voice laced with concern.

He placed his hands on my shoulders, and a soft trickle of sensation began at my head and cascaded over my shoulders and skin like falling water, gently coating me in its warmth as it drifted downward. When it reached the bruising on my belly from my scuffle with Joey the Bull's henchman, it paused and pooled, bathing the wound in warmth and washing away the pain. And as the magic moved on, it left my flesh whole and unharmed, and my mouth dropped open in a super not-sexy way. "You healed me!" I said.

The prince's lips curved into a perfect, gentle smile. He continued to move his magic over my body as if he was meticulously tending to each scrape, bruise, and blemish. I could feel his healing touch on my knees and arms, where his guards had restrained me. It was as if he was mending my body and stitching together the fabric of my spirit. His power seemed to rejuvenate every fiber of my being, leaving me feeling refreshed and ready to face the world anew.

There was no way I could thank him for that. For a start, the word thank you wasn't in my repertoire, and secondly, I wasn't eloquent enough. What did you say to a fae male who chose Healing powers so he could help others, when you were just a selfish human bitch who wanted to go home?

I had no words. So I did the cowardly thing and tipped

forward again, claiming his lips with mine. His hand was more like fire than flesh as it roved lightly down on my side, resting in the hollow of my waist, flooding me with warmth. But the tingling didn't intensify as I expected because I couldn't escape the guilt thundering through my stupid woodpecker brain.

I shouldn't be here. I shouldn't be using the prince like this. I should confess my inadequacies and let him send me home.

Jayke moaned softly as his lips moved against mine, but I couldn't get my head in the freaking game. Just thinking of home had me worrying about Grandma. I knew Kayla and Razelle were safe—I'd made sure of that. But who would look after Grandma while I was gone?

The question formed on my tongue. Could Jayke send supplies or gold to my family back home? I'm sure he could, but I wasn't in a position to ask. I was already deceiving him by pretending to be the passionate and political female he'd told his guards to bring him. I was already slick with guilt. I was already so completely the villain in the situation, so how could I ask him for more?

Besides, requesting help for my family in Hebes would be admitting I planned on staying here in the fae realm for longer. I'd told Jayke I would stay overnight but hadn't agreed to stay longer.

So I should forget my selfish grandma and lose myself in this delicious fae male.

Or, even better, let him lose himself inside me. Deep, deep inside.

I kissed him more intensely and pulled around the back of his muscled neck, hoping to force some excitement into my body, but it just wouldn't come. I was too distracted.

I broke our kiss. I still intended to chalk up a fae prince notch onto my bedpost, but not right now. Not tonight.

We would have plenty of time for that.

Jayke

Delphinium's lips were softer than I expected, and I couldn't get enough. I heard the muted sound of rain outside the window and the faint scent of a lily floating in the air as I tasted her sweetness. She was sensitive and warm beneath my touch and was utterly desirable despite her lack of fae grace.

I heard her heart pounding in her chest, pleased that she enjoyed this as much as I did. We were reclined awkwardly on the daybed, and I wondered if it would interrupt our momentum to suggest we retire to her bedroom.

I ran a hand down her cheek, and she shivered deliciously beneath my touch. I traced that finger over her shoulder, along her side at the very back of her breasts, then followed the dip of her waist and the swell of her hip.

She had none of the fae perfection of the females I'd bedded so many times, but that made her even more intriguing. Different, fascinating. What would she sound like in the throes of passion? She hadn't moaned yet, and I made it my first challenge to earn that delightful sound from her.

I leaned in close and pressed my lips to hers again, tasting her softness, my cock hardening with every lingering kiss.

She placed a hand on my chest, a subtle barrier between us, and pulled away. "Just a moment," she breathed.

I wanted nothing more than to keep kissing her, take her right here and now, earn the sounds of her pleasure, and pound away my insistent erection. But I didn't, of course.

I rocked back on my elbows, opening a little distance between us but keeping my hand on her delicious hip. Would I ever get used to her odd coloring? It was startling and utterly captivating. Humans were rare in Caprice and in all of Arathay, so I had never grown accustomed to their unusual complexion, the fact their hair and eyes didn't match.

Delphinium had pitch-black hair and vivid green eyes, and my gaze kept flitting between the two, trying to take it all in at once.

"Give me a sec," she said, and I detected a tinge of defensiveness in her tone.

I rushed to explain myself, not wanting her to think I was rude for staring. "Every fae has matching hair and eye color—" I began.

"Yeah, I noticed." She reached out to brush her fingers through my hair, and I pushed aside my twinge of annoyance at being interrupted.

I kept my tone kind and soft so as not to spook her. "You may not have noticed that the matched coloring applies to every fae in Arathay except the ruler of Caprice. He is Touched with Lightning by Gaia, and his eyes turn silver during the Ascension rite." She glanced at my irises, and irritation skittered across my skin. I knew my eyes weren't silver, but that didn't mean I was ineligible to rule. I could still be the interregnum ruler until Gaia chose another Lightning Touched.

Her brow furrowed, her emotions written plainly on her face. "Did King Athar have silver eyes?"

I rolled onto my back, and my erection softened. House Athar destroyed my family, wrenched us from our rightful place atop the Caprician throne, and prevented us from improving Caprice through our reign. I hated thinking about the male who was responsible for it all.

Delphinium didn't force me to answer, showing remarkable restraint. She shuffled around and followed my line of sight to rest upon my mother's portrait, her boots clunking on the floor. "Thank you for bringing me here," she said softly.

I was glad I had. I took a gamble bringing Delphinium in here to see this portrait, which looked like it had paid off. I needed her to support my bid to become king. Her support would tip the campaign in my favor in the eyes of the other Houses of Caprice.

Her support would be the difference between failure and success.

I also needed her to appreciate how disastrous the unfae King Athar had been for our realm. I hoped she understood because I wanted to rule Caprice right, making the best decisions to ensure our strength and prosperity into the future.

Opportunities to change kings were rare, and I didn't want to squander this one.

I turned my attention back to the female at my side, aware that her mood had dipped. Her regard was sad. Her intense green eyes flashed as she asked, "Why me?"

I tried not to sigh. My sign of exasperation was so small she would hardly have noticed it with her limited senses, having lived so long in the human realm.

I had to limit her fears, so I hid my response beneath a smile and rose to my feet, holding out my hands. She took them, granting me a smile that made my insides dance with the prospect of success.

"Because, young lady," I said, keeping the tone light, "you are a beautiful and passionate female, and I can't think of a better representative of the mortal realm."

I jolted her up fast, and she landed against my body, chest to chest, laughing.

Good, she was enjoying herself. And I had to admit I was too.

I didn't often bow to others, but I lowered my head and motioned to the door. "May I show you to your chambers, milady?"

She laughed a little, and I could see her natural wariness warring with her delight and perhaps a good helping of fatigue.

Delight and fatigue won out, her features softening into a smile. "Of course," she said. "That would be great, thanks."

This wonderful, motion-filled creature was intriguing, and in a short space of time, she'd gone from spitting at me to thanking me, so our relationship was heading the right way.

She walked in silence, her steps echoing softly as I led her through the ornate corridors of my palace. Her chamber was far from mine, so I wouldn't be tempted to visit her at night because Gaia knew resisting her would be hard enough.

Her silence surprised me. I expected a full repertoire of wows and oh-my-God's, but perhaps my intel on Hebes was wrong because she absorbed the finery of my palace without comment.

At her chamber door, she stopped on the threshold and faced me. "You still haven't answered all my questions," she said.

I swallowed my irritation at the veiled accusation and flicked through our conversations, trying to recall anything I hadn't shared with her that I'd intended to.

She smirked and placed a hand gently on my chest. "You never told me how you knew my name."

Her touch was light, but her gaze was heavy, as though she were issuing a final test—one I had every intention of passing.

I placed my hand over hers, both resting above my heart. "You told the guards, and they told me."

She held my gaze for a long moment, and I couldn't tell if she believed it was that simple. Then she nodded and withdrew her hand. "Okay. Good night, Jayke."

It was so foreign for anybody outside my immediate family to call me Jayke that I almost scolded her, but I wanted her to be happy here, so I refrained. I had instructed her to call me that, after all. "Good night, Delphinium," I said softly.

She turned to leave, her long black hair swishing through the air, but my fingers curled around her delicate wrist.

"Yes?" she demanded, glancing down at my wrist until I released it. Her behavior was presumptuous—I was in contention for the throne, and here she was berating me for touching her uninvited when I had the right to touch anybody I damn well liked.

But I let it go. I swallowed my natural response and focused instead on imparting the information she needed. "I told you how the realm is connected to the ruler—" I began.

"Yes," she said.

I took a deep breath at the interruption and calmed my voice. "I want you to understand the depth of the connection. The weather, for example, is influenced by his mood. The sun shone when King Athar was happy; when he wasn't, it stormed. Now that the ruler is dead, the realm has gone wild. It is diseased and dying and not a safe place to roam."

I could almost smell the sickly stench of rotting vegetation, the smell of death in a diseased land. As I glanced out the window, my gaze lingering on the stormy horizon, I was reminded of the vital importance of my magical wards. They kept the worst of the realm's affliction at bay.

Delphinium seemed intelligent enough, but I couldn't be sure if she was able to absorb the implication. With the king dead, the realm itself had gone wild, poisoned by Gaia herself. If Delphinium went outside my estate, she would be beyond my influence and power to protect. She needed to stay within the borders of my lands if she wanted to survive.

I opened my mouth to explain it further because her death was the last thing I wanted, but she nodded dismissively. "Got it," she snapped.

She closed the door in my face, leaving me half furious and half aroused, with my blood pounding and my cock jumping at the memory of her soft lips.

Delph

The more I saw of the prince's magnificent palace, the more I fell in love with it.

I spent the evening luxuriating in a bed the size of a car in my room. It was a full faerie-tale-princess scenario, four posters on the bed with sheer curtains hanging down that rippled like water when I ran my hand through them. The fittings and fixtures were golden, and an ornate makeup mirror had a matching cushioned bench with studded purple velvet that was soft to sit on.

The adjoining bathroom welcomed me with cream-colored marble walls gracefully laced with delicate veins of gold. It reeked of opulence and royalty. The air carried a subtle hint of floral fragrance. When I let out a solitary singing note, it echoed off the hard surfaces and made me sound like a better singer than I was.

I could have spent all day in that bathroom, chilling in the tub and staring at the details in the ceiling, singing made-up snippets of songs. But the Realm of Caprice beckoned.

Unfortunately, Jayke had to leave on business, so he wasn't there to breakfast with me, but he left me a cute little note with a love heart and a row of x's that I read way too much into. And that kind of made me want to barf.

Our sweet kiss last night hadn't eventuated into me notching up a fae prince onto my bedpost, mainly because my stupid woodpecker brain wouldn't let me settle into the moment. Apparently, it felt guilty about abandoning Grandma and about using the sexy-as-fuck fae prince for his body instead of confessing I wasn't a human ambassador, hand-selected for my political passion.

Stupid brain.

A walk outside would make me feel better.

I was itching to get out and explore. I dressed in my black jeans and T-shirt but left my leather jacket in the closet, strode along the corridor, and took the stairs two at a time, like I belonged. As I stepped to the front doors, a tiny winged faerie buzzed in my way. She was no taller than the length of my forearm, but she had an imposing manner that stilled my feet. Probably something about the way she hovered before my face without blinking.

"Hey," I began uncertainly. I had no idea if she was some kind of princess or held another fae rank. Perhaps I should be bowing to her and scraping along the ground, but that wasn't my style. With an impulsive grin, I held out a hand to shake, but she didn't even glance down at it.

Her voice was melodic, like a tinkling bell, and I had to focus on making out the individual words. "The prince requires you not to leave his domain."

I frowned. Jayke and I had established that I wasn't here under duress, so I didn't see why I should be *required* to do anything. "And why is that?" I demanded, cocking out a hip.

Compared to the faerie's delicate voice, mine was as loud as a trumpeting elephant. She flinched before replying, "It is for your own safety. The world is not safe for fae, let alone humans. You may, of course, wander wherever you please, but if you leave the palace grounds, you are unlikely to return in one piece."

Oh. If I left the grounds, I'd be in danger. Maybe I'd stick around the palace after all.

Damn me and my combative impulses. Jayke was just trying to protect me, not imprison me. He'd already told me of the link between the ruler of Caprice and Caprice itself. Apparently, King Athar's mood had dictated the weather, so if he was happy, the land was all rainbows and sunshine, but the sky split in two when he was in a foul mood.

Just another piece of evidence of how selfish that guy had been. Why require an entire kingdom to suffer just because you had the grumps?

Last night, he'd said something about how the realm had gone wild after the king's death, but I'd been so focused on him grabbing my wrist like he owned me that I hadn't paid much attention to his words. Plus, I didn't realize he meant it so literally. And so dangerously. The fact was, I didn't know exactly what he meant by the realm going wild, so I'd have to ask some more questions.

I wasn't stupid enough to set foot out there when I had no clue what I'd be facing. It was clear as day that fae were stronger and faster than humans, and if they were cautious of facing their dying world, I dreaded to think what it might do to me.

"Right, okay then," I said to the unblinking faerie. I shuffled on the spot, aware of my endless movements compared with the fae stillness. The only movement of the faerie before me was her slowly flapping wings, which managed to keep her body perfectly still. Her amber hair framed her small head like a halo, and her amber eyes bored into mine as though trying to read my soul.

With another lazy flap of her wings, she asked, "So you won't venture beyond the palace grounds?"

I shifted my weight. "No. Thanks. Sorry," I mumbled.

She drifted aside, letting me pass. I wondered what she would have done if I hadn't agreed. Was she strong enough to physically stop me? Or did she have some kind of lasso magic that could tie me to the spot? I really had to find out more about fae abilities.

The vast front doors swung open, and I stepped out into the sunlight, which rippled against my skin. I descended the stairs and crunched along the gravel pathway to the verge of soft green grass.

It certainly didn't look as though the world was dying. It was beautiful and exquisite. Magical. Every breath seemed laced with nectar, and my skin sang under the sunshine.

My last words filtered back to me. *No. Thanks. Sorry.* I barely recognized myself anymore. I never spoke like that. Obviously, I'd said *no* a bunch of times, but I usually sprinkled *thanks* and *sorry* like they were made of diamonds.

This world was changing me. Making me softer, and I'd only been here one night. I wasn't sure how I felt about that. Most young women would leap at the chance to land in a faerie book castle with a charming prince, but it sat oddly in my stomach. And, of course, I knew why.

It was because I didn't belong here. Nothing about Delphinium Smith played nice with being a faerie book princess. True enough, I'd never felt like I truly belonged in Hebes either, but the sheen of oily discomfort on my skin was even thicker here in Sansett Palace.

Like a dog, I shook it off, trying to get rid of that feeling. I passed beneath a perfect fir forest with trees in neat rows, precisely spaced and with consistent foliage all the way to their distant peaks.

Honestly, it was dreamlike. The fir needles at my feet absorbed the sound, and I wondered if this was another sensory deprivation setting, like the Aroma Room. It certainly didn't feel natural here—it was too perfect, too manicured, too orchestrated. And no hint of woodsmoke.

Was the silence of a pine needle carpet exactly what I needed right now? Was the castle's magic providing that for me to help with my emotional state? Like it had given me a scent of burning wood in the aroma room yesterday. And, by the way, what the fuck was that about?

This place and everything about it—and everyone in it—was too perfect for me.

I didn't belong. Even the kiss I'd shared with the prince was sweet but not ground-shaking. He deserved more than me.

As much as I'd like to be there for him and help him onto the throne, I couldn't shake the knowledge that I wasn't the person he needed. That I would never be good enough for him. That I belonged back in the shadowy Docklands, not in this paradise.

After walking for a long time, lost in thought, I noticed full sunlight on my skin and a different texture underfoot, where the pine needles had given way to grass. I was no longer in the fir forest but standing among large pink and purple mushrooms the size of sofas. Unable to resist the impulse—because I was a fucking child—I went over and plonked my ass on the nearest one.

Sure enough, I sank right in, just like that fantastic armchair in the palace. I closed my eyes and relaxed into bliss. Despite having had one of the best night's sleep of my life, my limbs grew heavy, and my head lolled back. Divine. The pink mushroom caught my lolling head, growing and transforming to meet my needs like that gilded chair had yesterday.

This place was freaking heaven.

Perhaps I'd stay a moment longer. There was no place I needed to be. Jayke could wait a few more hours before I told him the hard truth that I wasn't the person he needed on his side. Besides, he wasn't in the palace, he was away on business. There was no reason I should open my eyes or ever leave the comfort of this honey-scented pink mushroom.

The only needle in my bliss was the memory of Kayla and Razelle being ushered away from the Hebes town square. I knew they were safe—I'd sacrificed myself to make sure of that—but they reminded me of Grandma, who was vulnerable and helpless. If I hadn't wanted to leave her house for the bliss of free board with Joey the Bull, what business did I have leaving her alone while I lived through a faerie tale dream?

The needle sharpened, forcing me to a conclusion. Dammit, I would have to talk to Jayke and see about getting home sooner rather than later.

I fought the drugging bliss of sleep and opened my eyes. The pink mushroom had grown around me, encasing my wrists and ankles, forming manacles. I couldn't move. Horror lanced through me as I tugged my right arm, trying to free it. It wouldn't budge. The harder I pulled, the more the pink mushroom fought back. Where I yanked my arm, it turned black and started to smell of rot. The blackened rot spread outward from my thrashing arm, and I tugged harder while panic bubbled through my chest, but with each movement, the fungus thickened around my wrist, then crawled up my arm until I was fully immobile from elbow to wrist.

A cold steel blade pressed to my throat, and I thrashed, trying to get a hand to my neck to protect it.

Fuck. I must have wandered beyond the prince's border, lured onto a pretty seat by foul magic. Lured to my own demise. Lured like a fucking idiot.

But I'd been in tight situations before. An oversized mushroom wouldn't be my undoing, not when I'd survived the streets of Hebes alone.

I took some deep breaths, trying to figure it out.

"Think, dammit," I snarled at myself.

Despite my heaving breaths, I forced myself to stop thrashing, and the spread of rot slowed. It was focused around my right arm and still a sweet cotton candy pink over my other arm and legs. I wiggled my left arm slightly as though stirring in a reverie, and it started to blacken and harden, so I instantly stilled my movements.

This thing was trying to lull me to sleep and only responded aggressively when I tried to free myself. So I'd have to take it by surprise.

The fungus grew slowly over my shoulders, and I looked down, realizing it was growing from both sides, aiming to meet in the middle like a necklace. The sensation of cold steel at my neck grew stronger, but I couldn't free a hand to deal with it and bash it away. Was this mushroom partly made of steel?

I closed my eyes for a moment's focus and felt the lull of sleep calling, so I snapped them open. I counted to three, then launched into action, tearing the soft pink flesh of the mushroom from my ankles, ripping its meaty body and hurling myself free, renting the air with my scream.

I was standing, but the damn thing was still attached to my right wrist, dangling from me like a bloated corpse. Yelling, heart pounding, I tore away strips of the pink flesh and the rotting diseased flesh until the mushroom was in pieces at my feet.

I panted, unable to move, rooted to the spot by fear. My eyes remained fixated on the shredded fungus at my feet, a grotesque sight that sent shivers down my spine. To my horror, each torn piece seemed to burrow into the ground, transforming it into a writhing mass of maggots. My feet moved instinctively, leaping off the tainted ground, my movements awkward as I hopped up and down like an idiot trying to learn how to fly. Panic surged within me as I whipped my head around, scanning the landscape for the shortest route back to the safety of Jayke's lands.

There, fir trees grew in the middle distance, farther away than I remembered walking in the sunshine. I sprinted toward them, hissing and stomping on maggots and the shoots of growing pink mushrooms.

I had to get back to the prince's lands. ASAFP.

Delph

I sprinted across the open field, aiming for the fir forest that marked the boundary of Jayke's lands.

A sense of foreboding enveloped me, caressing my exposed skin like a deranged lover, and I shivered. It wasn't just the pink and purple mushrooms, which had returned to being beautiful and inviting with no hint of their poison. It wasn't just the buzzing heaviness in the air. There was a more specific threat nearby. Every fiber of my body told me so.

When I was nearly at the forest's edge, I slowed to a jog, sweeping my gaze along the tree line in search of threats. A large hooded figure stood between two tree trunks, radiating violence. Fear spiked through me as that cold blade slid flat against my throat. I inhaled sharply and moved a hand to my neck, checking for a knife but finding none.

I looked back up, and the figure in the woods was gone, and the cold blade against my skin was gone with him.

I started running again, panting with fear. I might be stronger and faster than most people in Hebes, but fae were a whole different species and a whole different level of predator.

I dived into the fir forest, and the world changed immediately. Gone was the drugging atmosphere of the mushroom grove, replaced by a cooling, soothing shade beneath the canopy of fir needles. My footsteps were silent on the bed of fallen needles, but that wasn't exactly comforting. Because the predator's footsteps would be silent too.

Even so, the panic gripping my heart eased because I was back in the prince's territory and, therefore, safe. Somehow I knew that hooded figure who radiated violence couldn't hurt me here. Feeling my neck, there was no sign of the cold steel blade I'd felt against it. What the hell was that? It had felt so real against my soft skin, but I hadn't felt anything with my hands.

I beelined for the palace, ran up the grand stairs, pushed open the ornate wooden doors with my shoulder, and barreled in.

Sweat coated me, and I realized how out of place I was. Not only was I out of the mortal realm, but I was out of my comfort zone. I had no business lounging about in palaces, getting my stinky sweat all over the prince's fine rugs and mosaic floors.

From the shadows, a fae appeared from nowhere, startling me. He was tall and fine-featured with ears that tapered to an elegant point, and he wore nothing but a fine green toga that wouldn't have been out of place at a college party. Except the draping was perfectly spaced, the material finer than silk, and he wasn't holding a red plastic cup or hurling into a nearby potted plant.

It wasn't until he spoke that I realized he was a butler. "The prince would like you to join him in the drawing room, my lady," he said.

The male swept an elegant bow and indicated a room to my left that I hadn't noticed before. I swear it appeared out of thin air, the door materializing from a wall of portraits. I blinked several times, having that strange fuzzy feeling like

I'd just woken up and couldn't yet focus. The fae looked at me patiently, and I figured I'd let him wait a moment longer while I gathered myself.

I took a deep breath, then swanned through the newly materialized doorway with as much grace as I could manage, given I was coated in sweat and my shirt and pants were torn from wrestling with a malicious toadstool.

Soft string music tinkled from somewhere, and the prince was reclined on a daybed beneath a flowering palm tree that seemed to grow directly from the wooden floor. I wanted to dive right in next to him, nuzzle into his side, and stare up at those massive purple blooms that had no business being in a palm tree.

But the prince's voice stopped me in my tracks. Irritation passed across his features at my bedraggled state but was quickly replaced with concern. In the next moment, he stood before me, and I swear he must have used muscles I didn't possess to make it look so graceful. "Delphinium, what happened to you?" he gasped. "Are you all right?"

I cocked out a hip and tried to look self-assured. "I met an unfriendly mushroom," I said. "But don't worry, I showed it who was boss."

His brow crinkled in what I suspected was amusement, then he opened his arms. "Come here," he commanded. My feet obeyed without checking in with my independence and carried me across the living wooden floor to the prince's arms.

"You're bloodied," he scolded, and I looked down at my ripped clothing. Red seeped through the tear in my sleeve, but I couldn't feel a thing. Maybe if I'd worn my leather jacket, I would be so leaky. Jayke tested and inspected the wound, which I now saw was blackened where the mushroom had grown around it.

Jayke placed a hand on my arm above the wound and closed his eyes in concentration. A warm tingle began under his hand, soaking the injury in warmth. The sensation spread from the wound along my arm, pausing and pooling at damaged flesh, chasing away the putrid rot and knitting my cells together. Warm water trickled through my veins, clearing the infection and healing everything it touched.

I wriggled my fingers and twisted my arm, feeling and seeing nothing but perfectly unmarred skin. Very fucking cool.

Jayke ran a finger along my jawline, and I looked up to find his lavender eyes filled with emotion. "Did you leave my lands?" he asked.

I bristled at the scolding in his voice—who was he to chide me like an infant? I straightened my spine, ready to mouth off, but the concern in his brow stopped the shit-talk dead.

The fact was, he was a fae prince, and I was a nobody mortal. He'd already given me so much, and I was here under false pretenses. I was not the passionate supporter and political enthusiast he needed in his fight for the realm. Plus, he'd just healed me. Oh, and he'd warned me not to leave his territory.

I bit back my anger and shrugged. "I was curious," I said instead of my natural barbed reply.

He pulled me into a quick hug, enveloping me in his lavender scent. "Do you feel better now?" he asked, and I nodded. "Then go freshen up," he said. "We have a meeting of the Houses to attend this evening and no time to waste." I opened my mouth to object, but he cut me off with a cool finger across my lips. "Please do this for me, Delphinium. Then if you still want to go home in the morning, I'll take you."

Gratitude washed through me, an emotion I was largely unfamiliar with. I knew anger, spite, and jealousy like bosom buddies, but thankfulness was new. I had to figure out how to navigate this strange new side of me. I started by forcing my lips to curve. "Sure thing, Jayke."

Perhaps if I acted the part of a decent human being, my personality would catch up.

Delph

An hour later, I descended the winding stairs to where the prince awaited me in the foyer. I wore a long green gown that fluttered at my ankles weightlessly. The material was so fine I felt naked and had to keep looking down to check that my bits were covered.

They were...mostly. Strips of material covered me horizontally and vertically, turning me into some kind of chessboard. The green ribbons crisscrossed my white flesh, putting on quite a display. The strips were just wide enough to cover my breasts. I gave a little deliberate jump, observing to check if the strip dislodged, but the material seemed to anticipate my movements and keep me covered. Even walking up a small step, I didn't have to lift the long strands, they magically swished aside so I wouldn't tread on them.

"You look ravishing," Jayke told me when I reached the first floor, his eyes hooded and an unmistakable hitch in his voice.

I smirked and put a little extra swish into my step, adoring the way his gaze devoured me.

"You look entirely lickable," I told him, and it was true. His outfit was similar to mine, but a lot more of his chest was on display. Yellow strips crossed diagonally over his chest but failed to cover his nipples. I glanced down, of course, but his junk was obscured by more yellow ribbons that fluttered to his knees like a kilt. His muscular thighs were on display as he walked, reminding me of gladiators of old, ripped as fuck and somehow rocking a skirt and making it masculine.

Jayke held out his hand with a query in his eyes, asking if I would accept it. Already, the presumptuous cocky side of this prince was melting away into a gentleman who asked for consent, and I couldn't be happier about it. I gladly accepted his hand, and the front doors opened as we approached, spilling moonlight across the threshold.

Hand-in-hand, we descended the broad staircase to the gravel path. I looked about for a sign of a carriage. "How are we getting there? Are we flying?"

Jayke grunted. "You know I'm a Healer, not a Hover," he said. I glanced up to figure out if I was just imagining that pissed-off tone and saw that crinkle in his brow I was beginning to associate with amusement. "We're walking," he said.

My soft silk shoes looked like ballet slippers but protected the soles of my feet like thick leather as I crunched across the gravel. Still, I wasn't up for a ten-mile hike. "Where are we going?" I asked. "Is it far?"

My arm was looped through Jayke's, with my hand resting on his forearm like a couple straight out of a Jane Austen novel. Warmth seeped through the place where our arms touched, and I squeezed gently on his thickly muscled forearm, enjoying the hardness.

He squinted into the distance. "We're going to the Spike forecourt several leagues away."

I had no freaking idea how far a league was, but it didn't sound walkable. "I—"

The prince cut me off, anticipating my concern. Being interrupted by anybody else usually left me shouting and stomping, but somehow I didn't mind. "Don't concern yourself, Delphinium," he said. "It is not that far by foot."

Now there was a riddle I could get lost in. How could something be closer by foot than by any other means of transport? And what did distance even mean if it couldn't be paced out?

Impatience curdled my gut as we approached the ornate marble gates that marked the edge of the prince's property. I squeezed his forearm, gaining strength from his strength. "This is so exciting! I can't believe I get to see the fae realm."

Jayke's tone had none of the giddy excitement of mine. "You'll be safe if you stick by my side," he said.

Oh yes, the dangers. I'd forgotten about them. I'd only been eaten by an oversized fungus a few hours ago, and already my emotions were sliding back toward excitement. Grandma always told Lexi and me that we had too much adventure in our spirit and should be more like Kayla or Razelle, and this was exactly what she meant. I was foolhardy and headstrong and plunged merrily into danger without considering the consequences.

Well, that would never change, I knew that much about myself. I didn't even want it to change. I loved being impetuous, daring, and headstrong, and even if I didn't, those qualities were so innate in me that if I were to change them, I would become a completely different person.

No, that would never happen. I would remain the thrill-seeking woman I always was. So I needed a levelheaded male by my side. I stole a glance at Jayke's grave face and smirked. He was precisely the kind of person I needed to keep me in check.

The marble gates opened at our approach, and as we stepped over the threshold and left the palace grounds, the moonlight intensified. It was so bright above us that shadows pooled at our feet, and I could see perfectly in every direction. There was no sign of poisonous toadstools, no sign of any danger. In fact, there wasn't much sign of anything – no neighbors, no shops, and just one single road that shot into the distance.

But magic lay thick in the air. That heavy foreboding I had felt in the mushroom grove laced the air, and with every breath I took, it inhabited more of my body. I released my hold on Jayke and took a few more steps, inhaling deeply and feeling the world's anticipation fill me. It was like a scuttling of roaches but silent. Or a pounding waterfall, but without the noise or water. Just the anticipation of something terrible. "What is that?" I asked.

Jayke closed the distance between us and held my hand. "Caprice is tied to the ruler. The realm is...waiting for her next king."

"Or queen," I interjected sharply.

"There are no females currently in contention for the throne," he remarked mildly.

Oh. So that *king* thing wasn't him being sexist, just a reflection of the current state of politics in Caprice. Good to know.

Jayke's phrasing was interesting. *The realm is waiting for her next king.* He made it sound like the land was alive and filled with emotion. Strangely, I felt that anticipation viscerally. It was all-consuming, soaking from the realm into my skin, like the land's anxiety to find its next ruler was contagious.

"And when will the king be crowned?" I asked. We resumed

walking along the road. It looked miles long, and I dreaded to think we had to walk the length of it. Jayke would probably end up having to carry me, which would be embarrassing.

"The coronation happens in sixteen days, right after the Ascension rite," he explained.

The Ascension rite. That was where young fae killed themselves to come into their power. The ritual at which Jayke had come into his Healing powers.

"Why then?" I didn't see why they should wait a moment longer to nominate a king. The tingle of anticipation in the air made me jittery, demanding that a decision be made as soon as possible. How could everybody stand to wait another sixteen days?

Jayke's expression grew thoughtful. "You see, there's this rare chance that Gaia might Touch a fae with Lightning to be the ruler during the rite. Though, it's been more than a millennium since that happened, and never during the interregnum phase."

"An interregnum what now?"

Jayke's brow creased again in amusement. "The period between rulers. In every instance when a king has died on the throne." *Or queen*, I interjected silently. "The next ruler has been determined through nomination and coronation. But formality requires us to wait. We are lucky the next Ascension rite is only sixteen days from now."

We walked on, our fingers laced together, a measure of comfort flowing from his hands to mine and counteracting the anxiety the realm's atmosphere induced in me.

The road we followed was wide enough for a horse and carriage and gave slightly underfoot as though made from rubber or wood rather than asphalt. Fields stretched on either side of us, with wildflowers closed up for the evening, bathed in the cool moonlight that leached all color from the world. I would definitely have to come back and see these fields in the daylight because if those pink and purple mushrooms were anything to go by, these fields would be a riot of color. I determined to take a peek tomorrow, danger be damned.

The world buzzed like a million insects were hovering nearby, but I had the odd sensation that the buzzing wasn't audible but just a sense of anticipation.

The moon lit the road before us, and our footsteps ate away at it. Then the moonbeams diverted and lit up a second path I hadn't noticed, enticing me to follow it. I tugged Jayke's hand toward the moonlit way, which was barely wide enough for us to walk side-by-side. I stole a glance at his face and found him frowning, but he followed me anyway.

As soon as I stepped onto the path, the world transformed. The fields of sleeping wildflowers blurred, and the moonlight formed streaks through the air, looking so tangible I could climb a moonbeam all the way up to their pearly mother.

I stopped in amazement, and the world charged back into place. The fields, the flowers, the road that I'd left behind me, although it seemed farther away than it should. I'd only taken a few steps along the secondary path, but the road was already dozens of yards away.

Delighted, I tried a little experiment and took a few more steps along the moonbeam path. Again, the flowers and fields blurred into streaks, and the moonbeams formed distinct lines through the air. I stopped and looked behind me, and the road was even farther away, just a dark line in the distance.

I laughed. "It's like a travelator," I said. Jayke frowned again, and I touched his hard jaw, feeling it soften beneath my touch. He was a grumpy host, but I wouldn't hold that against him. "Like they have in airports back home," I explained. "You walk along one, and it's like you're walking faster than the world around you."

"I see," he grumbled, although I could tell he didn't really.

"Only here, if I stop walking, the whole world stops, too," I gabbled. "I bet I could step off this path and—"

He grabbed my wrist as I made to step into the field beside us. "If you leave the path, you will get lost and unable to find your way back onto the moonway."

Okay, good to know. Do not step off the moonway—the perfect name, by the way.

My usual surliness was wrapped in a tight ball within me, and I couldn't be happier to leave it behind. Giggling—fucking giggling—I trotted along the moonway, alternating between sprinting, jogging, and twirling. I looked back and saw Jayke striding steadily behind me, not falling prey to my giddiness. I supposed he'd seen this a thousand times. Maybe a million times—God knew how old he was.

Standing still and watching him approach was the oddest sensation. The fields around me were not blurred because I was stationary, and Jayke wasn't blurred either because we were on the same path. But with every stride, he walked dozens of yards, seeming disconnected from the world around him though very much anchored in mine.

"Absolutely fucking wonderful," I grinned, watching him come closer.

Delph

When we reached the end of the moonway, we'd left the wildflower fields far behind and emerged in a bustling town. Sweet little cottages with doorways and windows of different shapes and sizes to accommodate beings of different shapes and sizes lined the cobblestone road. Fae darted in and out of homes and what I suspected were storefronts, buzzing and humming. The happy hustle and bustle of a prosperous city muted that anxiety-inducing anticipation in the air.

The colors were everything. One house was round like a giant beach ball and painted a peppermint hue that glittered in moonlight and changed colors as I walked past. I could stride back and forth in front of that little home for hours, mesmerized by the subtle shades and dancing moonlight.

As I watched, three tiny fae no taller than my calf, with gossamer wings almost as large as they were, fluttered out of the peppermint beach ball. I wondered if they were lesser faeries and how they felt about being labeled like that.

Every fae we passed nodded at Jayke or dashed away, giving him a wide berth. One girl with strawberry-red eyes bowed so low to him that her strawberry-red curls swept the cobble-stones.

The prince smiled generously at each and every one of them.

"They all seem to respect you," I whispered, although fae hearing was so much better than mine that perhaps my murmur was the equivalent of shouting through a loudspeaker.

Jayke swept my hand into his and kissed my fingers. "Of course they do. I am the prince."

There was that arrogant male I first met, but I let it go. After all, he was only speaking the truth. He was destined to be their next king, so I should hardly be surprised by the odd show of reverence.

As we walked, I kept an eye on the marvelous buildings. "You said we were going to some place called the Spike forecourt," I said. "That sounds kind of painful. Am I likely to survive?" I joked.

My quip fell flat, and I reminded myself I was in danger here, as those man-eating mushrooms should have taught me.

Jayke squeezed my fingers until they hurt. "I'll keep you safe," he growled.

"What's the Spike?" I demanded, fear lancing through me at his reaction.

We walked swiftly along the cobblestone streets until we rounded a corner and got a clear view over some rooftops. "That," he said, pointing to a tall tower in the middle distance that rose above everything else in the city and ended in a piercing point that gleamed wickedly in the moonlight.

I shivered. At least we were only meeting in the forecourt of the Spike, so presumably, I wouldn't have to go in. We turned left at the junction and plowed immediately into a forest, which greeted us with a cloying perfume of jasmine. What the fuck?

Not wanting to earn another amused brow-furrow from Jayke, I kept my question inside. Instead, I paid attention to my surroundings, determined to figure it out on my own. No, we hadn't plunged into another moonway. And no, we hadn't accidentally fallen into a different realm. It was just a standard street in Capricia. As we crisscrossed toward the Spike, I realized that forested roads were interspersed with urban ones throughout the city.

It was spectacular. This city was like the offspring of ye olde London mating with a hedge maze.

A ring of fae mounted on massive horses surrounded the Spike. A large black mare snorted as we approached, stamping her foot. Holy crap, these guys were serious about defense. Barely five inches separated one fae's knee from his neighbor, forming an impenetrable circle. Every second guard held a sword, and every other a lance.

My footsteps slowed as we approached, and I scanned the ring of guards for a break where we could pass through, inhaling the musky horsey scent. The prince strode directly forward and made an impatient gesture when the guards were slow to move aside.

But move aside, they did. Jayke wasn't kidding when he said he was respected around here.

Beyond the circle of guards, the paved ground outside the Spike was festooned with transparent globes, each filled with buzzing Lightning, like mini thunderstorms. These hovering globes lit up the forecourt with flashes of electric blue–white light. Soft music was playing, which thankfully drowned out the buzzing of bugs that was always just beyond my hearing.

Fae stood about in finery, wearing gowns and outfits every bit as outlandish as my own. One female wore a dress that flashed with Lightning, which was surely electrocuting her with every flash, but her dazzling smile never faltered.

Many fae wore outfits that matched their hair and eyes. A midnight blue gown with a midnight blue up-do studded with sapphires, above an intense midnight blue stare that seemed to recoil in shock when it landed on me.

After that woman's reception, I paid more attention, watching people respond to my presence. Despite the perfect control over their faces, I detected strong reactions in those fae eyes. Red eyes, green eyes, violet eyes, all dilating in surprise when they landed on me.

I had to resist the temptation to run my hands over my rounded ears. If I'd known how rare humans were in Caprice, I never would have agreed to attend this event. But it was too late now, so I rolled my shoulders back, stuck out my tits, and smiled back at every asshole who looked at me.

Clearly comfortable that I wasn't in imminent danger, Jayke melted into the crowd and began pressing palms. I supposed this was one of the significant events leading up to his coronation, so he had to schmooze. I didn't mind a bit. It allowed me to absorb my surroundings without feeling the intensity of the prince's attention.

It was just like the few housewarming parties I'd attended, just fancier. People standing about in small groups gossiping, others flashing smiles and telling stories to earn respect, or at least attention. And one male standing by himself at the edge of the group, sneering at anybody who approached him.

The man was tall, with skin as black as onyx and a slim but tautly muscled frame. His hair was golden, practically glowing under the Lightning globes, and when his golden eyes locked on mine, I saw they shone just as brightly.

Locked in his glare, I felt a cold blade pressed against my throat, and I gasped.

That same sense of foreboding from earlier, when I'd seen a hooded figure by the mushroom gorge, threaded through me. I put a hand to my neck, checking the knife wasn't really there because it felt so real, and a satisfied smirk crossed the dark stranger's face.

How dare he? How fucking dare he? Fury pounded through my muscles, and before I knew it, I was stalking toward him, my hands curled into fists.

"You were at the mushroom gorge this morning," I accused, jabbing a finger into his chest. I wished my fingernail were a bit longer so I could stab the asshole while I was at it. His chest was covered in dark, rough cloth, and unlike most fae here, he didn't display his flesh beneath finery but was demurely clad from head to foot.

That imaginary cold blade dug farther into my throat, and I swear I felt a trickle of blood down my neck.

The dark stranger sneered, and violence and mistrust rolled off him. "So what if I was?" he snarled.

I jabbed him again, digging past the rough fabric and really poking my forefinger into his pectoral muscle. "I could have died," I hissed. "Those wild toadstools almost bloody ate me, and you just stood around and let it happen. You could have stepped in and helped me, but you just fucking watched."

Electricity sizzled beneath my skin, and I wished I could manifest it and char this asshole where he stood. His golden eyes dripped with violence and beckoned to the anger and fury inside me, heating my blood into a frenzy. He brought out the worst of my nature, and I didn't give a damn.

The golden light in his eyes blazed for a moment, signaling his own anger. "Caprice takes care of her own," he drawled.

"What the fuck is that supposed to mean?"

"Only the strong survive here," he sneered. "There is no place in Caprice for the weak."

My fingernails bit into my palms as I struggled to contain the volcano within me. "So you just sit back and watch the weak die? Would you watch an infant be consumed by flames, or would you step in and save it?" Honestly, what kind of brutal being would just sit back and watch while somebody in need was demolished?

Those golden eyes flicked down to my toes and then worked their way slowly back up to my face. "You're not an infant," he said slowly.

I cocked my hip, owning every inch of my body. "You got that right," I said. "And I'm not weak either, so you can forget about your precious realm weeding me out."

The male's earlier flash of anger receded, and his tone became measured. He plastered a condescending sneer onto his face and looked at me. "You say you're not weak, yet you berate me for not treating you like a damsel in distress. Did you ever stop to consider the hypocrisy of that?"

"Asshole," I spit. "Any decent person would help somebody in distress whether or not they were weak."

His sneer turned positively sinister. "I never said I was decent," he snarled.

The blade on my neck felt cold, hard, and sharp, but I refused to feel for the phantom knife. I couldn't do anything but stare at the fuckwit who almost let me die and couldn't even be bothered to apologize. "And from your trashy language, you're clearly not decent either," the male added.

Anger buzzed inside me. I might be a savage bitch from the Docklands, but I didn't need this idiot to point it out. The hum of the crowd and the lilting music added to the buzzing in my ears as I prepared to get stuck into this guy. I was so riled up that a light tap on my shoulder made me jump, and I swung around with my fists up, my defensive instincts kicking in, but it was just Jayke. "It's time," the prince said, his breath warming the shell of my ear.

I threw one last furious glance at my tormentor, and he smirked. "Off you go, little pet," he growled. "Off to perform for your master."

Jayke whirled around, his face mere inches from the other fae, his porcelain white skin contrasting with my tormentor's onyx flesh. "Stay the fuck away from her," my prince snarled.

The other man was still relaxed, looking for all the world like he was at a tea party. "Or what?" he drawled.

"Or you'll have to answer to me," Jayke snapped.

We spun and walked away. As I put distance between myself and that horrifying male, the cold pressure of an imaginary blade at my throat finally released. I'd always prided myself on my ability to defend myself against Docklands thugs, but here, I was damn glad to have Jayke's protection.

Jayke

I introduced Delphinium to as many fae as possible, circulating around the forecourt with smiles and warm words.

It was the usual drab array of lick-spittles and sycophants, but they were armed in finery and smiles, and I hoped for Delphinium's sake she didn't see the way they scanned her with predatory eyes. I could smell the thrill of the hunt in them. Hopefully, the rumors of Hebes inhabitants' lack of perception were true, and Delphinium was blissfully unaware of the effect she was having on these fae.

Certainly, she seemed amazed at the pomp and circumstance, and her gaze flitted between hair and fabric and toothy grins with wonder and awe.

Many fae were gossiping about the Shadow Walkers in the East. Bastian and Bree Athar had returned from their last Ascension rite in Verda talking about the monstrous beasts who, apparently, had destroyed the celebration and killed several important fae, including Arrow Sanctus, the heir to the Fen throne. Rumor had it that the Shadow Walkers had crossed from the Shadow Isles to the East and turned their victims into lifeless husks who had to be salted and burned, or they kept walking around.

It was difficult to separate rumor from fact, particularly

with the hysterical tendencies of our previous rulers. But if it was a serious threat, I would deal with it in due time. But right now, I needed everybody's focus on the coronation. After I was king, I would deal with the Shadow Walkers.

So, whenever the conversation veered toward the Walkers, I moved Delphinium on to the next group of fae who were hungry to meet her.

I left the most important introduction to last. Gently tugging Delphinium toward a statuesque female who shared my pale skin but matched it with eyes and hair of the palest blue. "Delphinium, I'd like you to meet my sister Jayne."

My precious Hebes girl smiled, warmth filling her face. Honestly, I could read her emotions from the moon. For most of the evening, she'd been lost in awe and feeling out of depth among the glittering fae, but now she was suffused with pleasure.

"Jayne, how lovely to meet you," she gushed. "Jayke has been extremely—"

Jayne interrupted with her usual imperious voice. "Jayke?" She lifted a perfectly arched eyebrow in my direction, and my gut clenched. I didn't want her to ruin this moment for me by being a complete snob about the use of my first name.

"That's right," I said, grinning broadly to encourage Delphinium to continue.

She didn't miss the interaction between me and my sister but plowed on regardless of Jayne's rudeness, for which I had to admire her. "As I was saying," Delphinium began, "Jayke has been very welcoming and hospitable." Her slight emphasis on my first name had a smile tugging on my lips, but I clamped it down. No need to raise my sister's ire while I still needed her support to become king.

My sister's eyebrows were a paler blue than her hair, and she released her arched one and addressed me. "I like this one," she said tartly. "She has bite."

Both females relaxed slightly, the minor differences in their postures signaling it as clearly as a beacon calls a ship. I was pleased. Jayne didn't think I could pull off my scheme of fetching the most important person in Hebes to help my cause, but from the appreciative glint in her pale blue eyes, I could see I had won her around.

I observed Delphinium to see how she responded to the situation and saw her studying me just as closely. "Your hair and eyes are different," she mused, "but your perfectly straight noses and full lips are like mirror images. I didn't realize fae could be twins."

Honestly, this female was very impressive. Her powers of deduction exceeded what I would expect from a resident of Hebes. Most fae could not perceive that Jayne and I were twins, but that was because twins were so rare among fae. Even single live births were rare, let alone doubles.

Jayne's pale blue eyebrow quirked again, and she looked more impressed than I'd seen her in years. "Indeed," she said flatly, just loud enough to be heard over the soft music.

Oblivious to the current of meaning flowing between Jayne and me, Delphinium plowed along. "Do you have any other siblings?" she asked.

That was probably a common question in Hebes, but in Caprice, it was considered the height of rudeness. Many couples could not conceive one child, and very few conceived two. For somebody to stare a brother and sister in the face and ask if they had a third sibling was unthinkably crass.

But also, in this case, outrageously correct. The smile that tugged at my lips was genuine. "We do. Her name is Leena—"

This spectacular creature interrupted me again, which despite her perspicacity, still irritated me. "Is she here?" she asked, babbling like a brook. "Can I meet her?" She practically wriggled with excitement, and the green strips of her gown swooshed.

Jayne and I shared a look so loaded that even the citizen of Hebes noticed. I tilted my head ever so slightly at my sister, giving her permission to explain.

"Leena was brutally attacked by House Athar," Jayne said, and my attention zeroed in on Delphinium's reaction.

It was gloriously over-the-top, of course, as befitting somebody raised among humans. She gasped, and her hand flew to her mouth. "Oh, I'm so sorry," she said.

Jayne put a hand up to stop the display of emotion, and I hoped Delphinium read it as a gesture of comfort, though it certainly was not. "There is no need to be concerned," my sister said tightly. "All you need to know is that Leena cannot be here tonight."

Delphinium sucked her teeth. "And House Athar is to blame," she hissed. The steel in her voice rang through me, and I was proud of her response. She didn't back down from a challenge or cower in fear. This impressive female from Hebes stood taller and readied for the fight, which was exactly the reaction I needed.

Remarkably, Jayne carried on the conversation as though we were chitchatting at the spring equinox. "And you, Delphinium? Do you have any family?"

My sister somehow refrained from throwing me a loaded glance as she asked that innocent-sounding question.

Delphinium jutted out her chin as though facing an enemy.

"I was brought up by my uncle until I hit puberty. Then he had the twins, and my grandma took care of me from then on."

I narrowed my eyes, watching Jayne, wondering where she was headed with this line of questioning and praying to Gaia she didn't fuck everything up. My sister put a long painted nail to her lips. "And do you get along with your family?"

I held my breath, waiting for the answer. "Not really...That is, yes. I love my cousins with everything I've got. I would do anything for them. Actually, I did." She turned her face to me. "The youngest two were the ones chosen by your guards, Jayke, and I'm here only because I stepped in on their behalf. I thought they were coming here to be your sex slaves or something." She gave a small huff I couldn't interpret.

Her innocent face was upturned to mine as though making a confession, as though she was only here because of some kind of misunderstanding.

I would never take human children to bed, and my fists curled in anger that she had thought so. But I placed a hand on her cold shoulder, running my thumb over her smooth white skin, trying to calm her the fuck down. "That was very noble of you," I said. I wanted to reassure her, to assuage her fears that she didn't belong here, but she just shrugged off my hand.

"You don't understand," she said. "I'm not saying that so you'll think I'm a good person, I'm just trying to explain—"

Jayne tilted her elegant head forward and, thankfully, interrupted Delphinium's self-derailing monologue. "And are you close with your grandmother?" she asked, swirling her glass and sniffing her fruity wine.

Delph's jaw jutted out again as she struggled with her thoughts. "I... She isn't an easy person to love. And there's always tension between us. It's like I was made from fire and

83

she was made from water. Like…" She trailed off, her eyes looking beyond me and my sister, beyond and through us, peering all the way back to Hebes.

"Like you didn't belong," my sister said softly, and I looked up sharply. Why had she said that? Where was she heading with that line of thought? Perhaps my sister was trying to make the stranger feel like she belonged here.

I didn't know how to ease the suffering in Delphinium's chest, to untangle the writhing thread of thoughts that kept her from relaxing. But I tried anyway. "You're welcome here for as long as you want to stay." I shifted uncomfortably and lowered my tone, hoping nobody else could hear. "Regardless of what happens at the coronation."

Her eyes refocused to the present and bored into mine. Did she know how startling the effect of her mismatched hair and eyes was? Her green eyes flashed with uncertainty and guilt, but I could see my warm words worming their way inside her too.

She beamed me a grin that didn't match her posture, but at least she was trying. "Well, my prince," she said silkily. "Let's make sure things go your way at that coronation."

Delph

Jayne was an honest-to-God queen. It was all I could do to stop myself from prostrating on the floor before her and praying. She was intimidating as fuck. I could see how the fae and lesser faeries on the streets felt around Jayke, either bowing or fleeing, because those were my instinctual reactions to meeting his sister. Fuck me.

Despite her queenly voice, her words were pleasant enough. I certainly wouldn't trust her any more than I would put my head inside a crocodile's mouth, but this was one croc I would happily befriend.

I was saved from having to make any more small talk with Her Intimidating Highness by an announcement that the strength display would begin. The tension in the crowd mounted, eager eyes turning toward the stage as anticipation crackled in the air.

A woman wearing a tube dress that sheathed her body like a pale pink condom held the assembled fae's attention. "The two candidates for king will now display their inner powers. Only the strongest fae may rule Caprice, so these displays must factor into your decision about whom to support. Throw your weight behind the strongest candidate."

I couldn't wait to see this display. I'd only known the guy

twenty-four hours, but I was already buzzing with pride for my champion, Jayke. He was the first candidate called up, so my impatience to meet the second candidate from House Davin would have to wait.

Jayke looked every inch a king as he took to the center of the forecourt. As I watched, a stage grew up beneath him, elevating him above the fae who ringed him, all as silent and still as only fae could be.

I stilled my fidgeting fingers and tried to emulate their statue-like composure but fuck it, a woman had to breathe.

In his crisscrossing yellow outfit, Jayke's link to me was obvious. Even if they hadn't seen us arrive together, everybody would know he and I were a pair. Only where my clothes were feminine and flowing, his were sweeping and intimidating.

His voice bellowed, and I wondered if that was a display of strength in itself. "Bring out the wounded," he roared.

A female limped out from behind the crowd and approached the stage, her dragging feet scraping over the paving stones. A dangerous glint in Jayke's eyes had me concerned for a moment, but then he smiled and held his hand over her knee while magic poured from it and healed her.

I knew exactly how that felt. Warm and tingly and like a bubble bath was sluicing through your veins. The woman smiled and danced a jig, and a smattering of applause rippled through the audience.

The next injured male was more impressive, with his hand nearly severed at the wrist and dangling at an angle from his arm. I couldn't hold back the grimace of disgust at the sight of his bone poking out, but the other fae kept their expressions stony, of course.

The applause at the prince's healing prowess was louder and

more enthusiastic this time and lasted a little longer. A parade of injuries emerged from the crowd, each more devastating than the last, and as Jayke healed each one, the enthusiasm in the group at his powers escalated to a frenzy.

Finally, a child was borne from the crowd on a stretcher. She was close to death, and although fae came in all colors, her pallor looked unnatural even to my eyes. Spittle bubbled at her mouth, and poison leached her veins black, visible through her sickly yellow skin. I could smell the rot on her, like death made visible.

The fae beside me gasped, and my eyes practically bulged out of my head at the sound. A fae sounding emotional? Holy hell.

"She cannot be Healed," a voice behind me muttered, and other fae murmured their assent. Surely they were right. The faeling on the stretcher was a hair's breadth from death. Her black curly hair reminded me of Lexi's, and I had the urge to run over and ease her departure from this world with comforting words.

But Jayke's hand was already passing slowly over her body, his eyes closed in concentration and his jaw clenched. A bead of sweat rolled down his brow. We onlookers collectively held our breath and waited, watching Jayke push back the spidering black veins from the girl's frail body and bring her breathing back to normal. Her eyes fluttered open, and she smiled weakly, and Jayke staggered in exhaustion, his boots thumping on the wooden stage.

Wild applause went up from the fae, and one male to my right exploded with a bang. A female to my left levitated a few feet to get a better view, and the globes of Lightning above us fizzled and sizzled as though in support of Jayke's bid for the throne.

Pride and relief buzzed in my chest as the young faeling sat up and threw her arms around her prince.

The statuesque female with the pale pink condom dress reappeared and introduced the second candidate for his strength display. "Darzan Davin, the candidate for House Davin, will now demonstrate his inner power. As before, I encourage you to throw your support behind the strongest fae so that Caprice may have the strongest ruler."

I couldn't help the flutter of anticipation that wound through me and couldn't tell if it came from within or from the tense atmosphere itself. Caprice wanted to see what this second candidate was made of just as much as I did.

My mouth fell open, and my heart stopped dead in my chest when the second heir stomped angrily onto the stage. He was tall with glowing golden hair and eyes, and skin as black as night. His eyes locked onto mine, and that cold steel sensation pressed against my throat.

The candidate from House Davin was the asshole I'd sparred with earlier, who thought the weak should be tortured and killed.

Darzan Davin released my gaze and closed his eyes, summoning his inner power. Mercifully, the sensation of steel against my throat disappeared when his eyes left mine, but I could sense the violence growing within him as he mustered his magic.

"Bring out the victim," he snarled. His voice matched Jayke's in volume but was woven through with violent intent and made the hairs on my arms stand on end.

Victim? Seriously? What the fuck was this asswipe going to do to display his strength?

A fae male stepped forward from the crowd, the oldest I'd seen, with visible wrinkles and a slight stoop. He approached the stage slowly, his breathing labored and loud, then raised his head wearily and nodded slowly at Darzan. Surely whatever was about to happen couldn't be too bad if the old fae went willingly.

But I was wrong. A sneer of pure evil lanced across Darzan's face in the instant before he raised an empty hand and slashed the air before him with a finger, slicing the old fae in half diagonally from shoulder to hip. The fae's torso slid to the ground with a juicy plop, then his legs toppled over, spraying warm, sticky blood across the paving stones.

A fae in the front row let out a horrified shriek as blood spattered across her face, her body recoiling instinctively. Gasps and exclamations rippled through the crowd, mingling with the pungent metallic scent of fresh blood.

Then silence solidified into a physical entity that stilled my breath and stopped my heart from pumping. That disgusted look never left Darzan's face as he swept an ironic bow to the crowd and stomped offstage.

When I began breathing again, I couldn't tear my eyes from the body seeping blood onto the ground, red rivulets grouting the paving stones.

That did it. That brutal act of sheer violence and the nasty expression on Darzan's face convinced me to help Jayke win his kingship, even if it meant Grandma had to fend for herself a while longer.

I would do everything I could to ensure that murderous thug never sat on the Caprician throne.

Delph

The next morning, I insisted on visiting the field of wildflow-ers, and Jayke insisted on accompanying me.

"It's not safe alone," he growled, and I took that as an invitation for a lovely picnic date among multicolored blooms.

The petals were even more spectacular than I imagined. Blue, purple, pink, green, golden, silver, the flowers came in rich shades of every hue I'd ever seen—and some I hadn't. They smelled like the street outside a flower shop, like a place rich people would hang out.

Delighted, I trailed out my hand, and the blooms leaned toward it like preening kittens eager for a pet.

But Jayke smacked my hand away. "With the king dead, it isn't safe to interact with the flora," he grumbled.

Well, I knew that was true. Those mushrooms that looked so comfortable and inviting had turned the worst kind of cruel. So I supposed I should believe him about the flowers, too, although they looked as soft as velvet. After Jayke was king, I'd come back and roll around in this field.

"Why don't you just take over the kingship now?" I asked. I kept my fingers to myself but inhaled the heavy floral scent as I stared over the beautiful flowers. "I mean, I know you said the coronation is after the Ascension rite, but couldn't you just take the throne in the meantime to keep the realm happy? Surely that's better than being attacked by all the fucking wildlife."

Jayke regarded me solemnly, and I was glad he took my question seriously. I opened my mouth, but he silenced me with a large finger to my lips. "Fine," he grumbled, "I'll show you. In Capricia."

The buzzing anticipation of the realm grew louder, and I kept my eyes open, looking for the moonway, but without the moon shining, I couldn't discern it from the rest of the fields. But Jayke apparently could because before long, he swept up my hand and tugged me off the road. I traveled the moonway carefully, following behind Jayke so as not to step off accidentally, and we finally emerged in the same location as the previous night.

The peppermint beach ball house was now bubblegum pink and emitting a lollypop smell, and as I walked past, it morphed into a deep mauve.

Fae bowed and hurried away as we passed, their feet skittering over the cobblestones. I noticed more than a couple balk at seeing my rounded ears, so I stuck out my chest and held my chin high, determined to relish being the center of attention, seeing as I didn't have a choice.

Their reverence reminded me of how I'd felt meeting Jayne. Last night opened my eyes in many ways, especially regarding the other contender to the throne.

"That Darzan guy from House Davin was a right fucker," I muttered. We walked a few more steps, me clomping along and the prince gliding noiselessly while I figured out what I was trying to say. "Surely House Athar couldn't have been worse?"

Jayke's beautiful face turned toward me, the sunlight playing through his lavender hair. "House Davin is probably worse than House Athar, it's just they haven't had the kingship to prove it. But Darzan and his brother Pike have left a trail of atrocities dotting back through time since their birth."

I shivered. The air was a perfect temperature, warm but not hot, and if I ignored the terrible sense of anticipation, it was entirely comfortable. Even so, I shivered, remembering that look of pure evil on Darzan's face as he sliced the elderly fae in two. The memory curdled my gut and set my blood on fire. It was disgusting but also fucking infuriating, and I dreaded to think what would become of the realm if that monster became her king.

"Darzan has a brother?" I asked.

We reached a junction of cobblestone streets and forested highways and took a left down a grassy avenue lined with colorful treehouses. I swore this street smelled of jasmine last night, but now it gave off a robust piney scent. Jayke's brows knitted together. "It is impolite to ask fae about their siblings," he scolded, and the coldness of the comment washed away my anger at House Davin.

I removed my hand from Jayke's, and he tutted, making me feel like a petulant bitch. But I wouldn't trot along beside any male who reprimanded me like a child, prince or not. "I see," I said flatly. I knew I should be open to learning about fae culture, but his cold command was more reprimanding than informative, and I couldn't help my retreat.

I sighed. I supposed that was another way I didn't belong here. Fae were emotionless and composed, and I was neither. I knew I was being childish and far too human, but I couldn't control my reaction.

We continued in silence for a while. It became clear we were headed toward the Spike because that pointed stone tower grew closer with every turning we made, and we soon stood outside the ring of mounted guards.

I thought those horsey guards were only there for the ceremony last night, but apparently, they were a permanent fixture around the Spike. In the daylight, I saw their tunics were black with a silver horse engraved onto their breastplates, similar to House Sansett's uniforms but with different coloring.

Just like last night, the mounted fae took one look at Prince Sansett and moved aside, letting us pass without comment.

Silence had fallen between me and Jayke after his cold rebuke and my childish reaction, and I didn't know how to broach it, so I let it grow. The debris from last night's party was gone. No stage, no trash, no hovering balls of Lightning. Jayke crossed the forecourt and marched right up to the gaping hole that was the Spike's entrance, and I swallowed my fear and matched him stride for stride.

Inside, the Spike was just as dark and forbidding as the outside. Cold stone walls rose like a fortress, the air heavy with a sense of ancient power. A staircase hugged the tower's outside curve and probably wound all the way to the tip. It smelled dank and empty, like it hadn't been lived in for a hundred years, although there was no sign of dust or decay. A couple of grand soaring doors carved with ornate forest scenes led off the entrance hall, and Jayke motioned to one without speaking, letting me go first, and I wondered if it was punishment.

Great. I'll go first into the lair of doom.

I refused to show any fear, so I stepped in front of Jayke

and through the door, which led to a cavernous room with another sharply peaked roof that may have reached all the way to the Spike's tip. My footsteps echoed, a faint murmur bouncing around the cavernous space, and I abruptly stopped. Intricate pillars carved from marble, stone, and wood reached the heavens. Across the vast chamber was a throne shaped like a lightning bolt raised on a broad platform.

But the most remarkable thing about the room was the floor, which was a giant lake. A shiver crawled down my spine as I stared at the rippling expanse, the room's true centerpiece—a floor that appeared to be a liquid mirror, reflecting the throne's sharp angles.

The only way to get to the throne was to swim.

A nervous laugh escaped me. "Was House Athar part dolphin?" I joked.

Jayke's brow creased in what I was becoming increasingly convinced was amusement. "No," he said. "The floor is enchanted so those with evil intent will drown, and those loyal to the crown will pass safely."

"And get very wet," I said, watching the ripples play across the water's dark surface.

Poised and still, Jayke corrected me again. "For those who bear the crown no ill will, the floor is solid."

These constant corrections were beginning to irritate me, but I knew I should be more open to learning, so I bit down my angry response and held my tongue.

A voice rumbled behind me, and I whirled around to see Darzan leaning back with one boot propped against the wall, his dark skin melting into the shadows. Darzan's mocking voice broke the silence. "You've come to show your pet your toys, Jaykey boy."

Those golden eyes gave me the creeps, even though they weren't looking at me. Thank God for small mercies, I supposed, because without his gaze on me, I didn't feel that cold phantom blade against my throat. But on the other hand, the fact he wasn't looking at me made his comment even worse. Without bothering to glance at me, he called me a fucking pet, the same term he'd used last night.

Anger reared inside me. I was nobody's pet. I cocked out a hip. "If you wanna talk about me, Darzan, talk *to* me." The throne room floor lapped quietly behind me as I waited for a response.

The Prince of House Davin flicked his eyes to me, and that blade squeezed against my neck, cold and dangerous, but no way in hell would I give him the satisfaction of flinching. "Oh, I was getting to you, pet," he sneered. "I suppose you think your presence here will make everybody throw their support to House Sansett?"

No, of course I didn't think that. I had no reason at all to believe my presence here could be any help in Jayke's bid for the throne. I wasn't an emissary for the mortal world, for fuck's sake, despite what everybody seemed to think.

But there was no way I was telling that to Darzan. I narrowed my eyes. "I will do everything I can to get Prince Sansett onto the throne," I said. "You won't be getting your grubby little hands on it as much as you might want to."

"Prince Sansett," Darzan laughed. He released me from his glare, and that phantom blade thankfully disappeared. He addressed Jayke instead. "My, my, you do have your pet well trained. I must admit I'm impressed you garnered the support of—"

Jayke stepped forward, rising to his full height and looking magnificent, I might add. This was no time to admire his muscles, but the curve of those shoulders was like a fucking eye magnet. "Do not address my guest so rudely, Davin." He stalked closer, really working those muscles. "If you go anywhere near her again," he growled, "I'll personally see to it that your brother misses his Ascension rite."

Wait, that was news. Darzan's brother, Pike, was due to participate in the next Ascension rite? The one in sixteen—no, fifteen—days? I thought this was all about Darzan versus Jayke, and now there was somebody else in the mix?

I could see Jayke smirking at the reaction he'd provoked in Darzan, so he must've hit home. Good on him.

The dark prince pushed off the wall and got all up in Jayke's business, grabbing him by the collar. "If you mess with Pike's Ascension, you'll regret it every day for the rest of your fucking life, which will only be until I slice you in fucking two."

The image of that old fae's torso sliding off his legs and squelching onto the flagstones played through my mind in slow motion, and I knew Darzan was more than capable of carrying out his threat.

Jayke's muscles bunched. He was the larger of the two and would win in a fistfight, but I didn't see how he could win a battle when it came to magic. What could he do? Heal his opponent to death?

I had to intercede before this escalated any further, and the only way I could think to get the males' attention was by poking the bear. "But don't you want to be king, Darzan? I reckon you should play nice." My voice rang clearly through the massive chamber.

The dark prince's gaze landed on me, and that cold blade snicked against my throat. "What I want, pet, is for things to go back to how they were. I want nature to stop poisoning and attacking us, and I want House Athar back on the throne." He spit the words at me like an arrow, then continued with a wicked gleam in his golden eyes. "But since that apparently isn't going to happen, I want the next best thing. My brother to be chosen by Gaia in two weeks to lead Caprice to a better future."

I snorted. Sure, a better future where the weak were destroyed, and the king's brother was a bloodthirsty murderer.

Jayke's laughter rang through the room, filled with confidence. "You know the chances of that are next to nothing, Davin." His voice held a sharp edge, a challenge laid down with every word. Tension thrummed in the air, a taut bowstring ready to snap. "Gaia chooses kings neither lightly nor often. She will never select a weakling like your baby brother to lead our mighty realm. And once Gaia has overlooked Pike, the fae of Caprice will choose me as their king. So enjoy these last few weeks while you can," he added in a clear threat, matching Darzan's machismo.

The asshole prince didn't even glance my way as he spit, "Don't forget to look after your pet, Jaykey boy. Take her for walks and tell her she's a good girl. Make sure you keep her on a tight leash." He cast me one last sneer before he melted into the shadows and out the door, leaving me and Jayke alone.

Fury bubbled in my chest, the violence inside me responding to the violence inside Darzan, still simmering even after his golden head disappeared from view.

Jayke

Davin flounced from the throne room like a bratty faeling absconding from school, his footsteps echoing in the cavernous space.

Ice-cold determination filled me to wipe that casual smugness from his face and have him kneel before me, begging forgiveness. Which he definitely wouldn't get.

The anger simmering through Delphinium was the only solace to my frozen heart on the return journey to Sansett Palace. I had carefully maneuvered her to exactly where she needed to be, and her evident hatred for that Davin brat cheered me up.

But I didn't want to piss her off so thoroughly that she left Arathay altogether and scurried home with her tail between her legs. I had to tread very carefully, for her sake and mine.

I would start by limiting her interactions with House Davin. If he opened his big mouth in front of her and showered her with insults, I wouldn't be able to help myself anyway. I would strike before thinking, so deep was my protectiveness toward her.

I sighed minutely—not enough for human senses to notice. I would have to get my emotions under control. Only fifteen days remained of the interregnum period, and I would have to make every one count.

Back in the family palace, I headed straight for the stables without realizing Delphinium was still on my heels until she tapped me on the shoulder. "I will fight for you," she told me with fury in her eyes.

I thawed completely and pulled her into a measured hug, careful not to crush her fragile body. "Thank you," I murmured into her hair, breathing in her shampoo. Her soft body melted against my own, forgiving in all the right places, and I felt my cock harden against her. I had to admit that the prospect of her supporting my bid for king made me even harder than her supple curves. Perhaps she would go to her knees before me, too, only it wouldn't be forgiveness she'd beg for but to take my length into her soft warm mouth.

She placed her hands on my chest and pushed gently, and I released her. Knowing I had her fully on board allowed me to relax, so I let her go with just a kiss on the forehead.

But she didn't walk away, just stood there with her green eyes blinking up at me, so eerily mismatched from her jet-black hair. "Last night, you promised that if I attended your party, you would take me home today."

Gaia-be-damned, she wasn't going to call me out on that hasty promise, was she? I should never have told her I'd escort her back to Hebes, but I needed her to attend the strengths display with me, needed the powerful Houses to see her at my side. I hadn't expected her to actually want to return to the hellhole of Hebes.

My horse whinnied impatiently while I composed my answer. "You just told me you would help me onto the throne," I said.

She threw out her arms, clearly exasperated. The fabric of

her gossamer dress stretched across her hips at the movement, snagging my eye. "I can't help do anything to help you," she cried. "I don't know anything about Arathay or Caprice or any of it. And I worry about my family. Grandma has nobody to look after her, and without my help, she may starve. Plus, I don't even know if Kayla and Razelle got home safely the other day. For all I know, they're battered and bruised in some alleyway in the Docklands, waiting for me to rescue them."

Her love for those wretched people she called family surprised me. From all accounts, she'd never been treated particularly well and had fought tooth and nail to survive. Frankly, her fierce love for them was astonishing.

I ran a finger down her neck and over the curve of her shoulder, feeling her warm flesh igniting under my touch. My cock twitched again at her reaction, and I longed to press myself against her and inside her, fucking her right here against the stable wall.

But this conversation was too important to mess up. "I will send fae to look after your family," I said.

"But—" she interrupted, a habit that was quickly becoming tiresome.

I hushed her with a finger to the lips. "But nothing," I said. "I will station fae permanently with your grandma and with your uncle. Their job will be to ensure your family's safety and happiness without interfering or letting them know they are being observed. You surely can't doubt the fae ability to go unnoticed."

She rolled her tongue through her mouth before answering, which was very distracting. "No," she said uncertainly.

"Good. Then it's done." I turned to nod at my stable fae, who was readying the horses. The horsey musk was making me keen to get moving. I needed to ride the perimeter of my lands to reinforce the wards that prevented the rot in the realm from tainting my territory.

"But you promised I could go home," Delphinium said in a slightly whiny tone.

I took a deep breath and faced her, ignoring the stamping of horses' hooves. "And you promised you would help me onto the throne," I said sternly. She hadn't actually pledged that, but surely her word was as good as a promise. "After that, you can stay here by my side and help me rule, or you can return to Hebes and take enough of my gold to live an extraordinary life, for you and your loved ones. Okay?"

I chucked her under the chin and saw disobedience warring in her flashing green eyes.

She clearly wouldn't agree, so I ended the conversation before she could voice her opposition. She would come around to my way of thinking, and as much as I hated forcing her to go against her wishes, the future of Caprice was too important to leave to chance. Her sacrificing two weeks of her life to ensure the realm's future was a small price to pay and one I would pay a thousand times over despite the uncomfortable twinge in my heart.

The sound of Terabithia's steady breathing accompanied my thoughts as I watched Delphinium's figure disappear back into the house. With a well-practiced motion, I swung onto the saddle of my horse, Terabithia, a powerful gray stallion whose strong muscles twitched beneath me. The saddle creaked in protest before settling into place, and Terabithia's tail whooshed gently to acknowledge my presence.

Lucius mounted his mare, a smaller creature but no less spirited, and together we rode from the stables, the rhythmic clopping of hooves a promise of the task ahead. Together we would reinforce the spell work that protected our lands from the rot.

"I had the stable fae saddle a horse for my lady, too," Lucius informed me, with the unasked question of why I didn't bring her with me.

"She didn't want to come," I lied.

The truth was, she was a female raised and bred in a mortal realm who didn't need the thrill of a horseback ride to be satisfied—she would be happy in her room with a shiny toy.

Delph

I spent the next week exploring the palace and uncovering no end of wonders.

Whenever I passed by, I ducked into the aroma room, trying to take it by surprise and experience a new scent. But every damn time, I smelt burning or smoke, like my eyebrows had been singed. This was a magical palace, for God's sake, I expected nothing less than a sublime nectar of forbidden flowers or some shit. But all that damn room it gave me was charred wood.

Plenty of other rooms occupied my time, like the portrait room, where I often visited with Jayke's dead mom to find the courage to keep supporting him and to stay away from my family.

Not that I had much choice about that. I was freaking disappointed when Jayke broke his promise to let me return to Hebes, but he'd sent some fae to look after Grandma and the girls, so I really had no grounds for anger. After a few days, the simmering inside me settled down, and I began to understand why he'd done it. There was much more on the line than just the dust in Grandma's house. An entire kingdom depended on Jayke becoming king, and apparently I, a random Docklands skank from Hebes, was enough of a mortal ambassador to help him win.

I sighed and tried the handle of a tiny purple door that only reached my upper thigh but had an elaborate silver handle with miniature horses engraved in a ring around the outside. It was locked. Most rooms were off-limits to me, and when I complained to Jayke, he told me the palace didn't want me to enter. Apparently, only those of pure Sansett blood were allowed to roam freely.

I soon grew bored of smelling wood smoke and rattling locked doors, and I itched for more. I was a born wanderer. I'd spent my childhood in the streets, evading peril and growing stronger for it, so prancing about like a princess in a castle didn't sit well with me. It went against every fiber of my Goddamn being.

I asked Jayke to accompany me out of his palace grounds so I could explore safely, but he was always too busy reinforcing the wards or strengthening his inner power or planning policies for when he became king.

So I made my own rules. I couldn't sit on my ass doing nothing while an entire magical world begged me to explore it. I'd learned my lesson from the mushrooms, and I'd already visited Capricia city twice, plus I'd sparred with the most dangerous male in the realm, the vile Prince Davin, and come away unscathed. I was confident in my ability to survive.

So I developed my own routine. After dinner, when the moon cast her watery light over the world, I sneaked out of the palace grounds and along the moonway to the city. The wild buzz of the realm got beneath my skin, making me tingle with anticipation and excitement.

It was glorious. I'd gone out for four straight nights, and tonight was no different. I had to be back by midnight because we were attending some schmooze event, but until then, I could explore.

The little beach ball home was burnt umber today with flecks of gold that shimmered like hidden treasures as I walked by. I waved at the winged faeries who flew out of the little window, and the smallest one, a sweet faeling with light brown skin and pink eyes and hair, smiled back. "Hello, my lady."

I snorted. "I'm no lady. You may have seen me with Prince Sansett, but trust me, I'm no more a lady than that kitten is."

I pointed out a sweet ginger furball who wobbled up to me on unsteady legs and gave a tiny mew. When it got close, I bent down for a pat, unable to resist the cuteness. But my heart lurched as it suddenly sprouted massive fangs and lunged at me, oversized jaws snapping like a fucking alligator.

I jumped back and saw the faeries had gone. In fact, the street was deserted, with no sound but the rustling of a chill breeze that left my skin crawling with goosebumps. Even the realm's buzz had disappeared, leaving me utterly alone. Dark, clinging shadows enveloped the houses and storefronts, and the moon hung bone-white and pale in the sky, casting an eerie pallor over the deserted streets. A heavy sense of foreboding weighed on me, making my breaths come faster.

"Hello?" I croaked out, hating the uncertainty in my voice. Where the fuck had everybody disappeared to? The streets of Capricia were suddenly dark and barren, with no sign of life. Just a hovering sense of death. Even the ginger kitten had vanished.

A cold blade pressed against my throat, icy and painful, causing panic to tighten its grip on my limbs, my breaths growing shallow and frantic. I spun around with my fists up, but nobody was behind me, just that phantom fucking blade that scraped my neck whenever the War wielder watched me.

I snapped my head left and right, searching for the golden-eyed fae who must be lurking in one of the alley's shadows, but I found no sign of Darzan. My fists were raised, ready for a rumble, but I slowly lowered them. Who was I kidding?

It bloody killed me to back down from a fight, but how could I battle an enemy I couldn't see? And my street fighting, which could beat down even Joey the Bull's best men, was no match for Darazan's vicious War power.

Especially while he hid in the shadows.

"Fucking coward," I muttered. Why didn't he show himself and confront me face-to-face? But as I stumbled back to the moonway and sprinted along it, my own words echoed in my ears, taunting me, following me all the way back to the palace as I freaked out. I had a horrible suspicion that I was the fucking coward, not Darzan.

Back in my bedroom, I leaned against the chamber door, panting hard. My four-poster bed was cast from marble but topped with the softest mattress I'd ever known, which was apparently crafted specifically for a being of my shape and size. A cream rug laced with gold was slightly dirtier than when I first arrived, thanks to my muddy feet stomping across it, but it was still pristine, beautiful, and safe.

So safe. I'd never appreciated how good safety felt. I'd endangered it by venturing into the streets alone, ignoring Jayke's advice, and I wanted to hate myself for that, but I couldn't. Rebellion and adventure were etched into my very being, and I would never allow myself to become a princess in a cage.

Delph

At a quarter to midnight, I descended the curving stairs to the palace's grand entrance room, where Jayke was waiting for me.

Our outfits were far more conventional tonight than for the last pre-coronation event, but we still looked like we were wearing a couple's costume. Jayke was dressed head to toe in black, with a black-upon-black suit that wouldn't have been out of place in the high rollers room at Vegas. I wore layers of black chiffon, so light and airy that I could have been wearing nighttime itself. The layers of my dress landed at different points on my leg, making an overall effect of fluttering elegance that made me proud to wear it.

My long black hair was swept back and fastened in a sleek high ponytail with a clasp the shape of a lightning bolt. My maid, Elora, had told me that Jayke insisted I wear it, which was clearly a clever power play given that Lightning was the symbol of the realm.

"Absolutely ravishing, Delphinium," Jayke said as I reached the bottom of the stairs.

He said my name so silkily that pleasure tingled over my skin. I wanted to lean up and kiss him full on the lips, needing to explore the physical aspect of our relationship more fully.

We still hadn't had sex, and with every passing day, my body noticed it more and more.

It didn't matter that the few times we'd become intimate, I hadn't become swept away with need because I'd still been adjusting to being in the fae realm. But now, I felt more comfortable here and convinced this sexy fae male should lick me from head to toe—and everywhere in between.

I batted my eyelashes coquettishly. "You don't look so bad yourself," I purred.

He smiled, then we headed outside, my boots crunching on the gravel. Jayke surprised me by veering off the path and across the dewy grass toward the fir trees. Under their canopy, the carpet of needles devoured every sound, even from my clumsy human feet, and an eerie quiet tickled the air.

But when we emerged near the mushroom gorge, that heavy anticipation in the realm chased away any lingering eeriness. With every passing day, Caprice became more impatient for her king, and the buzzing anticipation grew more and more unsettling. We were now eight days from the coronation, and the atmosphere made me want to scream with impatience.

A moonlit path caught my eye, and I realized another moonway ran from there. I smiled. "There's another one? How many of these moonways are there?"

I was learning that Jayke didn't share information easily, so I was pleased when he answered my question directly. "All of Arathay is crisscrossed with moonways. Most travel short distances within a single realm, but certain moonways link Caprice with other realms of Arathay."

We stepped onto the moonlit path, and the mushroom gorge immediately blurred beside us, streaking the ground with bleached purple and pink. "Amazing." I looked up in alarm as a thought struck me. "This isn't taking us back to that place where I babble like an idiot, is it?" I remembered how I'd been unable to keep my thoughts and feelings inside me when I'd first landed in Arathay with Captain Peterson.

Jayke rumbled a laugh, and my heart swelled at the rare sound. "No, we aren't going to the Realm of Fen this evening. Though perhaps I should take you there one day to get a few truths from you." The wicked glint in his eye made that statement deliciously flirtatious. "But tonight, we shall have to settle for going to Jewettim Falls."

At the end of the moonway, we spilled out to the base of a magnificent waterfall that fell several hundred feet from a looming cliff face.

The pounding water kicked up a thick mist covering the grassy glen around us, so the dozens of fae were only visible from the waist up.

I traced a hand through the mist and watched it eddy and swirl around the movement. It felt more like smoke than spray, and my black dress didn't cling to my legs as I would have expected but stayed dry and fluttery.

The crowd turned at our arrival, and I saw a few familiar faces. Jayne, with her pale blue hair, aquiline nose and porcelain white face the feminine pair of her twin, and various other fae I'd met outside the Spike.

Deep green lily pads floated throughout the crowd, weaving artfully without bumping into anyone. They held glasses of bubbling liquid and tiny mouthfuls of creamy fish egg that tasted far more delicious than they sounded.

Jayke gave me a few minutes to settle, for which I was grateful. I swam among the crowd, following those hovering lily pads and sipping pastel-colored drinks that sent bubbles up my nose.

I had a chance to observe the networking and saw how accomplished Jayke was. He greeted every fae by name with a warm smile and a kind word, and I could see he already knew the game of diplomacy and would make an excellent king.

Darzan, on the other hand, scowled at anybody who approached him and jumped down the throat of one female who batted her eyelashes his way. Perhaps he wasn't that way inclined but preferred drinking from the male well. In fact, the only fae he tolerated was a male whose skin had the slightest hint of pale green, with emerald hair and irises. Perhaps he was the dark prince's lover? I observed them closely, hot on the gossip trail and realizing there was a whole world of who's-dating-who I could play to spice up these mingling events.

The setting for this event was spectacular. The waterfall poured down the cliff face and diverted sideways and even upward at the edges, creating curlicues of silvery blue streams that made intriguing patterns.

I leaned against a boulder, watching how the eddies and swirls of water on the cliff face mirrored the eddies and swirls in the mist as the fae moved through it. I nibbled on a butternut salmon cake that was softer than a marshmallow and twice as nice, somehow smelling like the night before Christmas.

Voices on the far side of my boulder, belonging to fae I couldn't see, buzzed around me while I focused on the subtle nutty flavor. They were discussing creatures called Shadow Walkers, which sounded like nightmares that could turn fae into zombies. But nobody seemed to agree whether these Shadow Walkers existed or were just tales invented to cause havoc. In any case, the threat was far away, in the far East of

Verda, and nobody was too concerned, so neither was I. We had enough to deal with already, with Gaia going crazy.

The voices kept droning, turning to different topics, and when I heard my name, my attention snapped.

"Delphinium is irritatingly passive, isn't she?" a female said. "Entirely insipid and so thoroughly disappointing. I can't imagine a less impressive being. She's more a detraction from House Sansett than an asset."

Other voices chuckled, and I dropped my nutty salmon into the swirling mist and clenched my fists.

Passive? Insipid? I'd never been accused of that before. Aggressive and impatient and a cold-hearted bitch? Sure, I'd heard those insults plenty of times, and I wore those barbs like a crown. But insipid? That fucking stung.

Another voice joined in, pitched low. "I agree, Melia. The girl is hardly more than a puppet, I haven't seen an ounce of backbone in her, and I don't think I will. She wouldn't last a minute if she appeared in Caprice without Sansett's protection. A thoroughly weak little thing."

Okay, these fuckers were really getting to me. What right did they have to judge my personality after only having met me once? True, I'd been on my best behavior in the Spike forecourt because I was trying to be fucking polite—would they prefer if I told them what I really thought of them?

Fuck it, I would. I pushed off the boulder but was stopped by a familiar rumbling voice cutting in. "Delphinium has more courage than that cockhead Jayke," came the deep voice of Darzan Davin. "She may not know our world, but she's learning. Give her another year, and she'll be formidable. If her puppet master lets her survive that long."

Okay, he was still a prick, but was Darzan defending me?

The shock froze me to the spot while I absorbed the implication. The dark prince thought I had courage and could be formidable? That knocked my tongue into next week, and I didn't reckon I'd be able to talk again until I caught it up. Holy fuck.

I tuned back in as he carried on insulting Jayke, describing him as weak and pathetic and all those words a warmonger typically used for a pacifist. So I didn't like the vile prince more than I had a minute ago, but hearing his lips singing my praises was still odd.

"We should go back to the Houses sharing power, in my opinion," Melia drawled, and I instantly hated the idea because it was hers. The conversation turned to the merits of power-sharing, and I strained to follow their logic and understand how that would work. Something about how in someplace called Verda, it worked just fine, and they could adopt the same system here.

A hand on my shoulder jerked me from my eavesdropping reverie, and Jayke showed me his perfect white teeth while his lavender scent wrapped around me. "Will you come and meet a few more fae, Delphinium?" he asked. "I know it's tiresome, but it really does help."

The words *tame pet* thudded against my eardrums, but I swatted them away. I was helping Jayke because I wanted to, not because I was a domesticated beast. Even though I was convinced I wasn't actually helping—even the dickheads I'd overheard thought I was a liability, not an asset.

Still, who cared what they thought? I smiled up at Jayke. "Sure. Lead the way."

He took my arm and looped it over his. "Thank you. As you know, your support as a mortal ambassador is..."

He carried on with his spiel about how much I would help his cause, but even with repetition, I didn't find the argument convincing, so I tuned him out and played over Darzan's conversation with Melia and co. They'd talked about the Houses sharing power, and I wondered if that was such a bad idea.

I squeezed Jayke's forearm as the mist eddied around us. "Would it be possible to share power among the Houses?" I asked. "That might keep everybody happy and avoid ill will. Perhaps that would be a better solution for Caprice."

Jayke whispered in my ear, his warm breath sending shivers down my spine. "We will talk of this later."

Resentment simmered in my chest. I wanted to talk about it now, so why should I wait? No matter how important he was, I was not this male's pet. I slid my hand off his arm. "I'd like to talk about it now," I said through gritted teeth.

He sighed in an over-the-top display of emotion for a fae, but at least he took me seriously. "House Athar will never agree to share power. The unfae monster Athar imprisoned my sister simply for speaking her mind," Jayke said as his lavender eyes bored into mine, holding an ocean of pain.

"Oh," I said, suddenly feeling foolish as my words tripped up. The pounding of the water suddenly seemed too loud. "I, er, I didn't realize that was the reason." I knew Athar had done something bad to Jayke's sister Leena, but I didn't realize they'd jailed her. And just for speaking her mind? That was like the worst kind of dictatorship.

His lips pursed, the pain etched on his face. "That's why she can't be here," he bit out, his voice tinged with bitterness. "She's still in jail," he continued, his voice dropping to a hush.

"What?" I yelled. The nearby fae looked up at my outburst,

and Jayke hushed me.

"Keep quiet, Delphinium." I bristled at the instruction but said nothing because Jayke was clearly upset about discussing his sister. "House Athar cannot be trusted," he continued. "Besides, the only potential candidate is an Unseelie and therefore not suitable."

Okay, fair enough."But what about H—"

Jayke nodded grimly, cutting me off. "House Davin is even worse," he said, his voice tight with frustration. "Trust me, Delphinium, if there were any other way, I would take it. I don't particularly want to rule, but I must. And for Caprice to have any chance at a peaceful future, I must rule alone."

His pain and intensity washed off his face as he replaced it with a bright mask and a warm grin. "Now, let's go and circulate," he said, his smile returning, though I sensed the weight of his burdens just beneath the surface. "Shall we?"

Delph

After the midnight event at Jewettim Falls, I slept late the next morning and woke with wet panties, recalling a dream of Jayke's vibrant lavender eyes and sculpted body.

Man, I had to get me some.

I went through my usual daily routine of rattling doorknobs and trying to take the aroma room by surprise—I swore that thing must be broken. Then I took a tour of the palace grounds, as usual. Only this time, I was also plotting sex. After dinner would be nice. Perhaps I could find whoever cooked our sumptuous meals and convince them to include oysters and strawberries. And if I could get my hands on whoever set the long wooden dining table, I could slip them a couple of bucks to lay out some candles.

Before dinner, I dressed in the most revealing outfit I could find in my cupboard, which was like trying to pick the hottest coal in a blazing fire—these fae were not big on modesty. I settled on a short dress that hit me mid-thigh and had cut-outs on either side of my hips and waist. It was a bright scarlet, which would hopefully get Jayke hot.

When I arrived in the dining room, Jayke wasn't there. My sexy smile dropped, and my whole body sagged. He often skipped meals while busy with his preparations, so I supposed

I wouldn't get any sex tonight.

I walked along slowly, trailing a finger along the smooth wood of the dining table, feeling dejected. The table was laid for two, but it always was. A rich aroma like red wine and stew floated in from the other room, so at least I'd get a good feed.

At a sound, I looked up and was relieved to see Jayke sauntering in. He wore an open-necked shirt in pale blue and cream pants that hung from his hips. It all hugged his muscles so perfectly that saliva started pooling in my mouth at the sight of him.

"Hello, beautiful," he said, looking me up and down appreciatively. Good, he liked what he saw—that made two of us.

I straightened up and grinned wolfishly. "Hey yourself, sexy." He took a seat, and on a whim, I turned my back on my chair and sashayed toward him suggestively, noticing how he watched my hips. I planted my ass on his lap and slung an arm around his neck. "How are you?" I purred.

He growled, taking in the deep view of my cleavage and resting one hand on the bare flesh of my hip. "Better now."

I felt his cock harden beneath my thigh, pushing upward into the edge of my ass, making me wet. I leaned forward and bit his lower lip, and he smiled beneath it so his lip tugged between my teeth. "Naughty girl," he growled. His fingers dug into the flesh at my hip. "I can be naughty too."

I looked up at him from under my lashes. "Do you promise?" I asked. I leaned into him, breathed in his musky lavender scent, and sucked on his mouth, then took him in a hard passionate kiss, pressing my side against his hard chest.

He groaned, and his hand squeezed my hip while the other roamed up my leg, past my knee, and along the soft flesh of my inner thigh. His fingers and palm were soft, so soft, unlike the other men I'd been with. Because he hadn't spent a lifetime working the ships on the docks or any other manual labor.

He hesitated for a moment, and I pulled him closer, snagging the back of his head and sweeping my tongue through his mouth. "Don't stop," I demanded, and his lips curved into a grin again beneath mine as he spoke through the kiss.

"If you insist," he growled.

His soft fingers on my thighs roved higher and reached the slick fabric of my panties, pushing them aside. He moaned when he felt my wetness and ran a finger up my slippery pussy until I moaned right back and pressed myself against his hand.

I should have done this days ago. I'd been living with a freaking God of sexiness and had barely laid a hand on him when all it took was for me to make the first move—if I'd known that, I would've struck long ago.

He slipped a finger inside me slowly, oh so slowly, then removed it completely and put it to his lips, then inserted it into his own mouth, sucking in and out. I watched mesmerized as desire swamped me.

I pushed away his hand and kissed him hungrily, tasting my salt on his tongue, and he returned his hand where it belonged, right between my legs. He circled my clit, and warmth seeped through my veins.

"Yes," I breathed. "Fuck yes." I spread my legs farther, needing him inside me, and he obliged by slipping two fingers in but keeping my thumb pressing my clit. One leg was slung across his lap, and the other was between his legs, opening me up completely to him.

"You're the most important being in Arathay, Delphinium, do you know that?" he moaned into my mouth.

The comment shook me from my daze, and I blinked at his hard jaw and full lips. "What?" I asked, feeling stupid. Was he seriously talking politics right now? He leaned forward and kissed my throat, his hand still moving inside me, but I was losing momentum, my thoughts snagging on his comment. "What did you say?" I repeated.

I knew what he'd said, I just didn't understand. Why did he keep telling me how important I was? Didn't he comprehend what I kept telling him—that I was no representative of the mortal realm. It was like he didn't listen to anything I told him.

He licked my neck. "You are my everything," he whispered.

The finger moving inside me stretched me uncomfortably like it was going through the motions, and it was suddenly unwelcome. I pushed his wrist away, and he looked up at me with hooded eyes, confused eyes,

I couldn't believe I was doing this, but I stepped off his lap, readjusted my underwear, and then wriggled down my short red dress to cover me. "I...Do you want to join me for a walk?"

My desire was quenched for some reason I couldn't understand. Perhaps because he didn't seem to know me for who I really was. Maybe those words *you are my everything* sounded shallow and insincere, like the worst kind of sleazeball's catchphrase.

Whatever it was, I was a fucking idiot because I seemed to be walking away from the chance to ride to the hottest male I'd ever bloody seen.

He blinked at me a few times, trying to figure out what was happening, and I couldn't exactly blame him. "I've got a little problem here," he grinned, pointing to his bulging lap.

I shrugged. "I'm not exactly satisfied either."

He reached toward me. "You could be."

But I danced away out of his reach. "So...How about that walk?" If I could finally convince him to join me along the moonway and explore Capricia together, I'd probably feel comfortable enough to bone his brains out.

Shadows clouded his face, and he took a long time to respond, and when he finally did, my heart dropped. "Not tonight, beautiful," he said. "I've got work to do."

"An empire to plan," I responded automatically.

"A realm to run," he grinned. "You understand."

But I didn't. I didn't understand why he would have plenty of time to play me like a violin but no time to stroll by my side. I didn't understand that at all.

But since I'd arrived in Caprice, I recognized myself less and less. My brash edges had been rubbed away, and I wasn't sure anything else was left.

I shrugged. "I'm going up to bed."

His gaze rode my body once more, but he nodded curtly and watched me leave without another word.

I wasn't going to bed, though, I was going on that damn walk with or without him. Maybe I'd find some dinner while I was at it.

The moonway was like my old friend, and I knew her twists and turns like the alleys of the Docklands. Before long, I emerged into the city's cobblestones and looked eagerly for my winged pals to see the color of their beachball house tonight. Lemon green with candy-cane stripes that reminded me of Christmas. There was even a slight frosting scent in the air that I swore was coming from the round house.

Despite the magical surroundings, my thoughts flicked back to Jayke. I didn't need that fucking male to keep me happy—although his dick could keep me satisfied—and I didn't need anybody to keep me safe. I was a survivor, and if Joey the Bull and the other Docklands thugs never bested me as a teenager, nobody would beat me as a kickass twenty-four-year-old.

I wound through the streets, not caring if I got a little lost. I kept to the cobblestone paths, though, avoiding the forested roads because they looked forbidding in the moonlight, and I knew nature wasn't exactly friendly around here. Perhaps I'd come back after Jayke's coronation and skip along those forested paths even in the darkest witching hour, but not tonight.

I turned the corner, wishing I'd changed my panties because now they were just soggy and uncomfortable, when a cold steel blade pressed against my throat. Fucking Darzan.

I couldn't see him. Just like my walk last night, the cowardly prince was hiding in the shadows, watching and not showing his stupid face.

Well, I was in no mood to tolerate it. I cocked out a hip and put a hand on it for good measure, only then realizing I was still wearing my skimpy minidress with the cutouts. "Come on out, Prince Davin. I know you're there, so you might as well show your mug. Perhaps we could share a cup of poisoned tea?"

His laughter rumbled from the shadows on my left, low, throaty, predatory. The first things I saw were his golden hair and glinting eyes. He wore black pants and a black T-shirt that pulled against his biceps and hid him in the shadows. "My, my, Sansett's pet has teeth."

"You better fucking believe it, asshole," I spit.

He grinned. "What happened to calling me Prince Davin?

Although I think I like your bite better than your purr."

Man, I wanted to punch that smug smirk off his face. "Come closer and say that," I threatened.

Not surprisingly, he did. A towering fae with War power would hardly be scared of a puny human like me, but my anger was big enough to inflate me.

When he got within kissing distance, I distracted him with one hand while I landed an uppercut in his gut with the other, putting everything I had behind it.

He released a satisfying whoomph and backed up a pace, which had me grinning like the Cheshire cat. "I'm nobody's pet, prince, and if you keep calling me that, I'll keep having to remind you," I said in another clear threat.

Everything about this evil prince brought out the worst in me. My natural violent instinct reared up to meet his, erasing all the gains of politeness I'd made since arriving in Caprice.

His snarl held a measure of respect. "Fine. I won't call you that anymore. Pet."

Lightning sizzled through my veins, and I struggled to contain my rage, knowing I was lucky to get away with that punch. I didn't want to enter a shouting match because that would only make me look like a fool. But him lurking in the shadows every time I went for a Goddamn walk was infuriating. "Better a pet than a coward, I suppose."

That knocked the cocky grin off his face. "What do you mean?"

I folded my arms across my chest. "You're the eldest heir of House Davin and yet you're hiding behind your younger brother, hoping he gets chosen as king," I said. "You know that's not gonna happen. Gaia won't choose him, and you're too much of a fucking coward to step up and make a real play for the throne yourself, so you'll end up under House Sansett's boot where you belong."

Emotions crossed the fae's face, more fervor than I'd seen on one of these creatures the whole time I'd been here. I smirked in satisfaction as he worked through anger all the way to disbelief, finally sparking with a glint of revenge. "And where do you belong, Delphinium?"

His lips twisting to say my name sounded like fingernails down a chalkboard—I almost preferred him calling me pet.

His question drilled into my vulnerabilities and pierced me to my core. It was everything I'd asked my entire life, and I didn't have a good answer. I'd never belonged with Jackson, and Grandma didn't exactly make me feel welcome. But no way would I tell him that.

Instead, I jutted forward my chin and let my voice ring strong. "I grew up in Hebes, where my family is. That's where I belong."

Darzan circled me slowly in a wide arc, his black boots silent on the cobblestones. "You don't always belong in the place you've spent the most time. Sometimes you belong in a place you haven't yet seen."

Those words sat heavy in the air between us like they'd been scrawled in the fucking sky. I couldn't let this violent male know how his words offered me hope because the truth was I didn't belong in Hebes. And I didn't belong in Caprice. But maybe, just maybe, I belonged somewhere else I hadn't even imagined. Somewhere I hadn't yet seen.

I didn't want to engage in any more conversation with this frustrating male, I just wanted to get the hell out of here and crawl into my squishy bed. But he didn't seem to be going anywhere, so eventually, I turned on my heel and headed back toward the palace.

The blade against my throat didn't disappear until I set foot inside the moonway.

Jayke

As I rode through the forest, my thoughts continued to churn.

Little over a week remained until the coronation, and I had to confess to being tired of the campaign trail. Warm handshakes, a string of fae I didn't care for demanding promises in return for their support, and an eternal fucking grin. Gaia only knew how exhausted I was.

Keeping Delphinium content was a little easier now, but even managing my own family was fraught with difficulties. Jayne, who you'd think would support her twin brother in his bid for the crown, kept needling me, poking her barbed wit into conversations where it had no place. She was still irritated that Father chose me as the Sansett candidate and kept taking out her frustrations in a million tiny ways.

Then there was Leena. Managing the fallout from her ongoing imprisonment was a balancing act worthy of a fucking circus clown. Whenever her name arose in conversation, I had to maneuver it delicately to convince anyone within earshot that House Athar was firmly to blame and that she was entirely innocent. However, the truth was more nuanced than that. Fucking family. Honestly, I would be relieved when this was all over.

Terabithia whinnied, and I tugged his reins, pulling us to

a stop. Lucius pulled his mount to a halt beside me while we listened for any danger. We were taking our daily rounds of the perimeter, scanning the protective wards for weaknesses that needed fortifying.

My steed was attuned to fluctuations in magic, so it was worth taking his whinny seriously. I sent out tendrils of power, feeling the air around us, and found a tiny crack in our shield.

I pointed between two whistlewood bushes. "Over there."

Lucius was the best Weaver in Capricia city, possibly in all of Caprice. And he was all mine. He'd killed himself with a powerful spell during his Ascension rite and came into Weaving with a strength that outstripped anybody else in the past two centuries. I could perform simple spells, but I relied on Lucius to weave the more intricate ones, lending him my power to add strength.

I watched carefully as Lucius knitted the tear in our magical defenses with deft skill, forming delicate shapes with his fingers and hands and whispering his will. He was more than competent.

I wasn't only here to watch him work and not even to lend him my strength, but to make sure he got the job done. The wards on our grounds were more important now than ever. Nature fought against the leadership vacuum with poison plants and vicious wildlings, a twisted manifestation of Gaia's displeasure.

But I also had fae enemies. So many enemies within the realm, like the other powerful Houses, but also outside the kingdom. I sighed. I would deal with the Realm of Ourea after I became king.

Lucius nodded at me. "All done, my prince."

I had already inspected the quality of his handiwork as he

performed, so I didn't need to respond and just nudged my heels into Terabithia's sides, urging him into a canter. Trees whipped past us as my horse strode powerfully through the forest, kicking up leaves beneath his hooves. Birds called distantly from outside my lands, although their twitters turned more and more into shrieks every day.

News had arrived that morning that sat particularly heavily on my shoulders. Darzan had declared he would compete more willingly for the crown rather than sitting back and hoping his brother ascended into Lightning. Gaia only knew what had spurred his change of mind, but apparently, he was no longer content to sit at the edges of gatherings and snarl at any fae who approached him. From now on, he would be shaking hands and baring his horrific teeth in the closest thing to a smile he could manage.

The prospect of him attempting to be civil and play nicely with others was almost laughable, except I couldn't muster a smile when the entire future of the realm was at stake.

I would just have to redouble my efforts to gather the support of the influential Houses. Game on, Davin. Game fucking on.

Davin's news had arrived first thing in the morning. One of my groundskeepers had found the spellbird fluttering up against the palace gates with its papery wings half broken. Spellbirds were the best means of long-distance communication outside of scrying amulets. Any competent fae could write the letter and fold it into an aerodynamic shape—usually a bird—then whisper a spell that sent it along the appropriate moonway. Spellbirds never stopped trying to reach their intended recipient until they were read or disintegrated on the wind.

In many ways, it was a shame human technology couldn't work in Arathay because a cell phone was a far simpler alternative. But their technology repressed fae magic and so couldn't be tolerated.

How anybody abided living in the mortal realm was unknowable. But Delphinium was here now and aligned with me. With her by my side, I would still beat Darzan even if he kissed the ugliest fae babies.

Terabithia reared up, and I had to squeeze my thighs to stay on his back. Both horses whinnied and stamped their feet, and I quickly sent out magical feelers to detect what had disturbed them.

We were near the border with the Drowned Valley, which was usually a magnificent wetland teeming with wildlife, but, since the king's death, had turned into a gray and noxious swamp.

With a flurry of bushes, a creature lunged out of the undergrowth from the direction of the quagmire, sending leaves and water droplets flying. It was unnatural, clearly not born from Gaia but a monstrosity cobbled together through the rot poisoning the realm. It had an alligator's snout with the claws of a lion, and it stank of sulfur gas like the swamp it hailed from.

The creature lunged for Terabithia's foreleg, and the horse reared out of the way. I pulled the sword from my back and sliced the monster in two, watching as black blood spurted from the wound, enjoying its piteous howl of defeat.

Lucius wove together the fraying strands of our magical ward while I hacked the unnatural behemoth into pieces.

I couldn't wait for nature to start behaving herself again after I became king. Law and order would ripple throughout the realm, bringing nature—and fae—to heel.

Delph

That evening, I was trussed into yet another gorgeous gown, and I had to admit I wasn't tiring of that anytime soon. This one was dusty rose pink with an asymmetrical hem and all sorts of straps and cutouts that I never would've navigated without my maid, Elora. Instead of another floaty chiffon concoction, this one was smooth and silky and gave me a sleek silhouette. It even smelled faintly of roses. It was all down to my personal maid.

"You're an absolute genius, Elora," I said, twisting to admire my ass in the mirror.

Elora was slightly shorter than me and way more slender, so she had to tilt her head up to answer. She shrugged a narrow shoulder. "It's my calling."

I bit my lip. "Your calling? What do you mean?"

She twirled a deep red gemstone into my intricate hairdo and winked. "I am a Dresser. I'm drawn to beauty and fashion and can't think of any better occupation than coordinating outfits."

I had assumed Caprice had some God-awful hierarchy where less powerful fae were given the crap jobs, but Elora explained that wasn't the case. Apart from a handful of so-called noble families, who had grand estates and vied for power, every fae was considered equal. No matter their job, no matter their gender, no matter their hair color.

Elora had creamy skin, with hair and eyes of ivory white. The effect was quite startling, and I supposed she made an excellent blank canvas for any outfit.

A thought occurred to me as I rotated to check out my hairstyle from behind. "Did you ascend to Fashionista or something? Like, did you have to kill yourself with a sewing needle so you could come into the Power of Clothing?"

The fae tradition of killing yourself at age twenty-five to ascend into your full magical power was terrifying. I wondered if there was an option to chicken out and keep your low-level power until you died.

Elora laughed. "I'm only twenty-two. I haven't ascended yet. And as far as I know, Fashionista isn't a power you can get...." A wistful look came across her face. "But maybe I should look into that."

I sagged onto my bed with a whoomph. "Oh Jesus, don't stab yourself in the eye with a knitting needle on my account. I can see you stumbling around for the rest of your life, missing an eyeball."

Elora mimed walking around with a needle sticking out of her eye, giggling. The morbid talk clearly didn't bother her. She pulled the imaginary knitting needle out of her eye and threw it onto the floor, laughing. "Anyway," she said. "I've always thought I'd like to be a Cleaver like my mom." She obviously read my confusion, so she explained. "Cleavers can split anything into their constituent parts. It's useful in construction, energy production, a bunch of things. Obviously, most of our energy comes from Lightning here in Caprice, but energy producers are highly sought after in other realms."

I ran a hand along the soft duvet, realizing its silken texture was the same as my dress. "Don't tell me you have to cut yourself in two to become a Cleaver?"

Elora grinned. "Yep."

Fucking hell on a stick, fuck that. No way. For the first time, I was glad I was human and didn't have to suffer the horror of slaughtering myself just to participate in some cultural tradition. Although I supposed the magical boost would be nice...

"Come on." Elora tugged me to my feet. I felt so much better about her helping me now that I knew she wasn't an indentured slave but was here by choice, following her passion for coordinating outfits for others. "Get downstairs, or you'll be late," she scolded me lightly.

Jayke and I were headed to one of the noble Houses for a seated dinner, which I figured ought to be interesting. I was to accompany Jayke, of course, and had to remind myself I wasn't there as his pet but to ensure the peaceful future of Caprice.

We arrived outside another grand estate that Jayke told me also lay on the outskirts of Capricia. Apparently, the city center and immediate vicinity were reserved for normal-sized homes for normal fae, and if the noble families wanted big-ass houses, they had to go farther from town. Sounded reasonable to me, but Jayke had a disgruntled tone when he told me.

A dignified fae with brown eyes and hair, who could have passed for human if it weren't for his pointed ears, opened the large oak doors at the manor's entrance. "Welcome to Ranson Manor," he said.

Jayke's palace didn't have a footman to open doors, they always opened of their own accord, so why was there some guy here letting us into Ranson Manor?" Probably just showing off to the other Houses, I supposed.

Sigh. I'd rather be in the cobblestone streets chatting with my winged faerie friends outside their beach ball home than walking into a stuffy manor filled with metaphorical peacocks.

We were ushered into a dining room large enough to park a couple of buses in. It was mahogany everything, as far as I could tell, although my knowledge of fine woods was admittedly limited. It seemed we were last to arrive, with dozens of fae seated around a long table and only two empty seats available, which, I saw with a sinking heart, were right beside Darzan's.

Jayke stepped in front of me and sat beside the vile prince, sacrificing himself to be a buffer between me and Darzan.

I scraped out my chair and sat, looking around. Two dozen fae were seated around the long dark table, most of whom I recognized by now. Darzan had brought his green-skinned companion, making me even more certain he was his lover. But when somebody referred to the male as Pike, I realized the emerald dude was Darzan's brother, not his lover. Disappointing.

"So good of you not to keep us waiting too long," Darzan growled, clearly pissed that we were late. He was swirling his glass of wine so vigorously that some sloshed out and left big red splotches on the table.

I hadn't even realized we were late. But maybe Jayke was employing a power play by ensuring we were the last to arrive.

Jayke smiled grandly, taking the insult in his stride. "Not at all," he said, raising his glass. "Allow me to propose a toast to our generous hosts, Dorot and Jimia Ranson."

Dorot Ranson, a female with tight mauve curls and irises,

simpered and fanned her face. Jayke really was awfully good at this schmoozing crap. From the corner of my eye, I watched Pike elbow Darzan, who grudgingly raised his glass to join the toast. I toasted, too, then took a sip of the wine and gasped—it was the most delicious thing that had ever passed my lips. I drank more while I considered the day's events.

Apparently, Darzan had declared his intention to win the kingship rather than just sitting back and hoping his brother ascended to Lightning power. Apart from the crushing horror that a Davin rule would bring, I couldn't help but be a tiny bit impressed at his change of heart. I wondered if it had anything to do with our conversation the previous night. I'd told him to stop being chicken shit and step up, and the very next day, he had. Surely that wasn't a coincidence.

And if it wasn't a coincidence, that meant Darzan was a male who could take advice. A rare quality for a male of any species.

So I begrudgingly admired him for that. But if this display was any indication, his people skills were even worse than I thought. Every shining eye in the room was on Jayke, with barely a glance spared for Darzan. He had no hope in hell.

A garlic butter smell wafted closer, and my toes curled in anticipation as food trays were brought out by serving fae who, if Elora was correct, must love sticking food on plates and offering it to others. The conversation turned in grumbled tones to the fact that the rhonas were misbehaving.

I leaned in close to Jayke, seeking clarification. "Rhonas?"

He tilted toward me, and it felt like a win, like we were developing a hard-fought intimacy. His natural musky lavender scent was subtle this evening, pared back with a hint of artificial cologne, but it still calmed me.

"The rhonas are placid animals useful in domestic settings

and even employed in schools. But they have been aggressive of late, so we must resort to using serving fae."

I swallowed hard. "Are you telling me animals, these rhonas, usually serve the food at fancy dinners like this one? Are they like super-intelligent monkeys or something?"

Jayke shook his head minutely. "No. Humans are super-intelligent monkeys, and we aren't allowed to use them as servants under current Arathay law." His tone of voice was wistful, and a twisting feeling in my stomach had me wondering if he would attempt to change that law if he became king. "The rhonas are large and placid, more like short cows, I suppose. Or gentle hippopotamuses. The Magirus—fae whose inner power is an affinity for cooking—place trays on their backs, and they roam calmly around the table while the diners help themselves to food. But the creatures are behaving abominably at the moment and cannot be trusted."

"Because of the power vacuum? Because nature is linked to the king?" I asked.

"Indeed," he said with a sigh.

Yet another sign of the realm's displeasure at having no ruler.

Dorot leaned forward, and I could just tell she was dying to share some gossip. "At least we're better off than the Realm of Verda," she said. "They're dealing with the Shadow Walkers." Her mauve eyes shone with excitement.

"And not doing a very good job of it, from what I hear," her husband interjected, taking up the gossip stick. "Serves them right, I say," he continued. "They're a filthy bunch, the lot of them. Nothing but harlots and gluttons." He wiped a line of goose grease off his mouth as he finished speaking, looking greedy and filthy himself.

I kept hearing about the Shadow Walkers, but nothing tangible. I opened my mouth to ask about them, but Jayke interjected with his charming smile.

"Let's not talk of such unpleasant things tonight," he said, grinning.

Darzan's snide voice cut through the chit-chat. "What a shame Lorca couldn't be here this evening," he said loudly, and I searched to see who he was addressing. "Lorca was always so good at keeping conversations light."

A shocked lull fell over the entire table. Fae were the stillest and quietest creatures I'd ever encountered, but even they managed to find new pinnacles of hush. I could practically hear the candle flames flickering.

Gossip alert. From the outraged atmosphere, Darzan-the-Dickwad had pulled another insult out of his ass, directing it at our beneficent hosts. If it wasn't for the somber atmosphere, I would have burst out laughing. That prick was shooting himself in the foot yet again.

His brother clearly agreed. Pike shifted uncomfortably and glowered at the dark prince, and I figured it was lucky the green-skinned male didn't have Glare Death powers, if that was a thing.

When our hostess finally spoke, it was with a trembling voice. "Our dear Lorca was killed by Bastian Athar. If it weren't for that unfae monster of a king, he would still be alive. So yes, Prince Davin, it is a shame Lorca cannot be here tonight," she said.

The moment passed, and general discussion resumed, covering the more familiar territories of Caprice's current difficulties with flora and fauna, and the realm's future. The tinkling of teeth on wine glasses and cutlery on plates sprinkled through the hum of conversation.

But I couldn't keep up. I was still stuck on wondering why the fuck Darzan would have made that comment. He wasn't a stupid man—far from it. He'd proven his intelligence time and again in the cutting remarks he made in my company. So what was his strategy in insulting our hosts when they were among the few fae who could support his bid for the throne?

My question was answered when Jayke excused himself from the table for a moment, presumably to take a dump.

As soon as Jayke quit the room, Darzan leaned across the empty chair between us and asked in a low voice, "Did Jaykey boy tell you about Lorca?"

Interesting. So Darzan raised the subject for *me*. But since when was he in the business of providing me with information? Certainly, I wouldn't trust anything that came out of his mouth.

But, despite myself, my curiosity was piqued. "Who's Lorca?" I whispered, hoping like hell the other fae couldn't hear us above their own conversations. I fingered the crystal of my wineglass, relishing the smooth, cool surface.

Darzan smiled darkly, his golden eyes glinting wickedly. "Lorca Ranson was Jaykey-boy's best friend until he got killed by Bastian Athar," he hissed.

I leaned closer, putting the palm of my hand on Jayke's still-warm seat, catching a whiff of ash coming from Darzan. "Why are you telling me this?" It only made him look bad and made me like Jayke even more.

"Ask your boyfriend about it," he murmured, then straightened up and turned to say something to Pike.

I jutted out my jaw and slammed my attention back to my dinner plate, which was overflowing with food. Darzan was just trying to cause a rift between me and Jayke, and I refused to allow it.

That damn golden-haired fae was like caviar and slugs and racism all rolled up into one disgusting ball of all the worst things in the world.

I just wished he would leave me the fuck alone.

Delph

After the dinner party, Jayke and I wandered back toward the moonway. As usual, the evening air was heavy with anticipation, and I felt like an adventure. I opened my mouth to suggest we take the long route and meander through town, allowing us to enjoy each other's company and explore the city.

But I closed my lips without speaking. He would say no. He would be too busy, and I was done with begging. I wasn't the type of girl to get down on my knees for any man unless there was something in it for me.

We walked silently to the moonway, but one question kept nagging at me, so I eventually voiced it. "Why did Darzan bring up Lorca's death? It didn't seem to win him any friends."

Jayke snorted. "That moron doesn't have a fae-friendly bone in his body and doesn't have the least clue how to influence others. The only fae he trusts in the whole realm, the whole of Arathay, is his brother, and even he doesn't like Darzan very much." He chuckled darkly. "Don't be surprised at that Davin scum misstepping. He could only walk in a straight line if a pot of gold was at the other end."

I slanted my eyes at Jayke. I was starting to think he didn't have as good a handle on this realm as he thought. Darzan was no fool, and although he may not have the soft skills of *smarmy* and *charmy* like Jayke did, he was intelligent and cunning, and I was sure he'd brought up Lorca's death as part of his underlying strategy.

But if it was part of his tactic to win the throne, it didn't seem to be working, or at least there were layers to the plan I couldn't unravel.

We exited the moonway, and I felt disorientated momentarily as the world slowed to a normal pace. That heavy anticipation in the air washed over me like a physical presence, and I instinctively reached out for Jayke's hands as a bird shrieked in the distance. "Who was Lorca?" I asked.

The prince breathed deeply and squeezed my hand. "He was married to my sister," he said.

I waited for him to elaborate, but the night's silence had more power than my question, so I probed further. "He was married to Leena, the sister in jail?" I asked. He nodded. "So he was your brother-in-law," I persisted.

That didn't quite reconcile with Darzan's description of the dead male being Jayke's best friend. I knew I couldn't trust Darzan, that every part of him screamed violence and mayhem, but I needed to figure out why he'd raised the bloody issue.

Fallen leaves crunched under my silk slippers, and I craned my neck to see how the fae prince walked over the leaf litter without crunching, but couldn't figure it out. Somehow his feet avoided the noisiest leaves.

The gates to the palace grounds swung open, and we entered. I crunched along the gravel path, and Jayke moved silently beside me.

I sighed. I might as well ask the question even though Jayke was far from forthcoming. "Were you good friends with him too?" I murmured.

Jayke swept my fingers to his mouth and spoke into them, his breath warming my hands. "He was my best friend until that bastard Bastian Athar killed him."

Oh. So, Darzan had been telling me the truth. Still, that didn't make him trustworthy, and it didn't answer my one burning question. "Why?" I asked.

The prince's brow furrowed in that familiar gesture, the one I presumed was a sign of amusement. But he was clearly pissed, so perhaps I'd read that expression wrong all along. His jaw clenched, and he shot a glance my way. "Why does a monster do anything?" he snarled. "Who can say why a wild beast without morals kills innocent prey?"

The tension in the prince's body ran down through his fists, which squeezed my fingers painfully. I extracted them from his grip. "It wasn't a rhetorical question," I snapped. And I wanted more than his bullshit dramatic answer.

"What do you mean?" he asked.

I huffed out a breath. "A monster kills prey for food or self-defense," I said.

Moonlight flashed off the prince's lavender eyes. "A monster does whatever he wants. There's no rhyme or reason to his action, no justification for blatant execution. I won't have you defending that monster Bastian Athar under my roof."

I bit back a retort that we weren't under his roof, although we were certainly on his palace grounds. The petulant child in me was rearing her ugly head tonight, and I had no idea why I was being so pedantic.

Jayke might be frustrating as hell at times, but he was still a good fae. And he was absolutely right that I had no business justifying the murder of his best friend—and I wasn't trying to do that, really. I was just prizing apart the gluey strands of this knot, trying to figure out what was hidden at its center.

I softened my tone. "I'm sorry, Jayke." His brow twitched again in what I now realized was anger. Fuck, I must have been pissing him off a lot since I arrived. All those times I thought he'd been amused by me, he'd actually been furious. I sighed. I would store that information away to dissect later.

For now, I had to make amends with the powerful fae who was hurting from the loss of his sister and friend. Not to mention the powerful fae who held the lives of my grandma and cousins in his hands.

I took a deep breath of the crisp night ear and tried again. "I'm sorry, prince." This time his jaw softened, and his pursed lips relaxed. "I didn't mean to defend Athar, and I never will," I murmured. "Not until my dying day. All I want is to see you onto the throne of Caprice, then I can return home to my family where I belong."

Even as I said the words, they rang hollow. I didn't really belong in Hebes. Like Darzan said, you don't always belong in the place where you'd spent the most time.

Since when did I take advice from that dark prince? Since his words started resonating with me, I guessed. My footsteps covered my sigh as we climbed the grand stairs to the palace doors, which swung open soundlessly as usual, with no sign of a footman.

The air inside was less crisp and fresh but was laced with a faint floral odor. "Good night, Delphinium." Jayke kissed my forehead, and a string inside me tugged at the contact. I wanted more. I wanted full-body skin-on-skin contact that lasted all night. Couldn't he and I lose ourselves in each other for one evening, put aside our concerns and workload and that never-ending question of how the fuck I was supposed to help him onto the throne while also protecting my family...Couldn't we put all that aside and get lost in each other's bodies?

But he was already turning away, already climbing the stairs, already showing me his back.

I went through the motions of undressing, slipping naked between the silken sheets of my inhumanly comfortable bed and closing my eyes.

But that string through the center of my body that had tugged at the prince's kiss only grew tighter. I ran my hands over my belly, up my soft skin, and cupped my breasts.

Fuck it. The prince might be too busy to accompany me on walks through the city, but he'd made it very clear he had time for my body. I shrugged into a robe, which was deliciously cold and silky against my skin, then I tiptoed along the corridors to Jayke's bedchamber. I let the robe fall open so it brushed against my nipples and the fronts of my thighs, and warmth pooled between my legs.

Yes, this was exactly the release I needed. It didn't need to be all night, it didn't need to be sweet, I just desired rough release, and I knew Jayke desired me too.

I knocked on the door and heard a grunt of acknowledgment from the other side, so I pushed it open, letting my robe flutter out behind me. I stopped just inside the doorway, shocked at the sight of a naked female kneeling on the prince's bed, her ass in the air, and him thrusting roughly into her from behind.

"Oh," I said lamely. He turned at my small exclamation, and I hastily closed the robe around my body. That fucking furrow of anger creased his brow, and he instantly froze, completely inside the naked female.

"What are you doing here, Delphinium?" His tone was

fatherly and disapproving, like I'd stayed out past curfew, and the condescending attitude sparked fire through me.

"Fuck off, Jayke," I snarled.

The naked female with her ass in the air gasped when I used his first name, and I snapped at her. "You're letting him fuck you, surely he lets you call him Jaykey-boy?" Darzan's nickname slipped out of my mouth.

"My prince wouldn't like that," she purred, wiggling her ass against his cock.

The hard expression on Jayke's face melted into hooded desire. He cocked a finger. "Would you like to join us, Delphinium?"

The hunger inside me was anything but satiated, but I wasn't interested in the sycophantic female, and frankly, my interest in Jayke was waning too.

I folded my arms across my chest. "No, I would like to go home to Hebes."

Jayke's brows knitted together again. "I already told you—"

I gained great pleasure from interrupting His Royal Highness. "I know, you mentioned." I didn't want him to drone on again about how I had to wait until after the coronation. The last thing I wanted from this dick was a condescending explanation about anything. "Well, don't stop on my account," I said, gesturing at them.

The female giggled and wiggled her ass, and Jayke thrust slowly out of her and then back in, never dropping his lavender eyes from mine.

He didn't owe me anything. He had never vowed that I was his one true love or that he would always be faithful to me. I mean, he did mention that I was his everything and that II was perfect and should stay by his side after he was king.

Dickhole. He was probably just using me to get onto the throne, and all those times he'd been too busy to join me for a walk, he was probably screwing his way through the eligible population of Capricia.

Well, I didn't need a man to get by. And I certainly didn't need a man to hold my hand while I went for a walk. I pulled my robe tighter and stormed out of the palace, determined to have an adventure of my own.

What could go wrong?

Delph

The beachball house on the cobblestone streets was murky gray, and tiny lightning bolts sparked across the surface. I marched right up to it and held out my hand, and the jagged lightning bolts skittered around my palm.

The weather was as shitty as I felt, overcast with intermittent gusts of wind that almost knocked me off my feet and made me pull my short silk dressing gown tighter around me. I strode along the street, trying to get lost—which turned out to be pretty easy. Before long, I was in a part of the city I'd never been to before, although with the forested streets changing and growing each night, it was hard to be sure.

I turned a corner and plunged into an overgrown alleyway with gnarled trees on either side that met overhead and formed a dark tunnel. I knew fae lived in homes along these forested streets, but some of these houses were definitely abandoned. One lilac door was open and hanging from its hinges, giving a view of a barren, dusty interior. I supposed living so close to nature was less appealing than ever when it would likely strike out in attack.

In the mood I was in, I didn't care. I marched along the undergrowth, practically daring the tree roots to strike me. Since arriving in Caprice, I'd become stronger and faster than ever. I was always one of the most powerful people in Hebes, able to defeat the burliest of Docklands thugs, but here in Caprice, I was weaker than most. But the disparity between our abilities had definitely shrunk as I got stronger with every passing day. Must be something to do with the quality of food or drink or just the magical atmosphere.

Whatever it was, I had never felt more capable of protecting myself, so I wasn't too concerned about plunging into this dark tunnel of twisted trees.

But when I marched right into an invisible barrier of air, fear clawed at my limbs. I took a deep breath and tried to walk around the barrier, but there was no way through. I wasn't in the mood for this crap, and I wasted precious moments—and precious energy—battering at the invisible wall before giving up with a groan and heading back the way I'd come.

But another forcefield barred my way, and fear's claws drew blood. A beast emerged between two blackened tree trunks, tall and thin like a fae but covered in scales that appeared to be made of onyx, shiny, hard, and black.

Time seemed to hang suspended as I stood there, frozen, barely daring to breathe. The creature looked at me through slitted eyes, clearly sentient, intelligent, and calculating. It had trapped me in a forcefield cage, and now it circled me slowly, its black eyes locked on mine. Every calculated movement it made as it circled me sent shivers down my spine.

If its hearing was half as keen as a fae's, the creature could probably hear my pounding heart, which I couldn't control, so I focused on my breath, measuring sips of air like they were rationed, doing everything in my power to stay calm.

The beast circled me lazily, roving its gaze over my legs, assessing my stance and strength, and I spun with it, not letting it get behind me.

It took a step closer, and the pressure inside my cage intensified, like the air was trying to crush me into sludge. My lungs could barely expand, and that dreadful sense of anticipation that had layered the air since my arrival whirled within me and around me like malevolence incarnate.

The fucking creature was nature personified, and he was pissed.

He took another step, and I got a brief whiff of rotting vegetation before my lungs refused to function anymore. The air around them hardened into cement, and panic flooded adrenaline into my limbs, begging them to move, but they wouldn't obey.

Frozen to the spot, my breath stolen, my heart pounding, I could only watch and wait as the black-scaled beast pressed closer. My lungs screamed for air, my mind shrieked in terror, and I could only stand motionless and prepare for my death.

Who was I kidding? I couldn't survive here alone, I really did need a fae to keep me alive. Where was Jayke now? I willed him to come to rescue me. If there was any bond between us, any tie at all, I needed him to feel me clawing at my end of it so he could come to find me. I needed my prince now more than ever, and I didn't give a damn about his sexual practices.

A cold blade pressed to my throat, and if I could control my arm, I'd fling a hand up to ease the pressure, although I knew the knife wasn't real. Darzan. While I struggled not to pass out and fought to keep my heart beating, I saw a flash of movement from the corner of my eye, heard the sounds of a scuffle, and hoped like hell that whatever was happening would finish soon.

I slumped to the forest floor, landing hard on the intertwining roots. I could breathe again, move again, think again. Darzan was at my side instantly, pushing my hair from my face. "Are you all right?"

I couldn't formulate a response. He pulled my head into the crook of his elbow, and I let him do it, lying limp while I gathered the energy to tell him to put me down.

He peered into my face, his fingers digging into my upper arm. "I need to know. Are. You. Hurt?" Desperation tinged his voice, and I managed to shake my head. "No. I don't think so."

He pulled me close to his chest, and I breathed deeply, inhaling his scent of ash mixed with the rich leaf litter of the forested avenue.

My sense regained slowly while he held me tight, making me feel protected. I wanted to stay there forever, my cheek rising and falling with each of his breaths, enveloped in safety, soaking in the warmth from his hard chest, looped within the strong cage of his arms.

But nothing could last forever.

"You're a damn idiot," he growled after several long moments.

Reality came crashing back, and I realized I was wearing a scanty silk dressing gown and canoodling with my enemy. Who was just as condescending as Jayke. What was with these men treating me like a damn child?

"Am not, asswipe," I muttered before I could stop myself and realize how immature that sounded.

His grip around my shoulders loosened, and he lowered me gently onto the ground and then rocked back on his heels. "I see you're feeling yourself again, wench."

I pulled my gown tight, covering my torso but wishing it

was longer because my legs poked out the bottom, as naked as a babe. I gasped for air, sucking in lungfuls, and glared right back at him. "Wench?"

He stuck a tongue in the inside of his cheek in a brief crude gesture I immediately thought I might have imagined. "Would you prefer *pet*? Or one of your treasured favorites, *asshole*?" he quipped, his words laced with sarcasm.

I tried to stand but fumbled and landed hard on the ground. "Asshole," I murmured, and he barked out a loud laugh.

I didn't see what was so funny. I didn't have the strength to stand and figured that scaled stone creature must have done something to me. "What *was* that thing?" And the biggest question of all, why was I always chasing Darzan for answers?

"That was a Seelor. A manifestation of Gaia's displeasure."

I sucked in a deep, sweet lungful of air. "And Gaia would be...?"

Ignoring my grunted protest, Darzan swooped me into his arms and strolled along the forested avenue without a care in the world. "Gaia is our goddess, Mother Earth, who created, creates, and will create the world."

I snorted. "Sounds woo." He raised a questioning eyebrow, so I explained. "Woo. Gaga. Totally batshit fucking crazy."

I didn't just mean the concept of a God. Obviously, I was familiar with that. But *did create, is creating, will create?* Come on, that sounded like it was straight out of a self-help spiritual video on a YouTube channel with four subscribers.

"And would you call the Seelor batshit crazy?" he asked.

"Definitely." But I frowned. Maybe he had a point with this whole Gaia business. Nature was undeniably beating her chest, and if he wanted to attribute that to some being called Gaia, who was I to object?

Fatigue swamped me, and I knew it was because of that Seelor. The creature was terrifying. It had left me empty.

This time, I didn't even have to ask the question, and Darzan provided an answer. "The Seelor feeds on power, which is why you feel so drained. You'll be okay in a couple of hours. You just need to rest somewhere safe."

My head bobbed against his hard shoulder as he walked, and despite being carried by my enemy, I felt like I was already somewhere safe, nestled against his chest with a view of his corded neck and golden hair.

It was a relief to be provided with information without having to extract it like blood from a stone, and I realized that was the one attribute in this male that surpassed Jayke. The Sansett Prince wasn't good at sharing. My eyes closed, lulled by the rhythmic motion of the evil prince's steps.

What must have been hours later, consciousness seeped back into my senses. I woke in a dark room with a familiar, comforting smell I couldn't quite place. I opened my eyes and saw I was in a strange bed with blood-red sheets and a black frame. The walls were paneled in dark wood, and Darzan was seated in a blood-red leather armchair by a crackling fire.

I sat bolt upright. "What the fuck?"

He smirked. "Good morning to you too, Delph."

I narrowed my eyes at him but didn't bother replying. The air was sweet, and my muscles felt strong again. My gown was flapping open, partially revealing my breasts, so I tugged it tight around me. "How long did I sleep?"

"Three hours. Do you feel better now?" Amusement squinted his eyes, which, I was pleased to see, remained squarely on my face and not my chest.

I couldn't imagine why he helped me last night or why he

was being nice this morning. Probably trying to soften me up to win me to his side. But it wouldn't work. I hummed out a noncommittal response.

"Did you ask your boyfriend about Lorca?" he smirked.

Goddamn, this male was so infuriating. *Yes*, I'd asked him, and *no*, I hadn't got a satisfactory response, just more propaganda about how terrible Bastian Athar had been, which I already knew. But there was no way I was confessing that to Darzan—he was just as smirk-nnoying as the other prince.

"He's not my boyfriend," I snarled. That was the truth. He was just some fucker who thrust his junk inside other females instead of taking me for moonlit walks. Man, I was pathetic.

"Are you beating yourself up about something again?" Darzan asked.

"No. What are you talking about?" I snapped. "I don't do that."

If I expected him to dig a little deeper into my psyche, I was disappointed. He came to my bedside, grabbed my hand, and yanked me roughly to my feet. "Well, I suppose you'd better be going now that you're feeling better." He practically pushed me out the door, and I couldn't say I was sorry for it. I was happy to get out of his depressing little hovel. His home was a far cry from Sansett Palace, little more than a two-story townhouse in the city center.

Before I had time to object, I was standing on his stoop with cold air blowing around my knees, feeling like he'd handed me my ass.

"Thanks for visiting," he said snidely. "Do come again soon." Bastard. I looked around, and he tilted his head in curiosity. "Don't you know where you are?" he asked.

"Why the hell should I know where I am?" I snapped. "I'm

new in town, in case you didn't remember."

His lips curved in a smile, but there was nothing friendly about it. "Interesting," he said.

My hands flew to my hips. "And what's so interesting about that?" The cool wind flurried around my knees, making me shiver, but I refused to hug myself warm and show vulnerability, so I stayed in my best piss-off pose while he answered.

But he didn't. He just narrowed his golden eyes and pointed along the street. "Your road home is that way."

I followed where he pointed, plodding along the streets on full alert and tugging my ridiculous dressing gown as low as possible. But I wasn't scared. Because although he didn't make a sound, and I couldn't catch sight of him no matter how many times I whirled around, I knew Darzan was following me by the press of that phantom blade against my throat.

Before long, I found the little beachball home. It was no longer gray but shone golden. How frequently did it change color?

When I stepped onto the moonway, the phantom blade against my neck disappeared, and dread crept back down my throat.

Delph

I fled along the moonway, the world a blur of washed-out blues and grays as I sprinted faster than I'd ever moved.

When I finally set foot in the palace grounds, the heaviness of the air lifted from my shoulders, kept at bay by the Weaver's wards. My feet crunched slowly along the gravel path, the sound soothing against the weight of my thoughts. I was dog-tired. Those couple of hours of sleep had only restored my energy but hadn't rejuvenated me. All I wanted to do was clamber into my soft bed and disappear from the world for a while.

But there was something I had to do first. Darzan had raised so many questions in my mind that only Jayke could answer, and this time I wouldn't be fobbed off even if he had a dozen naked fae in his bed.

It wasn't hard to psych myself up, I just summoned the evil bitch who lived within me and was never far from my surface. I was done with playing a princess in a palace, done with my pleases and thank-yous, done with being a good girl and doing as I was told. From now on, I would do things my way.

I started by not bothering to knock on Jayke's door but flinging it open and storming in. He was alone in bed, having obviously dismissed the female he'd fucked. His eyes flicked open, and a stern expression began to settle on his face, but I was having none of it.

"I don't want to hear a word out of your mouth that isn't in response to my question," I snapped. Who cared if I didn't have any way to back that up. He seemed to want me here in Arathay, so I could use that as leverage. I couldn't necessarily escape without him, but I could certainly stop attending his parties and smiling at his fan club. I cocked out a hip. "First, I want to know what happened to Lorca."

He sat up, and the silk sheets dropped down his body, revealing his hard chest. It was as alabaster white as the rest of him, almost glowing against the room's shadows, toned and lightly muscled. It was like nothing I'd ever seen; he looked eerily like a God, but I wouldn't be distracted by that.

His lavender eyes crinkled, and he beckoned me closer, patting the bed beside him. "Why don't you come here, and we can talk properly?"

I knew that if I hopped into bed beside him, I'd have difficulty thinking of anything other than sex because I was in a long drought surrounded by hot fae, and I was still wearing my skimpy silk gown.

So I kept my feet firmly planted on the parquetry floor. "Why don't you answer my question? All I want is the truth rather than these nuggets of nothingness you keep giving me. Why can't you be straight with me? Who was Lorca, and why was he killed?"

Darzan had clearly gotten to me. I hoped I wasn't just playing to his tune now, gobbling up breadcrumbs he'd laid out for me and walking into his trap. But it didn't feel like it. All I wanted was the truth, and I didn't see what could be wrong with that. I didn't have to act on it, didn't have to change my allegiance from House Sansett to House Davin, didn't have to do a damn thing. I just wanted to know what the fuck was going on.

Jayke sighed. "I didn't lie to you, Delphinium." I hated when he used my full name. It made me feel like I was getting in trouble from my grandma, and it no longer sounded perfect on his lips but pretentious. But I didn't interrupt his flow now I was finally getting some real information. "Lorca was my best friend and my sister's husband, and he was killed by House Athar on the same evening that Leena was imprisoned."

"But why?" I demanded. "I swear to God, if you don't tell me right now, I will march out that damn door and tell everybody I don't think you should be king."

His lavender eyes flickered to purple momentarily, and I sensed the angry monarch living within him. I wouldn't switch allegiance because I still didn't want that violent creature Darzan to rule, but it was the only ballast I had in this argument, and I wasn't afraid of using it.

"Very well," Jayke said, getting to his feet and walking shamelessly around completely naked, his long dick slapping against his balls with every step. His pubes looked to be a perfect match for the lavender hair on his head, or maybe a shade darker. He shrugged into a robe. "Lorca attempted to overthrow House Athar to take control of the realm. He did it for the good of the fae, but he was caught and executed for treason. That's the full story, there is nothing insidious or secret about it. Everybody knows what happened. My sister was imprisoned for her part, and my friend was murdered. All because they were trying to make Caprice a better place."

I stamped a foot. This was so frustrating. "Why didn't you just say so! I've been running in circles trying to figure this out, and you've been so cagey about it. Just tell me the damn truth next time."

Jayke came closer, swept up my hands into his, and held them against his mouth, brushing his lips against me as he spoke, his lavender scent muted with the musk of recent sex. "Lorca was only mentioned at the dinner party last night. I would happily have told you everything, but when you asked me about it, I was...busy."

True enough. He'd had his cock hilt deep in a female when I'd last broached this topic.

I withdrew my hands from his and circled slowly, folding my arms across my chest so he couldn't sweep them up again. "And why won't you let me visit my family?" I demanded.

I just wanted to check in on my cousins, Grandma, and even Jackson to ensure they were safe and cared for. My trust in Jayke was spiraling, and although I believed his story about Lorca and Leena, I no longer had blind faith in him. "I just want to see for myself that they're okay, then I'll return and help you with your campaign."

He shook his head sadly, like denying my request pained him more than it pained me, and he again looked like a fatherly figure doing what was best for his child. "I'm sorry, that just isn't possible. It isn't healthy for a mortal to cross the barrier too many times, and I can't risk anything happening to you."

I was sick to death of the doting father routine, and this was the first I'd heard of the barrier crossing being dangerous. It sounded like bullshit to me. "I'm willing to take the risk. I'll duck home, let my family know I'm okay, then return here immediately. All I ask is for one hour in Hebes. Surely that's not too much?"

"I can't risk you, Delphinium. I—"

"You don't get to decide that," I snapped, tapping into my inner street bitch. Heat welled within me. I was done being a fucking princess, and that included having somebody else make decisions about my safety. I was more than capable of making those calls for myself, and if I fucked it up, I was happy to live with the consequences. "Am I back to being a prisoner here?"

I had to get out of this house, and I had to go tonight. This felt like a final test for Jayke, and I wanted more than anything for him to take me home for an hour, if only to restore my faith in him.

Jayke's brow creased, looking for all the world as though my words physically hurt him, and guilt twinged through me, but I couldn't back down.

I hated the person I was becoming here, weak and forgiving and compliant. It just wasn't me. Even if being like that—being like Jayke—was *better*, it still wasn't me. I was a violent survivor with limited people skills, not a courtesan or politician. I had to reclaim my identity.

"I'm sorry, Delphinium. You only have to wait one week, and then you can spend all the time you want with your nasty old grandma." His expression was neutral, but his words were barbs. "In the meantime, Calaboose will escort you to your chamber."

That small winged faerie who'd tried to prevent me from going outside when I first arrived materialized beside me. How long had she been there? Did she follow me everywhere I went? And since when could fae appear out of thin air? I would have to ask Darzan about that because strange as it may seem, he was beginning to feel like the only fae who would answer my questions willingly.

I decided not to press it any further. I didn't want to end up an actual prisoner here. If I didn't have the freedom to roam the palace grounds or travel along the moonways of an evening, I might well lose my mind.

I allowed Calaboose to follow me to my bedroom, but I shut the door in her face, slipped into bed and settled among the cloud-soft pillows. But I didn't sleep. No fucking way. I wouldn't spend another night in this place.

Delph

I waited an hour in bed pretending to sleep in case Calaboose was lurking in the corridor. Then I shrugged out of my dressing down and into the outfit I'd arrived in—my black leather jacket and black jeans, which scraped my skin like sandpaper compared to the clothes I'd been wearing here. I strapped my dagger to my hip for moral support, although I knew it would be useless in a fight against fae. I went for a pair of black silk slippers instead of my old boots because they were just as tough and twice as comfortable.

As quietly as possible, I creaked open my bedroom window and climbed out, then lowered myself to hang from the marble sill. My fingers slipped, and I dropped to the ground one floor below, landing with a loud rustle on some puffy white bushes.

I rolled on landing like they do in movies, and it seemed to work because I got to my feet uninjured. I jogged across the palace grounds, sticking to the dewy grass rather than the gravel path. I didn't have a firm plan, but I had a definite end goal—I was going to Hebes.

If I'd known where Elora slept, I might have woken her for help and guidance because she was the closest thing I had to a friend around here. But she was a fae, and she worked for Prince Sansett, so she wasn't a sure bet.

Which meant the only person I could go to was the fae I liked least. The irony wasn't lost on me. But I knew he was powerful and connected enough to get me across the barrier, he definitely wasn't aligned with House Sansett, and he wouldn't give a fuck if crossing the border poisoned me. The triple win, yay.

When I stumbled from the moonway onto the cobblestone streets of Capricia, I closed my eyes, trying to remember the way to Darzan's city pad. The route to his house showed easily in my mind like I was staring at Google Maps, except the path I had to follow wasn't shown in blue. But I could somehow tell which way to go, probably because I'd been there before, and I headed off at a steady jog.

I was fitter than I used to be, even when I was heller tired, probably from all the long walks I'd been taking. Before long, I was banging on Darzan's dark-paneled front door, suddenly realizing what a stupid idea this was. *Why, hey, mortal enemy, whom I despise and insult at every opportunity, could you do me a favor?*

But I didn't have a choice. I wasn't going back to the palace, and even I couldn't survive a night on the streets so close to the Ascension rite and coronation, not with Gaia being such a dick. So I kept ringing. I told myself it wasn't begging, but it felt a lot like it.

Finally, the door swung open, and I stumbled over the threshold. Rough hands yanked me inside, and the door slammed. "What are you doing here?" Darzan growled.

Lovely. This murderous prick couldn't be more different from Prince Charming, but I sucked it up and spit out my request. "I need you to take me to Hebes."

Darzan stared at me for a moment. He was rumpled from

sleep, his golden hair tousled, and he wore loose pants and no top. His chest was broader and more muscled than Jayke's, and his body emanated a dangerous energy that called to the violent bitch inside me.

I backed away a pace, but he pressed with me, pushing me against a wall, his entire hard body up against mine and his hands caging my head. "And what makes you think I will help you with anything, pet?"

I shoved at his hard chest, but he was too strong, too fucking strong. "I just need to check on my family, that's all."

His biceps caged around my ears, and his chest heaved with each breath, his ashy smell enveloping me. "Is this a scheme your master Jaykey-boy cooked up?" he snarled.

I slapped his face. "He's not my master," I snapped. This was a fucking mistake. I wanted to duck away and flee into the streets, but the image of my twin cousins being roughly manhandled by the fae in the Hebes town square had settled into my head and wouldn't leave me in peace, and as much as I hated it, Darzan was my only choice. "And he didn't put me up to this. He doesn't even know I'm here," I spit.

The dark prince finally uncaged me, and I could breathe again. He shifted his weight onto his back foot, leaving a narrow strip of hot air between our bodies, and dropped his muscled arms to his sides. "Well, well, trouble in paradise," he drawled. "Let me guess, you asked His Royal Prickness to take you home, and he said no. Not until after he's crowned king, and then you can do whatever you want. Did I get that right?"

Spot on, but I wasn't about to admit that. I slid against the cold wall to get away and widened the gap between us so I could think properly. "I just want to check on my family, then

I'll come back here. Will you help me get across the barrier or not?" I said. He clearly wasn't convinced, although his golden eyes sparkled with mischief. "As an added bonus, I'll get weakened by the crossing, right? Surely you like the sound of that," I urged. "Humans get poisoned if they cross too many times."

His brows knitted together. "No they don't," he said. Then his forehead smoothed, and he chuckled darkly. "It sounds like Jaykey-boy's been feeding you more lies. Humans are no more weakened from the barrier than fae are." He smirked. "That is, not at all," he clarified.

I shook that information off. If that was true, that was another lie Jayke had told me. I would have to sort out the truth from the lies later, but right now, I needed to convince Darzan to help me get home.

I tried another tactic. "It can only help you if I disappear for a while, right?" I said, practically pleading. "I mean, apparently, my presence here helps Jayke onto the throne somehow, so if I'm gone, you'll have a smoother ride."

He stroked the rough stubble of his chin, and a wicked grin grew on his lips. "You are absolutely right, pet."

I wanted to punch him in the dick for calling me that stupid name, but now wasn't the time, not when I'd finally gotten him to agree to take me home. "Great." I brushed past him to the front door, feeling the heat off his bare chest as I passed. "Let's go."

I jiggled impatiently while he looked me slowly up and down, and I imagined he was using his fae senses to assess the state of my heart and every twitching muscle. It was like being scanned by a living X-ray machine. He clearly came to a conclusion. "Not now. Your fragile body needs rest. Come upstairs."

I was sick to death of being reminded how much weaker I was than every single bloody fae, but I couldn't deny the bone-deep fatigue in my body, so I followed him upstairs. His ass was juicy, and the muscles on his back were toned, so I gave myself the small pleasure of watching him as I followed. I might as well get something out of this shitbox of a situation.

"You're in here." Darzan opened the door to the chamber I'd woken in earlier, with the dark wood paneling and blood-red sheets. I'd assumed this was his room, but I supposed it was for guests. A small fire crackled on the far side of the bed, making the hovel seem cozy, at least.

I waited for him to leave so I could strip down and slide onto that squishy mattress I knew firsthand was soft and comfortable, but he didn't go anywhere.

I motioned to the door. "Whenever you're ready," I said snidely. "I'm a fragile human who needs her sleep, remember?"

He raised an eyebrow but said nothing, just walked to the bed and got into it. He slid underneath the damn covers and lay down.

"What do you think you're doing?" I asked. "I thought you said this was my room?"

He stroked his rough chin again in a mockery of deep thought. "No, I said you're in here. In fact, this is my room, and I'm doing you a favor by letting you stay here, so kindly drop the attitude."

"If this is your damn room, I'll sleep somewhere else," I snapped. "It's not rocket science. I'll see you in the morning."

I turned on my heel, but he was out of bed in a flash and grabbing my wrist. "You need to sleep in here so I can protect you."

"Like hell I do," I snarled.

He released my wrist. "It's your call," he said. "But this is the only room with enough spellwork to be safe."

I turned to look at him, annoyed at the amused glint in his golden eyes. "You're telling me your entire house isn't properly warded?" I demanded, keeping my gaze well away from his bare, muscled chest.

He shrugged, and the curve of his shoulder caught the light. "Not all of us have a house full of servants and master Weavers. And Gaia isn't usually so pissed off. This only happens once every couple of thousand years, you know."

I narrowed my eyes. "This what? This part where the king dies before a replacement has been chosen?"

"Or queen," he said, pissing me off even more. I was the feminist around here, and I didn't like being corrected on it. "Or queen, obviously. But Jayke said they were usually kings."

Darzan tilted his head. "Did he now? Interesting."

I breathed deeply, squeezing my hands into fists. I walked over to the blood-red leather armchair, unable to hold myself up a minute longer, and slumped into it. "Stop saying everything is interesting," I grumbled.

He barked a laugh, and I couldn't help but smile. My resting bitch face was tired too. "I don't see what right Gaia has to be annoyed if she's the one who didn't select anybody. Surely this is her fault. She should have zapped someone with Lightning at the last Ascension rite. She's the one who fucked up."

Darzan motioned to the mattress. "Take the bed. You're too tired to sleep sitting up, and you need to be well-rested before our journey." Gratefully, I hobbled over to the massive mattress, toed off my shoes, wriggled out of my jeans, and slid between the delicious soft sheets. "And," he continued, "Gaia only chooses those who are worthy, and sometimes a worthy ruler doesn't come along in time."

"Bastian Athar wasn't worthy," I mumbled, but I slurred so much he probably didn't hear. I was almost asleep when Darzan hopped onto the other side of the bed and lay beside me, pulling on the sheets so a cold silky patch slid over me. My eyes flew open. "What the fuck?"

He looked at me like I was an idiot. "I'm not sleeping on the stone floor," he said. "It's my bed. Feel free to shiver on the hard stone if you like, but I'll be resting on the mattress."

If I was less tired, I would have put up more of a fight, but as it was, I was happy to let my eyes flutter closed again, but I couldn't shake the awareness of the hot male fae just inches away, his chest rising and falling with every quiet breath. And half naked, for good measure.

Delph

At dawn, Darzan and I headed off on our journey to Hebes. He wore a light gray cloak over brown traveling pants and a cream shirt and thrust a similar gray cloak at me.

"Wear this," he grunted. I opened my mouth to object—my default response—but he cut me off. "Wear it, or we don't go."

I pulled it on and trotted to catch up with Darzan, who had already started marching along the street without bothering to wait for me. The cloak swished around me lightly, making me feel like a kid playing superheroes.

"Are these magical capes that will transport us to the mortal realm?" I joked, but it fell flat.

"They're so we blend in in Brume," he said flatly.

We zigzagged through unfamiliar streets, exploring corners of the city I'd never seen. I figured we weren't flying to the border, given that Darzan had ascended to War, not Hover.

"The Realm of Brume?" I'd heard some of the names of the other fae realms, but I hadn't pieced together how they all fit on the map of Arathay.

He nodded. "The fae of Brume wear cloaks like these, and I don't want us to stand out."

There could only be one reason he didn't want us to stick

out. A cool breeze licked my cheeks, and I shivered. "Is it dangerous?"

"Everywhere is dangerous," he said flatly, but I didn't see how that could be true. After all, when Caprice had a benevolent ruler, it was reportedly a beautiful place to live.

But I already knew Darzan was the kind of male who mistrusted everything and everyone, and that clearly extended to every place. He had a dark, brooding talk-to-me-and-die attitude that repelled everybody kind and generous, and I supposed that made him believe the world was dark and dangerous.

Still, I wasn't about to fight it. He could be all dark and dramatic if he wanted, as long as he got me home to Hebes.

"So we're not going via the Realm of Fen?" I said. Thank God for that. The truth-telling realm was the last place I wanted to go back to. I already knew that I splattered facts like shrapnel from my brief visit there on the way to Sansett Palace, and I had no desire to sprinkle my truth confetti all over Darzan.

He shuddered almost imperceptibly. "No way."

He didn't elaborate, but he didn't have to. Somebody with major trust issues wouldn't want to visit Fen. He'd be forced to be honest and forthright without any control, which was probably his worst nightmare. Kinda like it was mine.

Not for the first time, I realized Darzan and I had a lot in common. He was a violent murderous bastard, and although I'd never killed anyone, I couldn't be accused of pacifism. The violence inside me reared up at the violence inside him, and I supposed we also shared a mistrust of others.

Even so, as much as I would have liked to witness him dropping truth grenades in Fen, I was pleased we weren't taking that route.

Despite the fingers of sunlight creeping across the cobble-stones, it was too warm for this cloak, and I was beginning to resent having it tied around my neck. At least it weighed nothing, so I just flung it over my shoulders and let it trail out behind me like Superman's cape. Figured I might as well lean into the whole superhero thing.

Darzan set a fast enough pace that I got a little winded and had to stretch my legs to keep up. "How many realms are there in Arathay?" I asked after a little trot, my slippers louder on the cobblestones than his but not as clompy as my boots would've been.

He cast me a glance, his golden eyes shining brighter than the pale dawn sun. It looked as though he didn't believe my question, to be honest, like he thought I was playing him, playing up my ignorance. I wished that were true. I only knew about Caprice, Fen, and now Brume.

"Arathay is divided into six fae realms," he explained. "Brume is the largest, covering vast territories to the south and east of Caprice, and is mostly grasslands covered in mist. The Western spine of mountains holds the mountain fae of Ourea, the sworn enemies of Caprice, and if we don't get our Court in order soon, they will inevitably invade."

A fae war sounded awful, although I supposed somebody with War power like Darzan would get off on that shit. "And Fen lies along the Requin Sea to the north, right? And over the sea is Hebes," I said, wanting to show off what little knowledge I had.

"Yes," he agreed. "That leaves two realms. Verda to the far east, past Brume, is green and lush, a place of excess and indulgence—"

"Sounds nice. Are we going there?" I quipped.

Darzan didn't bother answering. He just flashed me another one of his intense glares. "And the Unseelie Realm of Dust is in the South. Trust me, you don't want to visit there."

Strangely, I did trust him. On that one thing, at least.

We finally stopped walking through the city, somewhere to the east of the Spike, which I deduced from the sun rising in our faces. I closed my eyes briefly and lapped up the warmth on my upturned cheeks.

"Are we traveling by moonway?" I asked.

We stopped, and Darzan scanned the ground, glancing up occasionally at the sky, clearly looking for something. "Of course," he snapped. "Don't just stand there like a lump, help me find it."

I cocked out a hip and checked to see if he was joking, but there was no sign of amusement on his face. "I can't see the moonway without the moon. I'm human," I said.

"Don't be absurd," he snorted. He kept up his odd routine of scanning the ground and glancing at the sky for a while before turning to me. "Hang on, didn't Jayke show you how to do this?"

"No," I said slowly. "That male likes keeping information to himself." My opinion of Jayke was dropping moment by moment. He had, in fact, told me a mortal couldn't discern a moonway without the aid of the moon, but it seemed that was a lie. "How do I find it?" I demanded.

"It helps if you know where it is, otherwise, it can take weeks to find one. But I know there's one here by that marking." He indicated a rock cairn stacked in a field beside a house constructed entirely from interwoven flowers that emitted a pleasant aroma. What happened at night? Or in winter? Did those flowers close up or die? If so, what happened to the house? Did it fall over? Did they have to water it?

"Are you paying attention?" Darzan drawled, and I snapped out of my reverie about the practicalities of living in a home made from flowers.

"What? Yes."

"You have to catch rays of light and just scan the ground looking for the edges of reality," he explained.

I snorted. "Sure, no problem."

He carried on, ignoring me. "You have to glance away every so often, or you lose focus. I find glancing at the sky helps to clear my mind."

I was determined to find this damn moonway now that I knew how, but I had a boatload of trouble figuring out what the edge of reality might look like. It probably didn't look like the wide grassy pathway leading between the flower house and a regular brick house, though that's where Darzan kept staring, so I did likewise.

I glanced at the sky, then back down, and it was as though some of the rays of light from the sky were glued to my vision and snagged and sparkled at the edges of a path to one side of the grassy field. "This way!" I cried, all pumped up, stepping onto where the light had danced. I practically danced, too, when the houses on both sides started to blur.

"Quick study," he said.

The reply '*good teacher*' was on the tip of my tongue, but I bit it back. We didn't have the kind of relationship that allowed for easy banter, and I didn't want to. Not with this villain. I reminded myself of the top half of the old fae's torso sliding off the legs and landing in a bloodied puddle in the forecourt outside the Spike. No matter how helpful Darzan was being,

I could never forget that he had to be kept as far from the Caprician throne as possible.

So I swallowed my friendly reply and walked ahead of him along the moonway.

We walked fast enough that the world beside us blurred into streaks, and I had a sense of covering a vast distance eastward. Darzan told me this moonway emerged in Brume, near the Requin Sea. From there, we would need to hire a boat—or engage a Hover—to take us to Hebes.

We emerged from the moonway into a different world. The foreboding heaviness of anticipation that weighed the air in Caprice had disappeared, replaced by ordinary air that felt freeing and delightful. I breathed deeply, and even Darzan moaned a small sigh of pleasure.

Darzan was right about the grasslands in Brume. Bright green extended in every direction as far as I could see, with floating islands of mist swirling over parts of it. It smelled moist and grassy, and I wouldn't be surprised to see a herd of zebra thundering past, if they even had such creatures in Arathay. If they existed, they probably came with fangs and a bad attitude.

"This way." The prince beelined toward the northeast, and I trotted behind him, feeling the tug of home. It was eerily quiet in the grasslands as though the swirls of mist devoured all sound, and even my clunky human feet made no noise on the damp grass. We came to the edge of a patch of fog, and Darzan hesitated a moment before diving in. He disappeared from view within a few footsteps, and my hackles rose. If there was any kind of danger, it would be hiding in the fog. I was enough of a predator myself to know that much. I stopped and peered into the swirling fog but couldn't see any dark shapes within that might be dangerous. Or that might be Darzan—he'd disappeared entirely.

"Bad idea, buddy," I called into the mist, noting how my voice was swallowed and deadened. "Didn't you say this is a dangerous realm? Let's skip the ambush central."

He was at my side in a moment, holding his hand over my mouth to hush me. "Also a bad idea to tell all those enemies we're here," he hissed, and I had to concede his point.

I slapped his hand away. "So we both have terrible ideas," I murmured. "Let's strike a deal. I'll stay quiet, and you stay out of the mist of doom."

He considered it for a moment, then nodded. "Deal." We skirted the fog, taking a longer route to Port Lonsdale, and although I hated delaying my return home, it seemed the prudent course.

I walked a pace behind the prince, watching his light gray cloak flutter as he moved. It really was excellent camouflage on these misty grasslands, and I could see why he'd insisted we wear them. Plus, it was colder here in Brume, and I was glad for the extra layer.

I heard a slight sound in the eerie stillness and scanned the bank of fog to our right, seeing nothing but the eddies and swirls that accompanied us every step of the way. But I couldn't shake the feeling of watching eyes.

Ever since I put the idea into my own head of dangers lurking unseen, I'd felt eyes on me and had no idea if they were real or imagined, but either way, they were enough to keep my senses alert and my hand resting on my dagger.

I was watching Darzan's boots when it happened. A leg swept out from the fog and tripped him up, so he landed flat on his back with a surprised yelp. He was dragged into the mist, and if I'd been glancing away, I would never have seen what happened. Before his head vanished, I pounced onto his disappearing torso and held on for dear life as we were pulled into the blinding white.

I unsheathed my dagger with a ringing of steel and slashed blindly around my head, listening for any sounds in the eerie quiet. A snarl and an exhale nearby had me lunging into the nothingness, although I kept one hand on Darzan's arm, knowing that if we got separated, we'd never find each other again.

I heard the sounds of scuffling and felt Darzan's arm tugging and moving, though he clasped his hand into mine and gripped so hard I heard my fingers crack. Clearly, he had the same idea I did about not losing each other.

We fought together, blindly defending ourselves against our invisible attackers. I crouched, hoping any blows would go over my head. I swore I heard a heartbeat to my right, and I lunged forward and up, striking with my blade, feeling grim satisfaction as it plunged into flesh with a loud squelch.

Behind me, I sensed Darzan slashing our opponents using his War power.

We were the superior fighters. Our enemies had the advantage of surprise, but with that gone, they were outclassed, outmatched. Darzan had killed himself to enhance his inner power of War during his Ascension. He had chosen to slice his own heart open with a sword so that Gaia would bless him with the ability to wield one. To be one.

And a fucking awesome one. I wasn't too shabby myself, ducking, reading the battle through movements in the air and the panting of my opponents, kicking and punching and lashing out with my dagger, until it was over.

Finally, it was just the two of us, an unknown number of bodies lying at our feet. I'd never killed anyone before and didn't know if I just had. Was I a murderer?

The question didn't bother me nearly as much as it should.

Darzan pulled me close, my back against his chest. He breathed hard, his chest expanding and contracting behind me, and urgency laced his voice. "Are you all right?"

I enjoyed the feeling between us for a few moments, the warmth of his hard body behind mine, his ashy scent, and his arm wrapped firmly around me. Why did this feel so good?

"Never felt better," I panted. And it was true. I may have earned a few scrapes and bruises, but the adrenaline coursing through my veins more than made up for it. I felt truly alive, as though I was born to fight. The unsettling notion occurred to me that if I were fae, I might choose to ascend to War power, too, because that felt fucking brilliant.

The prince and I gripped each other's hands, striding ahead with our best guess at a northeasterly path. I just hoped we weren't walking in circles. I pulled my cloak close to protect myself from the dampness in the air and for extra warmth because I was cooling fast after the fight.

"Happy for the cloak now?" Darzan drawled, and I just hummed in reply. I wouldn't give him the satisfaction of answering that truthfully.

Time passed oddly in the mist, with odd squeaks and chirps coming from every direction—even down—and it felt like hours before we finally emerged into clear air.

"Thank fuck for that," I exclaimed when I could finally see past the tip of my tongue.

Darzan glanced at me, but I saw a slight curve in his lips. "You really have an interesting way of expressing yourself," he said.

I remembered back to the first time we met, when he called my language trashy. I would have arced up at his comment and spit out a nasty reply if he wasn't almost smiling right now. Plus, I was still on a high from the battle and felt drenched in positivity.

I realized we were still holding hands, so I released my grip. As much as I hated the violence in him that tugged at the violence in myself, it had certainly come in handy back there. No point denying that he and I made a damn good team.

Delph

We entered Port Lonsdale, the harbor city of Brume that welcomed the Requin Sea. It felt different to Caprice—far safer and tamer but less colorful. People wore drab grays and browns, and even the houses were dull. Mist rolled through the streets, veiling swathes of the city from view, so it was an ever-changing landscape.

Darzan stopped outside a tavern with a swinging wooden sign of a cat and the words "The Misty Feline" in faded silver lettering. "Yes," he muttered before creaking open the door and charging inside, expecting me to follow. Not that I had anywhere else to be.

Inside was like a ye olde style inn with wooden everything, tables, chairs, floor. No big-screen TVs or arcade games, no electricity at all. Lightning powered everything in Caprice, but this room was lit by oil lamps hung from wall sconces and some hovering globes of light I couldn't identify. I knew human technology was banned in Arathay, but this was so medieval it was borderline ironic, like a pub from a historical replica town. It even smelled ancient, like rich stew and stale ale.

"Find a table. I'll arrange some food," Darzan said.

I hated taking orders, but food and a seat were exactly what

I wanted. I slid into a cushioned booth in the corner from where I could keep an eye on the whole room. A five-piece band played ragged rock in the corner that made my feet tap, and a sign with faded red lettering named them *The Fanged Five*. Darzan returned with two large frothing beers and two plates of a delicious-smelling beef ragout.

He forked a mouthful of stew. "You did well in the fight."

Coming from a War wielder, that was high praise. His entire schtick was battle and killing, so his words sent a flicker of pride through me. "Thanks," I said. "I feel fitter every day. Ever since I arrived here, I've gotten stronger." I swigged a mouthful of ale. "Must be something in the water."

Darzan looked around, making sure our conversation wasn't overheard, but the other patrons were noisy and drunk and singing out of tune to The Fanged Five's music, not paying us any attention. "That's because human technology suppresses magic," he said. "The longer you're away from Hebes, the more your powers will emerge."

I snorted and looked at him like he was an idiot. Which he was. "I'm not magic, doofus," I scoffed. It felt good to know more about something than somebody else. Since arriving in Arathay, I'd been on the back foot, but now I could play teacher. And it felt damn good. "Don't you know anything about humans?" I asked, putting extra derision into my tone.

His brows knitted. "Of course I do. We have Human Studies class at faeschool."

I almost choked on a mouthful of mashed something at learning that. Everybody in Hebes heard rumors of life in the fae realms, but since nobody ever returned from there, they were just that. Faerietales. Certainly nothing as concrete as classroom lessons. "No way!" I spluttered.

He quirked a lip. "Way."

I swallowed some stew while I processed that information. Kid fae went to faeschool. Cute. And they learned about humans in a class called Human Studies. That was less cute because it made me feel like a chimp or a gorilla or something, a lesser species to be studied. Which was even worse because it was kind of true.

But obviously, their Human Studies classes were shit because Darzan didn't even know the basics. "And didn't you learn we don't have magic?" I asked with a scoff, trying to make him feel stupid to push away the awful suspicion that I was the stupid one.

He narrowed his eyes and avoided the question, which I took as confirmation I was right and he was an idiot. Good. Rather him than me. Darzan leaned his elbows on the table, showing none of the good breeding and manners that his rival to the throne had. "Tell me about your family," he said, studying me closely like I was a moth in a specimen jar.

I sucked in a breath, considering my options. I supposed it was only fair to give him some goss about my family since he was taking me to see them, but telling the truth felt like pulling out my hair. I was tempted to give him a bullshit story about a picket fence and two doting parents, the kind I always gave to the cops, but I figured I owed him more than that.

I pushed my plate away, half-eaten, scraping it across the wooden table. "I grew up with Uncle Jackson until he had kids. He has three girls now, Lexi, Kalya, and Razelle. They're sweet." I glanced up to see if Darzan had caught my drift.

"Not like you," he suggested, showing he did.

"Right. I guess I always tried to protect them from the world and keep them safe. That's one reason I'm keen to check on them. Lexi's a fucking idiot, always wanting to explore the Docklands. She thinks she's a badass, but she's not tough enough. She'll get herself killed."

Darzan nodded. "That's actually rather...noble."

I shifted uncomfortably. The wooden bench was hard under my butt, and I didn't want praise I didn't deserve. "No, I'm far from noble," I said. He chuckled in what I guessed was agreement, so I barreled on before he could agree too wholeheartedly. "I just want to sleep at night, that's all," I told him. "It's selfish, really."

I watched him chew, his broad jaw working up and down, his black stubble dark against his chin. "You know time flows differently there, right?" he said between mouthfuls. "You've been here, what, a week?"

"Ten and a half days," I said. "Not that I'm counting."

He chuckled. "Right. So that's just over two days in Hebes."

That information should have calmed me down, but it just made blood thunder in my ears. If only forty-eight hours had passed, Kayla and Razelle could still be in the Docklands, either hiding somewhere or captured. Or they could be in the hands of the Hover fae. It was irrational, but I had to get there and make sure they were okay.

The urgency pulsed through me like an electric shock, and I stood abruptly. "Can we go now? I know it's late, but I want to get to them."

Darzan wiped his mouth with a napkin, marking him as more of a gentleman than the other patrons, who used the back of their hands. "You really care about them, don't you?" he asked.

"Of course I do," I snapped.

"Well," he said slowly, wiping his fingers on his napkin. "I cannot secure a crossing until morning."

Food and ale had renewed my strength—though the beer was damn disgusting—and my feet were itching for action. "Not good enough," I snapped, impatience getting the best of me. "Keep asking around until you find someone who can take us tonight."

Darzan tossed his napkin in his bowl and leaned back with his hands crossed behind his head, the picture of someone who didn't give a fuck. "That's not happening, Delph. So either take a seat and relax or keep standing like a fool. It doesn't bother me either way," he said. He took a long swig of beer, smirking up at me.

Most annoying of all, I had little choice but to sit down again like a good little girl. I hated being a good little girl.

Darzan watched me intently, but he wasn't smirking in victory, so I kept my scowl to a minimum. "Where did you go after the charming and generous Jackson kicked you out?" he asked.

I bristled at the veiled insult to my uncle. "After he didn't have room for me," I said pointedly, "I went to live with Grandma."

"Grandma Smith?" he asked, obviously having researched me.

"Yes," I admitted.

"Interesting." He drew the word out slowly, still examining me like a specimen.

I folded my arms across my chest and leaned back in the booth, trying to look as fuck-offish as him but probably looking petulant. "If you already know all this," I snarled, "why the hell are you asking me?"

He waved his hands dismissively, making me want to

strangle him. "No, no, just a lucky guess. Go on."

Was he making fun of my common-as-shit surname? That made me want to gouge his eyes out and give in to my inner violence. He really was a bad influence on me. "That's it," I said. "No more to tell. That's the whole sorry story of Delphinium Smith."

He smiled slowly, still boring into me with his golden gaze. I was almost getting used to the feel of the phantom blade at my throat. "And what was Grandma like?" he drawled.

I wasn't in the habit of sharing my darkest secrets with strangers, especially not with strange men who were my enemies. But Darzan was doing me a solid, so I opened up. Just a little.

Biting my lip, I said, "I remember telling Grandma about this fantasy I used to have." I paused to see his reaction, wondering if I was over-sharing. He probably wanted to know about my school, jobs, and stuff, not my inner imagination.

"A fantasy?" he growled and leaned in close, his golden gaze dropping down to my breasts, making it clear exactly what sort of fantasy he thought I meant.

Heat flushed through me, and I hoped like hell it didn't show on my cheeks. "Not like that, asshole," I snapped, covering my embarrassment with venom. "It was a recurring vision, and it was so vivid. For a while, I had it every night before I went to sleep, and it was like I was actually there, you know?" I avoided his gaze, feeling oddly vulnerable, but the cold blade against my throat told me he was still watching me.

"What was the vision?" he asked softly, surprising me with his sensitivity.

For a moment, I let myself fall back inside the vision that used to bring me so much joy, and I could almost see it around me. "It was a world of flowers running through the streets," I said in a dreamy voice, "blooms that reached out to my touch as I skipped past. It was so real in my mind." I finally met his gaze, daring him to tease me and wondering why the fuck I'd just told him that. "I was a kid, you know," I mumbled. I hated that I sounded defensive and quickly moved on. "Anyway, Grandma beat the crap out of me when I told her about it," I said, remembering his original question was about her. "So, yeah, she was loving but...harsh."

My pulse jumped in my neck, right beside the phantom blade, so close I was worried it would start bleeding. I waited for his response, tense and alert for his reaction. Grandma was the only other person I'd ever shared that vivid image with, and she hadn't exactly loved it.

Darzan sipped his beer, finally releasing me from his sharp-edged gaze. "Interesting," he said slowly.

Anger exploded through me. I slammed my glass on the table, and ale splashed out. "Stop calling everything interesting," I snapped. That vision of the flower-strewn street was so personal that I couldn't bear it becoming the subject of his derision. I never should have told him. What was I thinking? I was acting like this was the truth-telling Realm of Fen.

The prince held my gaze, but his golden eyes were soft. "You're describing Capricia City," he said. "Or another town in Caprice."

I scoffed. He couldn't be more wrong. I'd seen Capricia dozens of times, and it was nothing like my old dreams. "No," I said, shaking my head. "The street from my vision was wondrous and beautiful, not terrifying and dangerous. And anyway, it was just something I made up as a dumb kid." I wiped the sticky ale from my hand with a napkin, then took another sip, suddenly wanting to change the subject. Dread was creeping up from the floorboards and snaking up my legs toward my heart, bringing a sense of foreboding that I couldn't shake. I stared at the band and opened my mouth to comment on the tiny purple drummer, but I couldn't get in fast enough before Darzan spoke.

"Caprice was just as you described before King Athar died," he said, watching me intently again, that cold blade heavy against my neck.

I shuddered, the weight of his revelation settling like an icy grip around my heart. Was it the phantom knife at my throat, his intense stare, or the creeping dread that crawled higher and closer to my center?

"Don't even say that fucking name," I bit out, my voice shaking with emotion, a stark contrast to his calmness.

My emotions were swirling and wild after discussing my family and that fantasy of the magical streets, which I'd never even shared with my cousins, and I didn't want to do anything stupid like burst into tears or punch the serving fae. I twisted the napkin, turning my fingers white under the strain as I tried to predict his next question.

Darzan cut me a golden glance, watching my twisting fingers, seeing right through me. Maybe he could even see the dread that was curling around my spine. "You really don't know about your true heritage, do you?" he said slowly, his gaze never leaving mine as if he could read my damn thoughts.

That dread squeezed until I could barely breathe. Blood pounded in my ears, and I wanted to tell him to shut up, but I only managed to whisper, "I'm a human from H—"

"Your name is Delphinium Athar," Darzan interrupted, leaning across the table and practically hissing at me. His words struck like a thunderbolt, leaving me reeling. "You are the daughter of Bastian and Bree Athar and the true heir of that House."

Delph

The damn blood in my ears pounded so loud I could barely hear. The ragged rock music receded into the distance, and I stared at Darzan's face, looking for a sign he was lying but finding none.

He'd just told me my last name was Athar and that my parents were the fucking Athar monsters who used to rule Caprice. I waited for him to laugh, tell me he was joking, and rib me for the look on my face. But he didn't. He held my gaze with unsettling intensity, his expression unwavering, that golden hair framing his dark face.

I shook my head, back and forth, back and forth, while my fingers tortured a napkin. "No," I said.

He placed a hand over mine on the table, hot and large. "Yes," he said simply.

"I can't be," I insisted. He was wrong. So definitely, absolutely, entirely wrong. I had a family back in Hebes, for fuck's sake. I clearly had no magic. I was as mortal as my mean old Grandma. And my cousins. And Jackson.

"You can be, and you are," Darzan said. His golden glare held an intensity I hadn't seen in them before, and I noticed the flecks of brown in his irises for the first time.

I shook his hand off mine and shouted, "I don't want to be."

I knew I was vicious and violent and a nasty piece of street shit, but the daughter of the bastard king?

Darzan narrowed his eyes, still keeping me locked in his intense gaze, but he leaned back against the backrest, and his tone changed, moving from gentle to annoyed. Probably because of his House's link to Athar. "Bad luck, babe," he sneered. "You don't get a choice."

Nobody got a choice about their family, but that didn't mean he was right. I knew my family better than he ever could. But even as I had that thought, I remembered what I knew about my parents—next to nothing. Mom was definitely Mom, Grandma's daughter, and Jackson's sister. And her name was Bree, like the king's wife. But Mom was a drug addict who ran out on her family—ran out on me. She was a dirtbag junkie, not a fucking queen. "No," I repeated.

The prince finally released me from his gaze and glanced across the room, still leaning against the back of the booth and looking like he was discussing the weather, but I sensed he was still paying me close attention. "Suit yourself," he said.

"None of this fucking suits me," I snapped, still searching my memories for evidence that I was who I was.

It was true I knew nothing about my father. Literally zilch. Just that he'd knocked up my mom and hadn't been man enough to bother raising me himself. I didn't even know his name. All I knew was that Grandma hated him.

Come to think of it, Grandma hated the fae more than anyone, practically hissing every time they were mentioned. Could that be because she knew my father was fae?

I sipped my beer and wiped the froth from my mouth, trying to sort through my life, searching for a fact among all the bullshit and lies. It was a fact that my strength and speed more improving the longer I stayed here. Even my senses. I could smell that glass of red wine across the tavern, discern the peppery undertones and the oak. I never used to be able to do that.

What the actual fuck? Was that a fae thing? Was I half-fae? A junkie for a mom and a king for a dad? Could I really be half-fae with my powers returning now that I was away from human technology? The junkie mom part made sense—I'd always known that. But the fae king for a dad? Not a benevolent one with a kind smile, but an asshole who murdered and imprisoned his political opponents.

No. I refused it. No way was I part of House Fucking Athar. "You're saying I'm a hundred percent evil, like the monster king?" I bit out, the words dribbling from my mouth, dripping with venom.

Darzan sipped his beer, dragging this out. Asshole. "I didn't say that," he said. He was enjoying this way too much, relishing my discomfort, loving the way my whole life had just turned on its head.

I gripped the wooden table, hard. "You didn't have to say it. It's implied by the fact House Athar is full of vicious fucking a-holes." Shit, this actually made a lot of sense. My violent streak had always set me apart from my cousins, and now it was clear I'd inherited it from the worst of the worst. Bastian Athar.

Darzan ran a finger around the rim of his glass. "Athar isn't that bad," he said.

"Really?" I snapped. "So why did dear old Daddy lock up Leena Sansett just for speaking her mind? That is what happened, right?"

Darzan gave a lazy shrug. "That's one interpretation of the truth." He brushed a hand through his golden hair. "But I wouldn't get too hung up on Leena. She's a nasty piece of work who doesn't deserve your pity. Back in school, she..." He paused like he was reluctant to keep talking, which snagged my interest. "She used to be my friend," he said slowly. "She worked really hard on it, always approaching me, listening, until I finally trusted her. One day, I confided that I was scared of an upcoming excursion to the Calcile Caves and...It turned out she was just after some dirt on me, and as soon as she had it, she went and blabbed to the whole class. Told them I was scared and a baby, and they all laughed. They made fun of me for years after that."

That story was like running into a brick wall, and all I could say was, "Oh."

"Yeah. She'd planned the whole betrayal right from the start," Darzan said.

Bitch. The room was spinning, blurring everything I knew about the world, and the only thing piercing it was the damn rock music and that tiny purple drummer. "Huh," I managed to say, trying to slow the world down so I could catch up.

"So don't spare too much pity for Leena," Darzan said. "She deserves everything she got."

Okay, brain, I told myself, *you can make sense of this.*

Leena sounded like a bitch, for sure, but a schoolyard prank didn't exactly justify a lifetime in prison. It explained something about Darzan's trust issues, though.

But frankly, it was hard to focus on Darzan's flaws right now, even if that was usually a favorite topic of mine. My extremities felt numb, and my thoughts kept swirling with the idea that I hailed from House Athar. That my father was the dead king. That my mother wasn't a junkie but a queen. Or maybe she was both.

I couldn't handle any more information tonight. "I need to go to bed," I said.

Darzan nodded like I'd finally said something sensible, and I was glad he'd taken the time to secure our lodgings when we first arrived. He led the way up a narrow set of rickety wooden stairs that looked two centuries old and squeaked with every step into a small bedroom with one small double cot.

I stared at the bed, at Darzan, back at the bed. He had to be kidding. I sighed. "You're on the floor," I murmured.

For a brief, shining moment, I thought he might find an ounce of gentlemanliness in his soul and agree. But then he opened his mouth. "Not a chance, princess."

"Asshole," I said wearily, too tired to make a fuss.

He smirked. "That makes two of us."

After learning that Athar blood ran through my veins, I could hardly disagree. I snatched a blanket off the mattress and made a nest on the wooden floor, which was softer than regular floorboards, perhaps imbued with magic, but still uncomfortable and cold. I wriggled out of my boots and jeans and lay down. "Why can't I have my own room?" I complained.

Darzan stripped down to his boxers, exposing his firm muscled chest, which coiled and flexed as he clambered into the soft bed, sighing happily. "Too dangerous," he mumbled. "I can't protect you if you're in another room."

"If you really wanted to protect me, you'd let me have the bed," I sniped.

He patted the mattress beside him. "You're more than welcome up here, Delph."

I growled and rolled over, showing him my back. Awareness of the soft, warm bed just feet away made the floor feel even harder and colder. No matter how often I changed my position, I couldn't get comfortable. Every slight movement brought a new pang of unease, mingling with the whirlwind of shit in my head.

I waited until the prince was breathing evenly and slowly, hoping like hell he was asleep, then I clambered warily onto the mattress beside him, dragging the blanket behind me. I would sneak back onto the floor before he awoke, and he would never need to know I was there.

He rolled over and slung an arm across my belly, resting his hand on my hip. "I knew you couldn't resist," he murmured.

I harrumphed loudly so he knew what I thought of that, but I didn't move away. I pulled the scratchy blanket closer and breathed in his ashy scent. Better the snake in the bed than the hard wooden floor.

Delph

I woke with a soft moan escaping my lips. I dreamed of Darzan. In my dream, he had ended up with his face between my legs, licking for all he was worth, and I had an intoxicating orgasm on his tongue.

I really hoped that moan had only been in my dream and not aloud because it had undeniable sexual undertones. I went rigid and stared at Darzan's muscled back, his dark skin supple and strong. I really fucking hoped he hadn't heard that.

"Do you need help with something, Delph?" Humor laced his tone, and I squeezed my eyes shut in mortification.

"No, I'm fine." I put as much singsong falsity into my voice as possible, willing him to go back to sleep and not take this any further. Trust me to freaking orgasm in my sleep and moan myself awake with my worst enemy here to hear it.

There was no chance he would let it go. He was too much of an asshole. He rolled over, showing me the full smirk I'd heard in his voice, then looked down my body, resting his golden gaze on the spot where my pussy was clenched beneath the soft blankets. "Are you sure about that?" he growled.

His eyes seemed to burn right through the blankets, making heat pool between my thighs. The image of his dream tongue licking my clit was so vivid it felt like a memory.

I squirmed under his gaze, wanting him to look away and not wanting it at the same time. The phantom pressure against my throat set my skin humming. His blankets cascaded over his waist, leaving his onyx chest bare and very fucking appetizing.

Fuck it. I reached out and traced the circumference of his nipple with my finger, feeling it pebble beneath my touch, then I pinched it hard, and he jumped.

"Naughty girl," he growled.

I smiled. The dream was so vivid it felt like reality, like we were already halfway through having sex, and the sensation loosened my tongue. "You don't know the half of it," I murmured.

His tongue poked in the inside of his cheek for a moment, and all I could think about was cock. It didn't help when he purred, "So why don't you teach me."

My body practically melted into the soft mattress, and I had to remind myself that this male might be as tempting as sin, but he was still my enemy, the one murderous fae I could never let onto the throne.

Unfortunately, the more time we spent together, the more I realized that it was because he was so similar to me. Violent and spontaneous and far too much of a risk taker. Hardly the calm thoughtful leader a realm needed. So perhaps he wasn't my enemy so much as my twin, which was also a good reason to keep him off the throne.

But was it a good reason to keep him off my body?

Desire coursed through me, and my finger kept drawing lazy circles on his chest, roving over the contours and the soft skin covering the hard muscles beneath. His mouth was open and his eyes hooded, and I heard his breathing quicken and felt his muscles bunch beneath my touch.

He flung the cover off me, and I realized too late my long shirt was hitched up around my waist, revealing my red panties. Cool air kissed my thighs, making me feel even more exposed.

A low moan filled the hot air between us, and I didn't know who it came from. Lust wove a spell through my body, making every inch of my skin yearn for Darzan's touch, making my heart thunder, making it very fucking hard to remember he was my enemy.

No, I reminded myself, not my enemy, my twin. Another murderous villain who couldn't be allowed anywhere near the throne. But did that mean he couldn't be allowed near me?

"Fuck," he moaned, staring at my hips and thighs, obsessed with my panties and pussy, and with the answering heat in me, I knew nothing could keep me away from him.

I was ready to straddle him, to throw off the scratchy blanket completely, to rub my yearning body against his, and to drag my tongue up his muscled chest. My muscles clenched for movement just as the door to our bedchamber blew off the hinges on a gust of magic-born air.

Guards bearing the House Sansett insignia of a horse on red leather chest plates stormed into the room with swords held high.

My lust turned cold, and ice froze in my veins. It was very hard not to feel like a criminal when a bunch of soldiers stormed into your room, but I had done nothing wrong. I'd been kidnapped from my home and kept prisoner against my will, and all I was doing was trying to get back to my family.

I had to remind myself of that because it felt a lot like I was breaking an oath to Prince Sansett and committing an act of treason. I supposed that one woman's treason was another woman's bid for freedom.

Darzan was already on his feet, slashing guards with his War power, using only one forefinger to slice his enemies in two.

I fought too. I might not have come into my full strength yet, but I felt more powerful every day. And I was the daughter of the fucking monster king, so I wouldn't go willingly.

Like an idiot, I'd left my blade out of arm's reach, so all I had were my feet and fists, and I did what I could with those, but it wasn't enough.

We were outnumbered. The guards had obviously been told not to harm me, but they weren't nearly so careful with Darzan, and his blood dripped onto the woven mat floors.

After I punched a guard in the gut, hard, another grabbed me from behind and slammed me against his back, then a third slapped some handcuffs over my wrists. I was incapacitated with my hands secured behind my back, but the prince fought on. He whirled and sliced a finger off one guard while another lunged from behind and nicked his thigh. Blood splattered across the bed, bold and red against the muted beige cover. Some droplets caught my foot, warm and wet.

I could tell that Darzan was holding back his magic, restraining himself, not taking lives like candy as I knew he could. But Jayke's men weren't so controlled, stabbing and slicing until the only possible ending was Darzan's death.

"Enough!" I called out, and all movement in the room ceased. Darzan had an arm hooked around a guard's neck, and two more had their swords pointed at the prince. They all froze like a morbid painting of a still life. Even their snarls were fixed.

"We will come with you," I shouted. I couldn't bear the

thought of the guards killing Darzan when the only reason he was here was to help me get home. It didn't matter if his motives were selfish, that he just wanted me out of the picture to improve his chances against Jayke, he was still here on my wishes, and I was honor bound to protect him. I might be a savage bitch from the Docklands, but I wasn't heartless. "What are your orders?" I barked, needing information so I could get the upper hand.

Captain Peterson stepped forward, the gray-haired, gray-eyed male who'd scrutinized the line of women in the Hebes town square and selected my cousins to assist Jayke. Not for sexual partners and not as ambassadors to the mortal realm, I realized, but because of their names. Smith. The fae knew my mother was Bree Smith, and they had orders to secure me as a representative of House Athar. When I'd failed to give my real name, they'd taken the only other Smiths they could find, and I had taken the bait and stepped forward to protect them.

Just another reason I had to get home, so I could throttle the twins' necks.

The captain moved like a warrior, smooth and controlled. "Our orders are to take you to the palace alive," he said evenly.

"And Prince Davin?" I asked.

The captain's gray gaze slid to the prince, then back. "He needn't be alive," he said after a moment's hesitation.

My heart hammered at those words, and I had no reason to doubt them. But with my hands cuffed behind my back, I could do little. They had only come for me, and I was the one they were after.

"Don't kill him," I called out, but the fight continued as a guard suddenly lunged, attacking with a sword, while Darzan held himself back from outright slaughter. Fuck, I had to do something.

I cocked out a hip, trying to look authoritative, but that was difficult with my hands secured behind me. I ignored the pain in my wrist and planted my feet in a wide stance. "If Prince Davin dies, I will kill myself, and you'll have to answer to Prince Sansett for my death," I yelled, pleased that my words rang loud and true without the slightest hint of a warble. The threat was a gamble, and there was no way I would go through with it—I had zero intention of committing suicide for that asshole or anybody else, but these guards didn't know that.

In fact, suicide was such a part of their culture, part of the very fabric of the Ascension rite, that the captain barely blinked at my declaration. He considered my words for a moment, then nodded to a guard. "Drop your weapons and Heal him," he barked.

A pointy-chinned fae stepped into the room from where he'd been waiting in the hallway and placed his hands on Darzan's temple, and I watched as the color returned to the prince's face and his wounds knitted together. Relief pulled at my limbs, making me sag. He wasn't dead, and his death wouldn't be on my conscience. Not today, anyway.

I looked around at the guards, who stood warily in erect poses around the room. The Healer moved between them, starting with the most dead-looking, fixing whoever he could. I'd been so impressed and awed when I'd first laid eyes on these guards in the Hebes town square. Shit scared, sure, but also amazed at their height, their beauty, and their flowing grace. But now I was just pissed. They were lickspittles without a backbone among them, just doing the dirty work of the lying twat, Jayke. I'd told the guards we'd go with them, but that didn't mean I was happy about it.

When the captain grabbed my upper arm to escort me downstairs, I aimed a globule of spit at him, but, annoyingly, I missed and just got the woven mat. Still, I snatched my arm away and hissed, "I'm perfectly capable of walking myself." My hands might be tied, but my balance was okay.

As I walked carefully down the stairs and stumbled outside, my anger simmered and bubbled. What right did these fae have to capture me? A-fucking-gain. They had no business the first time and next to none this time. My thoughts swirled, borne by a hurricane, tinging my anger with panic.

Darzan had revealed that my father was King Bastian Athar. That made as much sense as if he'd mentioned that my great aunt was a porcupine, but somehow I didn't doubt his sincerity.

But Athar was the vilest, cruelest House in Caprice, and King Bastian was the worst of the lot. When he was alive, he'd committed murder, kept his people under his boot, made war with a neighboring realm, and been a general all-round dickwipe.

Which made me a dickwipe's daughter. Yay me. No wonder Grandma had slapped me when I'd accidentally described the streets of Caprice with their flowering alleyways and roads made out of forests. She must have known my father was the vicious King Bastian and was just trying to protect me from him.

I supposed that was how I ended up in the mortal realm. Presumably, my mother had whisked me away from the mad king to keep me safe. Perhaps he never even knew I existed.

I stumbled down the front stoop and sighed into the cold air. Mist swirled down the street, hiding our boots, making everyone look like floating torsos and adding dampness to the air. I sighed. I knew so little of my heritage. Grandma had always told me she never knew who my father was, but that was a lie—she was just trying to protect me.

I knew very little of my mother, Grandma's daughter. Grandma didn't like talking about her. Her name was Bree, and she'd had trouble with drugs and mashups with the law, and she'd disappeared from Hebes for several years before turning up with a young kid and dumping me. That was about the extent I knew of her.

I had to find out more. There must be more to her story. If the kindest fae House, Sansett, could kidnap an innocent woman, surely the vile House Athar was more than capable of the same. King Bastian probably stole my mother from the mortal realm and kept her prisoner. Perhaps she'd even undertaken a journey much like this one when she escaped and got home.

I clung to that thought as the captain gripped my waist and flew into the air, making fast work of the return to Caprice. As the mist swirled into the vacuum where our bodies had been, and the buildings of Port Lonsdale merged into a brown sludge far beneath my feet, I held tight to that thought. My dad might have been an evil bastard and the Head of House Fucking Athar, but my mother was probably a decent woman. She had to be. Otherwise, I would have to face the fact that I was 100% asshole when I was still hoping I was maybe 50% okay.

My senses had certainly strengthened in Arathay, that much was clear. When I'd first arrived, I could barely see the ground below, but now I could make out the details of rivers and mountains and even individual homes dotted on the landscape.

And when we passed from Brume into Caprice, my skin tingled. The dread in the air slammed down on me instantly, marking our return to the realm my father had once ruled and where I was now officially a captive. Home sweet home.

Delph

When we returned to Sansett Palace, those beefy guards manhandled me up to my bedroom, leaving nasty bruises on my upper arm. The door slammed shut behind me. At least they'd ditched the handcuffs, so I rubbed my sore wrists.

As soon as the door lock clicked, I stomped to the window to yank it open and bail. It was welded shut. Or magicked shut. Jayke was a tyrant, for sure, but he wasn't stupid.

I eyeballed the room and picked up a heavy vase made from a metal alloy and weighted down with precious gems, probably worth a million bucks. Perfect. I hurled it at the window, but it bounced off the glass and landed on the rug with a thud. The glass was bulletproof or something.

"Bastard!" I bit out.

I paced back and forth in front of the fireplace, too furious to sit on the plush armchair or the soft bed. Anger fueled my restless movements. "Screw you!" I grumbled, giving the universe a piece of my mind.

"Fuckwit!" I yelled, this one just for Jayke.

I eventually ran out of insults and paced in silence. Jayke hadn't even bothered to come and talk to me. Unbe-fucking-lievable. He wasn't even pretending I was a guest. Nope, I was officially a prisoner.

He could at least show his face and apologize for fooling me. For tricking me. He didn't choose me as a random human ambassador from Hebes because he knew exactly who I was—a descendant of the nutjob King Athar. And just by being here, it looked like House Athar supported House Sansett for the throne. This was just a fucking political ploy.

He'd lied to me all along. I'd slept in this bed, stared at this beautiful painted ceiling and thought I wasn't worthy of this place. Wasted so many hours thinking he'd mistaken me for a real emissary, that I couldn't live up to everything he needed from me. When all along, he'd been playing me for a fool.

He was no better than me, the lying scum girl from Hebes. Hell, he was no better than Darzan, and that was saying something.

I didn't know who I hated more, Prince Charming or Prince Asshole. Neither of them would make a decent king, that was for sure. Perhaps I should throw my Athar-shaped hat in the ring to become the Queen of Caprice, just like my mom.

Hollow laughter escaped me, absorbed by the plush furnishings. I didn't have the skills to be queen, and I sure as hell didn't want to. I just wanted to get home—wherever that was—and leave these conniving backstabbing princes in my dust.

I knew for sure that Jayke was a lying bastard, and Darzan might be too. Who knew? Maybe Darzan tipped Jayke off about where we were back at that dingy tavern in Brume. I hadn't exactly given him a choice about helping me, so maybe it was all part of his plan, some ploy to get me on his side. Another fucking deception.

The lies made my head swim, and I didn't know who to trust. Or rather, I knew exactly who to trust—nobody.

Navigating the noble Houses of Caprice was just as danger-ous as wandering the streets of the Docklands. The thugs wore pretty clothes and spoke pretty words, but they were just as vicious.

The only truth I had to hang onto was what I'd seen with my own two eyes and the memory of the strengths' display in the Spike forecourt. Jayke was a Healer, and Darzan wielded War. No matter how much of a prick Sansett was and how much he'd lied and betrayed me, he had to make the better ruler.

I'd choose healing over destruction any day.

It didn't mean I had to like him. The doorknob rattled, and I hoped it was Elora coming to visit me. She could pretend she needed to help me undress. I was pretty sure she liked me, which made her as rare as a fucking diamond. Plus, she had no vested interest, she didn't care if I smiled and acted like a princess. She was the closest thing I had to a friend.

But the doorway was filled with Jayke, his white face glowing against his lavender hair, those pale lavender eyes narrowed in fatherly concern.

He swept into the room. "You had me worried sick, Del-phinium," he said. "I'm so glad you're home safe and sound."

I was over his condescending tone. Even the way he carefully enunciated every syllable of my name was irritating.

"Don't be," I snapped. "I'm not your little plaything anymore. I won't follow you around, showing the world you have the support of House Athar."

I just told him I knew the truth about my heritage, and I watched for his reaction, but, annoyingly, his composure remained perfect. Did fae even have emotions? His precise mask of control never slipped. I thought back to his displays of feeling, like when that lonely tear fell down his face at seeing his mother's portrait, and I realized the truth. He'd manufactured the whole thing to draw me under his spell. Bastard.

He kept his lavender eyes on me. "You hated House Athar so vehemently I couldn't bear to cause you the pain of knowing that vile blood ran in your veins," he said with a crafted expression of sorrow.

"Bullshit," I spit. I clomped across the room and got up in his face as much as possible, though I didn't match his height. I wrinkled my nose against his cloying lavender scent. "You never cared about me. You only cared about your precious throne. Well, guess what? House Athar doesn't support you. Not anymore. But I would have if you'd been up front with me from the beginning."

That was true. Jayke would make a better king than Darzan, no question, and I would have happily supported him all the way to his damn precious coronation if he'd only been honest with me. But I couldn't stomach liars, and I couldn't stand cowards who hid behind masks.

That crease of annoyance furrowed his brow, the only indication he had of true feeling. How hilarious that I used to think that expression meant he was amused when he'd been irritated all along. Well, right now, his creased forehead said he was pissed. Good, I wanted him to be.

"We have a few days until the House dinner," he said slowly, "so you can rest in your room until then. I wouldn't want you to feel weak or overwhelmed when the time comes."

He meant I would remain in my room, a prisoner for two more days and nights. Anger heated my blood, and lightning sparked down my veins. He expected me to sit here quietly until he let me out to simper at some dinner party. No way in hell.

But I wanted as much information from him as possible, so I clenched my fists and said, "What House dinner?" Jayke wasn't in the habit of sharing information with me freely, and when he did, it was usually bullshit, but I had to ask.

He smiled beneficently. "Representatives from every fae realm attend the House dinner before the new coronation," he said. "In theory, it's an opportunity for all the realms to influence the chosen ruler—unless he is chosen by Gaia, of course."

"Or she," I spit.

"But in practice, it's a chance to network with the key players in the other realms," he continued as if I hadn't spoken. "Sometimes the kings come themselves—"

"Or queens," I interjected.

"But more often, they send their heirs," he continued. "So the House dinner is where we make connections that will last for generations." He reached out to palm my cheek, but I flinched away. "It is a great honor to be invited to a House dinner, Delphinium, and I hope you will respect your role."

Like hell I would. It sounded like an excellent opportunity to make some chaos.

The prince wasn't done monologuing; he clearly liked the sound of his own emotionless voice. "Let me touch your face, Delphinium. I only want to heal you," he said with those kindly smiling eyes that irritated the crap out of me.

He lunged toward me and got his palm to my face before I could get away, and his Healing power flowed through me, warming and tingling, chasing away the aches and pains from my days of travel and my fight with his guards. My torn flesh knitted together, and my bruises smoothed away, but it didn't feel loving and sweet. It felt invasive and creepy.

I jerked away before he was done. "Do not touch me again without my consent," I growled. I would rather have a thousand cuts and bruises than feel his magic inside my body.

He tutted, and his lavender eyes flashed purple. "Always the ingrate," he snarled. He turned to leave and called over his shoulder. "I do so hope you'll be feeling better after two days of rest," he said sweetly.

The door closed behind him, and the lock clicked into place, sealing me in silence with only my ragged breathing for company. I didn't need to feel better. I already felt perfect, more and more like myself every day. I was a survivor with a strong violent streak and lightning in my veins, and I planned to sow some damn anarchy.

Delph

The window wouldn't budge or break, no matter how many priceless objects I threw at it. It just stood there, mocking me. Finally, I flopped onto the bed, giving up. As the sun slipped behind the mountains surrounding the city, I slipped into sleep.

I was awoken by a loud crashing and jerked awake to find a grinning Darzan crouched in the window frame, surrounded by shattered glass.

Sunlight haloed his golden hair, so I must have slept the whole night through. Darzan leaped down and strolled toward me casually for all the world like he was meeting me for coffee. He nodded toward the window opening. "Are we going, or what?" he asked lazily.

I blinked a few times, trying to wake up my brain and figure out what was happening. "Is this a rescue?" I said sleepily. "Are you rescuing me right now?" I pulled my duvet close, loving its cozy warmth.

He snickered because, apparently, life was a big joke to him. "Don't look so surprised, pet. I'm not just a killing machine, you know."

My eyebrow shot up. "Really? Could've fooled me."

I still didn't trust most things that came out of his mouth, although I supposed he'd earned some respect.

Before I could get up, he whipped my duvet from my bed, exposing me to the cool morning air. My shirt was hitched up around my waist, and I wasn't wearing panties. But I wasn't lying in a cutesy feminine pose but was spreadeagled in the most unflattering way possible.

This had to be a new low for me. I curled into a ball. "What the actual—" I spluttered.

"Don't get all pissy," he said, throwing me my black jeans. "I didn't know you were half naked. That seems like a recurring theme for you," he added, alluding to our almost-sex in the tavern, which, thank God, had been interrupted. "Do you even have pajamas in Hebes?" he smirked. "I'll buy you a pair. Anyway, I've seen it all before."

I snatched up the jeans and grumbled, "You haven't seen mine before."

"Well, now I have." He said lightly. "I'll show you mine if it makes you feel better."

He began unbuckling his belt, and I threw a pillow at him. "Fuck off," I said.

He smirked. "Yeah, I figured you'd say that." Jesus, just when I thought this fae might be reasonable, he dived to a new low. "Hurry up. The guards will be here in a minute," he said.

I looked at the shattered window. "Hmm, subtlety isn't your strong point, is it?"

He shrugged. "I wield War, not Weave. My way's just as effective, though."

The doorknob was already rattling, and the lock unclicked as I shrugged into my black leather jacket. "Plus, this way, you get to kill a few fae, right?" I added.

He grinned. "Right. It's win-win."

That didn't horrify me as much as it should. I remembered how I felt after fighting the fae in the mists of Brume, the battle joy that had flooded my body all evening, and I knew my true calling wasn't peace but violence, just like Darzan's.

He swept a mocking bow pointing toward the window. "After you, milady."

I crunched across the shards of broken glass, glad for my tough fae slippers, and climbed out the window just as the bedroom door opened and guards poured into the room in single file. It was early, and we weren't exactly at war, so they weren't fully prepared. They wore a mix of armor and night clothes, but every one of them carried a sword.

The last thing I saw before I swung below the marble windowsill to dangle over the grass was Darzan whipping his forefinger across a guard, blood spurting out and splatting on the beautiful sheer curtains around my four-poster bed.

I left the sounds of battle behind and concentrated on dropping, aiming for my favorite soft white bush, which caught me neatly. "Thanks," I murmured, then sprinted for the palace gates, moving faster than ever. It was becoming harder and harder to deny the truth that fae blood mingled with mortal in my veins and muscles, powering me along the gravel path.

I heard the crunching of footsteps behind me and spared a glance to see Darzan sprinting, his golden hair whipping out behind him, pursued by half a dozen Sansett fae.

A single sentry was on duty at the palace gates, which was new—I'd never seen any fae stationed there before. He was surprised to see me running at him, and probably figured Darzan was attacking me, so he was caught off guard when I punched his ear with all my force. He staggered a few steps and then toppled to the grass with a thump.

I barely broke stride, running for the moonway and hoping like hell I'd be able to find it in the daylight. When I reached the right spot, I looked for the sparkling edges that were so hard to discern, knowing I'd be safe if I could get to Capricia city, where I could disappear.

There. That section of the wildflower meadow snagged my attention, where the bright flowers sparkled, and I diverted into the field, flooded with relief as the world blurred beside me.

Breathing heavily, I didn't stop running until I reached the city, where I hid behind the beachball house, which pulsed red with danger.

Moments later, Darzan emerged splattered in blood but with no pursuers, and I had to assume he'd disposed of them.

I ducked out from my hiding place, pleased to see him startle. He didn't hide his emotions nearly as well as Jayke, and that was one thing I liked about him.

"Nice rescue," I smirked. "Real smooth. I don't think they noticed I'm gone."

He narrowed his golden eyes. "Hilarious. Would you prefer I didn't come get you at all?"

I shrugged. "I had it under control." Liar. I was drowning in despair back there with no plan, just a burning desire to leave.

His golden eyes sparkled. "Sure you did," he said. "And I suppose you were coming to my place for refuge?" A light breeze played with his golden hair as he smirked at me.

"Nope," I said. I glanced at the moonway, looking for pursuers and finding none. Still, this didn't seem like a safe place to chat. So I tugged Darzan's large warm hand to get him moving, then let go when he fell into a trot beside me.

"I'm heading to a library," I declared, having just decided.

"A library?" Darzan raised his eyebrows.

Crap, maybe they didn't have them here. "It's a place with a bunch of books where you can learn stuff, like historical stuff," I explained. "Because I'm guessing you don't have the internet here."

He chuckled. "I know what a library is, Delph. I don't know why you want to find one."

My footsteps ate the pavement faster than ever, and I knew I was still tense from fleeing the palace. Even my words came out quickly and slightly jumbled. "I need to find out about my parents. My mom, specifically. I need to find out how Bastian got her to stay here, if he kidnapped her or..."

Darzan cut me a glance. "She came willingly," he said flatly.

I shook my head. He might think that, but it didn't make it true. "I want to find out for myself," I said.

"You don't want to go back to Hebes?" he asked, jogging alongside me without breaking breath. "We can try again and maybe pick a different tavern this time. I think the barkeep there was in Jaykey-boy's pocket."

If Jayke was bribing the innkeeper in Port Lonsdale, that explained how his guards had found us so easily. Or was that an excuse Darzan was making because he'd sold me out? But then, why would he come and rescue me from Sansett Palace? Damn, it was all too much.

"I'll go back eventually," I said, not wanting to be too specific. "But not until I find out about my mom. If I go to Hebes, I'll never find out, and I'll spend the rest of my life wondering how she got here and why she never left. I need to know." The houses and shops were flying past me as my pace kept increasing. I was in a flat-out run now, my leg muscles bunching and releasing and wind blowing back my loose black hair as my feet pounded down the streets.

Darzan grabbed my elbow, washing me in his ashy scent, and I figured he would try to stop me, so I jerked free and kept running. "Hang on a second, and I'll show you where the library is," he growled.

I stopped, barely panting, and whirled to face him. "Fine," I said, waiting for him to speak. His telling me where the library was would beat sprinting around Capricia at random. While I waited for him to speak, I tapped my foot impatiently. "Go on," I snapped, "spit it out."

He sighed. "Just shut up for a minute and concentrate," he said, brushing away a leaf that had blown into his leg.

I didn't see how that would help, but I swallowed my impatience and stared at him for a moment while he remembered where the library was.

Out of nowhere, an image formed in my brain, like a miniature map of the city with the library's location clearly marked. It wasn't far from here but was along a street I'd never visited before, so I didn't see how that information could suddenly be in my brain. My jaw fell open. "What the...?" I began.

Darzan grinned. "Fae can transmit a place's location. To other fae."

Holy crap. To other fae. He'd just zapped that mini map into my brain, so I was definitely fae. No denying it any longer. Shaking my head, I figured I'd work through that shitshow of emotions later. The part about being half magical creature with an inbuilt GPS.

Consulting the map, I took a left, the shortest route to the library, and Darzan tagged along. He might as well answer a few questions while he was here. "How long have you known I was half-fae?" I demanded.

"Since I saw you and heard your name," he admitted. "Delphinium isn't a common name around here. Neither is Smith."

I chewed my lip, trying to piece it all together. "And you knew I was from House Athar?" From the corner of my eye, I saw him nod. "Why didn't you tell me?"

That was the question I really needed answering. Darzan wasn't complicit in Jayke's lie about why I was here, so why didn't he just tell me the truth? He could have told me who I was and turned me against Jayke days ago, and maybe I would have stopped supporting Jayke's bid for the throne. But he didn't. He sat back and let me smile for the nobles and tell everybody how great Jayke would be as king.

Darzan puffed out a breath. "At first, I thought you already knew," he said slowly. "And then, when I suspected you didn't, you already hated me. It was too late." We walked in silence, and I noted how my feet made less sound on the cobblestones than they used to. I could curve my foot to match the contour of the pavers, and it felt natural and easy. A faeling ducked out of a stone cottage and squeaked when she saw us, then darted back inside. "Besides," he breathed. "Would you have believed me?"

I thought back to my short history with Darzan and Jayke. From the outset, I'd definitely cast Jayke as Prince Charming and Darzan as the evil prince, so I wouldn't have believed a word out of his mouth.

"No," I admitted. "I suppose not."

The adrenaline sparking through my body after fleeing the palace had dissipated, and I felt calmer and more in control.

I may be from House Athar, and the monster king may be my dad, but I would do my mom the justice of finding out everything I could about her and setting the record straight back home.

She wasn't a junkie, she was a queen. And I would prove it.

We reached the library, a lopsided building that seemed to be constructed from long, plank-sized seashells, but that couldn't be right. I tilted my head to make it out, noting the saltiness in the air. In any case, it was closed with a wonky sign saying to come back in two days. Disappointment flashed through me, but it didn't matter too much. What was one more day when I'd already gone a lifetime not knowing my mother?

I reached for Darzan's hand. "Thank you for telling me," I whispered. My anger had melted, and I was genuinely grateful for Darzan sharing the truth about who I really was. He might be my enemy and a terrible choice for king, but he was the only one around here who was honest with me.

Something flickered behind his golden eyes, and I had to wonder at his motivation in helping. I knew he hadn't told me out of the goodness of his heart, that he had his own designs and schemes, and whatever he did to aid me was out of pure self-interest.

And that was proven correct when he said nothing but just dropped my hand and walked away.

Delph

I spent the day searching through Darzan's study, looking for books, scrolls, or anything with information about my mother. He'd told me everything he knew about her, but he hadn't known her personally, just as a public figure. Hearing all his second-hand info just felt like I was reading a gossip column, but at least it was something.

Darzan described Queen Bree as kind, a softening influence on her husband and a benign ruler. But I needed to know more. I needed to know what books she read, what her favorite color was, and where she kept her secret stash of booze. Those details would be hard to uncover, I knew that. So I'd settle for discovering how Bastian trapped her into staying in Caprice.

But Darzan's study had no answers, and his lips only told of her public-facing facade. I would have to get into the library, but it wouldn't open for two more days.

Working life in Caprice wasn't divided into weeks and weekends but was tied to the throne, just like the weather.

So without a ruler, most public places were closed. The library wouldn't open until after the House dinner, which marked the official start of the coronation ceremonies, culminating in the crowning of the new ruler at Lurlin Forest, following the Ascension rite.

"Can't we break in?" I complained. We were seated in the downstairs living room beside a roaring fire that Darzan had spelled to give off little heat since we only needed it for the atmosphere. "Or just get the keys from someone? You're one of the goddamn heirs." I had lugged a few books down from his study but was sick of flicking through them and finding nothing useful.

Darzan snorted, expertly dousing my brilliant lock-picking plan. "It doesn't work that way," he said. "We can't break in because the library is warded by the top Weavers from history, and my spellwork doesn't come near matching theirs. It would take me a year to unravel the layers of magic."

I put down the book I was holding onto the armrest of my chair and folded my arms across my chest. "And you can't borrow the keys because you don't have any friends," I snapped. "Am I right?" I was being an ungrateful bitch. He'd let me crash in his townhouse and rifle through his papers, but I couldn't help snapping at him. I still considered him my enemy, though perhaps that was no longer true.

The prince narrowed his golden eyes and bit his dark lower lip. "Sorry, Ms. Popular, I didn't realize my social habits offended you so much," he said.

Petulantly, I pushed the book with a forefinger until it toppled from the armrest of my chair onto the floor rug. "Well, it wouldn't hurt if you had more people on your side," I said.

"More fae means more lips to spill secrets," he growled.

I leaned back in the plush armchair. My chair was cozy but not as orgasmically comfortable as Jayke's bespoke grown ones. I ran a finger along a fraying edge of the armrest. "Why don't you trust anyone?" I asked. "Not everybody's out to hurt you, surely?"

Darzan's eyes were locked on the flames, his golden eyes reflecting amber and red. His chin was locked rigid while he considered my question. He was a handsome specimen when he wasn't snarling and surly, and I watched the muscles in his jaw clench and unclench while he thought of how to reply. "My father learned the hard way that even the closest friends can turn into bitter enemies," he said.

I watched his corded neck flex as he struggled to remain calm. He was referring to something seriously close to his heart, and I was curious. "What happened?" I asked.

He ran a hand through his golden hair, and the muscles in his biceps flexed and relaxed while he remained staring at the flames. Time stretched between us, and I didn't know if he would answer. His reluctance didn't feel like he was keeping me in the dark, not the way Jayke's silences always did. It was more like he was battling with himself in the one war he couldn't easily win.

"It doesn't matter," he eventually murmured, barely audible over the crackling fire.

It clearly did, but I decided not to press the point. Perhaps he'd tell me later, although my time in the fae realm was fast running out. The House dinner was tomorrow, and the coronation just three days later. After that, no matter how it turned out, I would leave.

Sadly, I no longer thought of leaving as returning home. Home was a foreign concept to me. I'd never really felt I belonged in Hebes, and now I knew why—because I was part fae. But I didn't belong here either because I was part human. In any case, I would return to my family, to Grandma, to the one person I knew needed me, even if it was only to cook and clean for her.

"Could you be chosen by Gaia to lead?" I asked, still stroking the faded fabric of the armchair.

Finally, Darzan looked at me. "No. My Ascension was long ago. My magical path is set. I already chose my future, and my future chose me."

I bent down to retrieve the book I'd so petulantly pushed to the rug and returned it to my armrest. "Sometimes you speak in riddles, you know," I said. "It's annoying."

His lips curved. "I'm pleased to return the favor."

It took me a moment to understand the insult, then I scowled. "You're right, you know. Your path is definitely Warlordery, not Lightning."

His gaze flicked to me, and the phantom blade nicked the skin of my throat. It didn't feel cold today but warm, which was strange. Could it be affected by the temperature of the fire? "Yes," he growled. "Mine is the power of War. I'm glad you noticed."

I thought back to that old fae whose torso slid off its legs after Darzan cruelly sliced him in two, and I shivered. Even if we had a temporary alliance, I could never let myself forget who this male really was and the evil of which he was capable. "Oh, I noticed," I said.

A green-haired serving fae with tiny curved horns jutting out from either side of his head entered the room and announced dinner. As far as I could tell, Darzan only had a single staff member in his household, a far cry from the dozens of servants employed at Sansett Palace. Hell, I had my own personal maid, Elora, the fashion expert, available just to help me dress.

"Thank you, Bert," Darzan said, using the serving fae's name, which I hadn't seen done at Sansett Palace.

Life was very different at Darzan's house.

I followed Bert into the small stone room, where we dined at a table that wouldn't seat my extended family, let alone host a ball. I scraped out a chair and accepted a plate from the horned fae. The food was outrageously delicious, a million times tastier than anything human-made, but still simpler and less lavish than what Jayke served. There wasn't a single quail-egg sculpture in sight.

"What about me?" I asked out of the blue.

Darzan paused with a soup spoon halfway to his mouth and cocked his head. "What about you? Let me see...Would you like me to list your faults?" he asked. "Or your qualities? The latter will be much quicker."

I scowled. "What about me ascending into Lightning?" I said. "I'm the only heir of House Athar, and I'm almost twenty-five. Maybe Gaia will choose me."

He slowly ate his soup, ignoring the daggers I was sending his way. "You are half-mortal," he said flatly as though I didn't already know that.

I clenched my fists. "And your heart is made of coal," I spit. "Any other obvious facts you want to throw out there?"

He kept his calm, which was annoying. I was used to Jayke having a benign mask of nothingness, but Darzan usually gave me an emotion to work with. "I'm not just being rude, Delph—" he began.

"How refreshing," I interrupted.

He set down his spoon with a clatter and looked at me, his phantom blade still warm against my neck. "Gaia only selects the strongest fae to be struck by Lightning," he explained. "On the occasions she's chosen weaker fae, the power burnt through them completely. They didn't survive the Ascension."

"Oh," I said. "I see." That put a damper on things.

"Electricity strong enough to destroy a city cannot be wielded by an average fae," he continued, staring right at me, though the blade at my throat didn't bother me. "It sizzles right through them, leaving a charred husk. A half-mortal with no discernible power would die when struck and be unable to revive."

A brief picture flashed before me of me killing myself with electricity, twitching on the forest floor, and turning blacker and blacker until I was a smoking corpse with no hope of ever coming back to life.

"Okay," I said, shaking my head to clear the image. "I get it."

He wrinkled his nose and looked into the middle distance. "I can still remember the stench of the last one," he whispered.

Well, that was graphic. And gross. And a definite deterrent to my ambitions for the throne, which were shaky at best.

"Plus, being almost twenty-five doesn't count. Gaia has never chosen a twenty-four-year-old for anything, least of all Lightning," he added, putting the topic to bed.

I knew these Lightning Ascensions didn't happen often, and the last one must have been hundreds of years ago. And Darzan remembered it. It occurred to me I had no idea how old he was. Or Jayke. Or any fae other than Pike, who was the same age as me, and Elora, who was a few years younger.

But I didn't want to know. It would be hard to maintain my moral superiority over Darzan if I discovered he was centuries older than me. I slurped my soup deliberately noisily, like a little bitch. "So your only hope is the slim chance that Pike gets chosen by Gaia," I said.

"Or, failing that, I get elected by the noble Houses," he said, nodding seriously.

I snorted a laugh. "Because you're so good at courting their support," I scoffed. I slid my soup bowl across the table and pulled the next plate closer. I forked some creamy sweet-but-salty pudding into my mouth, savored the taste on my tongue, then swallowed, enjoying the defeated look on Darzan's face. "Buddy, you don't have a chance," I said.

I was done with simpering and lying. Jayke had put a roof over my head in exchange for my support, and that turned into a major shitshow. So, even though Darzan was housing and feeding me, I wouldn't blow smoke up his ass. He had woeful people skills, and it wouldn't do him any favors if I pretended otherwise.

He threw his napkin on the plate and scraped out his chair along the stone floor. "I suppose we'll find out tomorrow," he growled.

Tomorrow, the House dinner, where I would meet represen-tatives from all the fae realms and come face to face with my ex-jailer and newly minted enemy, Jayke.

My enemies seemed to be multiplying, and the only guy helping me was my ex-enemy and newly minted...friend? And I kept kicking him while he was down. As Darzan stalked from the room, my heart thudded. He was a powerful fae with killing magic and a serious contender for the throne.

Maybe I should stop pissing him off.

Delph

The House dinner was the following evening, and I expected a sedate sit-down meal with a bunch of politicians, but this was more like a carnival.

Brightly dressed winged faeries tumbled through the sky above us, shrieking with laughter whenever they collided with each other or with the Lightning-filled orbs bobbing below the copper ceiling. Food trays wobbled and weaved among the crowd, often bumping into the jostling fae and sloshing their contents over a sublime outfit. Nobody seemed to mind, and I couldn't help smiling as I watched the scene.

We were in a grand hall tastefully decorated in blue and copper. The floor and ceiling were copper, and the walls were blue inlaid with nature scenes and cavorting figures in glistening copper. The effect was stunning—more refined than the cream and marble chiffonery of Palace Sansett and way more comfortable than Darzan's grotto.

I relaxed my shoulders, feeling more comfortable than I had in days. Even the heavy air of anticipation seemed to add to the wild gaiety.

Something wet spilled down my back, and I turned to find a hovering tray that bobbed apologetically at me before zooming off and delivering a fizzing blue drink to a tall slender female with gray eyes and hair and a shimmering gray dress.

Who were all these people?

"Is there a representative here from every realm?" I asked, looking around.

Darzan shook his head and sipped a drink he'd taken from a passing tray. He looked flat-out intimidating tonight, wearing a black suit a shade darker than his skin with golden embroidery that highlighted his hair and eyes. "I doubt the Dread King of Brume is here," he said.

I hadn't heard that name before. "He sounds nice," I deadpanned.

"He's exactly as nice as he sounds," Darzan said as his lip tugged into a slight smile. "He isn't welcome at many parties. People tend to run away screaming."

"Good thing he's anti-social then," I joked.

"Indeed."

I accepted a drink from a passing tray and weaved deeper into the crowd. Lilting music played softly, and I strained to see where it came from. It had an ethereal element and such immediacy that I couldn't imagine the music was piped through speakers, it had to be playing live, but I couldn't see the source.

A creeping sensation slithered down my neck as three fae approached. Pike, looking very dignified in a mahogany suit, and two males I didn't recognize. Darzan introduced them as King Draylar and Taysin from the Realm of Dust.

I tried to still my shudder. The Realm of Dust was the Unseelie realm where, in my simple black-and-white terms, the evil fae chose to live. And Draylar was their king. He wore a stiff silver cloak and had his long violet hair slicked back into a bun.

His violet eyes narrowed at me dangerously as he drank in my appearance. "This must be the feeble-blooded human Sansett leads around by the nose. How surprising to find her here with you, Davin," he said.

He might be the King of the Unseelie, but he was in my fucking realm, and he would show me some respect. Heat bubbled from my belly, and I stood straighter. "I'm nobody's pet, Draylar," I snapped. "Don't make the mistake of thinking I am."

The king's murderous violet eyes finally landed on mine, and I forced myself not to look away. He regarded me long and slow, and that slimy feeling in my belly that I'd felt at his approach intensified under his glare. Finally, his lip quirked in the ghost of a smile. "I see you have some of your mother's spirit."

The fire in my belly hardened into red-hot steel. "You knew my mother?" I demanded.

"Well enough to know she couldn't keep her mouth shut," the Unseelie King said. "I could see exactly what Bastian saw in her if that's what you're asking." His gaze raked my body again, a lingering predatory look that had me leaping to my mother's defense.

"Bastian didn't deserve my mother," I snarled, letting my inner savage bitch from the Docklands speak for me. "And I'll never let anybody keep me here like he kept her."

Draylar's rasping laughter sounded like a rusty saw, and I narrowed my eyes as he continued to laugh at my expense. "Nobody ever forced Bree to do anything," he said, "though many tried. Myself included."

What did he mean? I curled my fingers into fists, then splayed them wide, working through the possible questions.

"Bastian forced her to stay here," I stated as though it were fact.

But in truth, that was nothing more than an assumption. I needed my mother to be good, I desired it with all of my heart and soul, so I'd decided she must have been here against her will. But perhaps that was wrong, perhaps she was complicit in all of Bastian's monstrous deeds, perhaps she was just as evil as he was.

"She loved that do-gooding bastard with all her heart," King Draylar said. "And he was foolish enough to love her back. A mistake that cost him his life."

A couple of winged faeries screeched overhead and then raced away, and I watched them zoom around the room, trying to understand what Draylar was saying.

The king referred to my father as a do-gooder. What the fuck? Numerous people had told me my mother was kind and benevolent, a softening influence on her husband. Did I have this all wrong? I was so fixated on the idea of my father being a monster that I hadn't considered the possibility that he wasn't. Perhaps he was just a decent king with a goodhearted queen for a wife, doing their best to rule Caprice.

That's what Darzan had always said; he'd never wavered from that belief. The primary reason I believed the worst of my father was Jayke's word, which was devaluing faster than Bitcoin after a pandemic.

King Draylar leaned in close, and I caught a whiff of his chalky scent. "If you ever want to visit the Unseelie Realm, I could find a place for you in my Court."

I turned my head so my lips were close enough to warm his ear when I replied huskily, "I'd rather be burned to a crisp than set foot in your Court."

His eyes glowed deeper violet as he glowered, then he spun on his heel and stalked away.

The second Unseelie fae, whom Darzan had introduced as Taysin, gave me a brief nod. He had orange curls and a startled look on his face that I suspected was permanent, probably due to his massive, round, orange eyes. "Bye, cousin," he said with a tight smile before following his king.

I stood with my mouth agape as the unsettling Unseelie were consumed by the crowd. I whirled on Darzan. "Cousin?" I had three cousins, Lexi, Razelle, and Kayla. And I had a mom and dad here in Arathay, but I'd never considered I might have extended family here in the fae realm too. "Cousin?" I repeated, my voice pitching squeakily high.

"His mother was Bastian sister, so he's your first cousin," Darzan explained.

I looked after the bobbing orange head, disappearing into the crowd. "But he's Unseelie," I said. How could I be related to an Unseelie fae?

Darzan shrugged, following my gaze and staring across the crowded hall. "Sometimes the Seelie ascend into Unseelie power," he said. "It's rare, but it happens." I was getting used to how Darzan shared information instead of hoarding it, like Jayke, and I appreciated it. But I was struggling to keep up with the flow of new information.

Darzan guided me by the elbow toward a fountain in the hall's center that seemed to bubble water flashing with liquid diamonds.

As we approached, I tugged against him, resisting his pull and coming to a stop. "Wait," I said, needing to get my head together before the next truth bomb hit.

"There are more people you need to meet," Darzan said.

"I don't need to do anything," I bristled. "Tell me what King Draylar meant when he said my father died because he loved my mother."

Darzan ran a hand through his golden hair. "Your mom died a few months ago. She lived longer than most humans because he transferred as much life force into her as he could. But in the end, mortality is inescapable, and she made the final journey." His eyes flashed amber. "They say King Bastian died of a broken heart. That he loved her so profoundly that he couldn't exist without her. That's one reason people call him an unfae monster because he sacrificed himself—and his leadership of the realm—just to follow a human woman to the afterworld."

That was why they called him a monster? Because he loved my mother so much, he couldn't live without her?

The world spun around me, the chat and laughter blurring along with the riot of color, and I swayed on the spot before collapsing against Darzan's chest.

Delph

"Stand on your own two feet," Darzan hissed. "This is not the place to show weakness."

His fingers and thumb dug into the flesh of my upper arm hard enough to hurt as he steadied me. He was right. I was done being a swooning princess—now was the time for strength.

I took a deep breath and a wide stance, and ignoring the whirling bodies around me, I looked up at Darzan. "Was my father a good king?" I asked.

This was a moment of revelation in my life. I'd grown up believing my mother to be a heroin-soaked junkie and my father just her one-night stand. Now it had turned a full circle. She was a queen, and he was a king, and maybe even good ones.

But Darzan didn't share my sentimentality. He growled at me instead. "I've told you he was good dozens of times," he hissed. "Dozens. But you don't listen to me, do you? You only believe it when someone else tells you...the Unseelie King, for fuck's sake. You believe the word of the Unseelie King over me!"

He was pissed, but I didn't have time for his tantrum. I was reeling from discovering my parents weren't trash or monsters and that the real monsters lived in House Sansett. The monster was Jayke.

I looked up to say so, but Darzan had melted into the crowd, though the aura of hurt and betrayal still lingered where he'd stood.

Well, fuck him. If he was selfish enough to make this personal revelation about him, I wouldn't lift a finger to make him feel better about it. He could go and huff around the party, terrifying fae with his War gaze, and leave me the hell alone.

I didn't mind being alone in a crowd, especially one this interesting. The old me would have loved to wind through the beautiful people, perhaps pinch an easy purse or two—although pickpocketing was never my forte—and generally observe the lascivious behavior.

But the new me, the heir to House Athar, drew way too much attention to pull that off. Every time anybody caught sight of me, they blanched, and now I knew the truth—it wasn't a reaction to seeing my rounded ears, it was a response to coming face-to-face to the long-lost watered-down half-blood heir to Athar.

I caught sight of Darzan talking animatedly with the most beautiful female I'd ever seen. She had dark brown skin with soft pink hair and wore a copper gown that spilled over her curves like liquid metal.

A low voice pitched in my ear. "She's Gabrelle from the house of beauty in the Realm of Verda. Isn't she perfection?"

She was. Perfection was the only adequate word to describe her, and seeing her laughing and batting her long eyelashes at Darzan made me nauseous. Irritation at him walking off mid-conversation, I supposed. Irritation at the mask he was displaying, all smiles and sexy winks. Irritation at being caught ogling the pair of them.

I looked at the male who'd addressed me. I was glad it wasn't Jayke because I still hadn't figured out what to say to him or if I should run when I saw him. Perhaps he had guards stationed outside the hall to arrest me as soon as I left. But it wasn't him. It was a male with vibrant blue hair and eyes, tanned skin, and a square jaw. "I'm Colzan Blunt from Ourea," he said with a grin.

The name resounded in a distant chamber of memory, and I finally remembered he was the heir to the Ourean throne.

I thinned my lips, in no mood to parry wit or trade compliments. "I see you don't have any more friends here than I do," I remarked. Ourea comprised the mountainous strip of land to our West that extended all the way down past Brume to the Realm of Dust, and it was Caprice's sworn enemy.

"That's rather astute," he said, without any venom in his tone, just mild curiosity, like I was an animal in a zoo.

I shrugged one shoulder, tearing my gaze away from where Darzan flirted with Gabrelle. The gorgeous female was sitting on his fucking lap feeding him a pastry, and it made me want to vomit.

I met Colzan's vibrant blue gaze. "It doesn't require much insight to figure out the heir of the enemy realm wouldn't have many fans in Caprice," I said.

"And what about the heir of the late king and queen?" he asked, his curiosity shining through. He spoke to me like I was the only person in the room...or the most interesting exhibit. "The real question is, why don't you have any more friends here than I do?" he mused. "Perhaps you've been sidelined by a certain prince?"

I glanced at Darzan sitting under Gabrelle's beautiful round ass. How did so many curves fit into such a tight damn dress? But I knew Colzan was talking about the other prince. Jayke. And I knew he was probably right—I had been played like a puppet and used only to improve Jayke's standing in Caprice and reduce my own.

Colzan blinked at me slowly. "I suppose I should thank you for hosting the dinner in Athar Hall," he said, watching for my reaction.

This was Athar Hall? I looked around at the copper and blue room, the perfect balance between Jayke's opulence and Darzan's cave. No wonder I felt so at home here—I fucking owned this place.

Darzan had mentioned that my family estate had been used as a community hall for the past few hundred years while the Athars lived in the royal chambers at the Spike, but I hadn't known this was it.

I didn't want to give away my ignorance to Colzan because no matter how friendly he seemed, he was the sworn enemy of Caprice. Which made him the sworn enemy of me. Man, I was acquiring enemies faster than a whore acquired lovers.

He seemed to pick up on my discomfort anyhow because his blue eyes glittered with malice. "It's a shame we couldn't hold the dinner in the throne room as usual, although nobody wants to meet the same fate as Lorca Ranson."

My mind cartwheeled as fast as that spinning ball of pink chiffon overhead that I knew to be a winged faerie, which slammed right into one of the Lightning balls with a loud sizzle.

Darzan was the fae I instinctively turned to for answers, but he wasn't here when I needed him. I tried not to look over to where I knew he was, I fucking tried, but I failed. There he was, grinning seductively at that gorgeous female on his lap, who wiggled her ass into his crotch and licked cream off his finger.

Gabrelle from the Realm of Verda. In that moment, I hated her more than Jayke.

No way was I interrupting their little fuck party. Since I couldn't rely on Darzan for answers, I'd have to seek them myself. Who cared if I came across as ignorant to this male I would probably never see again?

"What happened to Lorca? I thought House At—I thought my father had him killed."

The delighted malicious glittering in his blue eyes told me I was making Colzan's day. "Lorca entered the throne room with a plan to kill Bastian," he said. "The enchanted floor read his intent and swallowed him whole. I like to imagine him stuck under the surface, trying to break out and take another breath of air, forever banging his fists on the underside of the floor. He planned to murder the king, and the spells read his black heart correctly, and he drowned."

I took a couple of shallow breaths. "Fuck," I murmured.

"Quite," Colzan agreed with a smirk.

This whole thing sounded hocus. Like the prince before me was trying to put a spin on the truth, to twist it to his ends.

"What about Leena Sansett?" I asked, watching his reaction carefully. "She was imprisoned for speaking her mind." I didn't care who you were; putting your political opponents in jail made you a tyrant and a monster.

Colzan's eyes glittered like sapphires as he replied. "Leena was imprisoned for her role in the attempted coup and the attempt on the rightful king's life. She was lucky she got away with her life. That was only because of the kindness of Queen

Bree."

Holy crap. "My mother," I breathed.

"Yes," he smirked.

I played with the fabric of my dress. "Fuck," I murmured.

Colzan's smirk turned into a full grin. "Yes, you mentioned that already," he deadpanned.

So Bastian hadn't killed Lorca, not really. The fae had fallen subject to his own stupidity—surely he knew the floor was enchanted. Perhaps he'd thought happy thoughts as he stepped onto the floor and assumed that would protect him. But it hadn't.

Thank God for that enchanted floor. Otherwise, the treasonous Lorca could have killed my father years ago, and Sansett would already be ruling Caprice. My mind was swimming again, but I planted my feet firmly on the copper floor and stood tall.

I watched as Colzan wandered away, then I did likewise, heading in the opposite direction. I avoided the corner where I knew Darzan was bouncing Gabrelle on his knee and turned my back on them. I longed for the feel of a cold blade against my throat, a sign that he was watching me, but it never came. He was far too absorbed in somebody much closer to him.

Delph

My fists were clenched beneath the floaty blue layers of my ballgown. Darzan was off in the corner with the most beautiful woman in the world on his lap giggling like a fucking idiot, and he was lapping it up.

Apparently, I was a jealous bitch, and I didn't like this new side of me.

I took some deep breaths and peeled my fists open. What did I care if Darzan screwed the most gorgeous creature in the universe? He was nothing to me. He just provided a roof over my head while I figured my shit out, nothing more, nothing less.

So why was this red devil dancing on my chest?

I put my head down and weaved through the crowd, aiming to get as far away from Darzan and the curvy pink-haired siren as possible. I plonked myself on a padded bench in a small alcove, needing a break. My spot wasn't exactly secluded, but it was out of the way. A thick velvet curtain hung to my right, separating me from the next alcove, and the blue and bronze embossed wall behind me made a good backrest.

Fae were dancing and chatting, mostly looking like they were having a good time, and I kept my eyes firmly to the left, avoiding the golden-haired asshole with a basket of curves giggling on his lap.

The curtain beside me moved as somebody sat down on the other side, and muffled voices filtered through. I leaned in closer to hear—a natural survival instinct that I hadn't shaken after only a few weeks in luxury.

"The food isn't very good," a deep voice rumbled, clearly belonging to a male with a large lung capacity. "D whips up better snacks in his sleep."

I leaned close to hear the reply, which began with a big huff. "Stop whining, Thorne," a higher voice said. The voice had a sharp edge, and if I didn't know better, I would assume its owner grew up in the Docklands. But that couldn't be right. "It's better than rice and beans," she continued. "Or beans and rice." She paused thoughtfully. "Or, even worse, rice and beans."

I smiled to myself. She sounded like my kind of woman, somebody who knew what it was to struggle and who still appreciated a decent meal. Carefully, I wriggled back on my bench and lined up with a small crack between the curtain and the wall. From there, I could just see a sliver of a female with spiky blue hair wearing an ornate pantsuit with swirling ivory silk. She looked fierce and capable but was obviously fae, so I must have been mistaken about her living in the Docklands.

"I wasn't complaining," the male said. I couldn't see him, but his voice was loud, and I imagined a large fae with a barrel chest. "I was just commenting on a fact."

"Okay, truthenstein," the female said with a sigh. "Fine."

The male grumbled. "I hate that name," he growled.

I caught the edge of a cheeky grin from the female. "I know, babe. That's the point."

Trying to figure these guys out was keeping my mind off

the shitshow of a ball. I'd learned that my parents weren't monsters, which was obviously a good thing. But I'd barely absorbed that fact when I'd been slammed with the knowledge that Jayke was a monster who'd been playing me all along and, even worse, Darzan was flirting with Gabrelle.

No, hang on, that couldn't be worse. That didn't matter at all. Who cared if he screwed the most beautiful female in Arathay?

The name 'Gabrelle' snapped me back to attention. The female fae on the other side of my curtain mentioned her. "Aren't you jealous of Gabrelle flirting with that awful Davin heir?" she asked.

Jealous? What? Did that mean the male was Gabrelle's partner? I slumped against the wall as I realized he was probably just one of many fae obsessed with Gabrelle.

The male growled. "N-no," he stammered.

The blue-haired female cocked her head. "The growl says otherwise, Thorne," she told him, and that name rang a distant bell in the back of my mind. "You've gotta work on your lying game now that you're out of Fen. It's not just the words you say, it's how you deliver them."

He growled again, and the hair on my neck stood on end. "Fine," he grumbled. "I want to ring Davin's fucking neck. Is that better?" Holy crap, that male was intimidating. I still hadn't laid eyes on him, but he was growing taller and more muscled in my imagination, and I hoped he didn't find out I was eavesdropping. He sounded like he could kill me with just a look.

"Oh, now you're back to telling the truth," the female scolded with a singsong voice. She wasn't affected by the male's display of dominance, which made me think she spent a lot of time around dominant men. But with that Hebes street twang in her voice, I couldn't figure her out. Who the hell was she? "It's probably better that you stay out of the way while Gabrelle's working."

Working? What the hell? What did that mean? Her ass was on Darzan's thighs. His cock was probably poking into her. And they called that working?

"I don't see the point," Thorne grumbled. "Davin won't become king. We should keep focusing our attention on Jayke. He's the one we need to get on board to battle the Shadow Walkers."

The Shadow Walkers? This all had to do with those mythical creatures everybody kept gossiping about? The ones who walked around and turned fae into zombies? I shivered and must have gasped because the curtain beside me whipped aside, revealing the two fae I'd been spying on.

"Who the hell are you?" the male asked. He was just as intimidating as I pictured but less giant-proportioned. But with his black hair and eyes and black suit, he looked like a mafia boss.

The female was tinier than I thought but with a wiry muscled body beneath her ivory silk suit. She leaned forward and rested her elbows on her knees. "I know exactly who she is," the woman said, looking me up and down. "She's Delphinium Athar, the rightful ruler of Caprice. She gave her throne to the nearest male who asked for it nicely. Isn't that right?" she asked, her powder-blue eyes narrowing at me.

"No, it fucking isn't," I scowled, meeting her glare for glare. "I'm a mortal woman with a lot of damn questions. Like, who the hell are you?"

The two fae ignored my question. The female kept staring

at me like I was cowshit on the sole of her foot, and the male looked me up and down, assessing me. "I expected you to wear something more arresting," he said.

What the hell? He was lucky I was wearing a dress at all. When I fled Sansett Palace, I'd left my closet full of gowns behind, and Darzan didn't have so much as a scrap of silk in his place. I'd been delighted to find a frock on the blood-red armchair when I woke. It was a fairly ordinary floaty blue dress that reached my ankles and bared my back and arms. It would've earned paparazzi snaps at a human red carpet event, but the dress was positively dull by fae standards.

Darzan told me he'd borrowed it from a neighbor, and the thoughtfulness touched me. He didn't expect me to support his bid for the throne, yet he'd gone out of his way to find me something to wear to the House dinner that wasn't my trashy jeans and leather jacket. He'd done it personally, which was nice, rather than outsourcing it to a lackey like Jayke always did.

But now Darzan was off slipping his tongue down the throat of this rude male's friend. I didn't care if this dickhead was from the truth-telling realm, it didn't give him the right to be so obnoxious.

I tilted my head. "And I didn't give your outfit a moment's thought," I said. "Now, how about you tell me who the hell you are."

He ducked his head in a cursory bow. "I am Prince Thorne Sanctus from the Realm of Fen. I am very pleased to meet you." He turned and beamed at the woman. "See, I *can* lie," he grinned.

I coughed out a breath. "Prince?" I asked, my voice rising into an embarrassing squeak.

The female elbowed her friend. "Not anymore, babe. You're just a commoner in Verda now," she said. She nodded at me. "I'm Neela Flora, the heir to Floran throne of Verda. And I actually *am* a princess."

I gulped. Right. So these two royals were very influential, and their opinion would influence who became king.

I should be nice to them. I really should be nice to them. *Think of something nice to say*, I told myself. "Well," I began while my brain raced. "You might be royalty, but you're still rude assholes."

Fuck. That wasn't nice. That was brutal. Was some of Thorne's Fen truth-telling magic rubbing off on me? Oh well, who cared what some foreign princess thought of me?

I shifted my weight to leave, but amazingly, Neela Flora threw back her spiky blue head and laughed like I'd just told the best joke ever. She cackled like crazy, and it was contagious. Thorne smiled too, and even my lips quirked.

When she'd finally recovered, Neela put a small hand on my shoulder. "I like you. You suck, obviously, but I kinda like you."

I shook off her hand. "Erm...thanks?" What kind of a princess was this? Nothing like the grenade-up-their-asses fae I'd imagined the visiting heirs to be. "Well, I gotta go," I said. I turned to leave and caught sight of Gabrelle sucking on Darzan's thumb like it was his cock, and I swung away and blurted out, "Did you say Gabrelle was working? It doesn't look like it."

Thorne ground his jaw and growled while Neela answered with a chuckle. "She always liked a challenge, but even she wouldn't get that, er, close to someone with such strong War magic unless she had to."

"So, what's she doing?" I asked. "Surely the ties between realms don't need to be that, er, strong. If he becomes king, I mean."

Thorne's gaze was firmly on the bronze floor. "This has nothing to do with ties between realms," he gritted out. "And everything to do with the Shadow Walkers." Neela's powder blue eyes flashed at her friend, but she didn't stop him from talking. "The Stone of Veritas is the only thing that can kill Shadow Walkers," he said, still staring at the floor. "And we found it. But we need more pieces of the Stone if we have any hope of defeating them. There are just too many of the bastards."

Okay, so these guys were serious believers in the Shadow Walkers. The creatures hadn't made it to Caprice yet—thank God, because we had enough of our own problems with Gaia going feral and making nature mutiny against us. But, apparently, the Walkers had been causing chaos in Verda, which was closer to the Shadow Isles. At least, according to the rumors, which I didn't necessarily believe.

"And, Darzan can help you because of his War magic?" I asked, still trying to figure out the link between zombies and that beautiful princess wiggling her ass in Darzan's face.

Thorne harrumphed. "If only it was that easy," he scoffed.

Neela shifted her weight, cocking out a sassy little hip. "No, we need the ruler of Caprice to split the Stone of Veritas using Lightning," she said. "And Gabrelle's using her inner power of Lure to assess how open Darzan is to that idea."

I scoffed. "Oh, now we're calling tits an inner power, are we?" I grumbled, and Thorne swept an angry hand through his black hair.

Neela just chuckled. "Are you friends with Darzan?" she

asked me.

"I hate him," I spit out, though that was a big fat lie. But they didn't need to know about my stupid churning emotions.

"Right, well, in that case," Neela said, pausing for dramatic effect. "She's using her Lure to implant the idea of helping us with the Stone if he becomes king. Obviously, it'll only pay off if he gets the job and Gaia gives him a little Lightning to play with, even though he'll just be an interregnum. It's kind of an experiment. Pretty cool, huh? "

That sounded pretty psychotic, actually. Hopefully, she wouldn't mess around in his mind too much. Maybe I could hate her a little less, given that she was "working," but not him...he didn't know he was just some rat in an experiment, and his hands were roving all over her curves completely voluntarily. Neela reached out and snatched up her drink from a little bronze table and downed its contents in one. "Shame your parents aren't here," she said. "Bree would've made Bastian help us in a heartbeat."

My ribcage tightened at her casual use of my parents' names. I still thought of them quite formally as King and Queen of Caprice or as a monster and a junkie. I wished I could think of them as just Bastian and Bree. Mom and Dad. "Did you know them?" I asked, ashamed of the desperation in my voice.

Neela's blue eyes softened as she looked at me, and I felt a kinship in them. In her. As though she understood what it meant to want information about long-lost family. "I met them," she said, and her whole face softened. "But I didn't know them well. Ronan did, though. You can ask him any questions you want."

I looked around to find Ronan, whoever he was, but Neela laid a hand on my arm. "He isn't here," she said. "He's looking after things back home in Verda City. We couldn't afford to all come to this Ascension, not with the Walkers attacking every night."

Her intense gaze made me shift uncomfortably. "Are the attacks really that bad?" I asked. Maybe all the shit going down in my life was nothing compared to what these guys were going through.

Neela nodded. "Worse."

I squared my shoulders. The heirs of Verda had gone to the trouble of finding the Stone of Veritas thingy that could kill the Shadow Walkers, and all they needed from my realm was the power of Lightning to split the Stone and make more of them. As a fellow Seelie realm of Arathay, that was the least we could do.

If only my parents were still here to help. Instead, it looked like Prince Charming Smarmy Pants would take the throne, and I had to believe he was good enough to help.

But, deep in my heart, I knew he was selfish enough to keep all the power for himself, even if it meant throwing Verda to the devil.

As though I'd summoned him with my thoughts, I looked up and locked onto a pair of lavender eyes, watching me closely from a porcelain white face.

Delph

Jayke's white face stood out among the brightly colored fae, and his hard expression quickly softened into one of concern when he saw me looking.

I wanted to run away. I wanted to stamp on his foot and spit in his face. But I refused to behave like prey to his predator or like a child to his father, so instead, I excused myself from Neela and Thorne and walked steadily toward him, staring him down.

He excused himself from the nobles he was talking to and met me halfway across the room. "Delphinium, I'm so glad to see you safe," he said, pitching his voice to be heard above the string music and maybe overheard by the nearest fae. "When my guards told me you'd been taken by the dark prince, I feared the worst."

So many lies were packed into that small sentence I could barely tease them apart. He knew I hadn't been kidnapped but liberated. He hadn't cared for my safety or made any attempt to rescue me from Darzan's clutches. Even the gently concerned expression on his face was a lie.

I smiled sweetly, mirroring his courtly gestures. "And I'm glad you're okay, too, and that your oversized ego didn't kill you in your sleep," I purred.

His brow quirked in anger, which delighted me. "I only ever wanted what was best for you, Delphinium," he said.

I shuddered at his use of my formal name. It was hard to believe I'd found him charming when we first met when I could now see him for the ball of groveling slime he was.

"You never wanted anything but my name," I retorted. "You kidnapped me from Hebes, then lied about it. You never wanted me to be an ambassador for the mortal realm or any of that shit. A, what was it, a passionate supporter of politics? Bull. You only wanted me for my family name. Which you didn't bother telling me, I might add."

Jayke's mask was as stony as ever, still fixed in that conde-scending frown. "I already explained that I was protecting you from knowing the horror of your heritage. You would have panicked if you'd known you hailed from House Athar. All I wanted was to return you to your homeland and learn about the fae without overwhelming you with facts."

I snorted. "Facts are not overwhelming, Jayke. Facts are the foundation of truth, and truth is something we need more of around here. And I don't mean your power-hungry twisted version of the truth where you're the big hero and everybody else is the villain, I'm talking about hard facts. Like the fact that Lorca Ranson wasn't slaughtered in cold blood but threw himself onto an enchanted floor with evil intent. He died because of his own evil—or his stupidity, if you wanna be kind about it, Jayke. Oh, and here's another fact. People call Bastian an unfae monster king because he gave up his reign and his life for a human woman. Not because he did monstrous things like you told me. And my favorite fact of all? You kept me prisoner against my will, refused to let me return home, then hunted me like a fucking fugitive when I tried. Those are facts, Jayke. You should try using one."

Jayke blinked at me. He flinched every time I spit his first name, so I peppered my speech with it as much as possible. But his face regained his mask of composure, and the only hint of anger was the hardening of his lavender eyes. "I'm sorry if I mishandled the situation," he said carefully, and his tact and diplomacy only enraged me further. When I'd first arrived, I admired it, aspired to it, but now I saw it for the bullshit it was. Darzan Davin may be prone to violence and murder, like me. But at least we also shared the trait of honesty.

The prince and I stared bitterly at each other for a few moments before our silent fuck-off contest was interrupted by official proceedings. Apparently, the two contenders for the throne had had enough time to garner support, and now the visiting Houses and the Caprician Houses would declare their support publicly.

I refused to look into the damn corner where Darzan was *garnering support* from Gabrelle's ass, but when I felt that cold blade against my throat, I couldn't help the relief that flowed through me.

The phantom blade no longer felt menacing or predatory but somehow comforting. It felt more like a protective necklace than anything else, but the welcome sensation quickly disappeared as Darzan swept his gaze from me, leaving me cold and lonely.

The two princes crossed to their assigned positions, standing on either side of the dazzling diamond fountain. Darzan looked imposing and, frankly, evil in his black suit with gold embroidery. He should have gone for a more approachable look this evening, but it was too late to tell him. By contrast, Jayke wore ivory and cream, a complicated outfit between a suit and a toga. Together with the dazzling smile on his face, his clothes made him the good prince to Darzan's evil.

The Houses were called up individually to declare their support by standing beside their preferred king. This was the moment of truth.

I snagged a glass of wine from a passing tray and slammed it back. Even the amazing taste didn't distract me from the proceedings.

The first fae called up strode without hesitation and stood by Jayke's side, receiving a warm handshake and smile from the charming prince as a reward. My pulse raced as fae after fae went to stand beside Jayke, who grinned and nodded like a perfect statesman, with one hand tucked into his pants pocket as though he were posing for a photo shoot.

Jayne Sansett, looking composed and elegant in a long mint-green dress, went and stood by her brother's side, representing the Sansett vote. I didn't feel like worshipping her now that I knew she'd been deceiving me too. Plus, my fae senses were developed enough that I could see the arrogance in her smile.

When a fae finally moved to stand beside Darzan, the dark prince kept his expression stony, not even offering a word of thanks for the support.

When House Allura was called up to represent all five ruling Houses of Verda, who apparently ruled as one, Gabrelle sashayed forward, making a knife twist in my gut. I was no longer team Sansett, but I didn't want that gorgeous bitch to wiggle her ass toward Darzan, either. She glanced at Neela and Thorne, who nodded, clearly having agreed in advance who they would support.

My nerves jumped in my belly, and when Gabrelle sauntered

right past Darzan and stood beside Jayke, I almost fucking laughed. It served Darzan right for flirting with her and ignoring me, and the slight tick in his jaw only deepened my smirk.

The representative from the Realm of Fen was named to choose his candidate, and somebody called Erevan Reissan stepped forward with a broad grin, clearly enjoying his moment in the spotlight. I knew Thorne was an ex-prince from Fen, so I glanced at him to see his reaction and noted his face was red and his hands were curled into fists. He looked ready to murder. Clearly, there was some history between those two. Unsurprisingly, Erevan stood beside Jayke, lending his realm's support to House Sansett.

The next declaration came from Colzan Blunt, representing the Realm of Ourea. Given his father's betrayal of Darzan's father, it was no surprise when the larrikin prince took his place beside Jayke.

Every Seelie realm supported Jayke Sansett for king, as did most of the Caprician Houses. King Draylar from the Unseelie Realm of Dust threw his support behind Darzan, but that probably hurt his cause more than anything.

After a pause, I realized all the Houses had been named, and only four stood beside Darzan, including Pike, with the remaining dozen or more by Jayke's side.

House Athar hadn't been called up, and I supposed I wasn't deemed an acceptable representative because I was only half fae.

Well, fuck that. I stepped forward and made the announcement myself since nobody else seemed inclined to. "Representing House Athar," I called, mimicking the words and tone of the previous announcements. "Delphinium Athar."

The assembled fae were shocked into silence, but nobody stopped me. I looked at Jayke, who smiled benignly at me, telling me with a glance that he forgave my earlier outbursts. Everybody expected me to go to his side because I'd allowed him to parade me about town from party to party like a pet. Yes, a damn pet.

I looked at him deliberately, then strode past his group of lickspittles, past Gabrelle, whose molten curves were even more impressive up close, and rounded the fountain to stand beside Darzan.

I noticed Thorne looking at me with curiosity and Neela smiling at me with approval.

Darzan may be infuriating, murderous, and imbued with War magic. But at least he was honest, and he'd make a far better king than the Sansett prick.

Now that I'd made my opinion public, every eye in the room was locked on me. Tension crept into the atmosphere and made my skin tingle, and I wondered if I'd just declared more than I realized.

Darzan

Last night's House dinner was an unmitigated disaster.

I'd intended to introduce Delph to enough people that she wouldn't feel awkward and then slip away and grit my teeth while I courted the noble Houses.

It started off well. Delph held her own against King Draylar, which was more than could be said for most fae. But when she turned to me with wide eyes and asked if her father had been a good ruler...I exploded in fury. I'd been trying to convince her of that for days, doing everything in my power to portray her father's good qualities, hoping she would accept him and accept herself. Even if not to feel better about herself, then at least in memory of the king. He was owed respect from his own daughter, at least.

So when she'd asked that question, her eyes as wide as an ingenue, my control slipped. Emotions I'd been hiding since the day I met her bubbled to the surface and emerged as shouts spurting into her defiant upturned face. I couldn't contain myself. How dare she ignore my words for so long and then believe the words of the Dread King of Brume? Did I really mean so little to her? Why did I even care what she thought of me?

I hadn't handled my emotions well. At all. I'd beelined

straight for the most beautiful female in the room, the princess of beauty in the Realm of Greed and Excess. Verda. An immature bid to make Delphinium jealous. I wanted her to burn with rage the way I was.

But It didn't work. Of course it didn't—Delph didn't care who I flirted with or screwed. She didn't care if I lived or died, as far as I could tell. I'd just ended up torturing myself because all evening, I'd wanted nothing more than to pin my gaze on Delph as she worked the room, but I couldn't. She felt my gaze like a blade on her neck, so I fought every instinct in my body and kept it averted.

The evening had only gotten worse after that. Every fae and his damn dog had publicly supported Jaykey-boy. Except Delph...she'd stood by me, and I didn't have a clue why. I was burning to know why she'd changed her mind, whether she thought I'd make a good king, or if it was just out of spiteful hatred of Jayek. But she hadn't appeared for breakfast, so I couldn't ask her.

I sat by the downstairs fire in a dark brown leather armchair, watching the crackling and spitting of the flames, waiting for Delph to appear. We definitely needed to talk. A scuffle in the doorway had me turning with anticipation, but it was just my brother.

He dragged himself across the room and slouched into the opposite armchair, looking even greener than usual. "Thanks for letting me stay the night," he mumbled. He still wore his mahogany suit, which was crumpled and forlorn, looking far from the king we both needed him to be.

"Uh-huh," I said, my thoughts still on Delph. Should I confront her about ignoring my opinion of her father, or should I thank her for supporting me publicly?

Pike snapped my attention, cradling his head in his hands with a dramatic sigh. "My brain feels like it's about to explode," he groaned. "Do you have any night-cure tonic?"

I shook my head. I had no use for hangover potions. When I got plastered, I liked to sit in my misery the next day and pound through my well-earned headache. I figured I deserved it. I supposed that made me a masochist.

"Gaia-be-damned," Pike moaned, "when are you going to live like a fae instead of an animal?" He raised his head to glance around my living room, then slumped it back into his hands. His skin looked even greener than usual. "This place is dark and filthy," he mumbled. "You need some staff. And some tonics."

I let his grumbling wash over me. I didn't care to get into a conversation about my living habits with anybody, and that included my Unascended brother. We had far more important matters to discuss, given the upcoming coronation. "Last night didn't go well," I said, tossing out the understatement of the year.

Pike's emerald eyes flashed up at me before he resumed cradling his head. "You have even less support from the Houses than I expected," he mumbled.

I sighed heavily, watching the flickering flames light green sparkles in my brother's hair. "Quite," I said on an exhale. In truth, I had assumed that King Athar's support would flow to me. He had been a popular ruler, always working closely with me and my parents before me. Plus, all of Caprice—and beyond—knew that Jaykey-boy was a social climbing egomaniac who wanted power for power's sake and didn't give a crap about other fae.

Or so I'd thought. But that natural flow of support from

House Athar to me didn't happen.

Fuck.

Maybe Athar was less popular than I thought. His reputation was certainly tarnished when he gave himself up for the love of a mere mortal, giving up his crown and his life.

Even so, it was astounding how many fae had turned their backs on him. Turned their backs on me. Fen, Verda, Ourea, and Brume had all supported Jayke. The Unseelie realm had supported me, but that only made me look worse. Most of the Caprician Houses had supported Jayke, too, with only one or two exceptions.

Obviously, networking and kissing babies were far more effective than I realized.

"I messed up," I confessed bitterly. "I underestimated the power of Jayke's charm."

Pike groaned. "Underestimated the other fae's gullibility, you mean," he bit out.

I hummed noncommittally.

Pike shuffled his butt forward to rest his head on the back of the armchair, and he looked up at the peeling ceiling. "I was surprised you had House Athar's support," he mumbled. "How in Mortia did you swing that?"

The truth was, I didn't have a damn clue. Delph had never wavered from her view that somebody with Healing would make a better king than somebody with War, and no matter how I tried to convince her otherwise, I never made headway. So her last-minute decision to stand by my side stunned me as much as anybody else, especially after I shouted at her and stormed off mid-party.

I sighed. "It doesn't matter. The fact is, you and I can only trust each other," I said. "There is nobody else." Last night made that perfectly clear. Pike and I could only rely on ourselves and on each other. Even centuries of faithful service to House Athar hadn't been enough to earn anybody else's trust.

Pike groaned and threw a hand over his eyes. "Get some Gaia-be-damned medicine in your Gaia-be-damned house," he grumbled.

I leaned forward, examining his very unkingly pose. He looked like a damn street urchin in his rumpled suit, unable to even sit up straight. Sure, I had screwed up last night and failed to get anybody's support for my bid to be king, but that made Pike's role all the more important. "Get your head in the game," I snapped. "You need to ascend to Lightning to keep Jayke Sansett off the throne. You know he'll hoard the realm's resources for himself and let everyone else's lives go to shit. He's a selfish bastard with zero morals. We can't let that happen to Caprice."

Pike opened his eyes and glared at me through lowered lids. He shuffled to a seating position and leaned forward, resting his elbows on his knees. He suddenly looked wide awake and alert, but I could smell his hangover on his breath. "Gaia will never choose me," he said flatly.

I wanted to deny it, to tell him to pull his head out of his ass and start behaving like a monarch, to tell him not to give up, but the words wouldn't come.

He was right. It was a one-in-a-thousand shot that he would ascend to Lightning. No, the odds weren't even that good, more like one in a hundred million.

But we couldn't give up, couldn't just hand the realm to the selfish prince and wait for him to turn our home to shit. Delph once told me not to be a coward and to fae up—although she'd cursed a lot more when she said it.

She was right, though. This was about more than just making friends with other Houses—this was about the future of Caprice and everybody in it. And we needed to do something about it. "Then we need to change things up," I said, leaning forward. "We need to ruffle a few feathers. Let's bring the real Jaykey-boy out of the woodwork, the vindictive and vicious prince you and I know. He keeps that asshole hidden from most fae, so let's show all the Houses his true worth. Nothing."

A sly grin crept up Pike's face. "I'm listening," he said. "What are you going to do?"

I shook my head. "It has to be you. I want the Houses to swing their support my way, so I can't get involved in a petty squabble. I can't trust anybody, so it must be you." This was a final, desperate shot at keeping Caprice out of the hellhole it was falling into, with Jayke Fucking Sansett at the center.

"I'm still listening," Pike said, and some life was coming back into his face. Even his muscles had a little tension, and he sat straighter.

"Go to his home," I said, thinking fast. "Make some noise. Call him names, and he'll rise to the bait like a perfect brat and start a fight. If you can goad him into attacking you, he'll lose that golden halo of being the Healing Prince and hopefully lose some supporters too."

Pike's nodded, but his eyes fluttered closed again. "Okay, good idea. I'm in," he said, sinking back into his armchair. "But not today. I'm not doing anything today except trying to outlive this Gaia-be-damned headache. If I survive, I'll do it tomorrow."

My brother was in no fit state to do anything today, so I

agreed we should wait. I nodded in agreement, though Pike couldn't see me. An extra day would give us more time to plan, assemble a small crew to go with him and figure out how to capitalize on Jayke's tantrum.

It felt good to have a plan that didn't rely on winning the Ascension lottery. "Okay," I said, my thoughts churning, "tomorrow."

Darzan

Shortly after I kicked Pike out of my house and sent him to a Healer, Delph emerged from our bedchamber.

She wore a skirt and blouse I'd borrowed from my neighbor—I'd spoken more words to that fae in the past two days than in the previous two decades.

"Good morning," I said. Delph looked ravishing even in those simple clothes, with more natural style and personality in every step she took than even the most graceful female fae.

She looked me straight in the eyes, as defiant as ever, and we exchanged cordial greetings while she fixed herself some food. I noticed she favored grapes last night, so I had some delivered this morning. She didn't mention them, but I was pleased when she picked a small bunch.

Neither of us broached the topic of last night, of how I'd exploded in rage and stalked off, then ignored her for the rest of the evening until she did the ultimate solid of publicly supporting my bid for the throne. But the more I thought about it, the more ashamed I felt. Sure, she hadn't believed my opinion of her father, but that was hardly a crime. And I'd behaved like an idiot. Even so, I couldn't quite find the words to admit it.

Delph informed me, with that stubborn jut of her jaw that

made her look fierce and irreproachable, that she was going to the library to learn more about her parents. She said it like a dare, expecting me to lose my shit again, but I didn't. In fact, I thought it was a good idea. The more she learned about them, the more she would accept her heritage and herself.

But I couldn't let her go alone. She needed protection, now more than ever, as the realm became more and more impatient and nature grew wilder and wilder without a ruler.

She snapped her gaze onto mine, as direct as ever. "Are you going to walk with me?" she asked. "Or will you hide in the shadows and watch me from afar?"

My lips twitched at that question. She knew me too well. Ever since that first day I'd been testing Jaykey-boy's wards for weakness and seen her stumbling through the mushroom gorge, I'd followed her to watch over her.

She didn't usually need my help. From the outset, she was remarkably accomplished for a half-fae who'd spent her life severed from her inner powers. She had a sassy attitude and a mean right hook.

But I'd watched her from the shadows nonetheless. I never knew why Sansett didn't walk with her in the city after dinner, why he left her alone to the dangers of the world with no more than her wits to defend her. She had teeth and claws but was still just a kitten in our perilous realm.

So I found myself, night after night, waiting for her at the end of her moonway and following her through the shadows.

She sensed me as an intangible danger, just like everybody else did. That was one of the curses—or benefits—of wielding War. My gaze was a visceral thing that affected its recipient, who typically clenched their hearts in fear.

That was one reason I didn't schmooze easily. Fae tended to

clutch their throats while conversing with me, often trying to hide their discomfort behind a smile, but I knew how they felt. And it didn't make me prone to chitchat. So I usually ended up slouching in a corner, trying not to look at anybody.

Fat lot of good that had done me. My reluctance to socialize and network with the other Houses had now put the whole realm in danger of falling to House Sansett.

"I'll walk with you," I said.

Immediately after she'd eaten, I hunched into a coat, then we headed out. We walked in silence to the library and then went inside to the recent correspondence section, a magnificent vaulted hall with books lining the walls and archways as far as the eye could see. It had the faint scent of the sea from the enchantments that preserved the paper.

Delph had the idea that her mother's letters or diaries might be stored here, and while we searched, she finally broached the topic of the previous evening. "I spoke with Colzan Blunt last night while you were...busy." Fuck, I was glad she wasn't looking at me because I definitely would have reddened at that comment. I'd dandled Gabrelle on my lap like a fucking idiot. That beauty queen had been trying to conquer me for years, and I suspected I was the only one to ever say no to her. But last night, I'd given in and flirted with her just to make Delph jealous. And the damn human hadn't batted an eyelid. She'd barely glanced at me and Gabrelle all night.

Delph turned to a new shelf, cleared her throat, and continued, "He didn't seem as awful as everybody says."

The name Blunt set an edge to my voice that had me growling. "Never trust a Blunt from Ourea," I snapped. "They may seem friendly, but they are never your friend."

Her quick fingers paused in their dance along the books'

spines, and she glanced up at me. "What do you mean?"

I took a deep breath. This wasn't a story I'd ever shared before. In fact, I'd only ever discussed it with Pike. But after Delph's public display of allegiance last night, I owed her something. "Colzan's father, Traal Blunt, was best friends with my father," I explained. "The heirs and faelings of noble Houses often spend a decade or two in other realms to help foster relations and hopefully avert future wars. Fae births are rare, and fae lives are sacred."

Her fingers resumed walking along the covers and spines. "A decade or two?" she said. "So these kids, these faelings, they basically grow up in another realm? In another family?"

I knew family was important to humans—important to Delph. Maybe even more important than it was to fae, and outrage was clear in her voice.

"It's not always that long," I said. "My dad spent ten years in Ourea as a guest in House Blunt, aged five to fifteen. He and Traal grew up like brothers, and that's how my dad thought of him. As a best friend and a brother." It had been years since I'd thought about my father's stay in Ourea, and I realized I was re-reading the same line in a scroll again and again, so I rolled it up, taking a deep breath.

"What happened?" she asked softly.

It felt surprisingly good saying aloud the words I'd never uttered. Like I was letting Delph into my circle of trust, and although that feeling was terrifying, the terror was edged with relief. "My father confided military secrets in Traal and went on to tell his dad, who was the King of Ourea by that time. Based on my father's information, they razed an entire village in Western Caprice and destroyed the magical encampment there." I realized I'd carried my father's guilt as if it were my own and carried his anger too. At Traal and the entire Blunt line.

I looked up and saw Delph's beautiful face go pale, her full lower lip quivering, and her wide green eyes startling against her black hair. "I'm so sorry," she said. "What happened to the fae who lived there?"

"Every single one perished," I said flatly. "I was twenty-four at the time and learned a valuable lesson that day." A lesson I'd never forgotten.

Her fingers paused again, and she exhaled slowly, assembling the puzzle pieces. "That's why you chose to ascend to War?" she asked, but it wasn't really a question.

This female was so damn perceptive. I nodded. "So I would always be able to defend the innocent." The timing of Traal's betrayal changed the entire course of my life. I had been twenty-four, and just a few months later, I'd chosen to ascend to War. War suited me well, but I sometimes wondered how my life would have been different if I'd chosen Hover, like my mother or any other inner power. I'd have more friends, for a start. Not only because fae wouldn't feel their life was being threatened whenever I looked at them, but because I would trust them more easily too.

The words were unspoken between us but as plain as if they were written across the bookshelves. Traal Blunt's betrayal of my father was the reason I didn't trust anybody except Pike. And maybe, just maybe, Delphinium Athar.

After finding nothing in the book section, we moved on to the scrolls, working mostly in silence. Delph walked ahead of me, her hips swaying beneath her hypnotizing skirt. Everything about her was more pronounced than in female fae. Her walk, her emotions, her personality.

Her long black hair was loose today and flowed like a sleek curtain behind her. I wanted to run my fingers through it, to trace the curve of her hip and the hollow of her waist. I ached to caress her body with my hands and mouth.

I'd wanted it since I first laid eyes on her, but she, like everybody else, hated me at first sight.

"Here!" Her vibrant green eyes, which I always found so startling for not matching her black hair, glowed with excitement. "It's a list of engagements my parents attended after they were first married. There might be something in here, so I can figure out if she loved him or if it was one-sided." She stuffed the scroll up her shirt to hide it.

I frowned. "You can't smuggle it out of here. The library's humidity and temperature are controlled by protective enchantments. If you take the scroll out, it might disintegrate."

Her eyes shone with excitement. "It's too long to read now, I have to take it. It's worth the risk, trust me."

Trust me. Two words that held so much more power than she realized.

The problem was, I didn't know if I could ever trust anyone.

Delph

Strolling away from the library through the streets of Capricia, I felt buoyant. The sky was blue, the sun shone down on us, and the air felt less oppressive than usual. A few fae passed us and smiled, and I grinned back. As we ducked up a forest street, a large sunflower leaned toward us, seeking a pat, but I knew to keep my hands to myself.

"Next week, buddy," I told the flower. After the coronation, it would be safe to pet the plants again.

I was so glad I'd made that split-second decision to support Darzan last night at the House dinner. He just told me he ascended into War to protect the innocent, not to attack and destroy. And, when I thought about it, I realized that almost every time I'd seen him wield War had been in defense.

He'd protected me in that forested avenue when the Seelor almost suffocated me, and again in Port Lonsdale when Jayke's guards attacked. He'd even followed me around Capricia to ensure I was safe back when I detested the very sight of him. He'd used his War power to protect in every single instance.

Except one. "Why did you kill that old fae in the strengths display?" I asked. That bloodied torso sliding off the legs and splatting onto the cobblestones of the Spike's forecourt still haunted me. Death during battle didn't bother me, but the meaningless slaughter of an innocent fae was something else.

We were almost back at Darzan's house, with the contraband scroll tucked into the waistband of my skirt and the midday sun blazing down upon us.

Darzan cleared his throat in an oddly self-conscious sound I'd never heard from him before. "That was Lucerne, an old friend of mine," he said slowly. "He lived past his prime, he told me, and was ready to die. He begged me to end his life at the strengths ceremony, hoping he would gain a noble and painless death and also help my bid for the throne." He laughed bitterly. "His life was given for no reason, it turns out."

I had to scrape my fucking jaw off the cobblestones. I'd never been as wrong as I had been about Darzan. That fierce expression on his face the moment before he sliced the old fae in half with his outstretched finger hadn't been anticipation but a grim determination to carry out his friend's wishes. He wasn't a warmongering monster but a protector and defender of innocence.

When we got home, I ducked upstairs to our shared bedroom, hoping to read the scroll alone. But Darzan followed me up, so I placed the valuable scroll in a desk drawer to read the instant he left the room.

His golden eyes bored into me, and that comforting cold necklace graced my neck. "Why did you support me last night, Delph?" he asked.

I tried a flirty joke to change the subject. "Oh, so you've given up calling me pet?"

His lips didn't so much as twitch. "I thought you wanted Sansett to rule?" he said.

I crossed to the small window, my footsteps light on the blood-red rug and looked out across our little street. Close townhouses lined the opposite side of the road, like classic Victorian homes but with odd details like a balcony made of leaves and twigs, and one window that was always in a different place.

But I couldn't put off my admission of guilt forever. "I've been wrong about a lot of things," I eventually said.

Darzan walked toward me soundlessly, and I turned around to look at him. He looked more animalistic and wild today but more beautiful too. I was mesmerized by his shirt pulling across his muscled shoulders and broad chest. He closed the distance, and with every foot he gained, my heart beat a little faster until it was galloping. I'd been pushing this male away for so long that it felt odd to suddenly want him close.

He stopped before me and traced a finger along my neck. "How does it feel when I look at you?" he asked, staring at the skin on my throat.

I reached up and ran a finger along his collarbone, tracing the mirror path on his flawless dark skin. Electricity thrummed at the touch. "It used to feel like you were holding a steel blade to my throat," I murmured.

He leaned forward, ducking down so his hot breath warmed my throat. I thought he was going to kiss me, but he didn't. He just stayed there and asked, "And now? What does it feel like now?"

His breaths were hot against my neck, and his gaze was fixed on me. I closed my eyes and focused on the sensation, on that comforting cold necklace against my flesh that now mingled with his hot breath. "It feels like home," I admitted.

He tipped forward and kissed me gently on the collarbone,

and heat rushed between my legs.

I gasped and put a hand around his golden head, tugging him closer, pulling his ashy scent to me. He kissed me again, and heat poured from his lips into my body, desire rising within me stronger than I remembered it ever being before.

"Yes," I moaned as he licked along my collarbone, then kissed up my neck. "Fuck yes," I said as he nibbled my earlobe.

I turned my head so his lips dragged across my cheek and paused when the corners of our mouths met, each breathing into the other's cheek. "Very fucking yes," I murmured, then turned farther and pressed my mouth to his in a drugging kiss.

The kiss was long and lustful, and a bolt of electricity zapped from my lips right down to my pussy, as though those were the only two parts of my body, the only two things in the world.

His hands moved to my hips, sending flashes of awareness there, and he tugged me closer against him so the length of his cock dug into my lower belly.

Too high, it was too high, I needed it several inches lower and several inches inside me, but I couldn't articulate the words because only sighs and moans escaped from my lips.

Darzan growled when I tugged his hips lower, desperately trying to line him up with my pussy despite the layers of clothing between us.

"Where's the scroll?" he demanded, and God bless him for caring, but Satan curse him for interrupting.

"It's safe," I hissed, earning a quirk of his lips.

I ran my hands along his belly and under his shirt, trying to hold as much of his perfect hard chest as possible.

"You're as impatient as I feel," he growled, sending another pulse of desire through me. "I'm going to fuck you, pet," he said, and I dug my fingers into his corded chest muscles, thirsty with lust.

I fumbled with his belt, and he placed his calm hands over my frantic ones and guided them through the motions of unfastening, and his pants dropped but snagged on his hard cock.

I pushed firmly against his chest and forced him back a pace so I could see what I was dealing with here, then I bent to remove the snagged pants and dropped them to the ground. His soft hair was a tangle of dark gold, a deeper shade than his eyes.

"Holy fuck," I breathed. "Be careful with that thing. You could poke somebody's eye out."

He laughed, and his long thick cock wobbled as he did. I reached out and touched it, and it was even more perfect and softer than the rest of his skin.

He pushed my hand away. "Careful," he growled. "It's been a long time. And I'd like to last longer than two seconds."

That twinge of jealousy I'd felt last night reasserted itself in my chest. "What about Gabrelle from Verda?" I asked, and my fingers stilled by my side, not touching him, just dangling uselessly. A breeze from the open window played with my hair, cooling my neck. "Why didn't you fuck her?"

His gaze was locked on my belly and hips, and he ripped the fabric of my skirt in two, exposing me completely from the waist down, and he sucked his teeth when he caught sight of my light blue panties. "Because I wanted to fuck you," he growled.

Desire pulsed so powerfully through me that I wondered if he was using some kind of sex magic. An aching need swelled within me as he lifted me easily with one hand, holding my full weight in one arm. I wrapped my legs around his waist, needing to pull him closer, needing to touch as much flesh as possible.

He pushed aside my panties with one finger and hissed a low growl when he felt how wet they were, then he rested the tip of his cock at my entrance. "Are we doing this?" he asked as the flickering flames from the fireplace played in his golden hair.

I ached for him, I wanted to devour him, I fucking needed him. "Yes, we're doing this," I said. "And if you don't lower me onto your cock in the next two seconds, I'm going to bitch slap you."

He laughed, not shying away from my violent streak but leaning into it. Leaning into me.

His tip was still poised at my entrance, like a goddamn tease, and I tried to make myself heavy to push myself down over it, knowing I was slick enough to take even that massive beast.

He leaned forward and nibbled my lips, and my wetness dripped onto his cock.

Slowly, painfully slowly, he lowered me, with one hand clutching my ass and supporting my weight and the other pulling my head toward his so he could devour my mouth.

As I slid over and around, it felt good, so fucking good. I wanted all of him, and I wanted it now, but I also needed this moment to last forever, this long lingering sensation of him invading me, of me lowering onto a living God, of us being as close as two beings could be.

He smelled of ash and musk and arousal. I savored every second of him, the sensations of him inside me, but I was desperate for more. I wanted to keep going until I could no longer remember my name.

Then I was riding him, shifting my hips slowly, pointing my

ass back and forth, sliding up and down his shaft.

As we moved together, our bodies crashing against each other, I lost track of time and place. The intensity built between us, a deep craving neither of us could ignore. But at the same time, I was scared–scared of losing myself completely in this moment, scared of what might happen if I gave in to my desires.

His movements matched mine, his hips thrusting back and forth, and when we met completely, I couldn't help but breathe a little faster, sigh a little louder, lose myself a little more.

I wanted this male so badly that I was in danger of conflating lust with love. In real fucking danger.

I probed his mouth with my tongue, drinking up the taste of him and holding on around his shoulders and neck with no intention of ever letting go.

"I only ever wanted to fuck you," he growled into my mouth, and my pussy clenched around him, my heart igniting with the fire from his body.

God, I wished I could believe him. I threw back my head to catch my breath, clasping onto his biceps, feeling that slight breeze from my neck from the open window. He was still standing, holding me up. So strong, so powerful, so deliciously hard and ready for me. And I wanted him. I needed him. I had to have him.

"I was made for you, Delph," he said, his voice heavy with desire. Then he knelt on the ground and lay me gently onto the rug, and suddenly he was pinning me to the floor, his cock buried deep inside me, and I tried to catch my breath, tried to calm down and focus on the way he was moving, but it was practically impossible.

"You feel so fucking good," he growled, and his mouth was sharp and hard on my neck, biting my collarbone, kissing the soft skin between my breasts, suckling a nipple as his hips worked faster and faster. Was I moaning? Was I making a high-pitched sound, like some kind of desperate, pathetic little kitten?

He pulled my hips forward, and his cock sank deeper inside me. He slammed me back down, hard, and my teeth clenched as my pussy stretched to accommodate his girth, and I arched my back and was impaled again and again, determined to take all of him, to get closer to him, to be as one with him as I could be.

I gripped the back of his neck and pulled myself up to press my breasts against his chest, my nipples as hard as diamonds, and my entire body felt like it was on fire. I still wore my top, but pressing my aching breasts against him eased some of my need, even though I wished the fabric wasn't separating us.

I gasped a little, and that was all he needed to raise himself up to his knees, forcing me to slide back along the rug. He buried his face between my tits and immediately started sucking on them, hard.

He used one hand to hold my ass in place, so I couldn't move, and the other pushed both legs back to my chest.

He kept his face buried between my tits as he fucked me, and he pulled one of my nipples between his teeth and bit down hard.

I needed to get up, wrap my legs around his waist, and pull him closer, but I couldn't move. I was helpless to do anything but bear the pleasure of him fucking me, and that was what I wanted more than anything else in the world.

I gasped and groaned. I couldn't stop myself. He was

pumping his hips quickly, and my juices were slipping out of me, sliding down his cock.

His mouth found mine again, and he released my legs so I could move, writhing beneath him, desperate to taste his lips for eternity and grind myself against him. He tasted so good.

I kept fucking him, meeting him thrust for thrust. His cock slid in and out of me, and he wove a finger between us, rubbing my clit, and kissing me full on the mouth until lust and desire spiraled within me uncontrollably, and I burst into sparks of electricity. My orgasm lingered, long and delicious, as Darzan continued stimulating my pussy and clit with every thrust.

Darzan buried his face in my neck and clutched my whole body tight against his while he came with one last thrust and shuddered inside me.

He rolled off me and lay gently on the ground, but I didn't roll away from him. I leaned into his chest and felt his cool comforting necklace mingle with the heat from his body, and I relaxed completely as he folded me into his embrace.

Darzan

I placed a hand under Delph's knees and carefully swept her up, cradling her against my chest. I carried her to the bed, holding her gingerly as though she might snap, although I knew she was stronger than she looked.

I climbed onto the mattress beside her, and she rested her warm head against my chest, and my heart swelled up to meet it.

This female was everything I wanted. Powerful, strong, vibrant, a harsh shell over a loving interior that was undeniably similar to mine.

She placed a hand on my chest and curled in tight against me. "Your gaze feels comforting because I like you now," she murmured into my chest.

I had one arm thrown around her shoulder, and I squeezed her tight, marveling at her deduction. Sunlight flickered off the bedpost. "Nobody has ever figured that out before."

She tilted her face so she could look up at me. "That the feeling of your gaze is affected by our relationship?"

"Uh-huh," I agreed. I liked the word relationship rolling off her tongue.

"Well, that makes sense," she said. I waited for her to cut me to my marrow and tell me nobody could ever love me, but she just smiled slightly and added, "Most people are fucking idiots."

I rumbled a deep laugh, and her head bobbed in time with my laughter. "You never spoke a truer word," I said.

She fell asleep like that, nestled on my chest, cocooned inside the arc of my arm. I had no intention of moving a muscle and disturbing her. It felt as though my soul were waking up after years of slumber, that her skin against my own poured essential energy into my being.

So I ignored the hunger rumbling in my belly and stayed exactly where I was, watching the sun creep across the floor and out the window.

But awareness of her body crept through my limbs. My cock thickened and hardened as my eyes rolled over her exposed skin. She was naked from the waist down, and her hips and thighs were perfect torture, covered in smooth skin I demanded to worship.

But I didn't want to wake her, so I didn't move a muscle. I lay there, soaking in her beauty, torturing myself with her magnetic body.

I'd never seen a sexier female. The startling mismatch between her eyes and hair was intoxicating, and I'd been slack-jawed the first time I saw her. Her movements were otherworldly, wild and uncontrolled, brimming with savage passion compared with the disciplined movements of full-blooded fae.

Even in sleep, she was untamed and reckless. Her limbs splayed over mine, and micro-expressions flickered over her beautiful face.

My cock yearned for her touch, and when I couldn't bear it a moment longer, I gently ran a hand down the valley of her waist, behind her hips, and cupped her ass.

She murmured sexily and moved against me, leaving a trail of fire on every spot she touched.

"You're so fucking perfect," I whispered, knowing she wouldn't hear it in her sleep, so it was safe to speak my mind.

She startled me by flicking her eyes open and matching my hungry gaze with a ravenous one of her own. "I've always thought so," she said with a wicked grin that made me want to lick those smirking lips.

Without warning, she grabbed my cock, and sensation exploded through my nerve endings, desire transporting me to the top of a chasm and nearly tipping me over.

In one quick movement, I flipped her onto her back and caged her with my arms.

She blinked at me. "What time is it?" she asked.

It was almost morning. She'd slept the whole night while I lay awake in sexual torture. Instead of answering her, I forced her legs apart with my knees and rested the tip of my cock on her wet, wet pussy. "Time to act out those dreams you've obviously been having," I murmured. Her slick warmth almost undid me, and I limited my movements and stayed perfectly still.

She lifted her head to smash her lips against mine, and I drank greedily from her, our intense kisses erasing my night of agony.

She cried out softly when I broke our contact, but it turned into a moan when I feathered kisses down her neck and over her breast, moving my palms around the curve of her waist and squeezing both her ass cheeks.

I hoisted her hips higher and took a long look at her beautiful mound and the slick folds of her pussy. "Fucking stunning,"

I said.

She wanted to respond, I could tell from the odd moans and sounds, but they weren't coherent, which made me smile.

I leaned forward and breathed deeply, her sweet salty smell leaving me breathless. I licked her slowly and savored her taste, releasing a low moan into her perfect pussy.

I circled her clit hard with my tongue, and she bucked her perfect hips my way, giving my hands more access to her ass and filling my face with her. Her pleasure was my pleasure, each of her moans sending me dangerously close to orgasm, filling me with a heady mix of lust and desire.

I speared her with my tongue, and she gripped my hair with both hands and ground me deeper into her, letting out a small whimper as she did. This was intoxicating. She was intoxicating. Together, we were intoxicating.

I took her clit between my lips and sucked it into my mouth, loving the way her body jerked from the contact.

She was so responsive, honest and genuine, so wildly human.

I closed my lips around her and sucked, hard, and she let out a loud moan, her grip on my hair tightening even more and her entire body going rigid.

I teased her, alternating between fast pulls and slow licks, wishing I could have that honeysuckle taste on my tongue forever.

When I couldn't wait a moment longer, I crawled up her body and kissed her, and she kissed me back, moaning into my mouth. I devoured her, slow and deep, before hovering my mouth over hers and staring into her face.

She breathed slowly, her eyes closed, and I wondered if she would have stayed like that forever if I hadn't taken her up in my arms and brought her flush against my chest.

I brought her face to mine and moved my hips, the feel of her hot pussy against my shaft too much to bear, her lips brushing mine like agony and bliss. "Please, please. Just do it now," she moaned.

I angled my hips to position my cock at her entrance, then waited for her to open her eyes to look at me, and I held her emerald gaze as I buried myself balls-deep in her sweet, tight little pussy in one fluid movement.

She gasped, a small sound of surprise and lust, with her eyes hooded and lips parted.

She gripped my shoulders tightly, and I lay motionless inside her. I let her get used to the feel of me expanding her, and I grinned when she reached around me and gripped my lower back and ass, trying to pull me closer.

I groaned as I kissed her, and she devoured my kiss. Her hands moved up and gripped my neck tight, and she pulled me closer as we kissed, her tongue meeting mine and her breath hot against my face.

She didn't kiss like any female I'd ever met before. Her kiss was more like a promise than a question. A promise I wanted to fulfill.

I ground my hips, amazed by how good it felt to be buried in her and how amazing it was to be so close to her.

She moved with me, her back arched, her breasts bouncing with every thrust and grind.

So damn perfect. Her eyes were on my mouth, on my lips, and I knew that if I showed her how badly I wanted her, if I made her come, she would either love me or hate me, and either way, I'd fall.

But I couldn't help myself. I plowed into her, every thrust

slow and hard, and she responded with a heartbreaking moan. I kissed her again, and the sound of our bodies slapping together filled the room, and I'd never needed anything more in my life. She kissed me, her tongue darting into my mouth, and I fucked her hard into the mattress. Her nails dug into my back, and she held on tight, her lips busy on my neck.

I wanted this female like I'd never wanted anything.

It was too much, I couldn't hold back any longer. I gripped her ass cheeks and fucked her like I'd never fucked another fae, my balls slapping against her ass with each stroke. She was wet and hot and gripping me tightly.

I thrust into her again and again, her moans adding fuel to the flames of my lust.

I lowered my head, catching her nipple between my lips, and sucked hard, tugging at the peak. Her moans grew louder, and she yanked my hair back and slammed her breasts against my chest. She was so incredibly sexy.

She cried out softly, and her entire body went hard. Her pussy clenched tight around me, pulsing, and her eyes closed, her face contorted in pleasure as she orgasmed. I bent to kiss her lips, and at the contact, I came hard and fast, pulsing inside her, lost in the sublime feeling of her body around mine and her soft lips submitting to my kisses.

I slowed my pace and watched as she came down from her climax, her body shuddering and her lips open in a deep sigh. I loved how her eyes looked, her brows raised and her mouth parted. Her black hair was messy and her cheeks red, and I fell deeper under her spell.

Panting, we locked eyes. Her startling green orbs filled with such depths that I couldn't dare to think they were mine, could only hope.

She bit her lower lip, and my spent cock twitched in response. "That was actually better than my dreams," she murmured. "Well done."

I laughed, then rolled off her onto my back, dragging her with me so she lay on my chest, her breasts squished against my chest at the periphery of my vision. "Challenge accepted," I said.

She rested her cheek against my neck and mumbled a reply, her hot breath warming my throat. "What challenge?" she asked.

I rested a hand on her ass and replied, "The challenge to always outperform your wildest, wettest dreams."

"Oh really?" she asked with a touch of snark. "You have your work cut out for you. My imagination is unrivaled."

"And I'll be without rivals, too," I growled, clutching her ass. A pulse of possessiveness rang through me, forming a bubble around me and my female that matched and enhanced the protectiveness I already felt for her. Man, this fae was unraveling me.

She had been fucking with my head for weeks, and now she was fucking with my heart.

Delph

I woke from my second post-sex coma brimming with enthusiasm like an overinflated balloon.

I had never seen anything more clearly in my life. Jayke Sansett had to be stopped. Pike was unlikely to ascend into Lightning, so we couldn't rely on him. I would die instantly if I was struck by lightning and unable to recover, so my ascending to the throne was also out of the question. So if I didn't want Prince Not-So-Charming to rule, Darzan had to.

I was still lying face down on his chest and belly, with my legs stretched between his. I rolled off slowly so as not to disturb him. He hadn't emerged from his coma yet and breathed deeply and steadily, only stirring a little when I slid partially off him, though I remained in bed. The fireplace still flickered with flames, but sunlight streamed through the window, livening up the black and blood-red room. It definitely needed a makeover.

Darzan had told me Bastian and Bree had ruled jointly and been well regarded by most Houses and that he'd expected their support to flow to him.

But the Prince Not-So-Charming had flashed his perfect smile, fluttered his long eyelashes, and demonstrated his Healing power and the nobles had come running.

Fine, I just have to unravel that support. I would go into full campaign mode and muster whatever charm I had to convince everybody to vote for Darzan.

He couldn't do it himself because his damn War power made everybody shrink at the sight of him. Nobody liked the sensation of a steel blade at their throat, and that's all anybody felt when they talked with Darzan, so I would have to step up to the plate myself.

Fine, I could do that.

A sound startled me, and the bedroom door opened to reveal the horned serving fae, Bert. I snatched up the blood-red silk sheets to cover my nudity, not worrying about covering Darzan's junk because he deserved everything he got by not warning me Bert might ambush us at any moment.

I pursed my lips. "What is it?" I snapped. I was all for being nice to the servants, but anybody who walked in on me in the nude would get their head bitten off, no matter who they were.

Bert tiptoed into the room without disturbing even an air molecule. "I have an urgent message," he said.

I glanced down at Darzan's sleeping form, his broad dark chest slowly rising and falling. I hated to disturb him, but I couldn't ignore the word *urgent*. "Go ahead and wake him," I whispered.

The horned fae ducked forward and handed me a note. "The message is for you," he said.

What? I took the small scroll from his outstretched, green-tinted hand. What the hell was going on? Probably a disapproving-fatherly rebuke from Jayke for not supporting him at the House dinner last night.

I hissed out the word "Asshole" as I unfurled the scroll, but when I read it, I realized I was wrong. It wasn't about last night. It wasn't even about me.

My breath lodged in my throat.

I regret to inform you that Mrs. Adele Smith passed away last night from cardiac arrest. Sincerely, Prince Sansett.

The note fell from my fingers and fluttered onto the blood-red sheet. Mrs Adele Smith. Grandma.

Grandma was dead. Dead. Numbness rolled over me, and I dropped the silk sheet, not caring that I was naked and Bert was still there. I was only distantly aware of the sheet floating about my waist, exposing my top half, while I thought about Hebes.

If I had been home looking after Grandma, she might have lived. She might never have had the heart attack in the first place—she had probably over-exerted herself because she had no help. If I was there, I could have saved her. Called an ambulance, pressed on her heart, and kept blood pumping through her veins.

But I wasn't there, and now she was dead. Fuck.

The numbness crept through my limbs but grew a sharp edge of guilt.

I climbed out of bed completely naked, forgetting to be embarrassed by my nudity but dimly noticing that Bert had already left the room. It was late morning and already warm, and I pulled on the nearest clothes I could find, green leather pants and a black tunic that had appeared in the closet, maybe borrowed from the neighbor whose name I hadn't bothered to learn. Fuck me, and fuck my selfishness.

I had to get out of here and clear my head. I couldn't breathe in this coffin of a room, weighed down by deep reds and dark wood, those awful flames flickering their reflections on the roof.

I had to leave. At the doorway, with my hand resting on the cold knob, I remembered the scrolls. I'd gone to so much trouble to find those fucking scrolls I couldn't leave without them.

Though it cost me, I trudged through molasses back across the bedroom and pulled open the desk drawer, but where the roll of paper should be, there were only tiny scraps.

No. I fell to my knees and picked up the largest remaining scrap, only for it to disintegrate through my fingers. *No.* The only clue to my mother's true heart was destroyed, torn from the world through my carelessness. Just like Grandma. I'd destroyed her through my own fucking selfishness.

I fled down the stairs and spilled onto the street, running along the cobblestones away from the sun.

Fae looked up, startled, as I passed, reading my raw desperation. I must've been giving serious fuck-off vibes because nobody approached me or attempted to provide comfort.

A War wielder didn't need comfort; she needed revenge.

The need to return to Hebes burned hot through my blood as my feet clattered over the cobblestones, but with every corner I rounded, every stride I took, the fiery need cooled, ebbing away as clarity returned to my thoughts. By the time I'd lost myself in the winding streets, the desire to return to the mortal realm was nothing but a smoking log in my chest.

I had no reason to go back. My reason was dead. Literally. Grandma was gone, and it was my fault as surely as if I'd plunged my own knife into her heart. The girls didn't need me, not really. Lexi was almost twenty now, a fully grown adult who could look after herself...even if she had an overinflated sense of her own badassery. I could leave it to her to keep the twins in line.

The scrolls were gone too. The only link to my parents other than the distorted stories of fae who barely knew them had disintegrated, and again the blame was mine.

Darzan told me not to remove the scroll from the library, that it needed to remain in the temperature-controlled environment at a precise humidity level, but I ignored him. I thought I knew best. I thought that because it was related to my family, the rules didn't apply to me.

Fuck.

I slowed to a walk. There was no point returning to Hebes. Jackson had always resented my existence, and his daughters were perfectly fine without me. I didn't belong there, I never had, but now I belonged even less.

I was a mangy half-blood who didn't belong anywhere.

My feet stumbled to a stop, and I looked around like I was searching for where I belonged. The cobblestones from the street climbed up a cottage that looked like it was birthed from the road, and I definitely hadn't seen that before. I was thoroughly lost in the streets of Capricia, but I didn't give a fuck. My overfilled balloon had popped, and I was now just a bedraggled, limp shell.

But then I started walking again as a single idea overrode my despair. One thought powered me, kept my legs moving, my lungs gulping, and returned heat to my veins. Revenge.

Jayke had stationed guards to protect my family and promised no ill would befall them. His fae could have called an ambulance. They could have fucking Healed her.

But maybe they were following orders not to. Or perhaps Jayke never sent guards in the first place. Maybe they even gave her the fucking cardiac arrest. I had no reason to trust that male.

My breaths pounded, and the streets flew past as a single thought crystallized. There was no doubt in my mind that he caused her death, either directly or not. He was responsible for my being in Caprice and for preventing my return to Hebes.

Jayke Sansett bought Grandma's death with my imprisonment, and I wouldn't rest until I paid him back.

Darzan

I woke up with a soft smile, a memory of last night lingering like a kiss. Without opening my eyes, I patted the bed beside me, searching for Delph's warm body. Last night was amazing, and I wanted more of her. My cock was already getting hard as my hand slid along the blood-red sheets, but the sheets were cold.

My eyes shot open, and my heart sank.

She was gone.

She had been here last night, hot and writhing beneath me, and it felt like she was as desperate for me as I was for her. We had been making love—at least, that's how it felt to me. But not to her, obviously.

When did she leave? How long ago? Did she try to wake me? Why didn't she say anything? I felt abandoned. Devastated. I fucking shouldn't, but I did.

I pushed myself out of bed. I shouldn't be upset. I didn't really know her, and she didn't owe me a cuddle and a shared breakfast. I had no right to be upset. But I was.

Fuck her for doing this to me. Fuck me for allowing it.

She was never mine to begin with. I struggled to keep my anger at bay, but it roared to be free. Delph was a cruel tease. A seductress. A viper. A fucking succubus.

Heaving a shaky breath, I dressed quickly, determined not to let her ruin my day. It had been the best night of sleep I'd gotten in a long time. As I slipped into my boots, the black bedroom door opened quietly, and Bert scurried in silently.

"Good morning, sir," he droned.

"What is it?" I snapped.

He bowed slightly, unfazed by my rudeness. "I wish to inform you that Delphinium Athar has departed," he said. "She—"

"Yes, I can see that," I barked, dismissing him with a wave. "Get me some breakfast. I'll be downstairs soon. Then take the day off. I don't want to see you again today." I needed Bert out of the way before tonight's foray against Sansett Palace.

"But—"

"Go!" I roared.

Before I went downstairs, I needed to pull myself together. Delph pissing off shouldn't upset me this much, and I needed to get her out of my damn head so I could focus on what mattered.

Ruining Jayke's reputation.

I crossed to the small window and looked out on the street. This was where I'd breathed into Delph's throat and felt her soft, sweet pussy for the first time. She'd started off looking out the window at the narrow street, and when she'd turned at my voice, her lips were already parted and her eyes soft, her long black hair framing her white face.

Shit. My cock twitched at the memory, and I cursed and ground my jaw. She wasn't important now. She never had been. So why the hell wouldn't she leave my head alone?

When I could finally go thirty seconds without wanting to cry or getting a hard-on, I allowed myself downstairs to have my breakfast. It was dim and dark, as usual, and looked more lifeless and drab than ever. I didn't have a Magirus, and Bert was a terrible cook, so I made do with stale puffermuffins and a strong black coffee, sitting in the echoing stone dining room alone.

The day dragged like a snail on Valium while I tried to keep my thoughts on the plan for the evening's raid. In the late afternoon, Pike and his small band of warriors turned up at my door, and Delph mostly left my thoughts alone.

The group crowded around my dining table, rummaging through my kitchen for scraps and complaining when they didn't find much. The hustle and bustle were distracting, even though the scraping of chairs and clinking of glasses were interspersed with grumbling.

Pike wanted me to join the raid, I could read it in his emerald eyes. But that made no sense. "I need to keep my hands clean," I explained for the second time, as much for my benefit as his. "The whole point is to make Jayke look like a hothead, so I need to stay out of it."

Pike's green eyes flashed, but he saw my logic. The whole point of the exercise was to provoke Jaykey-boy into a petty squabble that revealed him as immature, and I couldn't get caught up as collateral damage.

Pike was an accomplished fighter, but he didn't wield War. I'd insisted on him taking another War wielder; his band of warriors was experienced, so he would have plenty of protection.

Finally, night fell, and the time arrived for Pike and his warriors to leave. They donned black armor and crept out under the cover of dark, heading for Sansett Palace.

The night crawled by on shattered knees as my thoughts

turned over. Without other distractions, I kept thinking about Delph. She was gone. I'd fondled her, fucked her, and fallen for her, and she paid me back by fleeing into the night. Trust was a rare and fragile commodity, and my trust in Delph was at risk of shattering. Why the hell had she run off? Why hadn't she sent word all day? When would she return? If ever...

But I couldn't focus on Delph, on my fucking heart. Not while my brother's life was in danger. He was leading the offense at Palace Sansett, following my instructions and hoping to provoke an attack and expose Jayke as an unstable and violent fae.

I imagined Pike and his small band walking the perimeter of the palace grounds, poking at the wards, dancing and joking as though it was a lark. I hoped they knew how dangerous House Sansett could be.

I tried to sleep, lying alone in my bed, staring at the flames from my fireplace flickering off the dark paneled ceiling and wondering if I should have gone with him.

I should have heard something by now. Pike should have banged on my front door and collapsed onto one of my armchairs, laughing and telling me how he'd insulted, galled, and enraged the prince. He should be shouting and joking and complaining about my lack of potions.

But Pike hadn't turned up. He wasn't here laughing, which made me worry that he was somewhere else, bleeding.

"Fuck it," I hissed. There was no point lying in bed staring at the ceiling while failing to sleep, so I dressed quickly and went downstairs with a book.

The book lay unopened across my lap as I swapped out staring at the dark paneled ceiling of my bedchamber with staring at the flickering flames in the living room fireplace.

The flames turned my mind to the fires of hell and the cursed demons who lived there. Gaia's curse had never affected Pike and me because we were never contenders for the throne. But now that I'd proposed myself as the next king, did that endanger Pike's life? I should never have sent him off on that fool's errand.

The fire warmed my face and should have been comforting, but my mind whirled just as chaotically as it had in my bedroom. But it was better down here because I wasn't constantly reminded of Delph's absence by the emptiness in my bed. Down here, I could forget I had fallen for her and forget she had disappeared in the night.

With a jolt, I remembered the scroll and ran upstairs, my feet thumping on every tread. In my bedroom, I yanked open the desk drawer only to find a million flecks of paper scattered inside.

My heart sank. She would be devastated at the loss. She'd pinned so much hope on those scrolls—pinned her entire identity on them, and now they were gone.

With a slow step, I returned to my watching post in the downstairs living room, picked up the leather bound novel and rested it across my knee, playing with its fraying cover while I resumed staring at the flickering flames.

I would wait until morning, then I would find answers. Like why the hell Delph had fled in the middle of the night. And whether my brother still lived.

Jayke

As soon as the unfae Bastian died, I'd commanded that every plant in my greenhouse be removed except one. I knew nature would turn against us, but I figured I could manage a single specimen.

The greenhouse hailed from my grandparents' era and was constructed of sandstone and glass cut in irregular shapes, the entire structure mimicking the form of a flower.

I used to come here to relax, breathing in the moist air and enjoying the scent of dirt, the scuffle of worms, and the faint whispers of the plants growing.

But now I came in here to practice. The remaining plant was vicious and snarling but couldn't get through the basic protective bubble I'd spelled around me. I closed my eyes and gathered my Healing power into the palms of my hands, then hurled it toward the plant, trying to calm nature's rage and bring it to heel.

My victory was so close I could taste it, could reach out and touch its golden form. Soon I would be king. And the inept rule of the Athars would finally be consigned to history.

But with that victory came an undeniable fear. Everybody knew that nature in Caprice was tied to the ruler. From the deepest tree roots to the falling rain, the king dictated every element.

What if nature remained unruly after I was elected? I'd searched every book and scroll I could find on the topic, looking for information on how nature responded when a ruler was elected rather than chosen by Gaia, and I'd found nothing. Would Gaia recognize me as a true leader after I was elected by fae?

If she didn't, and nature remained savage, my reign would be short. The fae wouldn't take long to rise against me, declare me unfit, and choose another ruler. I couldn't allow that.

Hence my attempts to Heal the wildness out of this plant. If I could channel my magic to cure a single plant, it logically followed that I could extend it to the entire realm, and my longevity would be assured.

So far, I'd had little luck. Every time I released my air shield to send a burst of Healing to the plant, it lashed out and scored me with deep lacerations. I Healed myself time and again, but impatience bloomed within me.

The moon shone brightly through the panes of glass, refracting into faint rainbows all over the greenhouse floor. It was beautiful, and I took a deep breath while I looked at the shimmering hues on the sandstone floor.

I didn't need to solve this problem immediately. Soon I would be king and have every resource in the realm available to solve the problem of nature.

The door to the greenhouse burst open, and I whirled around, my eyes blazing. My serving fae were under strict instructions never to disturb me at work. "How dare you—" I began, only to falter as I recognized Lucius, one of the few fae brave enough to ever question me. The look on his face stopped my reprimand cold in its tracks—something was seriously wrong.

If it had been any fae other than Lucius, I would have sent them away immediately, but the look on the Weaver's face gave me pause.

He bowed slightly, hands clasped in front of him. "My prince," he said. His voice trembled. "Our perimeter is under attack. You must come quickly."

I bristled at being issued an order and resisted the urge to rebuke him. I followed him without hesitation, my bare feet slapping against the cool marble floor as we rushed through well-lit hallways and climbed up the tower's winding staircase.

I peered through the night. A brigade of fae was attempting to penetrate the wards surrounding the palace grounds. I recognized one of them immediately, with light green skin and emerald hair. Pike fucking Davin, a would-be usurper who was finally showing his true colors as nothing more than an errand boy for his older brother, and an inept one at that.

"Send a troop of guards to repel them," I boomed.

Moments later, I watched with satisfaction as a dozen of my guards trotted in formation across the grass toward the intruders. The guards were heavily armed; each carried a sword and shield, and magic glittered along the edges of their steel blades. They battled at the palace perimeter, and every splash of Davin blood that spilled across the grass made me smile.

Ten years ago, I commanded my Weaver to construct a barrier around my perimeter that mimicked the enchanted throne room and would kill anybody who attempted to cross it with ill intent. That would be the ultimate protection. Anybody who wished me harm could either stay off my property or die.

But the enchantments were too complex, the intricacies of their spells lost with the ancient Weavers, and the best any modern spellcaster could manage was to erect a barrier to prevent entry.

Nevertheless, it gave my soldiers an advantage. They could charge through the barrier to attack, then retreat beyond it to safety. Even so, I saw that Pike's band included a War wielder, so although they were outnumbered two to one, the intruders held their own.

I barked another order without hesitation. "Send two more troops of guards—and tell them to show no mercy! If these intruders dare challenge me, let death be their only fate."

I didn't relish murder, and I never would have attacked the Davin brothers, but anger boiled hot inside me at their brazen attempt, and I watched with a smile as more of my loyal warriors marched across the grass to join their brethren in battle.

The sound of swords ringing was battle's symphony, each note intensifying my anticipation as I watched Pike Davin's band fight brutally. I didn't resent it. A few lives lost were nothing compared with the good that would come of my reign. I would end the weakness and sympathy that was the hallmark of the Athar era and replace it with strength that would make Caprice the envy of all the realms.

Several of my lesser Weavers stood within the perimeter and cast stunning spells at the attackers. They were rarely strong enough to kill, but they incapacitated for long enough that my swordsmen could make the final strike.

The intruders began to fall one by one, their lifeblood staining the ground and filling the air with an acrid scent of metallic death. And yet, despite his weakened state, Pike Davin managed to hold off three of my guards. He was impressive for Unascended faeling, parrying with his sword and meeting them stroke for stroke. But when a fourth and then a fifth surrounded him, I saw the widening of his emerald eyes and couldn't help the grim satisfaction that settled in my heart.

Pike Davin screamed, and I embraced the bloodcurdling sound. There would be no mercy here – only justice in a world that would soon bow before me in awe.

Delph

Anger coursed through me as I lost myself in the maze of cobblestone and forested streets.

I tried to direct the anger at Jayke, but it inevitably turned onto me. If only I'd avoided capture in the Hebes town square. If only I'd struck a better bargain with Jayke. If only I'd made more of an effort to return. If only I'd listened to Darzan and left the scroll in the library.

If only I wasn't such a fucking idiot.

I turned down a forested avenue that didn't look too intimidating, not caring about the overgrown roots that seemed to reach out and trip my ankles. I was beyond caring about anything.

A slight fae female with orange irises and orange curls tucked tight behind her pointed ears called out when I passed her home. "Good morning, Delph," she hollered. She sat on a stool made from an oversized sunflower that she clearly had under magical control because it wasn't trying to eat her.

I paused at her use of my nickname. I was used to being recognized wherever I went for being the infamous Athar daughter, the insipid, spineless pet of House Sansett. But apart from Darzan, everybody else in Arathay called me Delphinium.

I was in no mood for pleasantries, so I got right to the point. "Why did you call me Delph?" I asked.

The fae smiled and put down her work, which I had assumed was knitting but, on closer inspection, looked far more complicated. It used four separate pointed needles and threads of various colors, one floating in a very not-obedient-to-gravity way. "Your mother always said she would name you for the flower but call you for love," she explained.

My mouth fell open as I took in this female more closely. Her face was kind, perhaps beginning to show the faintest sign of age around her eyes, but crinkly smile lines that made her look wholesome and approachable. Her tight orange curls looked like they'd spring back in if I pulled them, and her gaze was soft.

And she had mentioned Mom. My heart leaped, but I couldn't get carried away. Still, I couldn't keep the hope from my voice as I asked, "You knew my mother?"

"We used to be neighbors," the female said. "She lived in that house for three years when she first arrived in Capricia." The orange-haired fae indicated a ring of trees growing so close together they formed a wall, a magnificent living wall shaped in a rough circle. A thought seemed to occur to the fae. "Would you like to see inside, dear?"

"Yes," I barked, unable to keep the urgency from my tone.

The fae smiled and nodded. "Of course you would. Follow me."

She got to her feet lightly, and I let her lead the way to the tree-trunk house. A narrow curved door painted red eased open to reveal an interior overgrown with crisscrossing roots and snapping flowers. Nature had taken over here. It was like a dystopian film.

"I'm Lilia, by the way," the woman said. Lilia shooed away a flower that snapped at her bubble skirt, and for some reason, it obeyed her.

"Do you have nature magic?" I asked. Her command over these wild plants was astonishing. I hadn't encountered any other fae who could control the wildlife. Most folks stuck to the cobblestone streets these days because at least the stones didn't bite.

Lilia huffed. "No, I ascended into Serpens." Her orange pupils narrowed into slits, and orange scales flickered across her skin as she began shifting into a huge snake form. But before transforming completely, she shook the change away and returned to her fae form. "I wouldn't recommend it, dear," she said as though we were discussing a film. "It's surprising how rarely being a giant snake is useful."

Holy crap. A giant snake sounded fucking awesome, and I figured that beneath her kind exterior, this Lilia chick was pretty kickass. She must have killed herself with a poisonous adder or something during her Ascension. I'd heard of Lupus, the giant wolf shifters, but I didn't know fae could ascend into other animals. That opened a whole world of possibilities for me as I neared my twenty-fifth birthday... if a half-fae could even ascend.

But War sang to me as a hum on the air itself, and I knew I would choose the brilliant aliveness of battle if given the chance. I never felt more alive, or more like myself, than during a fight. I just hoped I'd use it as nobly as Darzan did, to defend those in need, not to take what I wanted for myself. Given that I'd just killed my grandmother with my selfishness, I didn't like the odds.

Lilia shooed away a large beetle with piercing fangs, and it eyed her from its eight massive eyeballs before clicking and scuttling away with its antennae lowered in shame. "These plants and bugs just need a firm hand," she said as the beetle scurried under a fallen rhubarb leaf. "And obviously, they behave better while you're here."

What? That comment had me rocking back onto my heels. "What do you mean they behave better when I'm here?" I demanded. What the hell did I have to do with anything? I hadn't noticed nature being particularly obedient around me, that was for sure.

Lilia shooed a creeping vine with nasty thorns off a small wooden stool and motioned me to sit. "Nature knows your parents were king and queen, and they owe some allegiance to you," she explained.

I sat on the wooden stool, finding it surprisingly comfortable, and adjusted my green leather pants. "That's bullshit," I said. "A field of mushrooms tried to eat me, and a street came to life and started suffocating me."

Lilia trilled a laugh as though I'd just told a wonderful joke. "They were just saying hello. If they really wanted to hurt you, you wouldn't be standing before me."

"I'm not standing; I'm sitting," I said. It was fucking petulant, but it just slipped out, and she didn't take offense. She just trilled another laugh.

"Just like your mother," Lilia said.

I leaned forward and rested my elbows on my knees. Some of the tension in my shoulders melted away as I tried to absorb the fact I was sitting in my mother's old kitchen. If I squinted and used a lot of imagination, I could see a cozy wooden cottage with a blazing fire and pots hanging by the window. I sighed. "Will you tell me about her?" I asked.

Lilia sat on the stool opposite me and slapped away a thorn that tried to burrow into her ankle. "Your mother was a mortal woman who started her life here with little respect," she said, keeping one eye on the plants and the other on me. "She worked hard to earn the fae's esteem, and she ended up ruling over us as a much-loved monarch. She was a remarkable woman, and you'd do well to heed her lessons."

I deflated, sagging into the stool as I watched two worms wrestling with a flower. I could almost hear their wet slithering. "I can't learn from her," I admitted, "because I lost the only scroll I could find with any information about her."

Lilia scowled, and I knew I deserved it. "You won't learn about your mother from a dusty old scroll, Delph," she said sternly. "You can learn about her from me and from listening to your own heart. And there is one thing I am sure she would tell you if she were here."

Oh Lord, this was the closest I'd ever been to my mother. Grandma always talked about her daughter as a failure and a disappointment, a tale of warning. Never as someone who could dispense wisdom.

And here was this orange-hued stranger showing me a completely different person to the junkie I'd always pictured.

My toes tingled, and I wriggled them, trying to work feeling into them, but it didn't. "What is it?" I breathed, anticipation heavy in my limbs. I hoped this would be a golden nugget, not a shit nugget, and I told myself not to care too much, but my words tumbled out like a schoolgirl's. "What would my mother say? Please tell me."

Lilia looked at me, blinking slowly. Just when I couldn't bear the silence a moment longer, she spoke. "She would tell you not to listen when people say you can't do something but to follow your instincts." She paused and looked at me while I tried to figure out what the hell that meant.

"Um, okay," I began.

"You were born to rule, Delph," Lilia said firmly, "and you shouldn't let any nonsense about being half-human deter you. Your mother was fully human, and she was the Queen of Caprice for a hundred years. Her strength and courage are yours."

I'd known Mom was human, but I hadn't registered that she'd been a human queen of a fae realm. "But she was only queen because she married Dad," I said, searching for a flaw in her argument.

"Maybe, maybe not," Lilia said. "Anyway, you have your mother's strength and your father's magic. And his ferocity, if I'm not mistaken. You would make a better ruler than any of the bozos who've thrown their hats in the ring."

Yes, they were fucking bozos. Well, Jayke was, anyway. I didn't know what Darzan was...a sex God, sure, but also a warmonger without any people skills. Or fae skills.

But that didn't mean I'd be a better ruler. Did it? Was Lilia really suggesting that I should try to claim my throne? "But if I am struck by lightning, I'll sizzle," I said, still looking for flaws in her argument. "I don't have enough power to ascend to Lightning power."

I knew I was trying to find reasons why she was wrong, though I couldn't be sure why I was resisting. A blind sewer rat would make a better ruler than Jayke Sansett, and Darzan may have the right heart for the job, but he didn't have the people skills.

Lilia smiled gently, and more tension ebbed from my muscles. She really was a calming presence. I could see why my mother had befriended her. "Then find another way," she said in a tone that brooked no argument. "Lightning isn't the only route to the crown."

Not the only route to the crown? But it was, wasn't it? Unless I could get voted in. Perhaps Lilia was right and I could gather the support of the noble Houses to be elected their queen. After all, Jayke had gone to the trouble of kidnapping me from the mortal realm, so he obviously thought I had a lot of sway.

Those thoughts whirled in the back of my head while I spent the rest of the afternoon plundering Lilia's brain for information about my parents, listening to the scuttling of bugs and keeping an eye on the wriggling floor. She'd known my mother well, had been best friends with her for many years before Mom moved to the Spike, and had been received at the Spike many times during Mom's reign. She knew my mother a lot better than my father but had good things to say about both of them.

My deflated balloon husk grew a little plumper, a little firmer, as Lilia blew reassuring breaths into my hurting soul.

Darzan

Impatience clawed at me as I sat on the blood-red leather armchair staring into the fire, my book still unopened on my lap. I'd worn a patch into the leather cover, and the warmth from the popping fire was beginning to feel oppressive.

It was still early, but I couldn't wait any longer, couldn't sit back on my cushy ass while my brother's life may be in danger.

He'd only been supposed to taunt Jayke, not engage the fae in battle, and he should have been here long ago. He had promised to report to me before going elsewhere, but I just had to hope he'd forgotten or disregarded that vow and taken his comrades to a tavern instead.

But I couldn't sit around here a moment longer waiting to find out.

I dressed and pulled open my front door to find two fae on my stoop, a bloodied, ragged female from my brother's band with her fist raised to knock and a small but fierce looking faeling with a scowl on her small face.

I blinked and momentarily imagined that I had manifested my twin fears into reality—a bloodied soldier representing Pike and a fierce female representing Delph.

The soldier spoke first, her voice carried on a cold gust of wind that brought goosebumps to my neck. She was blood-soaked, her jerkin torn, and had clearly come straight from battle. "House Sansett overran us," she said steadily, her pink eyes blazing. "The prince sent dozens of guards to fight us with orders to kill. They reasoned that defense of their property was justification for our slaughter."

My blood pounded in my ears. I should have known Jayke would escalate it, use it as an excuse for murder. Fuck. "And Pike? What of him?"

The soldier swallowed thickly. "I'm afraid he didn't make it, my prince," she said. "He has taken the journey."

I stared at the soldier, trying to understand what she was telling me. Her pink hair was splashed with red, maybe some of it my brother's. Her bronze jerkin was covered in dark splotches that could be mud or more blood, and her expression was fierce.

"Dead?" I asked, trying to make sense of her Gaia-be-damned euphemism. Trying to make sense of the world.

"Yes, prince. I'm sorry."

My brother was dead.

I motioned jerkily behind me. "Go inside and clean yourself up," I barked, and the guard nodded, then swept past me into my house. My brother was dead. Pike was dead. Gaia had cursed him, and I would never forgive her, but the blame was mine. I'd made a bid for the throne and then deliberately put him in danger. What the hell had I done?

The breeze picked up, a cold gust that made me shiver. The other messenger still stood before me, blinking up at me. A young female with stubby blue horns who couldn't be more than twelve years old but had braved the pre-dawn streets alone. The one who reminded me of Delph. "And what of you?" I snapped, still trying to piece together the reality of my brother's death.

She looked in alarm over my shoulder to where the bloodied soldier had disappeared, then dipped a small curtsy and recited a message she had clearly memorized. "Princess Delphinium Athar wishes to inform you of her intention to claim the Crown of Caprice. She seeks the support of House Davin and the other noble Houses for this evening's coronation."

The faeling dipped another shaky curtsy before turning and fleeing up the street, her skirt blowing out behind her in the wind.

I couldn't contain my emotions any longer. They flowed through me as hot and pulsing as an erupting volcano, sadness and guilt and red-hot fucking rage.

I tore along the streets at a run, the cobblestones, bushes, and houses blurring beside me. My thighs pumped as I drove my anger and fear into my legs, pounding through the streets. Pike. Delph. It was too much. I needed the physical escape of running, smashing my thoughts into mush.

I dived into a moonway I hadn't used in years, though its location was seared in my memory. This path led to the place of my father's destruction and my family's downfall, and though I'd vowed never to return, I found myself sprinting closer.

My turmoil didn't lessen as I devoured leagues upon leagues, traveling west through Caprice until my legs ached and my breathing grew ragged. I panted heavily, not having run so far or so fast in a long time, just needing to pump blood through my organs and muscles so it couldn't flow through my brain.

It took me a few ragged gasps before I recognized Gameer,

the town that was razed to the ground by Traal Blunt's betrayal of my father. It looked bone white and lifeless in the early morning, and the only movement was a trail of leaves being rustled and blown by the cold wind, which had followed me all the way here.

Looking at the sad village, I reminded myself of a hard truth. This was the consequence of trust. I should have known better than to give my heart to a female, especially a half-human who didn't understand a thing about Arathay. I should have known better than to trust her. I should have known she would eventually betray me too.

And she had. I had done nothing but show her kindness, though she never recognized it as such, and she had thrown it all in my face by declaring her intention to run for queen. Didn't she understand how disastrous that was for our bid to keep Sansett off the throne? The little support I had would be split between our two Houses, assuring Jayke's victory.

By declaring she wanted the crown, she had just fucking handed it to Sansett.

Her betrayal stung deeper than I thought, and I felt a cleaving of my heart, but the sensation was distant, as though on the far side of a fog, because I couldn't overcome the fact of my brother's death.

My brother, the only fae in the world I truly trusted, was dead. And it was my fault.

I'd convinced him to foray into Sansett Palace and refused to accompany him. He wasn't even Ascended yet, and I wielded War, yet I sent him off to fight a battle on my behalf.

The cold wind gusted, roaring around me. Delph's betrayal pierced my heart, but Pike's death shattered my soul, and I knew the guilt would trail me for the rest of my life.

Jayke

I donned a long silver cloak with silver lines embroidered through it that reminded an observer of Lightning. Tonight I would be crowned the King of Caprice, and I wanted to draw every possible association between me and the realm. I wouldn't take any chances.

I strode along the moonway to the city to tie off the final loose ends. The wildflowers outside my estate would soon be obedient and sweet, and nature would be set to rights.

My cloak fluttered behind me impressively, and I allowed myself to smile. I no longer had to worry about Pike being chosen by Gaia. He had always been unlikely to ascend into Lightning, but even that dim chance had been removed because the youngest Davin brother lay shackled in my dungeon.

My men had surrounded him last night and captured him. He was the only member of the invading band I ordered kept alive because I didn't want his death on my conscience. And I didn't want to owe House Davin a blood debt. Too many longstanding feuds had poisoned too many reigns, and I refused to be among their number.

But he would remain in my dungeon until after the Ascension rite, so I had deftly removed the remote possibility of him becoming king. A smile licked my cheeks. Shame he would remain Unascended for his entire life, but that was a small price to pay for a bountiful future.

I emerged from the moonway onto the cobblestone streets of Capricia and strolled along with my head held high. The fae who saw me scattered or bowed, and I was pleased to note there were more in the latter group than there used to be. Already the lesser fae were expecting me as their ruler, and soon they would prostrate themselves before me.

Bastian never required that of his subjects, but I would. A king feared is a king respected.

The House dinner had buoyed my confidence to record heights. Almost every House made it clear they would choose me as their king over that warmongering monster Darzan. The Davin bid for the throne was dead.

Which just left the half-blood traitor, Delphinium.

Heat rose and thickened in my throat when I thought about her betrayal. I'd plucked her from obscurity and turned her into a fae princess, and she had thanked me by turning on me, aligning herself with my enemy, and then declaring her own bid for the throne. A messenger had arrived in the early morning to announce her bid, and my blood had been simmering ever since.

I would die before I allowed another Athar to rule Caprice. Her reign would be even more lax than her parents', and I dreaded how unruly the realm would become under her leadership.

No, I had to make sure that never happened. Hence my early trip to the capital.

I spent the morning visiting the key Houses and shoring up their support. I let them know there may be a last-minute grab for power from House Athar and was pleased by their responses.

My favorite was when Dorot Ranson said, "That mortal girl has already shown herself to be led by the nose like a compliant ass. First by you, when you paraded her from party to party, and now by Darzan Davin. She will never have my support as a leader."

I loved that image. It was exactly what I'd been doing, of course. By retrieving her from Hebes, not only was I giving myself an Athar's support, but I was taking her out of the running by showing her to be a follower, not a leader.

And she had walked the line willingly with smiles and thank-yous. It gave me a shiver of happiness to know that despite her inherently violent nature, I'd plied her into a caricature of submissiveness.

When her messenger arrived at my palace gates announcing her bid for the throne, I covered my fury with a laugh. The half-mortal's arrogance was breathtaking. She assumed she could announce that she would be queen at the very last minute without so much as having a conversation with a single House, and the whole realm would fall over itself to elect her.

Life didn't work that way. Every single fae I spoke to assured me their support would remain with me even if her parents returned from the grave. Every fae except Thorne, the cantankerous dick from Fen, who told me straight I'd make a bad leader and would swap his vote to Delphinium if he had one. Luckily for me, he didn't get a vote, although he was influential in Verda.

Well, his opinion wouldn't matter. Pike was in my dungeon, Darzan had already been cast aside by the fae who mattered, and Delphinium didn't stand a chance.

By the time I arrived outside Lurlin Forest as the sun dipped below the mountains, casting long shadows from the trees, I knew the future of Caprice was assured. Finally, a competent fae would be king.

Darzan

I stayed on the outskirts of Gameer because I didn't trust myself not to slaughter the first fae I saw.

Instead, I released my War power on the flora and fauna. A transmogrified version of a wild boar, with enormous tusks and fangs as sharp as any jaguar's, ran at me from behind a clump of rocks. I roared in satisfaction as I sliced its head from its body, letting the spurting blood splatter my tunic. I deserved nothing more than to be bathed in blood and have evidence of my guilt cover me from head to toe.

This wasn't the boar's blood, this was Pike's blood, and it dripped red from my hands.

Another boar charged after the first, and I hoped it would strike me down, stomp its ink-black hooves over my heart, but my War instinct kicked in, and I sliced this one vertically, cleaving it in half and letting its hot blood soak into my hair. Gaia's curse had felled my brother, and now I would fell Gaia's children.

Time and again, boars appeared from behind the boulders and charged me one by one, and time and again, I wished for them to be victorious, but I failed to die.

Finally, I sagged in a heap among the hulking corpses, panting in misery.

A sense of being watched descended over me...being watched by something other than lifeless eyeballs. An elderly fae walked closer, approaching steadily over the uneven grass, picking her way among the bloody debris. She should be terrified after witnessing me at my worst, yet still, she came on. Perhaps she was mad.

Lucky for her, I was spent of bloodlust.

Her voice was weathered with age. "Those boars have been causing us no end of trouble around here," she said shakily. "You've done us a great service."

I refused to accept praise for my violence. "I didn't do it for you, I did it for me," I spit.

I willed her to walk away. Who knew how long until my bloodlust reared inside me again and I sliced her into pieces, leaving her wrinkled body lying among the scattered tusks and hooves.

"Nevertheless, you've done us a service," she said, unfazed by my violence. "A bad action can have a positive outcome, you know."

I snapped my head at her. "A bad action is always bad, no matter how much lipstick it wears," I growled. "You of all people should know that."

She wasn't taken aback by my rude tone. I supposed she'd seen and heard all manner of acrimony during her centuries walking the earth. "Why me, of all people?" She asked, showing genuine curiosity like this was the first interesting thing anybody had said to her in years.

"Because you live in Gameer," I snarled, clenching my fingers into the blood-soaked earth, feeling the grit of dirt beneath my nails. "This place was destroyed by the Ourean Army. You must have known people who died, loved ones, family. The loss of life was immense, and every building was flattened, so how can you stand there and calmly tell me that even bad actions have a positive outcome?"

She nodded slowly, her sluggish movements flaming my anger. "Our village is more prosperous now than ever," she said. "We rebuilt it stronger and more practical, more beautiful too if you're into those things. Every fae has a good home, and the fields and lands are more bounteous than ever. The loss of life was a tragedy, but there's no point hanging onto the past. The past is a complete scroll, but the future is yet to be written."

This fae had seen more of the world than I had by a significant measure, and her tragedy and loss were even greater than mine. I bet she'd lost family members in the Battle of Gameer, yet she spoke calmly about forgetting the past and moving forward.

I watched the blood pool out of a dead boar and trail in rivulets through the grass. "If we forget the past, we'll never learn from it," I thundered, though some of the bite had gone from my tongue.

She looked at me, her watery aqua eyes looking into my own. "I didn't say forget the past, young one," she snapped. "I said not to dwell there. Your father's mistakes are not your own, and your life will play out differently."

The aqua-haired fae sat on a boulder and rested. She emanated peace, and although that was anathema to my War-born essence, her presence relaxed me.

Perhaps she was right. I needed to release the bundle of my father's errors I had carried around for so long. My path would be different from his. He trusted too much, but perhaps I trusted too little.

I climbed wearily to my feet, and although the air carried the scent of blood, the burden of guilt was slightly less on my shoulders. I could never excuse myself for my brother's death, and I didn't want to. I might never recover from Pike's death or my role in it, but perhaps I could learn to trust.

Princess Delphinium Athar had more chance of gathering the support of the noble Houses and the fae from other realms than I did, so perhaps her bid wasn't an act of betrayal but one of faith. Faith in our mutual plan to keep Sansett from the throne.

Faith I would have to carry.

Delph

I woke in a small but comfortable cot in Lilia's sweet stone cottage. Two small windows on the south wall let in the orange-gold light of the rising sun, which reflected off the bronze poker beside the stone fireplace on the wall opposite my cot.

As I slid out of the sheets, a loud creak and a pop of wood startled me.

I hadn't quite dared to spend the night in my mother's old home all by myself at nature's mercy because no matter how confident Lilia was that it wouldn't try to kill me, I certainly wasn't.

Pulling on the same borrowed green leather pants and black tunic as yesterday, I wandered downstairs to the kitchen, a cozy wood and stone room with a crackling fire and a delicious smell of freshly baked cake.

"Good morning," I said when I found Lilia awake and seated at the kitchen table. "That smells amazing."

Honestly, I was happy just to have survived the night in a forested street without being eaten by an oversized ant or strangled by an errant vine. But it looked like I was going to be fed too. Buttery fruit toast and fluffy vanilla cakes, from the looks of it.

Lilia wore a bright orange dress patterned with sunflowers which was very cheerful and worked beautifully with her tight orange curls. She was already knitting, which looked even more complicated this morning.

"Are you making a sweater?" I asked uncertainly.

"Oh no," she said. "I could never make anything so complex. I'm just making some wardrobe guardians." She balanced her four knitting needles precariously, with one in her mouth, while she slid a mug of berry-scented tea across the wooden table.

I sipped the hot tea, which was full of berries and honey and tasted divine. "Ta," I murmured. "What are wardrobe guardians."

Lilia picked up her needles and resumed her work. "Oh, just these little guys who look after your wardrobe. Protect it from moths and gnomes, you know, the usual."

I spluttered and spilled hot tea onto the table, which I tried to casually wipe away with my black sleeve. "You're knitting a creature? Like, a living, breathing animal?"

Lilia's orange eyes twinkled. "The trick is in choosing the right heartstring." She nodded at the floaty pink-and-gray thread that was defying gravity and weaving itself around the pointed tip of Lilia's right ear.

"Of course," I said, mesmerized by the naughty thread that was apparently called a heartstring and could imbue life into knitwear.

"And they're not really alive. But they're very committed to the job. I once got a nasty injury from one when it thought I was stealing a scarf." She shook her head at the memory, and her ringlets bobbed around her neck.

My shoulders tensed as I nibbled on the fluffiest vanillaiest cake I'd ever eaten. "Th-there's something I don't under-stand," I began hesitantly. "About Mom."

Lilia glanced up from her knitting. "What is it, dear?"

This had been swirling in the back of my mind since I'd taken the scroll and dared to truly believe in my Mom as someone special. If she wasn't a heroin addict, absorbed in her own technicolor world, then why the hell wasn't she with me?

"Why...why did she give me up?" There, the question thudded onto the table between us. I was scared of the answer because it couldn't be good. What could have forced the Queen of Caprice to abandon her child? It had to be something to do with my father. Had he forced her? But if so, why hadn't she found any way to come and visit me over all the years?

"Oh, honey, it's because of Gaia's curse," Lilia said. "Royal families can only have one child. If they are unlucky enough to have a second child, Gaia kills it. It's just the way of things. So they sent you away to keep you alive. Bree was scared to death of losing you."

I put down my vanilla cake and wriggled on my stool. It suddenly felt hard and unforgiving under my ass. "Scared of losing me? But I don't have any older brother or sister, do I?" I demanded. I leaped to my feet, and the stool clattered to the stone floor.

Lilia kept knitting, and I sensed it was calming for her. "Your older brother died, dear, many years ago."

"So why didn't Mom come and get me after he died?" Should I feel sad about a dead older brother I hadn't even met? Hell, I didn't even know he existed ten seconds ago, so I couldn't summon up any grief. But I did feel sad about Mom leaving me in Hebes instead of whisking me into her magical world.

Lilia's face was heavy. "Bree was terrified of losing you too, dear. She just couldn't risk it. And she always thought she'd have more time." The grandmotherly fae was mired in grief, remembering her old friend and her early departure from the world.

The fire crackled beside us, casting dancing shadows across the cozy kitchen and highlighting the orange in Lilia's eyes. I watched her knit, her old fingers moving in a complicated pattern across the threads and needles, darting, ducking, and weaving with practiced ease. Had her mother taught her how to do that? Or her siblings?

"But what about the other princes? They have siblings. Leena and Jayne Sansett, and Pike Davin. Gaia's curse didn't kill them," I said. It was hard to believe in a crazy old curse when the evidence showed it didn't exist.

"Oh, those old wannabes were never in true contention for the throne," Lilia muttered. "At least, not until recently. Gaia's curse only applies to those next in line for the throne."

My spine straightened as the implication hit home. If Gaia cursed the siblings of the next in line for the throne, then by throwing his hat in the ring for the crown, Darzan had put Pike's life in danger.

"So, Pike and Leena and Jayne are at risk now? At risk of succumbing to Gaia's curse?" I asked.

Lilia nodded. "Yes, and Gaia's welcome to them," she muttered. "They don't hold a candle to Bree Athar." My mom's old friend was clearly still grieving her.

But, despite her sadness, my heart was lighter. I would never get to meet my mother, but at least I knew she loved me. And she'd planned on coming for me one day. "Thank you," I said, picking up my slice of vanilla cake again. "For telling me about

Mom. I feel so much better today."

It felt wonderful to deliver a thank-you naturally rather than forcing it out through forceps. I'd spent my whole life behind a foot-thick barrier of attitude, and it felt amazing to lower it.

Lilia smiled, swapping one needle to her mouth and then into her other hand. "You can come and talk to me about your mom any time," she said. "I miss her now she's gone."

This female missed my mom. My lower lip pouted, and my ribs pulled tight. I envied that emotion. I'd never known my mother, so I was in no position to miss her, though discussing her with her best friend quelled an ache deep within me. Perhaps that was a type of longing too. In any case, I felt like I'd come full circle in my relationship with my parents and was ready for the next stage.

I placed my hands flat upon the smooth wooden table in what I hoped was a stately pose and made my big announcement. I'd turned it over all night, and this was the only next step that felt right.

I took a deep breath. "I've decided I will run for queen. I am the heir of House Athar, the most successful House to every rule Caprice, and I believe I will make an excellent ruler." It felt ridiculous to say those words aloud, but there was no going back now.

My heart fluttered in my chest as I waited for Lilia's response, which was slow in coming. She eventually nodded softly. "Of course you will, dear." She bit into a piece of cake and wiped an errant crumb from the corner of her mouth.

"Oh," I said, feeling somewhat deflated.

"In fact, I already sent out your declaration to Houses Sansett and Davin," Lilia said before taking another bite of her fluffy vanilla cake.

"You did?" My voice rose in a squeak so high I figured I might ascend into a mouse.

She nodded again, and I could tell the movement was over-exaggerated for my benefit. She was clearly accustomed to spending time with mortals. "Yes. The declarations must be in no later than twelve hours before the coronation, which is tonight. So I didn't have time for you to make up your mind," she said matter-of-factly. "I hope you don't mind, dear. But the next chance won't be for hundreds of years, and you might not live that long."

I should be angry. My initial instinct was always anger, but for some reason, I bypassed that and went straight to gratitude. I leaped up and flung my arms around the slender fae, my hands almost reaching my elbows on the other side of her. "Thank you, thank you, thank you. You're the best," I gushed.

Lilia glowed under the praise. "Now," she said, looking me up and down and assessing me carefully. "Let's get you ready for your coronation."

Delph

Lilia escorted me to Lurlin Forest, arriving just minutes before the Ascension rite was due to begin, yet fae were gathered at the forest's edge rather than inside it. The forest rose before us, an intimidating mass of trees and bushes that looked impenetrable. We'd need a machete to make it one yard.

"Do they always meet outside the forest like this?" I asked Lilia.

She shook her head. "No, I imagine the forest isn't letting them in. It always was a tricksy patch, and now that nature is completely unsupervised, it's naughtier than ever. Hopefully, your arrival will convince it to let us in."

Again with her insistence that nature somehow responded to me just because I was Bastian's daughter.

I didn't have time to argue the point. Nerves were jumping in my belly, and I almost broke into a jog but decided to try to keep a queenly air, so I kept to an infuriatingly slow pace.

Lilia had done a magnificent job with me. I wore a flowing gossamer gown that flickered between green and black as I walked, matching my eyes and hair perfectly. Lilia assured me we should lean into my humanity rather than trying to cover it up, and there was no better way than to highlight my mismatched hair and eyes.

My black hair was braided around my head in intricate circles that ducked and weaved, leaving my neck long and bare. Lilia had produced an onyx necklace for my throat and emerald studs for my hair, and I had to admit the effect was startling.

I might look the part, but I felt far from royal. I spotted many fae I recognized in the crowd, including the Unseelie King Draylar with my cousin Taysin who regarded me with open interest, plus Colzan Blunt from Ourea, who grew a sly grin when he saw my outfit. Lilia had only sent the declaration to Houses Sansett and Davin, so I still had to make my announcement public. From the look on Colzan's face, he could tell what was coming and the chaos that would ensue, and he enjoyed every moment of it. Jayne Sansett looked pristine, and even Elora was there, giving me an excited wave.

Fae darted glances at me and whispered to their neighbors as I approached, but there was only one face I desperately wanted to see. Darzan's.

I knew he had trust issues and that I was betraying his trust by running for queen. I only hoped he would forgive me.

I couldn't see him anywhere, but I felt that sweet cool necklace around my throat almost exactly where my onyx jewelry framed my neck. He was looking at me from the crowd, and he kept looking. The sensation didn't go away while I searched frantically for his golden hair and perfect black face.

There. His expression was stony as I walked closer, though his eyes roved over my outfit and hair, drinking me in. I remembered back to the last time I'd seen him, slumbering peacefully in his bed in a post-sex haze, and realized that he must've felt abandoned when he woke up to find me gone.

I hadn't said a word, just fled from the scene like a murderer from a crime. Then Lilia had sent him an impersonal note informing him that I was running for queen.

Betrayal of trust didn't come more obvious than that, though it was the last thing I'd intended.

Still, he met my gaze as I beelined for him and held it when I stopped an arm's length away.

He ran his fingers along his stubbled jaw, not even bothering to shave. "You look—"

"I'm sorry," I blurted out. "I never meant to betray you, I just got the news that my grandma died, and then I destroyed that scroll just like you said I would, and I had to get outside. Then I just kept running. I'm sorry."

His golden eyes glittered hard, nothing soft about them. "And the declaration?" he asked.

I wouldn't back down. I was done flitting from realm to realm, floating along the streets of Hebes and then Capricia like a discarded plastic bag. I was done harboring a sense of not belonging. I was a princess of Caprice, and I belonged on the throne.

I straightened my back and jutted out my chin. "I apologize for hurting you, for breaking your trust, prince, but I can't apologize for running for the crown." There. I'd said it. And I meant every word, but I still hoped like hell he'd accept it.

He stepped toward me and grasped my elbows in his fists, squeezing hard, somehow forcing the breath from my lungs. "You didn't betray my trust, Delph," he growled. "You never could. I trust you with the realm because I know your heart is as golden as my hair." His chest heaved with emotion as he stared into my soul. "I would trust you with my life, Delph," he whispered.

My heart filled to bursting, and I swore I must have been

shining golden at his words. After running out on him, he could have turned his back on me, and it would have been justified, but instead, he'd turned toward me.

I stepped forward and raised my voice to call for the gathered fae's attention. I kept it short and sweet, wanting to get the words out quickly. "A third candidate for the crown of Caprice was declared early this morning," I said, trying to ignore my sweating palms. A fucking human wanting to rule over the fae. What was I thinking? But I forced the words out. "I, Princess Delphinium Athar, am that candidate."

I looked around at the perfectly still fae faces turned toward me. Neela gave me a thumbs-up, and a massive grin engulfed her pixie face. I grinned right back. So much for handing my crown over to the nearest male—I could tell I had her support. If I'd declared this earlier, I could have won much more support.

But the important question was how fae were reacting now. The Verdan heirs stood together. Beside Neela, Thorne's face was unreadable, but Gabrelle was beaming, her happiness shining through.

The sly grin on Colzan Blunt's face had grown into a full smirk, and I could see he was loving every moment of the drama.

Jayke's face went even whiter than usual, and his lips curled into an inaudible snarl. If he was that pissed, I was obviously doing the right thing.

I scanned the crowd for a green-skinned male, wanting to see Pike's reaction to my declaration. Turning around to Darzan, I whispered, "Where's your brother?"

Darzan stepped up beside me. He blanched at my question but didn't answer it. "I retract my candidacy," he declared, his deep voice carrying easily across the crowd. "House Davin supports Princess Athar."

Even the poised fae couldn't hold in their gasp at that, and neither could I.

I whipped my head around to look at his chiseled face. "You don't have to do that, I —"

"I want to," he interrupted. "You'll make a much better ruler than I will. But perhaps I could be your advisor on certain matters." He grinned seductively, and I threw my arms around him in a very un-fae display of emotion, but fuck it, I didn't care. I just wanted to squeeze this male until his lungs popped.

I pulled away from our embrace at the sound of snapping twigs and creaking branches as the tangled, thorny wall of Lurlin Forest opened to reveal an inviting tunnel lined with vibrant purple flowers. Perhaps the forest had been waiting for me after all.

Nerves sprang in my belly.

The Ascension rite was about to begin.

Delph

Lurlin was a magical forest that transformed differently for every being that entered. I'd heard stories of fae being transported to sunlit plains where fantastical creatures lounged about, and of others being plunged into nightmare scenes chased by dark creatures with wicked fangs and claws.

When I first stepped foot into the purple tunnel, everything seemed normal. The forest was allowing us safe passage, with purple flowers lining the tunnel but snarling beasts and wicked vines visible just beyond.

However, as I walked into the forest, it changed, and the deeper I went, the more it mutated around me. The snarling beasts walking beside us among the trees, mirroring our path through the tunnel, became the thugs and low-lifes of the Docklands, growling at me with yellow teeth and glinting blades. I knew it wasn't a hallucination, but it was as real as any other natural environment, even if it was from my imagination. If I ventured too close to those grasping hands, they would pull me into the dark streets of the Docklands.

Meanwhile, the open purple tunnel became even more inviting and beautiful, luring me with its sweet scents of vanilla and jasmine and an ever-growing array of beautiful flowers. The solid purple blooms leached into pink, peach, and emerald green, with dewy raindrops glistening on lush leaves.

I reached down to brush at a furry lime-green creature with large blinking eyes, but Darzan grabbed my hand to stop me, clearly seeing something different.

"Is Pike here?" I asked, wondering why he hadn't shown up. If he ascended into Lightning, the question of who sat on the throne would be moot.

"He isn't coming," Darzan whispered. "You have to be queen."

Darzan clearly didn't want to go into details, but I didn't know what could have prevented Pike from attending his own Ascension. Didn't that mean he would never be able to ascend? We'd be having a long discussion about it after this all played out.

The forest tunnel stretched on forever. How would we know when we reached the place for the Ascension rite? It turned out to be easy. The tunnel widened into a perfect replica of Arathay, a giant map laid at my feet. Delighted, I walked between the different realms, sensing the differences in the atmospheres and how their very essences were governed by Gaia.

I hopped quickly through the Realm of Fen before I said anything I'd regret and felt a tug in my belly pulling me back toward the map's center, back to Caprice. Standing there, I felt I was in exactly the right place. Fae around me began disappearing, twinkling out of existence like Stardust until only a handful remained.

No great announcement was made or long speech droned out, but the forest herself let it be known it was time to begin.

An olive-haired fae named Lu of House Rarleen walked

into the center of the clearing, and a silver ring of sparking Lightning formed around him, holding him captive.

The poor fae looked terrified, as well he might. He was walking to his death after all, and the fact it would arrive by his own hand didn't make it any easier.

The forest posed the question without a sound being uttered. "To what power do you seek to ascend?" The question simmered through the air and through my body, and even the trees leaned forward to hear the answer.

The fae stammered a reply, his voice thin in the thick air. "W-water," he said.

The crowd murmured as a knee-deep pool appeared inside the ring of Lightning, no larger than an inflatable paddling pool but made of living stone that grew into shape. The pond filled with black water, and Lightning from the deadly circle skittered off its surface.

The fae stepped into the pool and fell to his knees, his body shaking. He went to his hands like he was preparing for a push-up, flung a final desperate look at somebody outside the Lightning circle, then lowered himself face-first into the dark water.

How bloody hard must it be to drown yourself? To keep your head underwater as your lungs ached for air and every muscle in your body tensed. The fae's muscles kicked occasionally, contracting unwillingly, as his survival instinct tried to force him to give up, to raise his head five inches and suck in lungfuls of oxygen.

How the hell was he doing it? I would definitely top myself with something fast when my turn came after I turned twenty-five, although I hated thinking about that. I didn't know if half-fae could ascend, but watching Lu with his head in the pool of water, bubbles of air popping to the surface beside him as he struggled against every survival instinct, I didn't want to. Half a weak magical skill was better than killing myself to get a strong one.

A whimper sounded from someone in the audience, and I wondered if that was real or the forest's manifestation of my own horror. The fae lay still, his body lifeless, his limbs now floating around him like a starfish.

He didn't move. How long was this supposed to take? I had psyched myself up to witness a suicide, but I hadn't known the resurrection would take so long. It had been minutes, surely. Wouldn't his oxygen-starved brain get damaged?

Sobbing broke out beside me, and it struck me that the dying—dead—fae had family witnessing this horror.

Fucking hell. Dread filled me, the feeling that this was horribly wrong, that Gaia would not allow this Ascension. The sense of wrongness emptied me, hollowing me out and creating a desperate void that could only be filled through action.

Gaia didn't want this. I didn't want this. I had to rescue that fae from this wrongful death. Without a king or queen on the throne, the earth goddess had no intention of allowing the fae to ascend; that truth resounded through my bones.

"We have to do something," I hissed.

Darzan, who stood beside me in his usual form but with eyes that glowed silver instead of gold, grabbed my elbow forcefully. "We can't," he whispered.

I shook my head. He didn't understand how wrong this was and that Gaia was playing us for fools. The earth goddess would never let Lu ascend without royalty on the throne. She may be the goddess of the earth, but she was also a complete

326

bitch. "This isn't supposed to happen like this," I spit.

"No fae can enter the Lightning circle while an Ascension is in progress," Darzan hissed, not letting go of my elbow.

I gritted my teeth, realizing my humanity might be useful for something after all. "Well," I said firmly, "I'm not fae."

Lightning ringed the stone pool, preventing anybody from entering, but it wouldn't stop me. I jumped through the sizzling barrier.

Light filled my vision, and screams collapsed the air around me. A tug yanked my elbow, but it was too late. I was airborne and flying through the ring of electricity, or had I already landed inside? The smell of charred skin assaulted me, my own burning flesh, and as I looked up at the starless sky, a bolt of lightning struck me down.

Delph

I awoke in a dark plane of existence without a body.

My senses were scattered, and it took me a long while to figure out what had happened. First to return was my sense of smell, and I detected a trace of wood smoke identical to the one I'd smelled in the Aroma Room. Perhaps that room had been trying to warn me to prepare for this moment, but I certainly hadn't listened. I'd just bitched about getting the same scent and trying to trick it into giving me something sweeter.

Next to return was my sight, and although the world was darkness, I saw a prick of light in the far distance in a direction I decided was up. Perhaps I was lying at the bottom of a very deep well that stretched from the Earth's surface all the way to its molten core.

Eventually, I figured out that if I could get up to the tiny pinprick of light, I would return to life.

But I didn't see how a bodiless being could move up or anywhere else.

Touch came next, and I realized I was lying on something hard and cold. That fitted with my mental image of a deep stone well. But if I could feel it on my back and legs, that meant I had a body, didn't it? I wasn't sure how things worked in the existential plane.

"Fuck it," I muttered. "I might as well take a shot." I tried climbing to my feet, even if I didn't have any, and it seemed to work. I propelled myself into more of a vertical position, and sensations returned to whatever body I had.

I pieced together what had happened. The flash of light, the smell of burnt flesh, the jolt of agony. I had been struck by lightning. Chosen by Gaia. I was the special being selected to lead Caprice.

Which was fucking hilarious because I didn't have the magical power to get up to that pinprick of light, and my Royal fucking ass was going to sit in this hole and perish.

At least my hearing worked because my own curses echoed in my ears.

So did something else. "Delph? Are you really there?" Darzan's disembodied voice came from beside me, and I kicked around to find it but couldn't make contact with flesh.

My heart leaped. "Of course it's me. Or did you think this was a manifestation of your deepest fantasies about me swearing like a sailor?"

He growled, and I watched as he went through the same process I just had, discovering his body, finding his mental faculties, and stumbling to his feet. I felt rather than saw him because that prick of light far above was little enough to go by. Even his eyes were dull and lifeless. But his ashy scent was still the same, and suddenly it made sense. Killed by Lightning. Gaia was a sadistic bitch.

"You're here too," I said. I figured no matter how dumb I sounded, it wouldn't matter for long because we weren't getting out of this place any time soon.

"I grabbed you to try to stop you..." I could hear the frown in his voice as he pieced together the events. "But lightning struck us both."

I stifled a hysterical giggle. "You already ascended, you can't do it again."

He groped out a hand, and something firm and tangible wrapped around me. "And you can't ascend because Lightning is too powerful. It pushed you too far from the light, and you don't have enough magic to get back up."

Fuck. I swallowed another freaked-out laugh. "Plus, I'm only twenty-four," I said. "So I'm not capable of ascending. I ain't going anywhere. I guess this is what it feels like to die."

"Yes," he said. "We're screwed."

He might be right, but there was no way I was giving up that easily. I tried jumping on my non-legs but got no closer to the light. I tried a running leap, but the pinprick didn't get any bigger. "How do we get up there?" I asked. "Do we just leap, or do we have to figure out how to fly?"

Darzan shook his head. "Only Hovers can fly. It can't be that."

"Well, what is it then?" I demanded. "You've done this before. How did you get up there?"

Darzan squeezed me hard enough that if I had a real body, it would hurt. "I can't remember," he gritted out. "Nobody remembers their Ascension. Gaia guards her secrets closely."

"Fuck Gaia," I spit. "She's a total bitch, from what I can tell. She had no intention of letting Lu ascend, but she still invited him to kill himself in front of his family anyway."

I couldn't justify knowing she never intended for him to ascend, but I felt it in my bones. I knew it as well as I knew my own name.

I started jumping again. I crouched really low and leaped as high as possible, but it made no discernible difference. I tried running at full speed to gain momentum before leaping up, but it didn't make a lick of salt.

"Give me a leg up," I said.

"Don't be stupid," he hissed. "That won't help."

I huffed dramatically, but he was probably right. No amount of physical effort would close the gap between me and that pinprick of light.

So I closed my eyes and tried to examine my way out of it. I cajoled the magic inside me to spark to life and whisk me out of there, but it stayed stubbornly silent.

I was growing weaker too. Obviously, we only had limited time to complete the Ascension before we were counted among those who never made it back.

I folded my arms across my chest. "Has Gaia always been such a dickhead?" I asked.

"Stop calling her that," Darzan said. "She is my goddess, and she rules over Caprice with power and love."

I scoffed. "And the odd murder."

Darzan didn't respond, but his words had gotten me thinking. Gaia rarely chose anybody by lightning, and she wouldn't have done so if she didn't think we could get there. But why choose both of us?

I jumped to my feet. "Because we're stronger together!" I shouted.

Darzan sighed deeply. "And the prize for best non-sequitur goes to—"

"Shut up and listen," I said, jumping up and down. "Gaia couldn't choose me because I wouldn't make the Ascension alone, plus, I'm not twenty-five yet, and she couldn't choose you because you've already ascended once. So she chose us both so we could help each other ascend." I danced a little jig at my genius, then found his hands in the darkness and tugged him to his feet. "Come on, get up. We have to do this together."

We tried holding hands and jumping in unison, leaping time and again but getting nowhere. I was growing weak, and I could see he was too. Our non-legs grew tired, and our non-hearts grew sluggish.

Darzan put a hand on my arm to still me. "Come here, pet," he said, pulling me close. His stupid nickname made my heart soften, and my whole non-body relaxed. If I was going to die here, I might as well do it in the arms of this perfect fucking male.

I melted against his embrace, inhaled his ashy scent, and relaxed against his broad chest.

"Thank you for rescuing me from the Lightning," I murmured.

He chuckled into my hair. "Some rescue. But there's something I want to tell you before...you know."

I kissed his neck and waited for him to go on, letting time stretch around me as I waited for my existence to dissolve into the inky dark. "I love you, Delph," he said. "And I will always rescue you no matter what happens. Always."

My body melted into his until I couldn't tell which heart-beats were his and which breaths were mine. He loved me, and I knew I loved him back with all my heart. It didn't need to be spoken, it imbued the very world around us.

I closed my eyes and leaned into him, content that my last breath would be of him, and a tug deep within me called me home.

The pinprick of light grew from within and between us and

expanded to encompass the universe before it flashed out of existence.

Delph

Awareness came over me again, only this time, it felt different. More anchored and real than at the bottom of the well. I had a body. I had all of my senses. Something warm and comfortable was beneath me, and something sparked beside me.

I opened my eyes to find myself lying in a strange bed holding hands with Darzan. He was the source of the electricity, and I wondered what went wrong. His eyes were closed, but I could see he was breathing, so some of my panic abated.

But not all of it. "Darzan, wake up," I said, shaking him. "Please, Darzan."

He made a small noise, then turned toward me and opened his eyes, but they were the wrong eyes. Gone were his compelling golden eyes, replaced with cold silver ones that sent another jolt of electricity through me.

"Your eyes," I said. Was this even my Darzan? He looked so different, like his essence had been swapped out for somebody else. They said eyes were the windows to the soul...did that mean this was somebody else's soul wearing a Darzan suit? I pulled my hand out of his.

He blinked a few times, then put a hand on my cheek, and at the tone of his voice, I knew it was really him. His soul blinked out at me through silver eyes. "Yours too," he murmured, staring into my face. Were my eyes silver too? "We were chosen by Gaia to rule together," he said.

The enormity of the statement took several long moments to sink in. We had somehow made the Ascension together. I remembered that tug from within me that called to Caprice, the same tug that had drawn me forward through the Lurlin Forest. The tug of home.

"Are you telling me my eyes are silver too?" I asked.

He nodded. "The chosen Queen of Caprice always has Lightning in her eyes."

"Or king," I corrected with a smile.

I was the Queen of Caprice. I didn't know what excited me more, the fact we'd beaten House Sansett or the fact my eyes were silver, and I now looked like a magical badass. Probably the latter.

I leaned forward to kiss Darzan but jerked away at the electricity that flowed through his lips. "Holy fuck," I murmured.

His eyes darkened with desire. "We'll have to get used to that because there's no way I'm staying away from you."

He leaned forward to kiss me again, and Lightning buzzed between us, heightening everything about the kiss and zapping directly down to my core.

"Ahem." A voice called from the corner, and we jolted apart. I took in my surroundings for the first time. We were somewhere very high up with a pointed ceiling that made me suspect we were at the very tip of the Spike. Wide doors were open to a balcony, and sheer curtains flapped lazily in a cool breeze. From the bed, I could see the mountains that ringed Caprice, and I knew that if I walked closer and looked over the railing, I'd see the city laid out beneath me, a crisscrossing of cobblestones and forested streets.

The fae who'd so rudely interrupted our Lightning foreplay was Pike, and as soon as Darzan laid eyes on him, he was across the room and folding his brother into his embrace. "You're alive," he said. "Thank Gaia."

"Thank Jayke, you mean," Pike said, grinning. But there was a sadness in his eyes that tore at my heart. Pike had missed his Ascension. He had missed the opportunity to reach his full power and would always remain weak. Forever.

"Not likely," Darzan growled.

Pike told us what happened at the battle outside Sansett Palace. His emerald eyes turned glassy when he described the deaths of his companions and how Jayke's men had captured him and kept him in the dungeon until after the Ascension. Silence sat heavy between us at the knowledge that his power would be limited. Forever.

Pike swallowed his sigh, seeming to put that sorrowful ache aside. "That was two days ago," he said, managing to sound cheerful. "You two have been sleeping a long time. Some said you may never wake up, and Jayke even tried to go ahead with his coronation after the Ascension rite, but even that charming bastard couldn't muster support for that after everybody witnessed you two being selected by Gaia." He smirked. "He was not happy."

Darzan squeezed his brother's shoulder, and that gesture contained a well of empathy. "Poor little Jaykey-boy," he hissed.

Pike went on to tell us our presence was required downstairs in the throne room as soon as possible because a bunch of fae wanted to wish us well.

"What if we hadn't woken up yet?" I asked.

"They would have waited another day," he said with a shrug.

I hunted around the royal chamber—my bedroom—and found a closet filled with gowns that were just my size. Apparently, two days were enough to outfit a sleeping queen.

I selected a silver frock that matched Darzan's new eyes, my new eyes, and twirled before the mirror. Darzan chose a silver suit that made his skin shimmer like the night, and he pulled me close for another kiss.

"Matching," he said with a grin.

"Badass couples costume," I agreed.

Pike intervened with another staged "ahem," and we followed him downstairs. A long winding staircase hugged the wall of the tall tower, and my thighs should have been burning by the time we reached the bottom, but they weren't. I loved this fae shit. Fae were gathered in the foyer and in the Spike's forecourt. Nobody had yet dared to set foot on the throne room floor. It still looked fucking dangerous to me, like if I took one more step, I would fall into its watery maw. But I figured this was the kind of shit the queen had to do, so I rolled my shoulders back and grasped Darzan's hand. "Are you ready?" I asked.

He huffed out a breath. "Together," he said, squeezing my fingers. "One, two..."

"Three," we said together. We stepped forward, and I tried not to dance a little jig or smash out a high-five when the floor remained solid, proving that Gaia approved of us. I walked in, trying to be queenly by imagining a stick up my ass that went high enough to balance a book on my head.

"His and her Lightning thrones," I quipped, noting that Gaia had provided a second seat.

Darzan smiled. "His and her everything from now on."

I didn't hate that. I didn't hate that at all.

As one, we plonked our butts on the silver thrones shaped like lightning bolts, and a warm buzz of acknowledgment zapped through me. The throne had accepted me. Despite being a savage bitch from the Docklands, I felt completely at ease as the Queen of Caprice.

The first to follow us onto the throne room floor were our personal guard, a team of six fae wearing black tunics engraved with a silver rearing horse. They stood beside us for hours, as a line of fae came to pay their respects, including those from other realms who came to bid us farewell.

Darzan had great difficulty maintaining his composure when Colzan Blunt stood before us with that inimitable cheeky smirk on his face. This was no time to start a war with Ourea, so I was beyond glad when Darzan pulled his shit together and managed a cordial greeting. It wasn't so hard for me because I kind of liked Colzan, and I didn't think the crap that had gone down between their fathers should influence the relationship between these two fae. And certainly not our two realms.

As the line of strangers and friends continued to come forward, I became more aware of the enchanted floor's power. Despite not knowing many of these fae from a blade of grass, I could feel perfectly comfortable and safe knowing that none with evil intent could come near.

King Draylar, Emperor of the assholiest of fae, didn't even dare set foot on the throne room floor. He and his posse of evil Unseelie just nodded at us from the entrance hall before turning and leaving.

Prince Charming did more or less the same, not daring to step onto the enchanted floor. Clearly, his ill wishes hadn't been eradicated by our Ascension to the throne, and I would have to watch out for him in the future. He didn't even bother with a nod. He just sneered at us from a distance as though we'd think that was a smile, then turned on his heel and stalked away. His sister followed close on his heels, not even bothering to nod at us.

Darzan leaned in close. "Prick," he muttered, watching Jayke Sansett leave. I was pleased to think of the sharp blade the prince must feel against his throat.

I couldn't hold in my laugh. "Oh, so now you're king, you use gutter language like me?" I joked, taking the opportunity to look my king up and down. He looked magnificent in that silver suit, and I foresaw some bedroom role-playing in our future.

He grinned. "I tried to elevate you to my level, but that didn't work," he said. "I see I'll have to stoop to yours instead." I slapped him on the elbow, and electricity sparked into my body. Man, that would take some getting used to.

But I was prepared to put in as many hours of work as required to ensure I could touch this male without flinching. As many hours as required.

Delph

After all our petitioners had left, the Verdan heirs appeared in the throne room door.

Darzan saw them first and growled, snagging my attention. "I bet they won't dare to set foot in here," he snarled.

But he was wrong. Gabrelle Allura, Neela Flora, and Thorne Sanctus marched onto the enchanted floor without hesitation. Darzan gave a surprised hmph and watched them approach, their footsteps pattering lightly but safely across our protective moat.

Gabrelle looked amazing in a dress of black and white silk trimmed in black lace that she made look fashionable instead of grandmotherly. Neela wore a utilitarian khaki outfit with plenty of pockets that looked more like a paintball costume than a princess one. And Thorne was dressed in bespoke black, looking like a male who'd recently upgraded from slob to sophisticate, and I suspected Gabrelle was to blame.

As they got nearer, Neela rubbed a hand along her throat, clearly feeling the cold blade of my king's magic. "That War thing he's got going on is really strong," she mumbled to Gabrelle, but with my improving hearing, I heard every word.

"Yes, it is," I said, hugging Darzan's arm. It was all I could reach of him from my throne.

Gabrelle smiled silkily and nodded gracefully. "Congratulations," she said smoothly, and I couldn't help gritting my teeth. But when she clasped onto Thorne's arm and beamed her perfect smile up at him, my jealousy eased. She had just been playing a part when she'd been flirting with Darzan. And, it turned out, he had too.

"Thank you," I said. "I appreciate it."

Thorne broke free from Gabrelle's grasp and approached our thrones. He surprised me with a gift of a necklace hewn from the boggy peat of Fen. It was black and shiny, and it was quite beautiful for a piece of compressed oxen poop. As a bonus, it didn't stink of feces.

"I always hoped you would stand up and claim your throne," Thorne said. "I'm glad you are not as weak as I first thought."

As compliments went, that was pretty bad, but his habit of honesty was clearly hard to shake, even though he was outside the Realm of Fen and had been living in Verda for months.

"Um, thanks?" I said.

"She is the furthest thing from weak," Darzan snapped beside me. "She is the strongest fae I've ever met."

Thorne looked like he would arc up, but Neela stopped him with a small hand on his arm. "Okay, lads, enough with the machismo. We get it. You both have giant cocks, okay? Now, can we get on with things?"

Thorne and Gabrelle nodded while Darzan and I looked at her silently. This was the oddest petitioner meeting we'd had all day. I was the freaking Queen of Caprice, and now a female I barely knew was talking to me about her friend's dick. Things were going from interesting to frankly bizarre.

"Good," Neela said as though we'd agreed with her. She removed her hand from her friend's arm and stepped forward.

"Gabrelle tells us you're open to splitting the Stone of Veritas with your Lightning power."

Darzan and I glanced at each other. "Actually," I said, "we haven't discussed it."

Neela cocked out a hip and put a hand on it. "Doesn't matter. Gabrelle has looked inside your minds and—"

Darzan's silver eyes pierced mine. "Splitting the what?" he interrupted. "Looked inside our minds? What the hell are they talking about?"

My jaw fell open. I wanted to fill my king in, but my brain was also hooked on that part about Gabrelle looking inside our minds.

Before I could formulate a response, Gabrelle explained the whole thing to Darzan. How the Shadow Walkers had come from the Shadow Isles. And yes, they were real. How they'd started by feeding on shifters to multiply, and now they were killing fae indiscriminately, feeding on their power and turning them into walking husks.

Apparently, these Shadow Walkers could only live inside shadows, which made them easy enough to avoid—you just summoned a globe of faelight or, in my case, Lightning, and they would stay away.

But that wasn't enough. Gabrelle's voice cracked in desperation as she described the hell the Walkers were wreaking in Verda, and I saw the real fae beneath her exterior of perfection. She wasn't just a walking orgasm, she was a human being—or fae, I supposed—with real emotions, fears, and weaknesses. I suddenly felt ashamed at my response to her beauty. I would do better going forward. Be less superficial. Be more like Darzan.

"How can we help?" Darzan asked, and I felt so proud of

342

him in that moment. He wielded War and made most fae want to flee, but he was good-hearted at his core.

Gabrelle explained how she had gone on a mission to retrieve the fabled Stone of Veritas from the Realm of Fen, and when she'd found it, she'd thought their problems were solved.

But there were too many Shadow Walkers and only one Stone of Veritas. They needed more, and the only way to do that was to fracture it with an enormous power source.

Darzan nodded from his throne, looking supremely regal. "And Lightning is the only source strong enough to fracture the Stone," he guessed.

Gabrelle nodded, her eyes shining with hope. "Yes. If you and the Queen of Caprice could combine your powers, it should be enough to split the Stone into four fragments that we can use to repel the Shadow Walkers."

Neela stepped forward again, her voice soft. "We'd be forever in your debt if you would help us," she said.

Darzan and I glanced at each other for a fraction of a second before turning back to Neela. We came to an unspoken agreement. We couldn't turn away from someone in need, especially when it came down to saving lives.

"We will help," Darzan said, standing.

I got to my feet, too, feeling graceful with my strengthening muscles. "We'll try, at least. Our control over Lightning is only shaky," I admitted.

Gabrelle produced a large gemstone from her pocket, which pulsed with an ethereal blue light. It was clearly the Stone of Veritas.

"Put it on the floor and stand back," I said, and the Verdan heirs obeyed. Gabrelle bent gracefully, placed the pulsing blue Stone on the enchanted black-water floor, and then joined her friends standing against a wall.

Darzan and I took our positions on either side of the Stone. We faced each other, palms outstretched, and our faces shone with determination. My heart raced in anticipation. A sense of rightness overcame me. This felt like the crowning moment of my life, the moment I'd been working up to.

We held hands and summoned our Lightning power, aiming it at the magical object. We worked together as one powerful unit, melding into a single entity—a brief glimmer of memory told me we'd done that during our Ascension and must always work together.

The air around us crackled with electricity as our Lightning powers collided into the crystal-like object. It glowed brighter and brighter as our combined forces clashed with its surface. A crack appeared in the center of the Stone, then spread outward like a web. The bright blue light intensified until I had to close my eyes, shielding them from its brilliance.

A gust of air blew my hair around my face, then it fell still, and the light faded, revealing a dozen equally-sized pieces of the Stone that glowed with their own inner blue light.

An awed silence descended on the room, deeper and heavier than ever after the wild crackling and power we'd just experienced.

Neela was the first to move. She scrambled to her knees and collected the four fragments of Stone, handing them all to Gabrelle. "We'll never forget what you've done for us today," Neela said. "Thank you." Her powder blue gaze landed on mine. "I don't say that lightly."

That sense of kinship with this foreign princess settled over me again, as if she'd survived the streets of the Docklands just like I had. As if she'd battled through a tough childhood and then somehow found her way to the castles of Arathay. But that couldn't be right, could it?

"I know," I said simply, and Neela nodded.

Gabrelle swept a deep curtsy, and I got the feeling she rarely bowed to others, which made her gesture all the more meaningful. "Verda is forever in your debt," she said formally. Then she winked. "Seriously. If you ever need anything, just shout."

I could tell that Darzan was itching to help them more, and I dreaded what he might say or what part of himself he might offer. I had only just found him—I couldn't lose him already. "I will come and help fight," he said, squeezing my heart. "I am strong in War, and—"

"You can say that again," Neela mumbled, fingering her throat where the phantom blade was likely drawing phantom blood.

"War wielders are no good against the Shadows," Thorne said. "Nor are swords or spells or sorcery. The Stone is the only weapon we have. So thank you, and we may call on you for the final battle, but for now, your realm needs you. Stay here, Darzan. With our thanks."

Relief flooded me. Darzan wasn't leaving me. He wasn't running off to war to put himself in danger. But if he did, I'd go with him, and then who would rule Caprice? That would make Gaia one pissed-off goddess, and who knew how much crap she'd pull on our realm.

I launched myself at Darzan and wrapped myself around his arm, inhaling his ash scent. "Thank God," I said, not bothering to hide my relief. But when Gabrelle's dusty pink eyes landed on me, and I glimpsed how much she'd given to the fight against the Walkers, I felt a simmering of shame.

"But if you ever need us, just call," I added.

The three Verdan heirs thanked us again and walked to the throne room door. But, as they were almost outside, I couldn't resist calling out, "Shame your Jaykey-boy didn't get the job. I know you backed him."

Neela stopped with one foot out the door. "Life doesn't always bring what you want," she said. "But sometimes that's a good thing." She threw us a wink and a wave, then took her leave.

Epilogue

After two months of ruling, I was starting to get the hang of it. I still didn't know my ambassadors from my ass, but I was making some good decisions and feeling more fae with every passing day.

I was even getting the hang of my Lightning power. Every morning before breakfast, I spent an hour conjuring Lightning and learning to control it. After the first indoor fire, I took my practice sessions to open plains until my control improved.

I could change the size of my Lightning, the amount of electricity behind it, and the direction. Next, I wanted to work on the accuracy of my aim and see if I could make shapes other than zigzags.

I wanted to visit Jackson and the girls in Hebes, but the prospect of all that human technology cutting me off from my magic was abhorrent. Now that I was beginning to tap into my fae side, I didn't want to lose it even for a day. Visiting the mortal realm would set back my progress, not only for that day, but when I returned home to Caprice, it would take weeks for my power to return. I couldn't handle that, not now.

But being queen had its perks. I could access a rare scrying amulet and send it to Jackson's house with a Hover royal guard. It was like a Zoom call powered by magic, so I could talk with my family whenever I wanted to, usually once or twice a week. I was due to speak with them this afternoon.

But this morning was special. I'd planned a surprise for Darzan that I hoped wouldn't make him freak out.

"Where are we going?" he growled, not for the first time, as he trudged beside me, the long grass whipping around our knees.

"You'll find out when you get there," I repeated.

We had to walk through fields and forests to reach our destination, but that was far less daunting than it used to be. Nature was not only compliant now but helpful. Rough branches eased out of the way when we walked through dense forest, and flowers strained to look at us as we passed, showing us their beautiful multicolored faces.

That heavy sense of anticipation that had weighed so heavily in the air when I first arrived in Caprice had gone too, and the weather now reflected my and Darzan's moods. When we were both happy, the sun shone and rainbows graced the sky. When we were fighting, storms raged, and fae cowered indoors to avoid the thunder.

And when we were in different moods, the weather became schizophrenic, with bluebirds singing songs beneath perfect white fluffy clouds while a gale blew rain horizontal.

Unfortunately, Darzan wasn't stupid enough to remain ignorant about our destination for long. After all, he knew Caprice better than I did. "We're not going to the Calcile Caves, are we?" he complained. "You know I don't go there."

Since Leena Sansett had announced to faeschool that Darzan was terrified of the caves, he'd avoided them. He'd spent decades avoiding those caves, and I intended to get him over his irrational fear.

"I'll take care of you," I promised.

He didn't rise to the bait, didn't growl that he could take care of himself like I expected, he just gripped my hand tighter. He really was scared of these caves, and I was beginning to worry I'd made a huge mistake.

Perhaps his fear was justified. For all I knew, wild creatures beyond Gaia's control roamed through the dark tunnels hunting for fae blood. Fuck, I should have researched this before we came.

Too late now. We reached the cave mouth, and I dragged Darzan into the gloom. We did not need torches because we had Lightning, and I kept a steady fork of glowing electricity ahead of us to show the way. A dank, wet smell assaulted me, and I hoped again I wasn't making a terrible judgment error.

The inbuilt Google maps that fae had was super helpful in these caves. I'd never visited before, but Pike had transmitted their layout to me, so I navigated easily until we came to a rock fall that wasn't marked on my internal satnav.

"This was a terrible idea," Darzan growled. "It's even worse than I remember. Why did you bring me here?" His silver eyes flashed as he looked around, taking in the close rock walls and the cold expanse, sniffing at the damp air.

I shrugged out of my backpack and laid out a blanket. "For a picnic," I said with a smile.

He looked at me like I was insane. Caprice had so many magical venues where we could picnic with stunning views of waterfalls that flowed upward, orange and purple grasses as far as the eye could see, and magnificent mountain vistas, and I had brought him to a pitch-black cave.

For a moment, I thought he might turn and walk away, but he grudgingly sat beside me. I sidled onto his lap, and electricity hummed between us. I straddled him, leaving a small gap between our bodies, breathing in his ash. We stared at each other for a few moments, our glowing silver eyes providing enough light to see each other's faces.

"Okay, this makes up for it a little bit," he grumbled.

"How about this?" I asked, leaning in to kiss him and mumbling into his lips. "Does this help?"

Electricity sparked between our lips, and my entire body thrummed. I would never get used to touching this man, never tire of the energy between us.

He wore loose pants, and his cock rose between us to meet me. "That helps a bit," he murmured. "Do it again, and I'll tell you for sure."

I leaned into him and claimed him with my mouth, drinking in his power and taste, feeling the electricity flow between us. I wore a loose skirt so his hardening cock pressed directly against my thin panties, only two sheer layers of material between us.

"Fuck, you're so perfect," he growled as he palmed my lower back and pulled me close to his chest. "So fucking perfect."

"Watch your mouth," I joked, remembering our first meeting when he accused me of being trashy. And loving that I had dragged him down to my level.

His eyes flashed at me. "Oh, you better watch my mouth." He dragged his lips down my neck and licked at my collarbone in long firm strokes that reminded me of him licking my pussy.

I reached between us and tugged down his pants and pushed aside my panties so his cock rested at my entrance, then I thrust my hips forward and sank onto him completely.

Lightning sparked from his cock inside me, flickering through every nerve ending and setting me on fire. I rode him desperately and pulled his face back to mine with both hands to devour his mouth.

Lightning flashed from both of us, reflecting off the cave walls as I rode my perfect steed.

He grabbed my hair with one hand and yanked me back slightly, preventing me from kissing him, and I groaned with annoyance.

"Tell me you love me," he growled, his silver eyes dancing with sparks.

"Get your hand off my head," I snarled. He did as instructed, and I stared into his eyes as I continued to ride up and down, taking in his length in wild strokes. "I love you, Darzan Davin, King of Caprice," I said.

Darzan gritted his teeth and ground out a moan that had my head spinning with lust. He pushed deeper into me and grasped my hips as I rode him harder and faster. He tugged at the hem of my shirt. "More," he groaned. "I want more."

"Take it," I moaned. I helped him pull the shirt over my head and was amazed to see Lightning skittering over my breasts and belly. I eased off his cock, resting back on my heels, and unbuttoned his shirt. I ran a hand across his smooth, firm chest and pinched his nipple lightly. Each button revealed more of his delicious black flesh and the Lightning bolts skimming across it.

I removed his shirt completely and then leaned forward and bit his nipple. "If you ever have sex with anyone else, you'll kill them," I told him possessively. It wasn't a lie either, I imagined this Lightning could never be borne by another.

He tilted my head up with a hand under my chin. "If you ever have sex with anybody else, I'll kill them."

For some reason, his possessiveness, which mirrored my

own, sent a bolt of Lightning straight to my pussy, and I couldn't wait a moment longer. I rocked forward and sank onto him again. It felt so good, better than ever before.

He put one hand on my ass and the other on my clit and stimulated me while I bucked like a wild fucking animal. Lightning flashed brighter and stronger off the black cave walls and sparked in the gap of air between our chests.

Every inch of my body was alive with Lightning, and I rode him harder and faster until I exploded with a cry wrenched from my soul.

As the waves of the orgasm rippled through me, Darzan threw back his head and came hard, joining me in my bliss.

Uncontrolled Lightning sparked from us and kicked the cave walls, and I collapsed forward, panting, watching the silver reflecting off the black, and then I rested my head in the crook of my king's neck.

Eventually, I eased off him, and we lay side-by-side on the picnic blanket, soaked in each other's scent, watching the display of sparks flickering over the walls, which slowly crackled out.

We lay on our backs, sides pressed together and hands clasped.

Darzan turned his head. "I admit it," he said. "You made the visit worthwhile."

"And?" I arched an eyebrow, waiting for more.

"And I'll come with you anytime you like."

* * *

Hi, I hope you enjoyed A Court of Caprice and Decay!

The next book in the series features Delph's cousin, Lexi... remember the one who overestimates her own badassery? That one. She wants adventure, and she'll get it. At the hands of the Dread King of Brume.

Free Novella

Grab your FREE NOVELLA set in the Realm of Caprice, where the weather is affected by the fae king's mood...and the king is NOT happy. A moody king, a badass heroine, and a beautiful but dangerous world—what's not to love?! This tells the story of Delph's parents, Bree and Bastian Athar.

By signing up for my newsletter, you'll also get all the latest info about new releases, some character art, and other good stuff.

About the Author

Zara has a pretty sweet life – hubby, kids, and a kick-ass Dyson hairdryer. But that doesn't stop her from inventing new worlds and having steamy affairs with her book boyfriends. Angels and demons and fae, oh my!

Lucky Zara, she gets to spend hours with those sexy beasts every day. The rest of the time she's working in health, negotiating with her kids, and beating her husband to the remote.

But mostly it's angels and fae.

You can connect with me on:
- https://zaradusk.com
- https://www.facebook.com/zaraduskauthor
- https://www.tiktok.com/@zaradusk

Subscribe to my newsletter:

✉ https://dl.bookfunnel.com/jtbq9u1oeu

Also by Zara Dusk

Fast-paced, twisty fantasy with plenty of smut. Bad men and badass women, some of them with wings.

Vestige - completed trilogy
Before he can return to heaven, she must die.

A Fallen Angel obsessively hunts a mortal woman who lives in the Undercity because she is the key to his return to heaven.

But she is driven by wild revenge and won't fall easily. Enemies to lovers steamy fantasy romance at its best, with captivating characters in a spellbinding world.